New York Times and *USA Today* bestselling author **B.J. Daniels** lives in Montana with her husband, Parker, and three springer spaniels. When not writing, she quilts, boats and plays tennis. Contact her at bjdaniels.com, on Facebook or on X @bjdanielsauthor

Delores Fossen, a *USA Today* bestselling author, has written over a hundred and fifty novels, with millions of copies of her books in print worldwide. She's received a Booksellers' Best Award and an RT Reviewers' Choice Best Book Award. She was also a finalist for a prestigious *RITA* Award. You can contact the author through her website at deloresfossen.com

Also by B.J. Daniels

Renegade Wife

Silver Stars of Montana
Big Sky Deception
Missing: Baby Doe

Powder River
Dark Side of the River
River Strong
River Justice

Also by Delores Fossen

Saddle Ridge Justice
The Sheriff's Baby
Protecting the Newborn
Tracking Down the Lawman's Son
Child in Jeopardy

Silver Creek Lawman: Second Generation
Targeted in Silver Creek
Maverick Detective Dad
Last Seen in Silver Creek
Marked for Revenge

Discover more at millsandboon.co.uk

ENGAGING THE DEPUTY

B.J. DANIELS

HER BABY, HER BADGE

DELORES FOSSEN

MILLS & BOON

All rights reserved including the right of reproduction in whole or in part in any form. This edition is published by arrangement with Harlequin Enterprises ULC.

This is a work of fiction. Names, characters, places, locations and incidents are purely fictional and bear no relationship to any real life individuals, living or dead, or to any actual places, business establishments, locations, events or incidents. Any resemblance is entirely coincidental.

Without limiting the author's and publisher's exclusive rights, any unauthorised use of this publication to train generative artificial intelligence (AI) technologies is expressly prohibited. HarperCollins also exercise their rights under Article 4(3) of the Digital Single Market Directive 2019/790 and expressly reserve this publication from the text and data mining exception.

® and ™ are trademarks owned and used by the trademark owner and/or its licensee. Trademarks marked with ® are registered with the United Kingdom Patent Office and/or the Office for Harmonisation in the Internal Market and in other countries.

First Published in Great Britain 2025
by Mills & Boon, an imprint of HarperCollins*Publishers* Ltd
1 London Bridge Street, London, SE1 9GF

www.harpercollins.co.uk

HarperCollins*Publishers*
Macken House, 39/40 Mayor Street Upper,
Dublin 1, D01 C9W8, Ireland

Engaging the Deputy © 2025 Barbara Heinlein
Her Baby, Her Badge © 2025 Delores Fossen

ISBN: 978-0-263-39714-7

0625

This book contains FSC™ certified paper and other controlled sources to ensure responsible forest management.

For more information visit: www.harpercollins.co.uk/green

Printed and Bound in the UK using 100% Renewable Electricity at CPI Group (UK) Ltd, Croydon, CR0 4YY

ENGAGING THE DEPUTY

B.J. DANIELS

There is nothing like the people you grew up with in a small town in Montana. It's like a family. Sometimes a dysfunctional family that can become dangerous—at least in this book.

This one is for those who remember West Yellowstone and Rainbow Point in the 1960s.

Chapter One

Ghostlike shapes of abandoned houses appeared on the darkening skyline ahead. Olivia Brooks had been nervous enough about this night but now felt a sense of foreboding she couldn't shake off. Why had she agreed to this? She hated this place and especially this fool idea of how to spend Halloween night. The settlement of Starling, Montana, was desolate and deserted, the anti-government group long gone but not forgotten. She hadn't liked the way it made her feel in the daylight, let alone late at night.

"The graves of lost dreams," her date said next to her in the back seat of his friend Dean's king-cab pickup. As Cody Ryan looked out his side window at what was left of Starling, she remembered why she'd agreed to this Halloween date. She'd missed Cody. He'd been the boy next door, her best buddy growing up, her high school sweetheart. When she thought of him, she thought of home.

The idea of spending time with him had appealed to her maybe more than it should have since it hadn't been all that long ago that she'd been engaged to someone else. She'd come home to heal. She'd missed having a friend whom she shared a childhood with. Now that she was home again, Cody was a huge part of those memories. Mostly, she missed the closeness they'd once shared as kids.

"Slow down," Jenny ordered Dean from the front seat of the pickup as he took a curve too fast on the narrow road. Weeds that had grown up between the two dirt tracks scraped the bottom of the truck like fingernails down a blackboard.

Olivia and Cody exchanged a look. Dean and Jenny both seemed tense, not that they didn't have every reason to be. She wondered whose idea this date had been, given they both were married to someone else.

Behind them, the headlight beams of the second vehicle suddenly filled the pickup's cab as Dean hit the brakes and came to a dust-boiling stop. Emery Jordan laid on his van's horn as he roared up, barely stopping before crashing into the back of the truck.

"Just like old times," Cody said, shaking his head as he looked over at her. He didn't sound as if he was enjoying this any more than she was. They'd run into each other at the local bar in town last night. Olivia had been the outlier, going away to college and not coming back for six years.

At the bar, they'd all been drinking and laughing about old times. She hadn't realized how much she'd missed this hometown comradery, especially with Cody. She hadn't talked to him since they'd broken up when she'd left for college. Like most of their other friends, he hadn't left the small Montana town. He'd been working at his father's local hardware store for as long as she could remember.

That night at the bar, being around old friends, especially Cody, felt so right that she'd questioned why she'd ever left. He looked the same but different in a good way. Mostly, he felt familiar and comforting, like finding an old worn flannel shirt she'd forgotten about that still fit perfectly.

Talking at the bar, it was as if they'd never been apart. When he'd asked her to come with him tonight, along with several of their old friends all now in their twenties, it felt almost as if she could rewrite history. She'd often wondered what her life would have been like if she had never left.

Inviting her must have seemed like a good idea at the time, even though Cody didn't seem so sure now that they were out there, especially when Rob's plan was that they all had to stay until midnight. Their friend Rob Perkins had been celebrating the other night at the bar. He'd been offered a really good position in Seattle. He was excited about the condo he'd purchased on the coast and this opportunity to change his life.

"Let's do something epic on Halloween," he'd said.

"Let's go to Starling!" Emery Jordan had said and thrown an arm around Rob.

"Great idea," Rob had agreed and grinned. "Let's go look for the gold." Everyone had groaned at even the mention of the legend—let alone going out to the abandoned community. Folklore claimed that the anti-government leader and founder of the Starling community, Elden Rusk, had taken all of his followers' money, converted it into gold and hidden it somewhere in the town before his mysterious disappearance. The gold, if it had existed, had reputedly never been found.

"But we have to stay until midnight," Rob had said. "That's when the really scary stuff happens. Unless you're all chicken," he'd taunted. Never the kind to back down from a dare, especially when they'd all had a couple of beers, their old group had quickly agreed. It was a date.

Olivia had looked to Cody, who'd given her that familiar grin. "What do you think?" he'd asked.

She'd nodded, warmed by the alcohol and her old friends. There was nothing quite like the people she'd grown up with, the boys she'd dated, the friends she'd known, the memories they'd made. She'd been the dreamer, determined to go to college, to have a career, not to end up like her mother had.

Six years ago, her friends hadn't understood her need to chase her dream—especially Cody, she thought as she looked out at Starling, unsure now what they were doing there together.

As they exited the truck into the darkness, she was having misgivings. She didn't want to give Cody the wrong impression. She wasn't interested in taking up where they'd left off. She just wanted that boy-next-door friend she'd missed.

Rob and Emery and their dates piled out of the van, shouting and yelling. She saw that Emery was helping Rob unload a cooler full of beer from the back of the van and realized what those two had planned.

Emery and Rob had brought dates as well, although the women were much younger than Olivia and the old crowd. Tammy and Whitney had their heads together, giggling over something. Clearly, that carload had been drinking on the drive out to the middle of nowhere and the remains of the Starling community.

"Okay, whoever finds the gold, remember, we split it," Rob said, laughing. "Except for anyone who wimps out before midnight."

Olivia took the beer Cody handed her and popped the top as they all stood around the cooler for a few moments. Rob and Emery retrieved their dates and headed down the hillside to some of the houses along the creek. She could hear Rob relating the story of Starling and its tragic end with relish as they went off to explore the dozen structures scattered across the hillside.

Jenny and Dean sat on the tailgate of his pickup, engrossed in each other even though married to other people. She saw that Dean had brought the mattress from his front porch futon and put it in the bed of the pickup. Seemed everyone had something in mind tonight. This wasn't going anything like she'd expected.

"Take a walk?" Cody asked as if as uncomfortable as she was. At the bar, they'd all been having fun together. Now they had broken off into real dates.

With growing discomfort, she walked away from the vehicles with Cody. It felt as though the bad part of their past had been hiding out here in the dark, waiting for them. The skeletal remains of one of the weather-beaten houses rose before them, etched against the night sky. She didn't want to think about the last time she'd seen Cody before she'd left town. They'd argued. She knew that she'd hurt him and hated that. But she also knew that was why she'd stayed away so long.

The air felt heavy, as if a storm was blowing in. Clouds scudded past as silent as wispy ghosts and blotted out the stars and moon, making the night darker than usual. Gusts of wind caught her long blond hair, lashing it across her face. She grabbed a handful and forced it into a ponytail with the scrunchie she'd brought.

"Aren't you worried that we might see the ghost of Evangeline?" she asked and took a sip of her beer, the eerie hillside scene making her jumpy as much as Cody's silence. She felt him glance at her as if he understood what she was doing. He knew her better than most anyone because of all those years they'd been inseparable.

"She probably ran away," Cody said. "Had enough of small-town living. Wanted something better."

She shot him a look. Was he really going to bring up her leaving now? She sighed, knowing that she couldn't explain why she'd had to leave when she had or why she hadn't come back. He hadn't understood six years ago. Why would he now? "The teen years are tough. Who knows what we want at that age?"

"I always knew what I wanted."

Olivia groaned inwardly and pulled her coat a little tighter around her as if the temperature had suddenly dropped. "You were lucky."

"Lucky? Right," he said without looking at her as they walked. "My dream was to work in my father's hardware store my entire life. Some of us couldn't just leave."

The wind picked up, stronger now. She could hear clanging metal on metal in the distance. Closer, a windmill's sails moaned as they spun restlessly, several of the blades broken or missing altogether.

She swallowed, feeling Cody's disappointment and hurt and wishing she could take it away as she took in the derelict-looking structure ahead. If he was being truthful, he hadn't wanted to go to college. He probably hadn't even wanted to leave. He'd always felt as if he were trapped here, but if he'd wanted something else badly enough, wouldn't he have found a way?

Olivia had put herself through college. It wasn't like her mother had been able to help. She tried to change the subject, not wanting to argue with him.

"Elden Rusk had a dream," she said, thinking of her own. "He wanted a little different life," she said without looking at Cody. "There's nothing wrong with chasing a dream."

"Yep," he agreed. "Had great plans for the future, sold everyone on building this community, putting all their hopes and dreams into it, thinking this would be their home. Then he up and bails on them—"

"His sixteen-year-old daughter disappeared." She was losing her patience with him.

"Or just took off. Either way, the Starling dream died when he abandoned his flock." He held up his hands to encompass the dark houses of Starling and their lost hope. '"Sorry,' he says, 'but I'm moving on.'"

"I'm sure it was very painful for him to leave like he did," she observed, hoping this would be the end of their discussion since they weren't talking about Elden Rusk. "He must have been brokenhearted, not just for his daughter, but his community and friends he had to leave behind."

She stopped walking and felt a chill as the deep shadow of what she recognized as Elden Rusk's house loomed in front of them. She remembered when this house had been in all the newspapers and on the television news. She wished they hadn't walked this way. Just as she wished they hadn't had to do a postmortem on their high school relationship after all this time.

Cody turned to her. "What happened with us, Olivia? I never thought you'd leave, let alone walk away from what I thought we were building together."

His voice was so filled with anguish, she wished there was something she could say.

"I used to talk about my dreams with you," she said.

He kicked at the dirt at his feet. The wind caught it and whirled it around them. "You just didn't mention that I wasn't part of them."

"Is this why you invited me out here tonight?" she asked, her voice cracking. "Cody, we used to be friends. I thought… It's why I came along tonight. I didn't realize everyone was going to go their separate ways."

"You didn't realize it was a date," he said and sighed. They stood only inches apart. He seemed to study her as if he'd never seen her before. "I thought I could do this, pretend you and I never happened, just be friends, no hard feelings." He shook his head. "Sorry, but I can't."

Her eyes burned with tears. "You picked a great time to

get that off your chest," she said, determined not to cry. "It isn't like we can just get in the car and leave now." Glancing back, she could no longer see Jenny and Dean or the tailgate anymore. Had they moved to the futon bed? Probably. Not the best time to go down there and ask for a ride back to town. "I don't know what you want me to say," she said, turning to him. "I'm sorry."

"I guess I always believed you'd come back to me," Cody said. "Even as kids, and later as teenagers, you and I were so close. I thought we'd end up together, that I would prove to you I'm the right man for you. I'm not going to work in that hardware store the rest of my life." He shook his head. "You never had any faith in me, but you know what the worst part is? After you left, I ran into Deputy Jaden Montgomery, the guy you fell for in college. We had a nice conversation."

She groaned. "Are we really getting into this now out here?"

"Maybe we should since I hadn't realized that the two of you had been *engaged* and apparently you broke his heart too. Now I'm wondering how many others there have been."

"Don't be ridiculous," she snapped. "You and I—"

They both started at the sound of a bloodcurdling scream followed by a burst of laughter and shrieks. Down the hillside, between the dark outlines of two houses, she saw Rob chasing either Tammy or Whitney, she couldn't tell which. But when she looked back, Cody was about to enter Elden's house.

For just an instant, she thought about going back to the truck, as embarrassing as it could have been. But she didn't want to go alone. She told herself that she could make it until midnight if Cody could. She hurried to catch up to him as the wind whirled dust around her. Ahead, she heard a door creak open.

Chapter Two

Cody wished he'd kept his mouth shut. He was mentally kicking himself for bringing up the past. He'd asked her to come along tonight because he'd missed her. He'd planned to keep it casual. Old friends. Nothing more.

Unfortunately, being around Olivia had brought back all the good memories from their childhood. She'd been his first real love. Maybe it had been puppy love, but it had been real to him. He'd really thought they would end up together; he always had.

He'd thought she'd felt the same way, not that they had ever talked about the future in high school. He hadn't realized he wasn't in her future until she'd dropped the bombshell. Not only was she going far away to college, but also she was breaking up with him. He'd never understand how she could leave seventeen years of life and all those memories and not look back, but she had.

So, what was she doing back in town?

When he'd seen her walk into the bar the other day, he'd realized that he'd never given up on his fantasy of the two of them being together. How could he not have thought it was meant to be? She had returned. She'd agreed to come out here tonight with him. But that was where the fantasy ended, he thought. They weren't kids anymore, let alone high school sweethearts. She just wanted to be friends. He swore under his breath. Maybe it was just as well, he told himself.

Standing inside the house, Cody hadn't heard her come up behind him—not with the wind whistling through the broken glass of the windows. He jumped when she touched his shoulder. He had stepped into Elden Rusk's dark house and stopped, realizing belatedly how dangerous this was as he felt the floor give under him. He couldn't see anything in the pitch blackness. For all he knew, part of the floor had caved in and he might step into the abyss.

"Don't come any closer," he warned as he pulled a penlight from his pocket. He wished he'd brought something larger and brighter. The LED beam did little to chase away the shadows from the dark corners.

At one window, a ragged white curtain suddenly billowed, making Olivia grab his hand as she let out a surprised cry. They stood like that, her hand warm in his. They could have been kids again standing there. But they weren't.

"I'm sorry," he whispered. He regretted spoiling this night and the time he had with her. He wasn't sure what had brought her back to town, but it wasn't him. He doubted she would be staying long. "Want to get out of here?" Her shoulder was against his, so he felt her nod and turned them back toward the open door they'd come through.

As they stepped outside, she let go of his hand. He wasn't sure what they could do to kill time until midnight. He'd be glad when they'd finally be able to leave. This idea of a "date" had been a mistake.

"We could search for the buried gold," she said, clearly only half-serious. Like him, she was probably looking for anything to do until midnight, when they could go their separate ways. He had a pretty good idea of what the other couples were doing as he glanced back toward the vehicles.

Dean and Jenny were probably still down there getting into trouble. Cody had been surprised and upset when Dean had told him Jenny was coming along.

"Where's her husband?" Cody had asked, hating to mention the obvious.

"Out of town. Angie's at her mother's. Don't say it. I know, but I never got over Jenny. If anyone should understand not being able to move on, it should be you."

Cody had let it go, realizing it was true. He hadn't moved on. Instead, he'd been stuck, as if he hadn't wanted to see a future without Olivia. As they'd swung by to pick up the two women before heading out to Starling, he'd realized that he'd been waiting for Olivia to return. He'd never seen himself settling down with anyone else.

Now he knew that it wasn't just Dean who was doing something foolish tonight. Standing in the creaking old house on the hillside in Starling, he knew he had been deluding himself. His wanting to believe that he had no future without Olivia had really been him not facing that he'd wasted years working at the hardware store with his father, waiting for his life to finally begin. Seeing her again had brought the realization home that it was time to change things. That was what he'd been working toward. Now it was time.

He finished the beer he'd been holding and tossed the empty can into the darkness of the house. A strong gust of wind howled off the eaves, pelting them with dirt. "Why not look for gold inside the houses?" he said. "Anything to get out of this wind." They dropped off the hill to the closest small dwelling below the founder's so much larger one.

He noticed Olivia glance at the dark shape of Rusk's house looming over the town. She looked as if she'd been expecting to see Elden Rusk standing in the doorway, watching them go. Another of the local legends out here at Starling was the alleged sighting of Elden's ghost searching for his daughter. Wandering around at night calling "Evangeline!" as he stumbled, heartbroken, through the deserted town.

Cody didn't believe any of it. If there had been any gold, he'd bet Rusk had taken it with him.

OLIVIA FELT A CHILL she couldn't quite throw off. After they'd walked away from the Rusk house, she'd sensed someone watching them and had turned to look back. Enough light had sifted through the clouds to illuminate a dark figure in what looked like a long black coat, wearing a floppy black hat, standing in the doorway they'd just deserted. In the blink of an eye, the image was gone as if it had never been there.

She shuddered, telling herself she'd imagined seeing the figure of Elden Rusk, and blamed the creepy place, the dark night and being back here, maybe especially with Cody. She hated the tension she felt between them. All that talk about Rusk and the past was making her see things.

She caught up with Cody, and they entered the small house. The door had been standing open. Cody turned on his penlight. Like the Rusk house, most of the windows appeared to be missing.

They'd only just stepped in when a shriek filled the night air from a house farther down by the creek where they'd last seen Rob and Emery and their dates. Everyone seemed to be enjoying themselves, Olivia thought. She wished she hadn't left her purse with her phone in Dean's truck. She had no idea what time it was, but feared midnight was still hours away.

She and Cody had barely gotten inside the house when a gust of wind literally shook the walls around them. Cody went to one of the glassless windows to look out. She could hear a distant howl, the sound seeming to grow in strength as the wind picked up even more.

"This is going to be some storm," he said, sounding nervous as another squall shook the house. "Do you hear that?"

Earlier, all she could hear were the creaks and groans of the walls, the whistles of the wind through the broken panes. But now she could hear what sounded like a roar. She hugged herself, just wanting to get out of the house, out of Starling.

"We should round up the others and head back," she suggested. Ending this outing early seemed like the best idea, given the way this night was going, especially with a bad storm brewing.

"I don't think there's time," Cody said, turning from the window, the beam of his penlight illuminating a spot on the floor at his feet. She could see his expression. "I think we'd better find a safe place to ride it out."

Seriously? "Doesn't it make more sense to go back to the pickup?" she asked, but he didn't seem to be listening. The house shuddered as the wind grew stronger, the howling sound louder. Dirt peppered the side of the structure as Cody moved toward her, his expression making her more anxious. The house shuddered again. "Cody?"

"When I was a boy at my grandmother's, we had to go into the root cellar because of a tornado." He had to yell to be heard. She remembered him telling her the story. "I think this might be a tornado. That's what it sounds like."

"That was Oklahoma. We don't have tornadoes like that in Montana, do we?"

"Come on. No matter what it is, we're finding a safe place until it's over." He grabbed her hand and led her deeper inside. He shone his light on the floor as they moved farther into the house until they reached the old kitchen.

"What are you looking for?" she yelled over the howl outside. The wind rattled the walls, shaking the floor under them.

"A root cellar. I think every house up here had one where

they kept their canned goods from their gardens." He moved the little flashlight beam around the floor until he found what he was looking for. "There it is. The trapdoor. Here, hold the light."

Standing back, the light making a small pool on the surface, she watched him reach into a slight indentation in the floorboards and pull. The wood groaned and creaked. It seemed to take all his strength, but finally he lifted the door, exposing a wooden ladder that dropped down into total blackness.

A musty, decayed smell rose as she watched Cody brush away cobwebs before reaching for the penlight again. "I'll check it out," he shouted over the deafening roar. The house shook. "We have to hurry!"

She could hear what sounded like objects hitting the walls on the outside. Not dirt or pebbles like earlier—large things that crashed against the side of the house.

He disappeared down the ladder. She moved to the edge of the hole that had been dug into the dirt beneath the house. She shivered at the thought of going down there, even as she heard what sounded like houses being turned into kindling. When she looked toward the glassless window, she saw large debris flying past.

"Cody?" she cried an instant before he reached up for her.

"Take my hand. Hurry."

She grasped his hand, falling into his arms. She'd barely dropped down a couple of rungs next to him when he slammed the trapdoor and locked it. Overhead, there was a loud crash that sounded as if the house had caved in.

"CODY?" HER VOICE came out breathless, making him think of when he'd been able to make her sound like that simply by kissing her.

"You're okay," he said as he slipped down the ladder and reached up to help her. They stood in utter darkness. He had the sense that he could no longer tell up from down. Snapping on his penlight, he saw her expression. She looked so vulnerable, so terrified. It reminded him of when they'd been kids and he'd been there for her; the few times he'd been braver than her.

He could see that she'd never been in a root cellar before and hadn't been anxious to enter into this one. He hadn't been either. Now he just hoped that he'd made the right decision. "I'll clean you off a place to sit."

He picked up a board that might have been part of the shelving system at one point and dusted off the dirt and cobwebs. "Here, sit on this."

She descended the last few steps and stood for a moment, clearly not wanting to sit at all. He knew the feeling. He watched her glance around, wide-eyed, in the faint glow of the penlight, making him think of that time at his grandmother's. There had been something terrifying about running out of the house in the middle of the night to crawl into a dirt hole in the ground. He recalled the panic he'd felt when his grandfather had closed the door and locked it.

Over their heads, the thundering had increased in volume, sounding now like a locomotive barreling down on them.

"What's happening?" she asked, her voice small in the contained space. The root cellar was tiny compared to his grandmother's. There were only two sets of heavy-looking wooden shelves with a couple of jars of canned goods on each. He pulled out more boards for them, knowing they would have to wait out the storm.

"We could be here for a while, though, so let's sit, okay?"

She lowered herself to the boards and he joined her, more

concerned about what was happening over their heads than he wanted her to know.

"It's a tornado." He could hear what sounded like the town ripping apart over their heads, but down here, it was relatively quiet. "I know it's rare, but I've heard of tornadoes in Montana. Usually, they're fairly small." This one didn't sound small at all.

She swallowed and looked as worried as he felt. "What if we're buried alive down here?" she whispered as if he hadn't thought of that.

"I think we're safer here," he said as he put a protective arm around her. It had to be a tornado. He couldn't imagine a thunderstorm doing the kind of damage they were hearing above them—not in Montana, where he'd lived his entire life. Rare windstorms tore off roofs, rolled over semis on the highway, swept in blizzards that closed all the roads out of town, but what was happening outside sounded as if the entire community of Starling was in the extremes of being leveled.

Just when he thought it couldn't get any louder or stronger, it did. The clatter was suddenly deafening. He tentatively tightened his arm around her and was glad when she curled against him, burying her face in his shoulder.

But when he looked up, he saw the boards being ripped off the kitchen floor. He pulled her down to the dirt floor, covering her body with his own. He could feel the wind pulling at his clothing, at his body, as if preparing to lift them both out of the earth and into the whirling maelstrom over their heads.

She cried out as he grabbed the heavy shelving unit and toppled it onto them to help hold them down, holding on to her as the house above them splintered apart.

"Don't worry. I won't let you go," he cried over the noise,

wishing he hadn't six years ago. He wasn't that man anymore, but he had no more chance of hanging on to her now than he did then as the floor over them disappeared.

THE SILENCE WAS suddenly deafening. "Olivia?" For a moment, Cody feared she wouldn't answer because she wasn't just buried under the debris and him—she was dead.

He felt her move under him. "Hold on," he said as he pushed the shelf off them, along with his weight on her. "Are you okay?"

"I think so," she said tentatively.

Cody sat up, shaking off the dirt and debris as he turned to look at her. Like him, she was filthy, but she looked unharmed.

"What was that?" she whispered.

"Definitely a tornado." They were still down on the ground, but there was a gapingly huge hole above them instead of the house's floor and once closed and locked trapdoor. He could see starlight overhead.

He could also see that part of the ladder to climb out was missing. He turned on the penlight and shone it around the space. Lowering the light, he looked at Olivia and found himself smiling.

"What?" she demanded, reaching up to pull a sliver of wood from her hair.

"You... Your face is a little dirty, that's all," he lied. "I must look filthy too."

She pushed to her feet. Her blue eyes were wide with the fear that still had her in its grip.

"We're alive," he said and laughed. "That was something, wasn't it?"

He saw her swallow and look skyward. "I need out of here."

"That might require some help. I'm not sure about the

ladder," he was saying as she grabbed hold of it and the rung tore off.

"Easy," he said as another part of the ladder fell away from the dirt wall, sending debris onto them. Fortunately, he caught the ladder before it hit him in the head.

"You have to be kidding," she said, sounding close to tears.

"Don't worry. I'll figure something out," he said as he noticed something he hadn't before. A portion of the root cellar behind Olivia had caved in. With the storm past, he'd just been glad that neither of them had been injured. But now he worried that the rest of the cellar might not be stable. They still could be buried alive if they weren't careful.

"Why don't you move over here by me?" he said as his light caught on a pile of something white lying in the caved-in portion of the cellar. "Easy," he warned again.

"If you're trying to scare me—"

The moment she reached him, he got a clear view of the bones that had been exposed when a portion of the wall had caved in.

"What is that?" Olivia cried, moving even closer to him as she took in his grisly discovery. "Are they...*human bones*?"

Chapter Three

Deputy Jaden Montgomery was already out assessing the damage left behind from the windstorm. Power was nonexistent in some areas and there was reported damage to a few buildings, including a couple of old barns that had lost their roofs. But no injuries or loss of life.

Until he got the frantic call from Starling.

"We need help!" Emery Jordan had cried. "We're out here in Starling, what's left of it. I can't find Rob. I can't find the others. Oh, man, it's really bad here. The town is almost completely gone. The tornado..." His voice had broken.

"How many of you are out there?" Jaden had asked and then told Emery to sit tight, that he was on his way. Starling was the last place on earth he wanted to go on Halloween night, of all nights. He had enough bad memories of the place. His parents had been members of the anti-government militant group years ago, long before Elden Rusk had left and the community had scattered, some a lot farther than Fortune Creek, where he now lived.

He had no desire to recall one of the darkest times of his childhood and had avoided going anywhere near Starling. He knew teenagers often went out there in an attempt to scare themselves with the ghost stories and alleged sightings of

Elden Rusk. Kids! But Emery Jordan wasn't a kid anymore. What had a bunch of them been doing out there at their ages?

As he drove toward the abandoned community, the closer he got, the more eerie it felt. But he hadn't expected almost total destruction. In his headlights, he began to see the piles of debris the storm had left, houses leveled to the ground. It looked as if a bomb had gone off, turning some buildings to kindling and sending others hurling off their foundations to pile up a quarter mile away.

The devastation shocked him, not that he hadn't hoped years ago that the place would disappear forever. Reports of a tornado had come in late last night. But they usually did little more than tear up a barn or shed, wipe out a few telephone poles.

The brunt of the storm had missed Fortune Creek, yet had pretty much wiped Starling off the map, from what he could see in the moonlight. According to Emery, he and seven other twentysomethings from the closest town of Libby had been partying in the empty buildings when the storm had hit. Right now, five of them were missing and others had minor injuries.

Jaden had called in medical help as well as a search party on his way to the scene. As he came over the rise, he saw a van sitting sideways in the road and a pickup lying on its side, buried in debris. What appeared to be the roof of a house had piled up beside the road.

A bad feeling settled in his stomach as he parked and got out.

OLIVIA SCREAMED. SHE WOULD have kept screaming for help, but Cody pulled her to him in a tight hug.

"No one can hear us down here," he said. "Do you have your phone?"

She shook her head, her mind whirling like the tornado. They were trapped in a dirt hole with human bones. It was too easy to imagine her own bones decaying down here when no one found them. She was trying so hard not to cry, not to panic, but it was useless. She'd never been so terrified.

"I left my phone in the truck," Cody said. It was still dark outside, except for the stars and moonlight. She had no idea what time it was without her phone. Why had she left it and her purse in the truck? Because they'd only been going for a walk? Who'd known a tornado would hit and they'd end up almost buried alive in an old root cellar?

She shivered, avoiding looking at the pile of bones as she tried to pull herself together. "You think it's Evangeline Rusk?" Olivia asked, her voice trembling.

Cody shook his head. "It could be anybody."

"Hello!" she called, her voice echoing, her throat raspy. "Anyone out there? We need help!" No answer.

It didn't help that Cody was trying so hard to reassure her. "Someone will come looking for us."

"If anyone is still alive." Her eyes burned with tears.

"Let's just keep our cool. I'll see about using some of the shelves as a ladder, but we have to be careful, so we don't make the dirt cave in any more, okay?"

She nodded, trying not to think about the rest of the dirt walls toppling down on them.

"Hey," he said, putting his hands on both of her shoulders. "Breathe. You're fine. You're here with me."

Her vision blurred but she nodded again. His words both soothed and hurt. Earlier, Cody had been angry with her, unforgiving. But he'd saved her during the storm. Probably saved her life by insisting they find a place to ride out the storm. He was still trying to protect her. "I'm so sorry," she cried.

"You're okay. We're okay." He held her tighter.

"You saved my life," she said, sobbing into his shoulder.

"Not yet," he said. "Come on." He pulled back to look into her eyes before taking the tail of his shirt and gently wiping her face. "Even now, you look beautiful."

She scoffed but made an effort to stop crying. She'd always prided herself on her strength and determination. Where was that woman right now?

"Can I help you with the shelves?"

He smiled. "That's the girl I used to know," he said. "Too bad we found old bones instead of the gold."

The silence was getting to her. Where were the others? Suddenly, she was even more afraid. "What if everyone is—"

"Hey," he said. "They're probably just like us, digging themselves out."

"Sure." Except she didn't believe it. It was too quiet.

As he walked up the road, Jaden spotted three of the survivors huddled together by the van. They were some distance from the demolished community, as if wanting to be as far away from it as possible. The largest of the group rose as he approached. He recognized Emery Jordan, but not the two young women with him. They were all filthy—their faces blackened with dirt, their clothing torn and dirty—but they didn't appear too badly hurt.

Emery, he saw, had what appeared to be superficial cuts and bruises, except for the one leg he was favoring. Mostly, he looked scared as the deputy walked toward him.

Jaden felt the weight of the quiet that had settled over the place. It made his skin crawl.

As he reached them, the two young women began to cry, holding tight to each other. "My mother's going to kill me," the brunette sobbed.

Seeing that they didn't appear to need medical attention, Jaden pulled out his notebook and took down their names, Tammy Bell and Whitney Clark. Both were underage to have been at a party where alcohol had obviously been served. Both said they had already called home and their parents were on their way to get them.

"I can't find Rob," Emery said. "He was there one minute and then…" He put his head in his hands.

"Give me the names of the others with you," Jaden said.

"Cody Ryan and Olivia Brooks. Rob Per—"

"Olivia Brooks?" Jaden stopped him. "She's back in town?" This was definitely news to him.

"Yeah, she's back," Emery said, sounding like it was no big deal. Probably wasn't to him, but then, he'd never been engaged to her. "Rob Perkins, Dean Marsh and Jenny Lee."

"Where was the last time you saw the others?" the deputy asked.

"Cody and Olivia went off that way," Emery said, waving toward what was left standing of Elden Rusk's house on the side of the hill. "Jenny Lee and Dean Marsh were here at the truck. Rob Perkins and I and the girls went down by the creek." His voice broke with emotion. "I thought we were all going to die."

Jaden looked up the hillside to where Emery had last seen Olivia headed. Even from this distance, he could see that only some of Elden Rusk's house was still standing, while the one just below it on the hill, where Jaden and his family had lived, was completely gone.

He desperately wanted to go looking for Olivia himself, but three other vehicles arrived. He needed to talk to the EMTs and search and rescue personnel. Too many people were still missing.

"Did you hear that?" Olivia whispered as she lifted one end of the heavy shelves and turned them to stand against the wall of dirt. "Voices."

He'd heard the voices and was as anxious as she was to get out of this root cellar. "It's probably the others."

"Maybe someone called for help," she said excitedly.

"Told you we would be found."

"But we aren't staying down here until they do, right?"

He shook his head. That was definitely not part of his plan for the night. "I'm going to help you climb out. Just stay low when you get near the top. Lie on your belly and crawl away from the edge so it doesn't cave in any more than it has." All he needed was for her to topple this damn hole on top of him.

She looked scared again. "You're going to be right behind me, aren't you?"

"Right behind you," he assured her, hoping that the shelves held enough to get her free. "Once you're out, head for the road we drove in on. If someone called for backup, that's where they'll be."

"I'm not leaving you down here," she said.

"Olivia—" He cursed under his breath. How had he forgotten how stubborn she could be?

"No. I might have left you once, but not again. Especially not like this." She shook her head adamantly. "We're both leaving here together."

He didn't want to argue, so he agreed. He didn't want to

waste the time. The root-cellar walls felt unstable. He didn't think either of them should stay down there any longer than they had to.

"I'm going to be right behind you," he told her. "Just climb up and out. Don't look back."

She mugged a face at him, and for a moment, he thought she was hesitating because there was something she needed to say to him. "There's plenty of time to talk when we're out of here, okay?"

She nodded, grabbed hold of the old shelving and, with his hands guiding her upward, climbed, not hesitating, and was up and out before several of the wood shelves broke apart. The nails used to hold the boards together had barely held with her light weight.

Not a good sign, he was thinking when he realized that she'd just disappeared over the edge of the hole when she appeared again. She'd taken off her coat and, lying on her stomach, was dangling it over the side. "Your turn," she said, a dark silhouette against the lightening skyline.

"The shelves aren't going to hold me. I can hear rescuers. Go get some help." He didn't mean to snap, but he knew the clock was ticking and she was determined not to leave him. If only she'd felt that way six years ago. "Go! Please. I'll wait right here for you."

She hadn't been gone but a few moments before he moved the last shelving unit over against the wall. He hadn't told Olivia, but the last thing he planned to do was stay down there if he could help it. He could hear crying and someone calling Rob's name.

His weight broke the first shelf right away, but he'd gotten high enough that he could see over the rim of the root cellar in time to glimpse a dark figure move past. He started to call out but stopped himself. The person wasn't going for help—but in the opposite direction, deeper into the nearly-destroyed Starling community.

Just before disappearing from sight, the figure turned, as if looking back in Cody's direction. Cody dropped out of sight, hoping he hadn't been seen. He was trapped in this hole. If anyone wanted to harm him, it would be like shooting fish in a bucket.

ONCE JADEN GAVE the information he had to search and rescue, they began grabbing their gear.

He turned to Emery. "How did you and Rob get separated?"

Emery wiped his nose and looked down the hillside. "Whitney and I went over to that small house by the creek to give him and Tammy some privacy."

Jaden looked to Tammy, who was huddled with Whitney on a large boulder beside the road. "You were with Rob when the storm hit?"

"We'd been visiting down by the water. I got scared and went to find Whit. She'd come looking for me, so we ducked into that little stone shed."

"Rob didn't go with you?" the deputy asked. They both shook their heads, but he caught her sneaking a look at Emery. "You stayed where you were, didn't go looking for Rob and Tammy?" He saw Whitney and Emery share a glance, both looking suspicious. "I can tell that there is more to the story. I need the truth."

Emery sighed. "Whit was panicked about her friend. I tried to get her to stay where it was safe, but she took off."

"You didn't go after her?" Jaden asked.

"I'd had so much to drink," Emery said in his defense, "I was having a hard enough time just standing up, and then all hell broke loose."

The deputy wasn't through with these three, but he figured whatever they were hiding would come out eventually. He'd been waiting impatiently for news on Olivia Brooks and was becoming more anxious by the minute when his cell phone rang. He saw it was the head of the search and rescue party and quickly picked up, afraid the news wasn't going to be good.

"We found Rob Perkins. I think you'd better come take a look. It appears his death wasn't accidental."

"I'll be right there," Jaden said, taken aback. What had been going on out here even before the tornado?

Chapter Four

Jaden shone his flashlight beam on the body crushed under the old block wall before calling for backup to secure the scene where Rob Perkins had been killed. He'd seen at once what the rescue crew had. Deep footprints in the dirt, where it appeared someone had stood—and waited?—before struggling to push a portion of the wall over his victim—who hadn't been dead very long. The deep tracks in the soil were a dead giveaway this hadn't been an accident.

Perkins lay on his back, his body crushed under the blocks and cement. Only his head and shoulders were free, his arms raised as if he'd been trying to ward off what was coming for him.

At the sound of a bloodcurdling scream from higher up on the hillside, Jaden felt his heart drop. Wasn't that the area where Emery had told him Olivia had gone with Cody?

He turned to the state law-enforcement officer who'd arrived. "If you keep everyone away from here until the rest of the state Department of Criminal Investigation arrive, I'll see to whatever that is," he said and took off up the hill. It was hard getting around in the debris. He'd had to make a wide circle to get to the small crowd on the hillside.

As he drew closer, he saw several people standing over a hole in the ground. Behind Jaden, the sun was starting to rise over the mountains, turning the sky pink. One of the two rescue workers was attempting to climb down into the hole with the help of the other. The woman was standing off to the side. Olivia?

"What's going on?" the deputy called to them.

"We have an injured man down in an old root cellar," he called back as Jaden advanced on them.

As the woman turned, Jaden felt a start. Relief made his knees go weak. It was Olivia and she didn't seem to be injured. She seemed startled to see him.

"I hadn't heard that you were back in Montana," he said as he glanced in the hole. He'd gotten only a glimpse of Cody Ryan lying awkwardly in the bottom of what was left of the root cellar. He appeared to be unconscious.

As he felt the ground shift under him, he quickly stepped back. Taking Olivia's arm, he drew her away from the hole as the search and rescue team did their work.

Living in Fortune Creek to the north, he'd only recently met Cody. He was the high school sweetheart she'd told him about. After what Cody had told him about how she'd broken his heart, he hadn't expected to hear that they'd been together out here.

"He was fine when I left him," she kept saying now.

"He wasn't injured in the storm?" Jaden asked.

"No, he was fine. He couldn't climb out. I told him I would go get help, but when I came back…" She began to cry. "I don't understand what could have happened. And…" She motioned to a spot along the wall away from Cody's body. "We found those bones. Cody said they're human."

The deputy shone his light on the bones. Cody might be right, he thought. They appeared to be human bones. They'd know more once the coroner had a look at them. His mind was more on what Olivia was doing out there, of all places, with her old boyfriend. Not that it was any of his business. Not anymore.

Jaden had agreed with Cody on their chance encounter that Olivia was indeed a heartbreaker.

With a sigh, he pushed that thought away. He already had one suspicious death. Now this. "You climbed out and went for help?" He couldn't help but wonder why it had taken her so long. "How long ago was that?"

"I don't know. I got turned around trying to navigate this mess out here." She sounded close to tears. The debris had made it difficult to move. Look how long it had taken him to make it up the hill. But he couldn't wrap his mind around what Olivia was doing with Cody out here, in the middle of nowhere, in the middle of the night. If Cody had been injured after she'd left him, could it have been the same person who'd pushed a wall over on Rob Perkins? Where was Olivia when that was happening?

One member of the search and rescue team, a paramedic, confirmed that Cody's vitals were strong. His only injury appeared to be a blow to the head.

"Deputy," he called up. "There's a rock down here with his blood on it. Would you like me to bag it for you?"

"Please," Jaden said and saw Olivia shoot him a look.

"You think someone did this to him on purpose?" She seemed shocked at even the idea.

"Did you see anyone else around before you left Cody?" he asked, telling himself whatever his problems were with Olivia, she wasn't a killer.

"No, it was dark, and all I could think about was getting him help out of that hole."

"But you're sure he wasn't injured when you left him?"

"He was fine," she repeated more adamantly. "He just

couldn't get out. He insisted I go get help." She started to cry. "If I'd stayed—"

"You might have been injured as well," he told her. "Do you know anyone who might have wanted to harm him?"

She shook her head. "No. That is, I don't know. I've been gone all these years."

Exactly, he thought. "How long have you been back?"

"Only a few days."

Jaden nodded. "You and Cody together again?" He knew she and Cody had been close from the time they were kids. They'd grown up next door to each other and had years of history.

She seemed surprised by the question. "No."

"But you were out here with him." He hated that he sounded like a jealous lover. He needed her to tell him why, after being gone for years, she was here with her old boyfriend at what was now a murder scene. A double murder scene, if Cody didn't make it. And they still had people missing.

"We're just friends." She shook her head. "After tonight, maybe not even that anymore."

He felt his pulse jump at her words. "Did the two of you have an argument?"

She seemed to realize what he was asking. "I didn't do anything to him," she snapped indignantly. "I told you he was fine when I left."

At the sound of more sirens headed their way, Jaden stepped away to make two calls. One to the coroner, the other to the EMTs to tell them that they were needed high on the hillside to help get an unconscious man out of a root cellar.

Disconnecting, he stepped back over to where Olivia was standing, hugging herself. Her face was streaked with dirt and tears. Still, she looked beautiful.

His cell rang. He stepped away to talk to the state crime team. Photographs of the scene had been taken and they were ready to get the body to the morgue. A helicopter had been arranged to airlift Cody Ryan to the hospital. One of their biggest problems was moving through all the wreckage left by the tornado.

Jaden kept looking back at Olivia, standing alone as a team worked to maneuver Cody out of the hole. There was still some speculation about where the helicopter would be able to land. At least the sky was getting lighter, visibility better.

He caught a glimpse of Cody and his head wound as he was brought up. Clearly, it had bled a lot, as head wounds tended to do. The rock he'd been hit with was large. Too large for the average person to throw down into a hole onto a man. But it could have been rolled. Not that Jaden had noticed any rocks like it nearby, none especially in the hole, except for the one that had injured Cody Ryan.

Jaden couldn't believe he had one suspicious death on his hands and an assault, along with two missing people: Jenny Lee and Dean Marsh.

As Olivia watched an unconscious Cody Ryan being lifted from the hole in the ground, Jaden observed her. He didn't want to believe she'd had anything to do with what had happened out here tonight. But he couldn't stop questioning what she'd been doing there with Cody to begin with.

More rescuers arrived to help dig through the debris for bodies as the sun rose behind the mountains, announcing the new day. The deputy took statements from everyone, let the parents of Tammy and Whitney take their daughters home, and then made calls to both Jenny Lee's husband and Dean Marsh's wife.

To his surprise, Jenny was home, her husband said. She'd

called him to pick her up. From the emotion he heard in the husband's voice, he was aware that Jenny had been out in Starling with Dean Marsh.

"Did you happen to see anyone else when you picked up your wife?"

"You mean someone like Dean Marsh?" Tom Lee asked sarcastically. "No. I didn't see him."

Jaden asked to speak to Jenny, who sounded contrite. She swore that she and Dean had gotten into an argument and she'd taken off, walking down the road, where she'd called her husband and he'd come to pick her up. They'd just missed being caught in the tornado.

The deputy thanked her and kept the rescue workers searching for Dean Marsh's body as the new day began. He called his boss, Sheriff Brandt Parker, to let him know that he had one suspicious death, another man unconscious with a suspicious injury, and a missing man who'd been involved with another man's wife.

"That's all?" Brandt said.

"No. The storm uncovered some human remains. Oh, and my former fiancée is here with the unconscious man who is being transported to the hospital."

His boss swore. "And I thought I had a rough night with all the storm calls. Any suspects?"

"Lots of them, including Elden Rusk's ghost. I wouldn't be surprised if they all tell me they saw Rusk in the storm, walking away from Starling, carrying something heavy."

"The gold," Brandt joked. "What the devil were they doing out there?"

Good question, he thought. "Some kind of Halloween dare, apparently. Though one of them could have had an ulterior plan to commit murder. The confusion during the tornado gave him or her the perfect opportunity." He shuddered as the sun rose so he could see the devastation and how little was left of Starling. "It's a miracle any of them survived."

"Let alone Rusk." For Jaden, Rusk was no laughing matter. He was the boogeyman who'd come out of his closet at night all during his childhood. "Good luck narrowing down the suspects."

"The coroner says there are two sets of human remains. One a teenage girl and the other a man somewhere between twenty-five and thirty. Apparently, they were buried together in the root cellar."

"All in a night's work," the sheriff said. "I'm finishing a case up here or I would help you."

"I'm good," Jaden said, then thought of Olivia. Not as good as he was pretending to be. What was she doing back here, let alone with Cody Ryan?

THE MORNING WAS almost gone by the time Olivia walked into her mother's house. She'd gotten a ride into town with one of the rescue team after giving her statement to Jaden. Just her luck that she'd been in Starling with her former high school boyfriend and the investigating deputy had been her former fiancé.

"You're not planning to leave town, are you?" he'd asked her. "I need you to stick around because the state boys might want to talk to you about what happened out in Starling."

"I'm not going anywhere."

"You staying out at the house with your mother?"

"I am."

He'd been all business, all sheriff's deputy, not the man she'd almost married, so she'd done her best to do the same. She'd imagined seeing him again but never under these circumstances. She wished that she'd called him as soon as she'd returned. She'd definitely thought about it. But after the way they'd left things when the engagement had ended, she wasn't sure he'd want to talk to her—let alone care that she was back in the area.

"Jaden?" It was the first time she'd said his name in so long, it had sounded strange on her lips. "Was Rob really murdered?" He'd nodded. "They still haven't found Dean?" He'd only shaken his head. "You can't really believe that I had anything to do with what happened out here. That I did something to Cody."

"Like leave your former boyfriend to die in that hole after clobbering him with a rock? Someone killed Rob and I suspect someone attacked Cody. The same person could have done something to Dean Marsh as well. Or had help with all three."

She had felt her eyes widen, alarmed that he would even say something like that. "You know me," she'd cried. "You know I had nothing to do with any of it."

His answer had been evasive. "The investigation is ongoing." He'd sounded so cold, not that she could blame him. He'd even asked her about the last time she'd seen Rob Perkins. If she hadn't gotten turned around after leaving Cody in the root cellar, it wouldn't have made her look so guilty. It had been dark and there'd been so much debris to try to get through... But she'd said all of that to him and it appeared he hadn't believed anything she'd told him. What he must think of her.

He'd asked if she'd seen anyone after she and Cody had gone for a walk. "I only saw them from a distance when I heard the girls with Emery and Rob screaming. I glimpsed them down by the creek playing around. After that I never saw any of them again." She'd registered his expression and felt her ire rise. "*You know me.* You know I'm not a killer." He hadn't commented. "I can't believe this."

"Let's get you a ride home" was all he'd said after that.

Her mother was pouring herself a cup of coffee as Olivia came into the kitchen. "You've been out all night?" Then Sharon Brooks took a good look at her. "What happened to you?" she demanded, alarmed.

"I got caught in a tornado." She poured herself a cup of coffee, even though the smell made her stomach roil. Cupping the mug of hot coffee in her hands, she tried to quit shaking. "I almost died. Cody..." Her voice broke and she couldn't continue.

"Cody Ryan? You were with him? I thought that was over a long time ago?"

Olivia shook her head, too exhausted to explain why she'd gone out with him tonight, let alone everything that had happened. She kept seeing Cody down in the root cellar, bleeding and unconscious. If that wasn't awful enough, she couldn't forget Deputy Jaden Montgomery's expression when he'd questioned her. He actually believed she could be responsible for what had happened to Cody, let alone the others?

"I should never have come home."

"Why did you after six years without hardly a word?"

She looked at her mother and felt a wave of guilt. Cody was right. She hadn't looked back when she'd left, not even to do more than occasionally keep in touch with her mother. But if anyone should be able to understand why she'd left, it was her mother.

Sharon had left small-town Montana, only to return home after she'd realized she was pregnant with Olivia. She'd moved in with her parents. Her mother and her grandparents, to make ends meet, had both raised Olivia. After her grandfather had died, Olivia had gone off to college, but her mother had stayed to take care of her own mother until her death.

Olivia took a sip of her coffee. "You came back here because you had no place to go," she said. "I came home for the same reason."

"You're pregnant?"

She shook her head. How could she explain that her dream hadn't turned out the way she'd thought it would? She'd gotten her degree in business administration and had no trouble getting a job. But she hadn't been able to explain the hollowness she had felt. She'd been haunted by the feelings that she'd made the wrong choices and not just with her job. She'd felt as if she'd left something undone back here and that she'd needed to go home.

"Don't you think I know why you fell in with Cody Ryan and then broke his heart when you hightailed it out of here? You didn't want to be me."

"Mom—"

"It's all right. I don't blame you. I never resented it. You had to leave. I wish you had at least come home once in a while to see me, but I understand that too. What I don't understand is why you came back now. I suppose you know that Jaden Montgomery is now a deputy over in Fortune Creek. Is it true what I heard, that the two of you were engaged?"

Olivia waved that away, definitely not wanting to talk about her broken engagement. "I saw him last night. He's in charge of the investigation out in Starling, where the tornado hit, almost destroying the entire community. Rob Perkins is dead, Cody's unconscious and Dean Marsh is missing."

Her mother shook her head. "I won't even ask what you were doing out there." Her expression softened as she asked, "Are you still in love with one of these men? Is that what brought you back?"

Olivia felt tears blur her vision as she shrugged. Maybe she was only in love with the past and that feeling of being silly and a fool in love with her whole life ahead of her. "I missed them both in their own ways."

Her mother rolled her eyes and rose to pour herself more coffee. "Your grandmother was right about you. She always said you were too much like me, just give your heart away willy-nilly. Go get a shower and go to bed. You look like you're going to fall on your face. I'll make you some breakfast later."

She kissed her mother on the cheek and headed for the bathroom, knowing it was going to take more than a shower and sleep to make this nightmare go away.

Chapter Five

Jenny Lee finally opened the door after the deputy had pounded on it, repeatedly calling out, "Sheriff's Department." He knew she was inside, curtains drawn, car in the drive. When she did finally answer, she only opened the door a crack, so she could peer out.

"I need to speak with you, Mrs. Lee," Jaden said. He could see only one of her eyes from where she hid behind the open door. It was red and swollen. He'd waited until her husband had left for work, needing to speak with her alone. "We can talk here or I can take you down to the sheriff's office, if you prefer, as part of my murder and assault investigation."

"I don't know anything," she cried. "Can't you just leave me alone?"

"I'm sorry, but I can't."

She didn't move for a moment, then finally pushed open the door to let him in as she turned and retreated into the house. As soon as he entered, he saw that there had been a struggle. A coffee table was splintered in one corner, broken glass from what appeared to be a lamp glittered on the worn wood floor, and he could see a shattered mirror over the fireplace.

He swore under his breath as he closed the door behind him and followed her to the rear of the house. It wasn't until she turned that he saw her black eye. She was a petite young woman with shoulder-length dark hair and a cowed expression, as if she'd had a rough life. "If you'd like to file charges against your husband—"

"No," she said with an adamant shake of her head. "I'm fine."

He could have argued that, given the painful way she was moving. He'd seen enough women like her to know her situation would only get worse if she stayed. But he knew she wouldn't want to hear it.

"Let's go out on the back porch," Jenny said. "I haven't felt like cleaning up yet. Watch where you step."

Gingerly he worked his way through the broken glass. Once on what was a closed-in sun porch, she sat down, pulling her legs up under her. She wore a sweat-suit set, the long-sleeved top smeared with blood.

Jaden still hadn't learned how to deal with domestic disputes. It was obvious that Tom Lee had physically abused his spouse. Jaden's first instinct was to go to Tom Lee's work and drag him outside. But unless Jenny filed charges…

"I need to get a statement from you about what happened last night in Starling," he said, pulling out his notebook. "You were there with Dean Marsh?" She nodded. "How long have the two of you been seeing each other?"

"For a while," she said.

"Weeks? Months?"

"I don't see what that has to do with—"

"Dean is missing, presumed dead. With one man murdered and another assaulted and in a coma, I need to know what was going on last night in Starling besides a tornado."

"You think Dean's dead?" There was a catch in her voice. Her eyes filled with tears for a moment before she bit her lip and made a swipe at them. "We'd been meeting secretly for a few months."

"Were you with him when the tornado hit?" Jaden asked.

She shook her head. "We'd had an argument. I left and walked up the road. When I saw the storm coming, I called my husband to come get me."

"What did you argue about?" he asked.

Jenny gave him an impatient look. "Dean wanted me to leave my husband so we could be together. He was going to tell his wife."

"You refused?"

"I realized we'd both been kidding ourselves. Neither of us could leave our spouses. It's financial suicide and that's if they didn't kill us. I'd realized that it had to stop or it might cost me my marriage."

"You told him you were going to tell your husband?"

She nodded. "He got really angry, accusing me of leading him on, and bringing up things from our past. He said I would destroy both of our marriages, and for what? We wouldn't be together and our spouses would put us through hell. I told him I didn't care—that it was over. I got out of the truck and walked away to call my husband to come get me."

"What did Dean do?"

"I don't know. I didn't look back. All I could think about was getting home." She looked down at her hands, picking at something under her fingernail.

"Are you regretting that now?" He'd had to ask.

She slowly lifted her head, determination a brittle gleam in her gaze. "I love my husband. This is all my fault."

He wanted to tell her that most abused wives blamed themselves—even those who hadn't had an affair with another man. That her husband had no right to beat her, no matter how upset he was. But Jaden saved his breath. He'd send over a rep from a local counseling agency. Hopefully, someone would be able to give Jenny some perspective.

"Where was your husband last night after the storm, after you came home?" he asked.

"Here with me."

"All night?"

She nodded, almost daring him to argue differently.

"You'll testify under oath to that, knowing what happens if you perjure yourself?" he asked.

"Yes."

The deputy put his notebook and pen away and rose. "If you change your mind about filing charges against your husband—"

"I won't."

"If you think of anything else that can help us find Dean Marsh, or if you hear from him, please give me a call at the Fortune Creek sheriff's office."

With that, he tipped his Stetson and made his way to his patrol SUV, telling himself all he could do was his job, but sometimes it was very difficult when he couldn't save those most vulnerable who needed saving.

OLIVIA HAD TRIED to sleep but couldn't. She kept thinking of Cody and wishing she'd never agreed to go with him to Starling. Now he might die. She'd never forgive herself for leaving him alone down in that hole. She had no idea who might have attacked him after she'd gone for help. The whole night had been a nightmare. She couldn't believe that Rob was dead, murdered, Cody unconscious in the hospital and Dean missing. How was that possible?

At a tap on her bedroom door, she looked up from where she'd been trying to sleep to see her mother in the doorway.

"The deputy is here to see you." The deputy. Jaden.

Her pulse kicked up a beat at the thought of seeing him again. He'd been just doing his job last night, but he'd been so distant. It had hurt her heart. She took a breath and let it out. "Tell him I'll be right out." As her mother closed the door, Olivia rose. She had showered and changed clothes after returning home earlier. Still, she went into the bathroom to brush her teeth and at least run a comb through her hair.

She stared at her face in the mirror for a few moments, surprised by the dark circles under her eyes, the paleness of her skin. Her injuries were all minor, including the cuts and bruises on her face and hands, but she felt weak from the shock of everything that had happened.

How could she not feel lucky to be alive? But the thought brought her no comfort. Cody was in the hospital, possibly fighting for his life, Rob was dead, and who knew what had happened to Dean.

And now she was being forced to confront her past. The decisions she'd made, the pain she'd caused. What choice did she have with Jaden being the deputy in charge of the investigation? There was too much history between them. Last night, he'd asked if she and Cody were together. How could she explain that she'd felt comfortable with him because he was familiar? That he'd felt safe. That she'd missed that closeness they'd once shared. He'd been a friend from a less confusing time.

What she hadn't considered was that Cody might have a different memory of their time together, especially of how it had ended. What if he never regained consciousness? Or what if, she realized with a start, he did wake up and he thought she was the one who'd attacked him?

But the real question was why she hadn't contacted Jaden when she'd returned home, knowing he was close by in Fortune Creek and a deputy sheriff now. Because she hadn't thought he'd want to hear from her. Still, wasn't he the real reason she'd come home? It was more complicated than that, she thought. Much more complicated.

Olivia found him waiting for her in the living room. Her mother had made coffee and poured him a cup. Both seemed nervous. "Is this about Cody? Is he…?" She couldn't bring herself to say the words.

"He hasn't regained consciousness yet, but he's still alive," the deputy said. "I just needed to ask you a few more questions about last night. If you have a minute?" He glanced past her. "If you don't mind, Mrs. Brooks…"

Her mother seemed a little surprised but acquiesced. "Then I'll leave you two to it," she said, then looked to Olivia. "If at any point you feel the need, you can call our family lawyer."

She waved her away with "I'm fine." Once her mother was gone, she stayed standing, unsure where to sit or what to say. "I don't need a lawyer, do I?"

"That would be up to you."

She shook her head. "You know I didn't harm anyone last night." When he said nothing, she felt as if she might cry. "You *know* me."

EARLIER, JADEN HAD been sitting across from Sharon Brooks, turning the brim of his Stetson nervously in his fingers, when Olivia had finally come out of her bedroom.

He'd risen to his feet, his gaze taking in the lack of color in her face, the cuts and bruises, the dark circles around her eyes. She'd appeared exhausted, hurt and scared. He'd been struck by how vulnerable she looked. His heart had gone out to her.

For a moment, she was his Livie, the woman he'd fallen head over heels in love with. He wanted to pull her into his arms and assure her that everything was going to be all right. But he couldn't promise that since he wasn't sure he knew this woman as well as he'd once thought.

Did he really believe she'd had anything to do with what had happened last night in Starling? He'd known Livie intimately back in college. But when she'd gotten her dream job after graduation and talked about postponing the wedding indefinitely, he'd been shocked. No way had he seen it coming.

She was the woman he'd been ready to marry right after graduation. Heck, by now they could have a child or two. The thought hurt his chest. He'd been looking forward to marriage, kids, their own house. Worse, he'd been ready to follow her anywhere her career took her—even if it meant leaving Montana.

After the breakup, he'd taken the job in Fortune Creek. He'd found he loved being a deputy, helping people, putting away the bad ones. It wasn't perfect, but then, it was such a detour from the life he'd had planned with Livie, it felt right.

Seeing her again had knocked him off-kilter. He hadn't expected her to come back to Montana—let alone here, so close to Fortune Creek and him. And now she was mixed up dead center in his investigation.

Determined to keep this official and not dig through the past, he pulled out his notebook. "Tell me again how you ended up in Starling."

Olivia blinked as if she hadn't expected him to ask about the investigation.

"Nice to see you, too, Jaden. Yes, I'm glad to be home. No, I wish I hadn't run into old high school friends and decided to go with them out to Starling on Halloween." She took a seat in the chair her mother had vacated across from the couch. Jaden sat back down in the same spot on the couch where he'd been earlier and took out his pen, warning himself to keep this professional.

"So how long had you been back when this was planned?" he asked, not looking at her.

"A couple of days. It wasn't planned. It was just spur-of-the-moment."

He shook his head. "I don't think so. Whoever wanted to kill Rob, possibly Cody and Dean, too, planned this. It might have seemed spur-of-the-moment to you, but someone was behind this."

She stared at him in obvious shock. "No, I can't believe that."

"You think it was just old friends getting together where possibly three of them might have ended up dead?"

She stood up and began to pace. "It wasn't like that. We had a couple of beers. We were reminiscing, laughing and having fun together."

"Who suggested it?" he asked, and she frowned.

"Emery. Or maybe it was Rob. I don't remember."

"You sure it wasn't Cody?" She shook her head. "How was it that you and Cody ended up at Starling?"

"He asked if I wanted to go. At the time, it sounded like fun. I didn't know everyone was going to pair off and disappear or I never would have gone."

"Tell me again who all was at the bar," Jaden said, his eyes on his notebook.

"Cody, Emery, Rob and Dean," she said.

He looked up at her then. "They weren't with dates or their wives or girlfriends at the bar that night?"

"It wasn't that unusual in the old days," she said, sounding defensive. "I used to hang out with them, play pool, go fishing. We were all just friends."

"Just you and the boys, huh?"

Her eyes narrowed with anger. "I told you about them when you and I were in college. They were old friends. That's why I agreed to go that night. I thought…" She shook her head. "It turned out to be a mistake even before the tornado."

"A mistake?"

"Cody still resents me leaving. He feels trapped here and…" She waved a hand through the air. "They're his issues, but me getting to leave is a bone of contention between us. Why is my relationship with him so important to you?" she demanded with obvious irritation.

"So you did argue."

She groaned. "Do we have to do this, Jaden?" Their gazes met. "You know I didn't attack Cody."

He wished he did. If she had rolled a rock down into that hole, she might not have realized it would hit him in the head and knock him unconscious. It could have been impulsive, like ending an engagement without any warning.

"Describe for me again what happened that night."

He listened as she told the same story she had last night. She'd left Cody to get help. He'd been fine.

"Any idea who might have wanted to harm him?" She shook her head again. "What about Rob or Dean?" Another shake of her head.

"I've been gone, remember?"

"I remember." He held her gaze for a long moment. They didn't have anything to say to each other, but there'd once been a time when they used to talk for hours. He had often called her at night, lying in bed. He'd loved the sleepy sound of her voice and had imagined her lying there.

But that was back when they'd been engaged. Back when he'd thought that one day she would be lying in bed next to him, talking about their day or their kids or their new dreams, shared dreams.

"Tell me where everyone else was when you and Cody left the group to wander up the hillside."

With a sigh, she repeated everything she'd told him before.

"Cody and I were fine. He saved my life when the house above us was ripped away in the tornado."

"Must have been terrifying." He couldn't imagine what she'd been through, but Livie had always been strong.

"It was. Then the tornado moved on. We saw the bones that had been dislodged from the soil. The ladder had been ripped away, but Cody helped me climb up the shelves. Unfortunately, they barely held my weight, so he couldn't use them to get out. I didn't want to leave him down there, but he insisted I go for help."

"That's the last time you saw him conscious?"

"I still don't understand what could have happened." She shook her head. "When I came back, he was lying down there motionless."

"Had you seen any rocks down there? Any that could have dislodged and struck him?"

She straightened her shoulders. "Like you said, I was terrified. I wasn't really looking around. But I think it was just dirt. That's why Cody was worried about it caving in more." She met his gaze. "You think someone purposely tried to hurt him?"

"Who of your group would want to do that?" Jaden asked.

"No one. They were his friends."

"Including Rob Perkins? There wasn't anything going on between them…? Any disagreements?" He saw her hesitate. "What?"

"Cody wasn't happy with Dean for bringing Jenny. He thought it was going to lead to trouble since they were married to other people."

"And Cody is close with Rob and Emery?" he asked.

Again, she hesitated. "I got the impression that Rob and Emery haven't matured. They brought those girls, you know—they're out of high school, but not old enough to drink."

Jaden thought the whole bunch of them were trying too hard to bring back their high school days. They appeared to be holding on to a past that was long gone. But then again, he realized that he'd been holding on to thoughts of Olivia and the imagined day she might return to him.

And now here she was.

"You and Cody were together the entire time last night? Neither of you left the other until you got out and went for help?"

"Yes, we were together the entire time. When the storm hit, we climbed down in the root cellar. Cody locked the overhead door, but then the tornado ripped it away, leaving us stranded down there. If you're asking if either of us climbed out and killed Rob..." She shook her head. "Why would we?"

"Why would anyone want Rob dead?"

She seemed to think for a moment before glancing up. "Rob and Emery talked about finding the gold last night. Maybe he went looking for it. You're that sure his death wasn't an accident?"

Jaden nodded. "Was there anything that happened back in high school, an old grudge involving a girl maybe?"

"Not that I can recall. You should ask someone who's been here this whole time."

"I will." He closed his notebook. She hadn't changed her story. He didn't think he would get anything else out of her. Yet he hesitated. "So how long are you back for?"

"I don't know."

He hated that spark of hope that filled his chest like helium. He'd never gotten over her, and seeing her again had brought back all those memories and feelings. He reminded himself that Cody Ryan must have felt the same way. They'd both loved this woman and she'd left them both.

"Are you thinking about staying?" He'd strayed away from the investigation into dangerous territory and mentally kicked himself. But he couldn't help it. He had to know.

She met his gaze. "I'm not sure."

"What about your dream job?" He hadn't been able to help himself. "Never mind. It's none of my business." He rose, telling himself to leave it at that. The worse thing he could do was ask if there was a chance for the two of them. She'd made her feelings clear enough when she hadn't called to let him know she was back in town. Instead, she'd accepted a date with her old high school boyfriend.

He hated how pathetic he felt, but finding her in the area had left him off balance. It had been easier to tell himself she was gone and that he was fine when he couldn't see her. But with her back…

"If I have any more questions, I'll call," he said as he headed for the door. "Goodbye, Mrs. Brooks," he called, knowing she hadn't gone far.

"It's Sharon," she called back. "Since you were almost my son-in-law."

He felt his jaw tighten and glanced at Olivia. She looked as uncomfortable as he felt. He gave her a nod, settled his Stetson on his head and left.

Once outside, he took a deep breath and let it out. He told himself to stick to his job. He had a killer to find. Maybe of more than one person, if Cody Ryan died. He turned his thoughts to Dean Marsh as he climbed into his patrol SUV and headed for the Marsh house.

Chapter Six

With her mother plying her with questions about what Jaden had wanted, about what had happened on Halloween out at Starling and about her plans for the future, Olivia couldn't take it anymore and left the house. She drove to the hospital, hoping for good news about Cody's condition.

Unfortunately, he was not able to have visitors. Deputy Jaden Montgomery had restricted all visitors to Cody's room, the head nurse told her, so she couldn't even see him—let alone find out his condition.

She was starting to leave when she looked down the hallway and saw a young woman come out of Cody's room. Slim, with blond, straight hair, wearing jeans and a T-shirt, the woman glanced toward the nurses' station. Olivia's gaze met hers. The woman quickly turned and took off in the other direction.

"I just saw someone come out of Cody Ryan's room," she hurriedly told the nurse.

"Are you sure it wasn't one of our nurses?"

"Yes. She was wearing jeans and a T-shirt, and when I saw her, she took off."

The head nurse rushed down the hall to check on the patient but quickly returned. Olivia wanted to admonish her for not keeping a closer eye on his room, but could see how upset the nurse was for letting it happen.

Leaving the hospital, Olivia glanced around, hoping to see the woman again as she drove down the main drag. She had no idea what she would do if she found the woman. But who she did see was Emery. He was just going into the bar where they'd all recently reunited.

Without questioning her intentions, she pulled into the first parking place she came to, got out and followed him. Jaden's questioning had more than bothered her. He'd gotten personal at the end and she'd seen how much it had upset him. He'd been trying so hard to keep it professional.

He'd left her feeling as if maybe he did still care. That gave her hope. If it wasn't for this investigation… That, she told herself, was why she was headed into the bar to see Emery. This wouldn't end until whoever had killed Rob and attacked Cody was found and arrested. And, like she'd told Jaden, she'd been away too long and didn't know what had been going on in her absence.

That first night in the bar, it had felt like old times. But by the time they'd reached Starling, she'd sensed that it wasn't—and not just for her and Cody. The old gang wasn't as close as they'd been. Still, she couldn't believe that one of them was a murderer.

Stepping into the dimly lit bar, she had to give her eyes a moment to adjust before she spotted Emery. He had taken a stool at the bar some distance from anyone else. He had a drink in front of him, even though it was still morning. All his attention seemed to be on his drink, as if he could find answers in the glass in front of him.

As she approached, she wondered if he was meeting someone. She'd never been as close with Emery as she had been with the others back in high school. He was the bad boy, the biker, the kid who'd lived, so to speak, on the wrong side of the tracks. Even in small towns without railroad tracks, there was sometimes a part of town less desirable.

"Is this stool taken?" she asked as she started to join him.

He seemed surprised to see her but smiled and appeared glad for the company. "Have a seat. What are you drinking?"

"I'd take a cola."

He laughed. "Teetotaler," he joked and signaled the bartender. Like her, he had scrapes and bruises but had miraculously survived the tornado, as had the two young women with him and Rob. "You been over to the hospital?"

She nodded. "They wouldn't tell me anything about his condition or let me see him."

He gave a shake of his head. "I heard he's still unconscious. My aunt knows someone who works there. I can't believe what happened."

Olivia wasn't sure if he was talking about Rob's murder, Cody's injury, Dean's disappearance or the tornado. "I know what you mean," she said as the bartender put a napkin and her drink in front of her. She thanked him and turned to Emery. "What happened after I left town?"

He frowned. "What do you mean?"

"The old gang. I picked up on what I thought was good-natured jabs that first night at the bar, so I didn't think too much about it. Rob was leaving town, going to his dream job. Now I realize that not everyone was happy for him."

"I was. Why wouldn't I be?" Emery said almost irritably as he reached for his glass. He drained it and signaled the bartender for another.

"I know you and Rob have been best friends almost since you were born. At least, you were best friends when I left. Did that change?"

"Why are you asking me these questions?" He eyed her suspiciously.

"I'm just trying to understand what might have changed since I left."

He sighed. "A lot changes in six years." The bartender took his empty and left a fresh drink, but Emery didn't pick it up right away. He seemed lost in thought.

Olivia took a sip of her soft drink and waited.

"Rob and I weren't as tight as we used to be, maybe." He shrugged. "That's why I was excited about going out to Starling on Halloween. We hadn't done anything like that in a very long time. As for the old gang... We're not in high school anymore. We all have jobs, responsibilities."

She definitely knew that feeling of a job becoming her entire life. She'd thought it would make her happy. She was making money, and she had her own place, though it was small and the neighbors noisy, and the hours at work long. She'd woken up one morning to realize she wanted more.

Emery looked down the bar for a moment before he said, "A lot of our friends left, greener grass, like I have to tell you. It's not like only the losers stay." He picked up his drink and took a gulp, his eyes on the back bar.

"Have you ever thought about leaving?"

He shook his head. "I left for a while after you did. Just got on my bike and checked out other places." He smiled over at her. "I found out that there is no place like Montana, and I hightailed it back. You're thinking that whoever killed Rob was jealous he was getting out of here and they weren't?" His expression said he didn't believe that was the case.

She was reminded that it was Rob who had wanted to go out to Starling and stay until midnight. If he'd been worried that one of the others resented his success, he certainly hadn't shown it. "Do you really believe there is gold still hidden out in Starling?"

Emery chuckled. "Doubtful. But it's like the other legends about the place. It gives people something to talk about, dream about."

"What would you do if you found the gold?" she asked and took another swallow.

"Depends on how much is there."

She smiled over at him. "Enough to take a trip around the world."

"That's just it. I wouldn't go anywhere. I'd buy me a place on the lake. I wouldn't have to work, but I probably would. I'd stay right there." He laughed. "I guess I don't need any gold. I'm…content. Some people think that's just laziness talking, but I like my life. I wouldn't change it."

She studied him for a moment. "I understand completely." She told him about her dream job. "All those years of college and then the job…" She shook her head. "I realized it wasn't what I wanted." At the heart of it, she'd missed Montana, the familiar, the place she'd grown up in. Wasn't that why she'd come back? At least, that was what she'd told herself, not that she could deny Jaden had also been part of it. The problem was…even before Halloween night and what had happened, she'd held out little hope that Jaden would ever be able to forgive her for hurting him.

JADEN FOUND ANGIE MARSH loading suitcases into the back of her SUV as he drove up. The petite, slightly built brunette didn't look happy to see him as he got out of his patrol vehicle and walked toward her. "Going somewhere?" he asked, eyeing the suitcases. He saw that she had loaded numerous boxes in the back. None of it looked like anything of her missing husband's.

It had crossed his mind that she might be going to meet Dean somewhere, the two of them on the run together after Dean had killed Rob and almost succeeded in taking out Cody as well. What struck him was how much Jenny resembled Angie. Clearly, Dean had a type.

"I don't have time for this, Deputy," she said, pushing past him with a load in her arms. She wore jeans and a T-shirt with a band's name he'd never heard of. Her long dark hair was pulled up in a ponytail. But what really caught his eye was that she wasn't wearing her wedding ring.

On her way back to the house, he stopped her. "I just need a few minutes to talk to you about Dean." She hesitated, looking as if she'd prefer not to. "We can talk here or down at the sheriff's office."

With a sigh, she dusted off her jeans and motioned toward the house. "Let's make it quick. I don't want to be here when he comes back."

Did she really think he was coming back? She'd be in the minority, from what Jaden had heard around town. Pretty much everyone assumed he was on the run, either a murderer or just a philanderer. Some thought that Jenny Lee's husband, Tom, had probably found him that night and killed him. Why Dean's body hadn't turned up was anyone's guess.

The deputy followed Angie into the house, not surprised to see there were more items by the front door that she was apparently planning to load into her vehicle. She was clearing out, leaving not just her missing cheating husband, but town.

"You said you wanted to leave before Dean returned," Jaden said once she led him into the kitchen and pointed to a chair at the table after he declined coffee.

"Does that mean you've heard from your husband?"

She poured herself some orange juice, then turned her back to add something to it. When she sat down across the table from him, he could smell the vodka. "I haven't heard from Dean," she said. "I don't expect to."

"Why is that?"

Angie lifted a brow. "Wouldn't you be too ashamed to show your face in this town?"

"Because of what happened out in Starling on Halloween?" he asked, confused.

"We all know what happened. Dean was with that tramp, Jenny Lee."

"I thought maybe you were referring to Rob Perkins being killed and Cody Ryan being assaulted and in the hospital, still unconscious. You're that sure Dean didn't do it and that's why he's disappeared?" Jaden asked.

For a moment, she looked as confused as he was. Then she let out a bark of a laugh before picking up her drink. "Dean? A murderer?" She laughed some more before taking a large gulp of her juice. "Dean's a cheater, a liar and a ne'er-do-well who burns his bridges. Smell that?" she asked with a sniff. "That's a bridge burning. Clearly, you've never met my husband." She took another drink of her orange juice. "Dean's a lot of things, but a killer? No, he wouldn't have the stomach for it. He's gotten caught cheating and now he's afraid to come home and face the consequences."

Jaden told himself that maybe Angie was just a woman spurned who'd had enough and was cutting her losses. Yet he couldn't help feeling like there was more going on. "You're that sure he didn't have any conflicts with his two friends?"

"He was jealous of them, especially Rob, since he was leaving here to start a better life. But Emery?" She shook her head.

"I know you're angry with him, but there's a chance his body might still be found out in Starling," he warned. "The area is still being searched."

With a shake of her heard, she said, "Oh, he'll turn up, alive and well and lying through his teeth."

He felt himself studying her ring finger. There was only a ghost of a white line where it had been on her finger. He wondered if she hadn't taken it off sometime before all this.

"If you hear from him, please call me," he said as he rose to leave.

"Oh, I will. I'll want you to keep him away from me because I want him gone. I wish he was capable of murder. Then you could drive him to Deer Lodge to the state prison and we'd all be shed of him."

"One more thing," he said as if the thought had just come to him. "Where were you on Halloween night?"

She glared at him, then shook her head as if amused. "If I wanted to kill my husband, I wouldn't have driven all the way out to Starling in the middle of the night, Deputy. I would have just cut his throat while he slept next to me. Halloween wasn't the first time he was with Jenny Lee, by the way."

After leaving Angie, Jaden drove over to Whitney Clark's house and questioned her about Rob and Emery's whereabouts just before the tornado. He then stopped by her friend Tammy Bell's and got pretty much the same information from her.

Both had been scared and foggy on what had happened.

"Had Rob and Emery been arguing?" No.

"Had either been acting strangely?" To that, he'd gotten confused looks. Clearly, neither girl had known either of them well enough to know. Both girls were grounded and still shocked and upset that they'd almost died.

As he was leaving the Bell residence, the hospital called.

Cody had regained consciousness.

Chapter Seven

Cody felt himself falling in and out of sleep as he waited for the doctor to come back. Earlier, he'd told him that he had a severe concussion from a blow to the head. Cody had touched the bandage on his forehead, but he couldn't remember how he'd gotten it. His head hurt and he felt confused and anxious.

When the door opened, though, it was the deputy. He groaned silently, having learned that when a cop showed up, it was usually not a good sign.

"How are you feeling?" Jaden asked as if he really cared.

Cody doubted it since they'd been in love with the same woman. He wondered if the deputy had gotten over Olivia. He had his doubts.

The lawman dragged up a chair and, pulling out his notebook and pen, sat down. "Need to ask you some questions about Halloween night at Starling."

Cody frowned. He'd awakened in a hospital bed, wondering how he'd gotten there. "Halloween?" Why couldn't he remember? Actually, he was having trouble retrieving his last memory. "What is today?" Jaden told him. "I've lost three days?" He couldn't help being scared. He had no idea what had happened in those three days. They were now a dark hole.

The deputy studied him, no doubt thinking he was lying. But why would he need to lie? Why was the deputy here asking him questions unless something bad had happened?

"What do you remember?"

"Work." He frowned in concentration. "Friday, getting off work and going to the bar."

"And after that?"

Cody shook his head. "Nothing until I woke up in this bed. Are you going to tell me what happened?"

"I'd rather you remember on your own. The doctor said once the swelling goes down in your brain, you should remember more."

"Great," he said, leaning back in the bed. "You can't tell me how I got hurt?"

"There was a tornado."

"No kidding?"

"You probably don't recall who you were with or what you were doing in Starling."

Cody frowned. Of course he hadn't been alone. But a tornado? What had he been doing in Starling? "Sorry, nothing. I have no idea what I might have been doing out there."

"Let me know if you remember something," Jaden said as he saw the doctor coming down the hall. His time was up.

AFTER THE DEPUTY LEFT, Cody stared out the window, his heart pounding. He blamed his aching head for why he hadn't caught on sooner. Had someone tried to kill him? Why else was the law asking him all these questions? Something had happened at Starling. It had happened to him. He squeezed his eyes shut, grimacing at the pain as he tried to remember. For a moment, he thought he saw something on the edge of his memory, a fleeting image of a dark figure standing above him. But it was quickly gone. What scared him was that if he really was in danger, he wouldn't have any idea who he had to fear.

At a sound, his eyes flew open, startled to find someone right beside his bed, standing over him. "Krystal? What are you doing here?" he demanded, drawing back instinctively.

"Keep your voice down," she ordered. "I had to see you." She reached out to touch the bandage on his head.

He grabbed her hand. "You shouldn't be here. The deputy thinks someone tried to kill me."

She mugged a face at that and pulled up the chair close to the bed before sitting down. "Who'd want to kill you? That old girlfriend of yours. That's who you were with Halloween night, right?"

"Old girlfriend?" he asked, even more confused.

"Olivia Brooks," she snapped, no doubt thinking he was faking his confusion. "She's back in town. Why would you take her out to Starling?"

"I have no idea. I don't remember anything. I have a concussion."

She studied him with squinted suspicious eyes. "You don't know if she's the one who coldcocked you?"

"No." He frowned, making his headache worse. "I didn't even know she was back in town."

"You were with her at the bar the other night," Krystal snapped. "You're telling me you don't remember that either?"

He could understand why she was suspicious. "I guess it's a major concussion since I lost three days of memory. You didn't happen to be out there at Starling, did you?"

Krystal laughed at that. "Why would I want to hurt you? Whose idea was it for you and Olivia to go out there together?"

He groaned and pointed to his head. "You probably know more about it than I do."

"I know you cheated on me," she said and pulled a pout.

"We aren't together, so it's not cheating." He wished he'd rung for a nurse the moment he'd seen Krystal beside his bed. "I can't do this right now. I'm supposed to be resting."

She stood abruptly but stayed standing over him in a way that made him nervous. "Did you know that they didn't find Dean's body in the rubble left from the tornado? No one knows what happened to him."

Had someone mentioned a tornado? "Dean's missing?"

"Haven't they told you anything?" She sounded both surprised and delighted. "You know you were all out in Starling on Halloween night when the tornado hit, right?" She didn't give him time to answer. "Dean, Jenny, Emery, Rob and a couple of young girls. Then you don't know that Rob is dead. *Murdered.* Seems someone pushed a wall over on him." She made a pained face.

He felt as if she'd dropped an anvil on his chest. What the hell had happened out in Starling that night? "Rob was murdered?"

"Isn't that what I just said?"

He knew that Krystal had never liked Rob or Dean, especially since Jenny was married to Krystal's brother, Tom. "You sure you weren't out in Starling that night?"

Krystal smiled. "If I had been, then the head count would have been much higher. Olivia Brooks among the dead or wounded."

"Excuse me," a female voice said as the hospital room door opened. A nurse stood framed in the doorway. "Mr. Ryan needs his rest. Only family can visit."

"I'm his girlfriend," Krystal said, meeting his gaze as if daring him to argue otherwise.

"I'm sorry, but you'll have to leave," the nurse said.

Krystal kissed Cody on the mouth before turning to walk out the door.

"Are you all right?" the nurse asked him.

"Fine." It was a lie. He wouldn't be fine until he remembered everything about that night.

CODY WAS CONSCIOUS. Olivia felt weak with relief after the call from Emery with the news. She cared about her former best friend, boyfriend and neighbor. She'd been so afraid for him. She felt a second wave of relief. His being awake meant he could tell Jaden who had attacked him. Finally, she would be cleared of any wrongdoing.

Before she could rush to the hospital, the deputy called.

"Cody wants to see you. The nurse said you could see him for a few minutes because he is so insistent."

"I'll be right there," she said, anxious to find out what had happened after she'd left him to go for help.

Cody was propped up in bed, his head bandaged. He smiled as she walked into his hospital room, making her think they'd put any nastiness from Halloween night behind them. She realized he was staring at her as if just as relieved to see her as she was to see him. "Did Jaden tell you?"

"He said you wanted to see me. Did you tell him who attacked you?" she asked.

He started to shake his head but quickly stopped himself. His eyes closed for a moment. When he opened them, he was staring at her again. "I'm sorry. I thought Jaden would have... I can't remember *anything*. When I woke up, I didn't even remember you were in town, let alone that I'd apparently seen you at the bar. You're back in town?"

He sounded so surprised at that, but not half as surprised as she was to hear that he didn't remember anything from Starling. "Wait. You don't remember Starling, the tornado…?"

"Nothing. What were we doing out there? Were we together?"

She sat on the edge of the chair next to his bed. That was when she noticed the deputy standing in the doorway, watching them. "What did Jaden tell you?"

"Not much. He said he'd prefer that I remember on my own. But I heard there was a tornado that hit Starling and you were there with me?"

Olivia fought to swallow the lump that had formed in her throat. "It was just a bunch of old friends doing something foolish." She explained how Emery had come up with the idea at the bar the night before Halloween.

"We couldn't have known there would be a tornado," he said, frowning. "How was it that we survived?"

Before she could answer, the deputy stepped into the room. "That's enough for now," Jaden said. "I know you have a lot of questions. The doctor said you need to rest. Once the swelling goes down in your brain, you'll probably remember at least some of it."

Cody looked at Olivia. "Thanks for coming to see me."

She smiled and rose. "Just get well."

On the way down the hall toward the exit, Jaden stopped her.

"I couldn't let you tell him. I want him to remember on his own," the deputy said.

She couldn't hide her frustration. "I need him to remember so that I'm no longer a suspect." His expression didn't change. "You being angry with me isn't giving me confidence that I'm innocent until proven guilty. The way you're looking at me right now feels as if it's more about our broken engagement than what happened to Cody."

"How am I looking at you?"

"Like you want to see me behind bars," she snapped.

"Sorry, that's not my intention. I'm only trying to get to the truth."

"I've told you the truth." She shook her head, seeing that he still didn't believe her. "None of this has anything to do with me."

"Right. You were just an innocent bystander who just happened to be down in the root cellar alone with Cody. You wouldn't have hurt him," he said, studying her closely. "But aren't you at least curious to know who tried to kill your boyfriend?"

"He isn't my boyfriend," she declared. "We're just old friends."

"'The old gang.' Isn't that what you used to call them? I think you know more about them and what happened out there than you're telling me. They're still your friends."

Olivia wondered about that. Friends didn't kill each other. What was he asking? "They've had years together while I was gone. I hardly know them anymore."

"Right. You've been gone so long that none of this probably matters to you."

"That's not true." She had to look away. She knew what he was doing. "What is it you want from me?"

He looked down at his boots for a moment. "You know these people. They trust you. You're one of them." His gaze rose to meet hers and held it. "Someone's lying. If you hear something…"

"You want my help?" She hadn't meant to sound so shocked. With a sigh, she said, "I'm really not sure anyone will be telling me anything, but you have to know that I'll help any way I can." She started to turn away, but stopped.

"What did you find out about the bones we discovered in the root cellar?"

"They're checking dental records and DNA, but the coroner said the remains are those of a young girl of about sixteen."

"Is it Evangeline?"

He shrugged. "We'll see."

Olivia couldn't believe that he could doubt it. "Whose house was that root cellar in?" she asked, keeping him from walking away just yet.

Jaden hesitated. "My family's."

She felt her eyes widen in surprise.

"Please don't jump to conclusions. We left there before she disappeared. I don't know who moved into the house. Maybe no one."

"What about Elden Rusk?" she demanded. "Is he still alive? Could he have been in Starling that night?"

The deputy groaned. "If he's still alive, I really have my doubts he was in Starling on Halloween."

"Because you want it to be one of my old friends. Or better yet, me."

He shook his head. "Believe it or not, I'm just doing my job. I'll try to find Elden. I'll find out if he's been in the area." With that, he turned and headed down the hall to the nurses' station.

Olivia felt sick to her stomach as she watched him leave. What had she thought would happen when she came home? Certainly not this. Jaden was angry with her, which scared her. What if Cody remembered that they'd argued and thought she'd been the one to attack him down in the root cellar?

Glancing back down the hall, she saw the young woman she'd seen earlier exiting Cody's hospital room. She started to call down to the nurses' station to Jaden, but he was already gone and the head nurse was on the phone.

Turning toward Cody's room, she saw the blonde disappear around the corner. She went after her. As she passed a nurse, she alerted her that a patient in Room 9 needed help. Then she kept going after the blonde, determined to find out who she was.

By the time she reached the corner, the woman was halfway down the hallway. She called, "Excuse me! Could you please wait up?"

There was no way the woman hadn't heard. Quite the contrary. The blonde increased her speed.

Determined to find out who she was, Olivia ran after her. "I asked you to stop," she said when she drew closer.

The blonde said something rude and kept going.

Olivia grabbed her arm, spinning her around until they were face-to-face. "Who are you?" she demanded.

"Let go of me."

"Not until you tell me who you are and why you were in Cody's room."

The young woman's expression turned ugly. She jerked her arm free and, spitting out the words, said, "I have every right to see Cody. More right than you do. He's *my* boyfriend."

Olivia blinked. "Your boyfriend?" But before she could get more information, the blonde took off down the hall to the exit and was gone.

Staring after her, she realized that she should have known Cody would have been dating someone. He could have even been married after all this time. Cody Ryan had never gone long without a girlfriend—even back in grade school.

Chapter Eight

Jaden couldn't help being frustrated by this case, by everything. As he climbed into his patrol SUV, he admitted that seeing Olivia again had him so far off-kilter, he didn't know which way was up.

Worse, if she and Cody had argued the night of the tornado, which he suspected they had, she could have picked up a rock and flung it at him without thinking. While she'd never been impulsive, her decision to return home seemed that way. She didn't seem to have an answer for why she'd come home or how long she planned to stay. That wasn't like her.

After interviewing her, he'd checked. She'd quit her job, one that she'd worked so hard, apparently, to get since it was what she said she'd dreamed of since she was a girl. Why would she do that? He'd assumed she was happy with the decision she'd made after wanting to postpone their wedding indefinitely so she could fulfill that dream.

His cell phone rang. Pushing aside his suspicions and concerns about Olivia for the time being, he saw it was the crime lab.

"Thought you'd want to know about those bones uncovered up there," the technician said. "I'm not sure if you were informed, but there were two sets in that pile. The one set is from a teenage girl. The second set is male, somewhere from twenty-five to thirty."

"Will you be able to get DNA from them?" Jaden asked.

"Doubtful, but with the girl, quite a bit of her clothing had also been buried with her." Even before he described it, Jaden knew the bones were going to be Evangeline Rusk's.

"Were there any other remains, like a baby's?" No. That meant she hadn't been pregnant, the baby had been too small and its bones had deteriorated, or Evangeline had already given birth. Jaden thanked him and disconnected, thinking that he needed to find Elden Rusk, if he was still alive, and give him the news.

Meanwhile, he needed to talk to Emery Jordan. Starting his SUV, he headed for Emery's bike shop.

He found him working on what looked like a vintage Harley, all the parts spread out on the floor around him. Seeing the man at work, he was reminded of the expression "happier than a pig in mud."

Emery looked up, but it had taken Jaden yelling his name several times over the rock music playing in the garage area before he acknowledged him.

The deputy motioned toward the bike shop office and headed in that direction. Emery came in a few minutes later, wiping his greasy hands on a rag before he turned down the music. It was more tolerable in here than in the garage, but still loud.

"More questions?" Emery asked and took a seat behind a cluttered desk. "Have a seat."

Jaden pulled up a padded army-green chair from another era and sat. Emery had bought the old gas station furnished when he'd started his bike shop, the deputy recalled. "How's business?"

With a shrug, he said, "So-so. It will pick up. It's always

slow this time of year. Is that what you wanted to talk about, my business?"

"Actually, I wanted to talk about your relationship with Rob Perkins," Jaden said. "I understand Rob was an investor when you started the shop."

Emery's eyes narrowed. "You think I killed him so I wouldn't have to pay him back? He was the first person I paid back when I got the shop running."

"Okay, if not financial, did you two have any other kind of disagreement?"

"I know what you're looking for. An argument over a girl or a bet or jealousy because Rob was following his dream. Sorry, there was none of that. No girl, no bet, and I was happy for Rob. This," Emery said, indicating the bike shop, "has always been my dream. You're barking up the wrong tree. I would never have killed him or anyone else."

"What about Dean Marsh?"

"I don't have a gripe with him either. Did I approve of what he and Jenny were doing?" He shook his head. "None of my business."

"What about their spouses?" the deputy asked. "You involved with either of them?"

Emery laughed. "Involved? Me and Tom? Or me and Angie?"

"Either."

"Now you are just being silly."

"What about Rob and Dean or Rob and Cody? How'd they get along?"

The bike shop owner hesitated a little too long. "Fine, as far as I know."

Jaden studied him, picking up on something. Putting his notebook and pen away, he asked, "Why Starling? I heard it was your idea to go out there Halloween night."

"Really? I might have brought it up, but Rob's the one who suggested it to me. We'd gone out there before on Halloween growing up, so why not for old times' sake?"

Yes, why not? "Did anyone from your old group who was at the bar decide *not* to go?"

Emery thought for a moment before shaking his head.

"What about other people at the bar the night you all decided to do this?" the deputy asked. "Anyone in the crowd have a reason to be listening to your conversation? Anyone with a grudge against you or Rob or Cody or Dean?"

This time there was no mistaking it. Jaden knew he'd hit upon something. Emery looked away for a moment. "Krystal Lee. She and Rob used to date. They broke up when he started talking about a job on the West Coast. I remember seeing her at the bar that night. It was strange."

"Strange how?"

"She was with Jenny Lee. Neither of them drink alcohol. Jenny's in AA and Krystal's pregnant. I got the feeling that they were trolling, you know."

"So, they could have overheard your plans for Halloween?" Jaden asked.

Emery nodded. "They both left right after that, so maybe they heard what we were talking about."

"You said Krystal's pregnant? Is Rob the father of her baby?"

"He swears he's not." He seemed to realize what he'd said. "I guess it doesn't matter now."

Straightening his Stetson, Jaden rose. "Thanks. If you think of anything else…" He knew there was more; he could feel it.

He still had so many questions. Anyone with a grudge could have been at the bar that night, could have overheard the group's plans for Halloween—including Jenny and Krystal. He wondered how Jenny and Dean had ended up together at Starling that night, sans their spouses. His guess was that Jenny's husband's sister, Krystal, wouldn't have been all right with it.

But there was one way to find out. He'd ask Krystal.

AS OLIVIA LEFT the hospital, she couldn't get the blonde off her mind. How could she not have realized Cody was in a relationship? A memory surfaced from that night at the bar. When she'd come up to the table, she recalled Dean elbowing Cody. She hadn't caught what he'd said. At the time, she'd thought Dean was kidding Cody because of his surprised look when he'd seen her.

Had anyone mentioned a girlfriend? The guys had all been there without dates or wives. But now that she thought about it, she knew Cody would have had a girlfriend. Back in their high school days, before they'd become serious, he'd never been without a date. He'd been like a magnet, always drawing the opposite sex to him. He might even have been serious about one or two of them. Like the blonde she'd seen at the hospital?

As she drove, something in the rearview mirror caught her eye. A dark-colored SUV behind her. She recalled it had pulled out behind her as she'd left the hospital parking lot. She hadn't thought anything of it, only noticing when she turned out of town—and it did as well.

She couldn't see the driver's face with the sun shining off the windshield, but she felt a prickle of concern as she sped up and the driver behind her did the same. Squinting in the mirror, she tried to read the dirty license plate on the SUV but couldn't make out the numbers and letters. Maybe it was someone she knew following her home.

Or not. Her instincts told her not. She started to reach for her phone, only to stop herself. Was she really considering calling Jaden and telling him...what?

Slowing down, Olivia hoped the driver would pass her before they got very far out of town. Her mother's house was still a couple of miles up the road. It sat on five acres, with no other houses nearby, with no one around since Sharon had said she had a hair appointment in Eureka today.

The driver behind her slowed as well, even though there were no cars coming in the other lane, no reasons not to pass. Except for one.

Her heart began to pound. She gripped the steering wheel, trying to decide what to do. She wasn't about to try to outrun the driver. Why would anyone be following her?

Rob Perkins had been murdered and Cody attacked the other night at Starling. She'd been there. Was it possible the killer thought she'd seen something incriminating?

She flinched as she noticed in the mirror that the driver of the SUV came racing up behind her. Automatically, she hit the gas to keep him from crashing into the back of her. But when she looked up, she saw a deer standing next to the road.

Startled, the deer jumped forward onto the pavement. Olivia swerved away from it, but the driver behind her must not have seen it until it was too late. In her rearview mirror, she saw him also swerve and lose control as the deer bounded away and the SUV careened into the ditch. It came to a stop in the soft earth.

Olivia tried to catch her breath as she reached for her phone to call the deputy.

JADEN HAD HOPED to find Krystal Lee at home. He left a note for her on her door to call him when she returned and was heading for his patrol SUV when he got the call from Olivia.

The moment he heard her voice, he knew something

had happened. "Slow down," he said, trying to assure her. "What happened?"

"Someone followed me after I left the hospital. I don't know if they were just trying to scare me or planned to run me off the road."

He listened as she described the dark-colored SUV and told him about the deer and the driver losing control and ending up in the ditch. "Where are you?"

"I'm at home. Mom's in town getting her hair done."

She was alone. He could hear the fear in her voice. "Stay there. I'm on my way."

The drive out of town didn't take long. He didn't bother with his lights and siren since there was so little traffic. Had it been summer with all the seasonal tourists, it would have been a different story. Still, he drove fast, worried about Olivia. The woman he knew didn't scare easily. But she'd been through a lot lately. He reminded himself that he still didn't know what had happened out at Starling to Rob Perkins. Or to Cody Ryan, for that matter, let alone Dean Marsh.

What he did know was that his former fiancée seemed to be dead center in the middle of it. If she was right about someone trying to run her off the road, her being back in town was becoming more dangerous for her.

He hadn't gone far when he saw the skid marks on the two-lane blacktop. Slowing, he saw the deep tracks in the earth at the edge of the road and even deeper tire tracks in the barrow pit. But the SUV had managed to drive out and was now gone.

Speeding up, he headed for the house Olivia had grown up in with her single mother. She'd told him stories about her life there before he'd met her at college. She'd said she was afraid of becoming her mother—if she didn't get away from the small town and make something of herself.

He could relate. He'd also wanted to distance himself from his parents' life when he was younger. His parents had chased every alternative lifestyle before ending up living off the grid in Alaska. Fortunately, by then, he'd been on his own.

So, as determined as Olivia had been about getting away from here, what was she doing back? he asked himself as he pulled into the drive and she came running out.

Chapter Nine

When Jaden drove up in his patrol SUV, Olivia felt such a surge of relief that she ran out of the house and into his arms. Just seeing him had brought back such a rush of emotions after her earlier scare. As he closed his arms around her, she leaned into him, breathing in his familiar scent, soaking up his warmth and strength. She'd always felt so safe in his embrace.

He held her tight, his breath in her hair as he called her "Livie," his nickname for her. Just the sound of it was almost her undoing. She'd missed hearing it on his lips, missed the intimacy they'd shared, missed him.

"You're all right," he whispered. She was now—now that he was there. "It's okay."

She drew back to look into his handsome face and felt a pang of regret. How could she not miss what they'd had together? Worse, she could only blame herself that he was no longer in her life. When she'd heard that she'd gotten the job of her dreams, she'd thought only of postponing the wedding for a while. He was on his way to law school. She'd never considered he might want to go with her and, instead of postponing the wedding, would break off their engagement.

No wonder he'd thought she wasn't ready for marriage.

He released her now. Her heart fell as she saw the change

in him. She ached with a longing she hadn't expected for him not to pull away. Wasn't this why she'd come home? She'd feared that she'd made the biggest mistake of her life by letting him go without putting up a fight for them. Now, as he went back to business, she feared it was too late. Cody had a girlfriend. What if Jaden did as well? She'd been such a fool.

Fighting tears, she tried to be as down-to-business as he was. "Did you find the SUV? Was the driver still there?" She felt bereft of his arms. Hugging herself, she looked down the road as if expecting the dark vehicle to appear.

"The driver was already out of the ditch," he said. "You happen to get a license plate number?" She shook her head. "How about a description of the vehicle?"

"A large, dark-colored SUV. Maybe a dark gray. Could have been dark blue."

He looked disappointed in her, and not for the first time. "You think whoever it was followed you from the hospital?"

She nodded. "I saw that blonde woman again at the hospital, coming out of Cody's room." She described her. Jaden made no comment as he pulled out his notebook and wrote it down. "I didn't see what she was driving, but it could have been her who tried to force me off the road."

Having him here made her feel better, stronger. She felt a little foolish for being so frightened earlier. So what if someone had followed her? They hadn't crashed into her. Maybe they were just trying to scare her. If it had been the blonde, she could have only been warning her to stay away from Cody.

Olivia knew it wasn't just today's incident that had her shaken. It was everything since she'd come home. She and Cody at the bar like old times, the disastrous trip to Starling that had ended so tragically, Jaden being the lead deputy on the case and the distance she felt between them.

Nothing had gone as she had wanted it to. That feeling of being a part of this town, her old friends, all of it was gone. She'd thought she could just fall back into that comfortable place she'd left behind. She couldn't have been more wrong.

What she should have done was go to see Jaden right away. She'd thought she had time to settle back in and sort out her feelings before she had to face him.

"You didn't recognize the SUV?" he asked and looked up from his notebook when she was so lost in her thoughts that she didn't answer right away. He repeated his question, studying her openly.

She shook her head. "You think it had something to do with the other night in Starling?" she asked Jaden.

He pocketed the notebook and pen. "I think you should be careful. Maybe stick closer to home."

She wanted to ask if he was close to finding Rob's killer and the person who'd attacked Cody, but hesitated. She didn't think he was or he wouldn't still be looking at her with suspicion. "Any news on Dean?"

"No. Dogs were brought in for the search because of all the tornado debris. His body wasn't found in Starling. It's possible, if he wasn't sheltered, that the tornado swept him away. They have widened their search."

Olivia could tell that Jaden had little hope of finding Dean alive. Her heart hurt to think about all of it. The tornado had been so destructive, but it hadn't caused Rob's death or Cody's concussion. Instead, the chances were that the killer was someone she knew. One of the old gang? That didn't leave many options. Emery? Or Dean?

She thought about the dark figure she'd glimpsed when she'd looked back at the Rusk house. It had appeared and disappeared so quickly, she'd thought she'd been seeing things. But what if she hadn't?

What if Elden Rusk had been there Halloween night?

JADEN HAD BEEN ANXIOUS to get back to town and was glad when Olivia's mother drove into the yard from her hair appointment. He was finding it harder and harder to be around his former fiancée. Only minutes ago, he'd had her in his arms. The memory made him ache. How could he forget the familiar feel of her body against his? He couldn't, and that was part of the problem.

When he'd thought he would never see her again, he'd thought that eventually he'd get over her. Now he knew he'd only been kidding himself.

"Remember what I said about being careful," he'd told her before driving away, unable to mask the edge to his voice. Why had she returned? Why had she gone to Starling? And the big question: Why had she gone with Cody?

He doubted she would listen to his advice as he left and drove into town, hoping to catch Krystal Lee at home. He'd recognized Krystal from Olivia's description she'd given of the blonde she'd seen at the hospital. The woman had not been home earlier, but he had a feeling she might be back by now.

Krystal Lee answered the door, wearing a robe. Her blond hair was wet and her feet bare. She was an attractive woman, except for her blue eyes. There was a brittle hardness there, as if she hadn't gotten what she'd wanted out of life and resented the devil out of it.

"Did I catch you at a bad time?" the deputy asked.

She smiled and leaned suggestively against the door frame. "Depends on what you have in mind."

"I need to ask you some questions. Perhaps you could get dressed. I don't mind waiting."

She pushed herself off the door frame, her smile vanishing. "Fine. I guess you'd better come in. You can wait out here in the living room." With that, she turned and disappeared down a hallway.

Jaden pushed the door all the way open and entered the house. He knew that she rented the small house, worked part-time at the convenience store and drove a small, compact, older-model car. She'd had four speeding tickets, but other than that, she'd kept her nose clean.

As he waited, he looked around since he assumed she was going to take her time. He spotted a pair of dirty boots by the door. Several jackets and coats hung above them, one jacket with fresh dirt on the sleeve. The house smelled like leftover pizza and the lingering scent of stale beer.

He was standing at the front window when she returned.

"I hope I didn't keep you waiting," she said snidely.

"Not at all." He turned to look at her and smiled. "I looked around while I was waiting." His gaze went to the dirty boots by the door as he pulled out his notebook and pen. "Let's start with where you were this morning." He turned in time to see her expression. It was enough to tell him she'd been up to no good.

Without her offering, he took a seat on the end of the couch and waited for her to sit. She had several options, one of two worn recliners or the other end of the equally worn couch. She chose the couch and turned toward him.

She'd changed into a T-shirt and jeans. Her feet were still bare, her hair pulled up in a ponytail. The look on her recently made-up face said he would have to drag the truth out of her.

"Why don't you start with what you were doing at the hospital this morning?" he said and clicked on his pen.

"Who said I was at the hospital?" she asked.

He waited, holding her gaze until she finally cursed and said, "That skinny nurse, huh."

"You were visiting Cody, and not for the first time," he said. "What's your relationship?"

"Relationship?" She made it sound as if she'd never heard the word before.

Again, he could have outwaited her, but was quickly losing his patience. "Maybe I should take you down to the sheriff's office for further questioning." He started to put his notebook and pen away, but she stopped him.

"Fine. Cody's my boyfriend. I have every right to see him."

"Does he know he's your boyfriend, because I believe he was with Olivia Brooks Halloween night?"

Her eyes narrowed into a glare, her jaw tightening before she said, "*He* knows, but apparently Olivia doesn't."

"Is that why you followed her when she left the hospital and tried to run her off the road?"

"I don't know what you're talking about," she snapped, leaning away from him and the accusation.

"I can have the dirt on your boots compared to that of the barrow pit where your SUV ended up," he said. "This time of year, it isn't quite mud, but close."

She grabbed on to the one thing she thought could save her and gave him a haughty look. "I don't own an SUV."

"No, but I'm betting you borrowed one." Before she could argue further, he asked, "Where were you Halloween night?"

The question caught her by surprise. Her eyes widened for a moment. "Home."

"Anyone with you?" She shook her head. "See any trick-or-treaters who can verify your story?"

"I had my lights turned off, so I didn't get any. Migraine headache. I went to bed early."

"You often get migraines?" Before she could answer, he said, "I can check with your doctor."

"My first migraine. Really a bitch."

"So I've heard." Seeing that he wasn't going to get any more from her, he put away his notebook and pen and stood. "I hope I don't have to come back and arrest you for anything, but I will be keeping an eye on you," he said as he walked to the door.

"Thanks. I appreciate that," she said sarcastically as he left.

Jaden didn't have to go far. A few blocks away, he stopped at the home of Jenny and Tom Lee. Tom's truck wasn't parked in the drive and neither was Jenny's car. But when he got out and looked in the garage, he found a dark gray SUV. He'd been bluffing back at Krystal's about comparing the dirt on her boots with that of the dirt in the barrow pit near Olivia's mother's house.

But even peering through the dusty garage door windows, he could see the large SUV's tires were caked with fresh earth.

OLIVIA HADN'T BEEN anxious to go back into the house after the deputy left and her mother went inside. She'd lived in this community for seventeen years before she'd left for college and hadn't returned until a few days ago. She'd never been afraid. But then, she'd never had anyone who'd wanted to run her off the road.

Her cell rang. She saw it was Jaden and felt her pulse jump like it used to when he called, back when they were together. She had loved the sound of his voice, been lulled by it. She let it ring again before she picked up, reminding herself that he was probably calling because he was a deputy and she was a suspect.

"Hello?"

"Hey," he said in a familiar way that set her pulse off again. "I just wanted to let you know that you shouldn't be having any more trouble from the person who threatened you earlier."

"You know who it was?" She heard him hesitate.

"It had nothing to do with Starling and what happened up there. Just a jealous girlfriend of Cody's."

"The blonde from the hospital. Who is she?"

"Krystal Lee. She's Tom Lee's sister, Jenny's sister-in-law. But I've spoken to her. I think that's the last you have to worry about her," he said.

Olivia wondered about that, given how aggressive she'd been on the road earlier. "You didn't arrest her?"

"No, not enough evidence to do that. I warned her. Just didn't want you to worry."

Good luck with that, she thought. "Any news about what happened at Starling?" She realized she was trying to keep him on the phone. Just the sound of his voice made her feel better. She'd missed it.

"Not yet. I'm getting another call. If you... Gotta go." And he was gone.

She stood holding the phone. If you...what? What had he stopped himself from saying?

"You going to stand outside all day?" her mother called from the porch.

Olivia pocketed her phone, turned and headed for the house. She could feel her mother's questioning gaze on her.

"Who was that on the phone?" her mother asked.

"Jaden. It wasn't anything." She stepped into the house, knowing her mother wasn't going to let it go. She headed for the kitchen to make herself a sandwich, her mother on her heels. "You want a sandwich?"

"I ate in town. What did Jaden want?"

Digging out what she needed from the refrigerator, she said, "Earlier, someone followed me from the hospital, running up behind me like she was going to run me off the road."

"She?"

"Cody's girlfriend, Krystal Lee."

Her mother's expression told volumes as to how she felt about Krystal Lee. "Cody forgot to mention he had a girlfriend when he asked you out for Halloween night?" Sharon shook her head. "You still worried she'll come after you again?"

Olivia concentrated on slicing a tomato before she answered. "I'm not worried." That wasn't entirely true, but she didn't want her mother doing something foolish like going over to Krystal's house and threatening her. It wouldn't be the first time her mother had done something like that.

"So why do you look worried?"

She spread mayo on the bread, then layered on ham, cheese, lettuce and sliced tomato. "It's the whole Starling thing," she said as she completed her task and reached for one of the small bags of chips her mother kept on hand. "What if he never finds out who killed Rob and injured Cody?" she added as she sat down at the kitchen table. She took a bite of her sandwich.

"Jaden doesn't really think you had anything to do with that," her mother said as she joined her at the table. "He's just angry at you for breaking off the engagement."

Olivia looked up, finished chewing and set down her sandwich. "I didn't break it off. Jaden did."

"What?"

She shook her head. "He didn't think I was ready to get married—let alone to him." She'd seldom seen her mother unable to speak.

"Why would he think that?" Sharon Brooks finally asked.

"I don't know what he thinks. He was headed to law school. I'd just gotten my job I'd hoped for. We were going in separate directions. I suggested postponing the wedding."

"Law school? How'd he end up being a deputy in Fortune Creek?"

"Turns out we both changed our minds about what we wanted to do," Olivia said.

"Was he right about you not being ready?" Before Olivia could answer, her mother said, "Well, obviously, because the first thing you did when you got back here was to go out with Cody Ryan, your high school boyfriend."

"It wasn't like that," she protested, knowing how it looked. She regretted it more than she could say. "We're just friends."

Her mother had always preferred anyone over Cody, saying she couldn't bear seeing her daughter organizing nuts and bolts down at the hardware store for the rest of her life. *What kind of life can he offer you? You think Cody and his dad wouldn't have you working down there in the hardware store?*

"I guess it wouldn't make that much difference, working at a hardware store or being the wife of a deputy and living all the way up there in Fortune Creek," her mother said now.

Olivia groaned. "Well, that's not going to happen."

"But for some reason both men thought you were going to marry them," her mother just had to point out. "One of them must be the reason you're back home."

Pushing her sandwich away, she snapped, "Do we have to talk about my past mistakes?"

"Only if you keep making the same ones," her mother quipped.

"I just wanted to hang out with some old friends Halloween night. Cody and I used to be friends. He was my best friend for a lot of years. I thought we could have that again. I was wrong."

"I should say so since now one of your old friends is dead, Cody's in the hospital and another friend is missing."

She shook her head, telling herself that her mother had good intentions and was only trying to protect her. "I just came from the hospital. Cody has regained consciousness, but he doesn't remember anything. He didn't even remember I was back in town."

Her mother got up from the table, returning with a knife. Olivia watched her cut the sandwich in two before sitting down to eat it. "I didn't have much for lunch," she said, grinning before taking a bite.

Olivia opened the bag of chips, dumping them on the side of the plate so her mother could reach them. She picked up the other half with her one bite out of it. Sometimes she wished she couldn't remember the past.

"I love them both," she said between bites. "Cody just as a friend. Jaden..." Her voice broke with emotion. "I can't seem to get over him. All right? It's why I came home."

Her mother nodded, smiled and reached over with her free hand to squeeze her daughter's. "That's what I thought. Don't worry. You'll figure it out."

Her laugh sounded more scared than bitter. "If only it were that easy."

"What a problem. If it's Jaden you're in love with, then I guess you'd better let him know you're serious. If you are..."

Olivia nodded. "But right now, he just sees me as a suspect in a murder investigation." She didn't mention that him finding her on a night out with Cody hadn't helped, and neither did her mother. She'd been such a fool to think she could recapture the fun times she and Cody had in high school for even one night.

Her phone pinged. It was a text from Emery. He wanted to meet her at the bar. Said it was important.

Chapter Ten

Emery was the last person Olivia had expected to hear from. They'd been friends but never close growing up. She'd hesitated before responding, wondering what he could want. Jaden had told her to stay close to home, and after the road race with Krystal Lee, she was inclined to do just that.

The problem was that, earlier, at the hospital, Jaden had asked for her help. *Someone's lying*, he'd said.

She was curious why Emery wanted to meet. What was so important?

"I'm going to meet a friend," she told her mother as she quickly left to avoid her questioning whether going into town tonight after what had happened was a bad idea. Olivia was already questioning it herself as she drove to the bar.

It was one of those pitch-black nights when the clouds hung low, blotting out the stars. She could barely see the outline of the mountains that rimmed the valley against the dark sky. Like her future, all she could see was the few feet her headlights illuminated ahead of her. When she finally caught the lights of town, she relaxed a little and tried not to think about the ride home.

There were only a few cars in the bar parking lot because of the time of the year and the weekday night. She found Emery sitting in a corner booth at the back, alone. He was staring into his half-empty glass and didn't look up until she slid into the booth, across from him.

He seemed startled to see her for a moment. She'd never seen him nervous, let alone on edge. Until tonight.

"Has something happened?" she whispered.

"Let me get you a drink," he said, hurriedly getting to his feet. "What would you like?"

Thinking of her drive home, she said, "Just a cola."

He hurried away to the bar and came back a few minutes later with her soda and another drink for himself. He took a gulp of his before he said, "You heard about the human bones that were found?"

"Cody and I discovered them after the tornado left them exposed down in the root cellar."

"They're Evangeline's. I have a friend who works at the sheriff's office."

"I'm surprised they already have the DNA back," she said.

Emery shook his head. "They don't, but there was some clothing found buried deeper in the grave that matched what Evangeline was wearing the night she disappeared."

Olivia shuddered, thinking of the dark figure she'd seen standing in the Rusk doorway. "It's so creepy. Do they think she's been there this whole time?"

Emery nodded and took another slug of his drink. "There was a man buried with her. Probably the father of her baby." He raised an eyebrow. "You know he killed his daughter and the man who'd impregnated her."

She didn't know that for a fact, although it did seem likely, didn't it? Was this why Emery had gotten her here tonight? He could have told her in the text.

"There's something I didn't tell anyone about that night," Emery said as he ran his finger through the moisture on his glass without looking at her. "I saw him."

"Saw who?" She realized she was whispering, although there was no one around who could hear. The only patrons were a handful at the bar. The bartender had the television on a loud ball game.

Emery looked up at her. "Elden Rusk."

She didn't know what to say, but she could understand why he hadn't mentioned this to anyone, maybe especially Jaden. She certainly hadn't told anyone what she thought she'd seen. "When was that?"

"When I was looking for Rob. The wind was so strong, it had knocked me down. I looked up and there he was, all dressed in black, his head covered by a big hat."

She swallowed the lump in her throat. "You're sure it was him?"

He nodded, not at all upset that she would question him. "It wasn't the first time I've seen him. I'd know those eyes anywhere."

"You'd seen him before?"

Emery took another gulp of his drink. His hand shook as he replaced the glass. He seemed to be avoiding her eyes. "When I was a kid, I used to ride my bike out to Starling. The houses were all empty, everyone gone, but, like you said, creepy. It always bothered us that the people left so quickly, leaving a lot of their stuff behind."

"Us?" she asked.

"Rob and me. We used to joke that a spaceship zapped them all up." He toyed with his glass that was now almost empty. "We used to talk all the time about what we would do when we found Rusk's gold." He looked up then, his gaze connecting with hers. "We saw him. He was loading something into the back of his old truck. We sneaked up on him, but he saw us."

Emery turned then toward the bar. "Could use another

drink over here," he called before he finished what was in his glass and looked at her again.

Olivia realized she'd been holding her breath.

"Rusk picked up an old rusty shovel and came after us. Rob could always run faster than me. I'd never run so fast in my life, but it wasn't fast enough. Rusk caught me, dragging me to the ground. He lifted that old shovel. I thought he was going to kill me. If Rob hadn't come back when he had..."

The bartender dropped off his drink and took his empties. "How about you?" he said to Olivia, who could only shake her head. She hadn't even touched her cola.

"Rob saved you?" she said when Emery didn't continue.

"He grabbed the shovel and brought it down on the man's head. Knocked him out cold. My legs were so weak, I could barely stand. I was shaking all over. I thought Rob had killed him, but we went back the next day. Elden and his old truck were gone. But I'll never forget the look on that man's face when he raised that shovel. He was going to kill me and would have if not for Rob." Emery picked up his drink and took a healthy gulp.

"Why are you telling me this?"

"Because," he said as he put down his glass, "Rob saved my life. I would never have hurt him, let alone killed him. But I know who did. It had to be Rusk. I thought I saw him right as the tornado hit. I swear it was him, all dressed in black, his head covered. He looked right at me."

"Why didn't you tell the deputy this?" she asked.

He scoffed. "Come on. Who would believe me? How many times have people said they saw Elden Rusk out at Starling? I'd be the laughingstock, but worse, the deputy would think I was trying to save my own skin. Other than whoever killed him, I was one of the last people to see Rob alive."

Olivia took a sip of her cola before she had to ask again, "Why are you telling *me*?"

"I don't know. I needed to tell someone who might believe me. Didn't I hear that you once saw Rusk out at Starling?"

She suspected his motivation had more to do with having heard she'd been engaged to Deputy Sheriff Jaden Montgomery. "You think Rusk recognized Rob as the kid who'd coldcocked him and that's why he killed him?"

"Why not? If you had seen the look in that man's eyes when he had me down on the ground with that shovel in his hands…"

"You said he was loading something into his truck."

Emery nodded. "Something heavy like…gold bars."

"Then why would you and Rob still be looking for gold at Starling if Rusk had taken it?"

"Because we think he hid it all over the side of the mountain," Emery said. "Maybe he didn't get it all."

"Are you really telling me that, after Rob knocked Rusk out, you didn't go see what he'd loaded in the back of his truck?"

"We were terrified we'd killed him."

"Even more reason to take the time to see what he had loaded in the truck."

Emery looked away, seeming defeated. "It wasn't gold. It was a bunch of old scrap iron he'd scavenged from the place."

She let out a huff. "Did you and Rob start the rumor about the gold?" she demanded, pretty sure they had.

"I think I heard it before that," he hedged. "The thing is, I didn't kill Rob. I had no reason to."

"You should tell the deputy. Coming from me wouldn't carry any weight. I'm a suspect as well as you."

Emery drained his drink and sighed. "Well, it was good to get it off my chest. I appreciate you listening."

"Thanks for the cola." She took another drink of it to be polite as she wondered if that was all Emery had wanted to tell her. She couldn't help feeling like there was a lot more. "So, you and Rob have been good friends all these years." He nodded, seeming a little distracted. "I know the deputy asked, but did Dean get along with Rob?"

"He and Dean were tight. It wasn't one of us." He lowered his voice. "It was Rusk."

She felt a chill and was about to ask Emery if he could follow her home when he got a call. He excused himself and stepped away from the booth, leaving her to mull over what he'd told her. That he was running scared didn't surprise her. His best friend had been murdered, and like her, he was a suspect.

"I'm sorry. I have to go," he said when he returned. He looked even more nervous than he had earlier.

"Is everything all right?" she asked. Clearly, it wasn't.

"Fine. It's a friend who needs my help. Thanks so much for coming in and listening. You believed me, didn't you?" She nodded and he smiled. "I hope things work out with you and Cody." He grabbed up his jacket and headed for the door before she could tell him things weren't going to work out between her and Cody—at least, not the way Emery probably hoped.

The bar was even more empty than it had been, the night even darker as she stepped outside. She couldn't help feeling spooked after everything that had happened. She hurried across the nearly-empty parking lot, anxious to reach her car.

She was already opening the door and about to climb in when she realized she wasn't going anywhere. In the glow of the neon bar sign, she saw that her driver's-side front tire was flat. There was a screwdriver sticking out of the side of it.

It was late when Jaden got the call. He hadn't expected to hear from Olivia again so soon and was immediately worried. "What's wrong?"

"I need your help," she said, her fear making his skyrocket. "I'm in the bar parking lot. My tire is flat. Someone stuck a screwdriver in it."

Bar parking lot? Hadn't he advised her to stay close to home? He didn't have to ask which bar. "I'll be right there."

The motel where he was staying while in town on the case wasn't far from the bar where Olivia had said she'd met up with Cody and her old friends the night they decided to spend Halloween at Starling.

He found her sitting in her car in the almost-empty lot and pulled alongside in his patrol SUV, spotting the flat tire. She climbed out into the night at once. He couldn't tell if she was more scared or angry.

"What are you doing here?" he demanded when what he really wanted to know was who she'd been with at the bar. Cody Ryan had been released from the hospital. Had he felt up to going to the bar his first night home?

"What you asked me to do," she snapped, clearly not liking the tone of his voice.

"I believe I asked you to stay close to home."

"Before that, you asked me to keep my ear to the ground with my old friends," she said. "Emery texted me. He said it was important."

Jaden pulled off his hat and raked a hand through his hair. Not Cody. He hated that he was jealous. He had no right to be, but that didn't stop him.

"Sorry. Why don't you go back into the bar? I'll join you when I'm finished here." He pulled on a latex glove before opening an evidence bag. She watched him remove the screwdriver from the tire and drop it in the bag.

"I'd rather stay out here," she said as he secured the bag in his SUV, then opened her car door and pulled the lever that opened her trunk. "Emery says he didn't kill Rob because he owed him his life."

As he changed her tire, he listened to the story she said Emery had related to her in the bar. When she finished, he asked, "Why didn't he come to me with this? Why you?"

"I asked him that. He didn't think you would believe him."

Jaden couldn't argue with that. Being suspicious came with the job, but he found himself more interested in where Emery had taken off to from the bar. "Doesn't it seem suspicious that he gets you into town, takes off suddenly, and you find your tire punctured in the lot? He didn't tell you why he had to leave so quickly?"

She shrugged, arms crossed over her chest, and looked upset that he wasn't more interested in Emery's story about seeing Rusk on Halloween night at Starling. "He said a friend needed him. Why would he flatten my tire?" Good question, he thought. "You don't believe him, do you?"

"I didn't say that." He replaced her jack and loaded the ruined tire in the back before slamming the lid. "You'll want to get a new tire tomorrow."

"Thanks for your help." She started toward her car, clearly intending to get in and drive home. But she'd have to get him to move out of the way to do so.

"You have no idea who called Emery?" he asked.

"No." She frowned. "Maybe. It sounded like he was talking to a woman."

Jaden nodded. "One of those girls from Halloween?"

She shook her head. "Older, more like someone he knew well. But I'm just going by his tone of voice. That's all I could make out."

OLIVIA REALIZED THAT Jaden seemed in no hurry to leave. What was he waiting for? "You know I wouldn't have called unless—"

"You needed me. You can always call. I hope you know that."

The cloudy darkness felt almost intimate as they stood looking at each other. The music coming from the bar seemed louder than it had been. The neon bar sign threw shadows across the parking lot. She stood only inches from him, feeling the intensity of his gaze.

"You're in my way," she said, her words coming out in a whisper.

"Remember this song?" he asked, cocking his head to listen to the music coming from the bar.

As if Olivia could have forgotten the song, let alone forget being in his arms slow dancing. It had been something they'd done often when they were dating. A song would come on, and no matter where they were, he would reach for her.

Like now. He reached for her in the darkness as she said, "We used to dance to this."

Without a thought, she slipped into his arms. He drew her close, the two of them moving to the rhythm as they danced between the two vehicles as if they'd been doing it for years. She could feel his breath in her hair. She closed her eyes, relishing his hard body, the strength of his arms around her. This was the one place she'd ever felt truly safe and secure.

In his arms, she'd had no doubts. She'd known what she'd wanted and needed—something she apparently couldn't have since he'd broken off their engagement.

The song ended and she pulled back to look up at him in the dim glow of the bar sign. The urge to kiss him was so strong that she felt herself leaning in, her lips only a breath away when a horn blared, making them both jump apart.

Headlights washed over them as a pickup pulled into the parking lot.

Jaden swore under his breath. "We need to get you home. I'll follow you."

It was exactly what she wanted, yet she started to tell him it wasn't necessary. One look at his expression and she knew it would be a fight she'd lose. It was a relief. She nodded since she'd been dreading the drive home.

Jaden opened her car door. His hand brushed her shoulder as she climbed in, sending shivers up her arms. They'd been so close to kissing. Why did she believe in her heart that with one kiss, he would know that they belonged together?

Foolishness, she told herself as she started the engine and pulled out, Jaden right behind her. The glow of his headlights behind her seemed to warm the dark autumn night even more as she drove toward home.

Her body still quaked, emotions running hot and wild. Being in his arms... Holding her like that, dancing, he had to remember how good they were together. She couldn't get the almost-kiss out of her mind or the ache of disappointment that they'd been interrupted. She wondered if Jaden was feeling the same way right now and shook her head.

You need to tell him how you feel.

"Now? I'm a suspect in his murder investigation. Do you really think right now is the time?" she demanded of herself.

No answer, which was an answer in itself, wasn't it?

"You really need to quit talking to yourself, too," she said and glanced in the rearview mirror to see his headlights. They stayed a safe distance behind her until she turned into her mother's driveway and parked.

Jaden pulled in behind her. For a moment, she thought he might get out, but instead, he flashed his lights and then left.

She felt bereft as she watched his vehicle lights disappear

down the road. "Don't let one dance make you think anything has changed," she said to herself. She was still a suspect and would be until the killer was caught.

But she knew it wasn't just that keeping her and Jaden apart. She'd known this wouldn't be easy. Wasn't that why she hadn't gone straight to Jaden when she'd returned home? She hadn't been able to stand the thought that he might turn her away and not hear her out.

Patience, she told herself with a sigh. But even as she thought it, her only other option had to be something besides hanging out here at the house with her mother watching her every minute, wondering what she was doing with her life. She needed to figure out who'd killed Rob, who'd attacked Cody, who'd flattened her tire. And maybe why Emery had left the bar so fast when he'd gotten that call.

As her mother came out on the porch, she cut her engine and lights, and climbed out, determined to clear herself.

JADEN CURSED HIMSELF all the way back to town. What was he doing? Just racing headlong toward heartbreak. He'd broken off the engagement because he'd felt in his heart that Livie wasn't ready. Did he really believe that something had changed? She'd come back to town and gone straight to her old boyfriend. Her going out with Cody the minute she'd hit town… What more proof did he need?

But dancing with her, holding her in his arms, almost kissing, had felt so right. He'd wanted that kiss desperately. Like one kiss was going to chase away any doubts he still had.

Yet just before they'd almost kissed, he'd looked into her eyes and he'd known heart deep that she still loved him. He couldn't be wrong about that. Not that it meant she'd ever want to be the wife of a small-town deputy.

He slammed his hand into the steering wheel. He didn't

have time for this. He had a job to do. Determined to concentrate on work, he recalled what Livie had told him about Emery. He didn't know what to believe. Emery's story sounded like boys would be boys. Did he believe Elden Rusk had planned to kill Emery and Rob with a shovel? He thought of the boogeyman from his nightmares while living in Starling. Maybe.

Rusk had scared him as a boy. It was the man's eyes. When they lit on you, it felt as if he could smite you on the spot. Jaden had been terrified of him. He couldn't imagine what he would have done if Rusk had ever brandished a rusted shovel at him.

Yet something felt off about Emery summoning Olivia to the bar to tell her about his and Rob's run-in with Rusk—especially with someone flattening her tire. Could it have been some kids looking for trouble? Unfortunately, he didn't believe it. Krystal? Maybe. He cursed at the thought since he'd told Livie that he had handled it.

The woman kept crowding his thoughts, reminding him of her in his arms, in his bed, always in his head and still lodged deep in his heart. He needed to stay away from her, but he was working a murder investigation—and Livie was right there, right in the center.

He should never have taken her in his arms to dance. He should definitely have not almost kissed her. Especially in public and not in the middle of an investigation involving her. He didn't know who had been in that pickup that had pulled into the bar parking lot, but he knew how quickly word spread in this town. The deputy and his suspect just a breath away from kissing in the parking lot would be all over town by morning.

The worst part was that he had wanted that damn kiss more than his next breath and now he couldn't get it out of his head. He kept remembering their deep, long kisses, the passion they'd ignited, their need for each other. Olivia Brooks had done more than stolen his heart. She'd ruined him for any other woman.

So why in the hell hadn't he ignored his doubts and married her? If he'd offered to follow her to her job— He pushed the thought away. She hadn't wanted that, or she would have suggested it. She'd needed her freedom to chase her dream. She'd needed it more than him. But what about now?

He knew he wasn't going to be able to sleep. It didn't help when he got a call the moment he walked into his rental.

Elden Rusk had been found.

Chapter Eleven

Olivia hadn't been inside the hardware store in years. It had the same smell, the same narrow aisles between high shelves loaded with every household necessity she could name and many she couldn't.

She wasn't surprised to find Cody working. Apparently, he had the same schedule he'd had in high school. Just like he'd never missed a day of school or work, he hadn't let a concussion keep him from his spot behind the counter.

The bandage on his head had been replaced with a smaller one. Like her, he still had the scrapes and scratches, the bruises and bumps on his face and arms. But unlike her, he looked pale.

"What are you doing working?" she demanded, unable to stop herself. She glanced around for his father and didn't see him.

"Dad had to run an errand. I'm just filling in until he gets back," Cody said. His voice softened as he asked, "How are you doing?"

"Fine." She reminded herself that the reason she was there was that he'd lied to her. "You didn't tell me you had a girlfriend."

He reddened. "Krystal isn't… We aren't… That is, we—"

"She tried to run me off the road yesterday."

"No. Seriously?" He shook his head. "I'm sorry. She's a little hot-tempered and unpredictable sometimes, but she's not dangerous."

"Are you sure about that?" she said, noticing a basketful of screwdrivers on sale. "After that, someone flattened my tire with one of your sale items here."

He swore. "I'll talk to her."

"The deputy already did. He didn't think she'd give me any more trouble. Apparently, he was wrong." She met his stare and felt her anger dissolve. This man had once been her best friend. She still cared about Cody. "Has your memory come back?"

"Bits and pieces. Nothing I can understand."

"It does make me wonder what Krystal would have done if she'd caught you out in Starling with me."

His hand went to his head and the dressing over the wound. "She wouldn't..." His words dropped off as his father came in through the back to relieve him.

"I should get going. But one question before I go... Did Krystal have something against Rob or Dean?"

Cody made an impatient face. "I'm sorry the two of you got into it, but Krystal isn't like that."

"Keep telling yourself that," she said and left.

ELDEN RUSK WAS alive and staying in an assisted-living facility in Kalispell. Not that far from Starling, the deputy noted. It was a pleasant enough drive this morning, the sun sparkling on the dew in the thick pines that bordered each side of the road. The mountains shone against a cloudless blue sky. The air smelled of fall, just cool enough to remind him that winter wasn't far behind. He didn't want to even think about a long, cold winter in Fortune Creek after seeing Livie again.

He found the facility without any trouble. It was one level, brick, and on the edge of town. There were benches still outside under the pines. But they were all empty this morning.

Jaden pushed through the front door and into the lobby, heading for the reception desk. "Hello. I'm looking for Elden Rusk," he said to the young dark-haired woman sitting there.

"Room 214," she said without looking up from her paperwork.

"Thank you."

He started to turn and head down the hallway in front of him when she called, "Other way." He swiveled, passing a woman leaning on her walker. In a large room, he saw a few elderly people playing cards at a table. A television was on in the room. Several women were sitting in front of it but didn't seem to be watching the game show that was playing.

He found Elden's room at the end of another hallway. The door was closed. He knocked. Hearing no response, he knocked again, then looked down the empty hall before he tried the door.

Earlier, he'd seen a couple of women in scrubs he took for staff, but no one paid him any mind or asked where he was going. The knob turned in his hand. He pushed and the door swung open.

At first, all he saw was blinding brightness from the sun streaming through the large window. He'd expected to see the Elden Rusk he remembered from when he and his parents had lived in Starling. A large, gruff man with a tuft of dirty-blond hair and piercing blue eyes. The boogeyman.

But the man sitting in front of the window was shrunken and bald. Or maybe it was the wheelchair he was slumped in that made him look so small and harmless. The only thing that was the same were those ice-blue eyes when Rusk turned to look at him standing in the doorway.

Chapter Twelve

As Jaden drove toward the hospital, the sun rose high over the snowcapped mountain peaks, casting a glow over the Montana landscape. He hardly noticed. His mind had been on little else but this case since it had begun. The case and Olivia.

He couldn't quit thinking about the story Emery had told Olivia. He kept asking himself why Emery hadn't come to him with it. Why tell Olivia? Something felt off and had since the beginning.

He'd been as ready as Emery to blame Rusk for what had happened out there Halloween night. But after seeing the man again, he knew that whoever Emery might have seen, it hadn't been Elden Rusk.

Jaden had attempted to tell the man about what had been unearthed. Along with the clothing found with the bones, he let him know that there was no doubt that they belonged to Evangeline.

"He can't understand you," the nurse had said when she'd found Jaden in Rusk's room. "Advanced dementia."

"I thought that, when he first saw me, he might have recognized me."

She shook her head. "I'm sorry. Are you a relative?"

"No, we haven't seen each other for years. I had some

news for him." But when he'd tried to tell Rusk about Evangeline, the man had looked blankly at him. When Jaden had tried again, Rusk had become agitated, tried to say something, spittle on his lips as he'd begun to moan loudly.

The nurse suggested Jaden take a walk around the facility and try again. "You might have better luck later."

He questioned whether or not Rusk had understood about his daughter's remains being found. But one thing was clear. Elden Rusk hadn't been out at Starling on Halloween night. If Emery was telling the truth, though, someone had wanted him to believe Rusk was alive and out for blood. It would have been easy enough to dress in all black, head covered with a big, floppy black hat, and try to frighten the group partying in the abandoned community. Given the storm and the confusion, it would have made revenge easier. Someone had taken advantage. Someone was lying.

Maybe they were all lying.

OLIVIA WAS SURPRISED to get a text from Cody later that afternoon. Her mother was watching one of her favorite old black-and-white movies in the other room.

I need to talk to you. It's important. Meet me?

She glanced into the living room. Her mother was laughing and motioning for Olivia to join her. "You really should watch this."

"I've seen it. Not as many times as you have, but enough," she said as she walked into the room. "I might run into town and get some things from the grocery store."

"We have ice cream. What else do we need?"

She smiled at her mother. She loved seeing her this content. Was it from giving up on men, on love? Olivia suspected it just might be. She hesitated, not sure that meeting Cody was a good idea. Worse, not telling her mother the truth about where she was going might also be a mistake.

But she wasn't up to an argument, especially when her mother was in such a good mood. "I won't be long," she said and headed for the door.

"We could always use more ice cream," her mother called. "Chocolate!"

The door closed behind her. As she walked to her car, Olivia still hesitated to text him back. She felt as if she and Cody had said everything they'd needed to.

When he texted back to meet him at the park down by the river after he got off work, she was glad she'd hesitated. Apparently, he was back at the hardware store. She couldn't imagine why he wanted to see her after what they'd said to each other Halloween night—let alone at the hardware store before.

Then she recalled that he had little to no memory of Halloween.

She figured she could kill some time in town before she met him.

JADEN HAD TAKEN the nurse's advice. He'd walked around, circling back to Elden Rusk's room after he'd had his lunch.

Elden looked up the moment the deputy walked into the room. This time, Jaden was sure the old man recognized him. He pulled up a chair in front of the wheelchair.

"I'm Deputy Jaden Montgomery," he said. "We believe your daughter Evangeline's remains have been found in a root cellar in Starling." He was unsure of what kind of response he would get—if any.

"Too pretty," the man rasped. "Tried to warn her mother. Evangeline—" His voice broke. "My sweet Evangeline."

Eyes narrowing, he said, his voice gruff, "Tried to protect her. They came like bees to honey." His eyes filled with tears.

Jaden had to ask. "Did you kill her?"

Rusk seemed to freeze, his gaze foggy with tears and memories. "Too pretty. Tried to warn her mother." He coughed and fell silent. Jaden thought that was all the man was going to say.

He rose to leave when Rusk said, "Criminal— Did what had to be done… Destroyed everything." He began to cry in chest-heaving gulps, the noise bringing a different nurse into the room.

"I gave him some sad news," the deputy said. "About his daughter. It's part of a murder investigation."

"Evangeline," the nurse said as she put an arm around the man to try to soothe him. "I heard on the news that her body had been found. Broke my heart."

"Did he ever tell you what happened?" Jaden asked.

She hesitated a moment. "She was murdered?" He nodded. Sighing, she said, "When he was first brought here, he talked about her. He didn't say it in so many words, but it seems she'd gotten pregnant at sixteen but refused to tell him who the father of her unborn baby was. Apparently, some man in the community where they lived."

The other body in the root-cellar grave, Jaden thought.

"I think what's haunted him all these years was that he never knew who the man was. When she disappeared… Well, he seemed to think they'd run away together, and he never saw her again."

"You know he started a community called Starling up in northeastern Montana. When Evangeline disappeared at sixteen, he walked away from it and the community died," Jaden said. "He'd started Starling to escape the outside world. He'd built his utopia, only to have what happened to his daughter and some man in the community destroy his dream. Has he ever mentioned his wife?"

"No. I got the impression she's been out of his life for a long time. A neighbor was the one who brought him in here."

The deputy stared at the old man in the wheelchair.

He didn't look much like a murderer. Nor a boogeyman anymore. He looked like a broken man haunted by his past and what he'd done as he quit sobbing and stared out the window, his blue eyes glazed over.

Jaden stopped in a small café after he left Elden Rusk's assisted-living facility. Seeing Rusk like that had unsettled him. It was the man's eyes. No matter what the nurse had said, Jaden couldn't shake the feeling that Rusk had recognized him.

He was leaving the café when he got the call. Dean Marsh had been found wandering down a road, miles from Starling. He was being treated for his injuries at the Kalispell hospital.

"Keep him there," he said. "I'm in town. I'll be right over."

WHEN HE WALKED into the hospital room, he found Dean sitting up, wolfing down lunch with a fork clutched in his left hand. His right arm was in a cast. Like the other Starling tornado survivors, he had cuts and bruises. But unlike them, he'd been missing since Halloween night.

Jaden pulled up a chair next to the bed and dragged out his notebook and pen. "Glad to see you've turned up," he said as Dean finished his lunch and pushed the tray away.

"I haven't eaten in days," he said, his voice gravelly. He took a sip of water from the glass on the table next to his bed.

"Where have you been since Halloween?"

Dean stared at him for a moment, as if considering the question. "When was Halloween?"

"A few days ago."

"Really? I don't know. I remember waking up in a ditch. I didn't know where I was or how I'd gotten there. My arm was broken, I knew that. I found a piece of wood and ripped off part of my shirt to make a splint. Then I just started walking."

"What do you remember before waking up in the ditch?"

Dean frowned and reached up to touch the bandage on his head. "Not much."

Memory loss. There seemed to be a lot of that going around, Jaden considered, questioning Dean's story. He recalled what Dean's wife, Angie, had said about her husband reappearing soon with some fantastic story about where he'd been. "You remember Halloween night?"

His frown deepened. "Halloween."

"You'd gone to Starling with some friends."

"Starling?" He sounded surprised by that.

"There was a storm." There appeared to be no recognition in Dean's expression. "A tornado."

"No kidding?" He shook his head. "Sorry, I don't remember a storm. Is everyone else all right?"

Not everyone, he thought as a nurse came in to take Dean down for more tests and Jaden left.

WHILE THE SUN had set, it wouldn't be dark for a couple of hours yet. Olivia drove to the spot where Cody's dad used to drop them off on weekends. The Ryans had the property next door, so Cody's dad would pick Olivia up on his way to town to work at the hardware store. She and Cody used to spend hours by the river skipping rocks and wading in the water until he returned—or her mother got worried and would come to take her home.

Too cold for playing in the water now, she mused as she parked next to his SUV and climbed out. She felt a chill and wasn't sure if it was the time of year—or finding out what was so important that they had to meet here. Jaden thought she hadn't gotten over her high school boyfriend. Meeting him down here at the river would only reinforce that misconception, but there was nothing she could do about that.

How could she explain that Cody was part of her every memory of growing up here? He'd always been there for her. Look how he'd been during the tornado. He'd saved her life. How could she not care about him?

She spotted him sitting on top of a picnic table close to the river's edge, chucking rocks out into the water as she walked up. "You came," he said, sounding surprised. Or maybe it was just relieved. She recalled the argument they'd had that night in Starling. Even if he couldn't remember Halloween, she knew he was still upset with her for leaving him and this town.

When they'd seen each other at the hardware store earlier, she'd been angry with him. She hadn't wanted to leave it like that. "What's up?"

"You want to sit?" he asked as he moved over to give her room.

"I'm fine standing."

"You're still mad at me," he said, nodding to himself. "Not that I blame you. I should have told you about Krystal."

"I wouldn't have gone to Starling with you if you had."

He chuckled. "Probably why I didn't tell you. I wanted to spend some time with you."

She had wanted the same thing. "You weren't very happy with me Halloween night."

"Sorry, I don't remember," he said, giving her an embarrassed grin. "But I'm sure I said some things I shouldn't have. I was hurt when you left."

"I know, but you've moved on, and I'm sure Krystal wasn't the first."

He gave her a bashful look. "You know me so well."

"If this is what you wanted to talk to me about—"

"No," he said, hopping off the table to walk down to the water's edge. He picked up a rock and skipped it across the dark surface of the cold river before turning to look at her. "I'm hoping you can help me remember what happened."

"You really still don't remember any of it?"

He shook his head. "I've talked to Emery. I know we all went out to Starling, there was a tornado, you and I were trapped in a root cellar. Somehow, you got out and went for help, and when you came back, I was unconscious and bleeding. That about cover it?"

"Pretty much, except for the part where you saved my life. We would have been killed if you hadn't talked me into going down into that root cellar to begin with. When the tornado hit, you pulled some heavy shelves over us and sheltered me with your body."

"Wow, I can't believe I did all that."

She smiled. "Yes, you can. It sounds just like you. You like being a hero."

That made him laugh, but it was as if he were holding back.

"Are you worried that whoever attacked you will try again?" she asked.

"I hadn't thought of that… Thanks. Something more to worry about."

"I'm serious. I can tell something's bothering you."

He looked at the ground for a few moments before he said, "When you went for help, did you see anyone?"

"No."

"How about when you came back?" She shook her head. "You came back alone, didn't you? Ahead of the others?"

"Yes." She frowned. "How did you know that?"

He shrugged. "I thought I heard you calling my name in this dream I had when I was in the hospital. I figured it must have been when I was unconscious because, in the dream, I couldn't answer."

"Maybe your subconscious is trying to remember."

"Maybe. Are they finished searching out at Starling?" he asked. "I thought maybe Jaden might have mentioned."

"Why?" She couldn't help her surprise. "You wouldn't go back out there, would you?"

"If it would help me remember, of course I would. You have no idea what it's like not knowing what happened, who attacked me and why."

"Maybe once Jaden finds out who killed Rob, that will help fill in some of the blanks for all of us."

"Yeah, it might have been the same person who attacked me."

"You have no idea why someone would want to hurt either of you?"

He met her gaze. "Not a clue. That's why I have to remember."

She thought about Jaden saying "Someone's lying" and felt as if the temperature had suddenly dropped. How could she have forgotten that whoever had attacked Cody was probably still a threat? How could he not have realized that?

He stepped toward her. "You're cold. I shouldn't have dragged you out here. I just didn't like the way we left things at the store."

"I didn't either. I'm sorry I can't fill in more of the blanks for you," she said as he walked her to her car.

"Oh, but you have helped," he insisted. "You told me I was a hero. I feel a lot better," he joked.

She swatted him on the arm. Just like old times. Smiling, she climbed into her car, started the engine and drove off. When she checked her rearview mirror, he was still standing beside his SUV. She thought he was watching her leave until she realized he was on his cell phone.

Chapter Thirteen

The next morning, Deputy Montgomery drove over to Emery's bike shop. He hadn't slept well, no surprise. He'd lain awake worrying about Olivia, worrying he wasn't going to get this case solved before someone else lost his—or her—life.

He'd finally roused this morning feeling as if he was racing against a ticking time bomb. But as he swung by the shop, he found that Emery hadn't opened yet. As he drove away, he saw Krystal pull up to the shop, apparently also expecting Emery to be at work. She pulled in, saw that the shop was closed and took off again as if in a hurry.

Curious as to why she was looking for Emery and why in such a rush, he turned around and followed her. When she made her way into Emery's apartment house parking lot, he stopped up the block and waited.

She seemed in an awful rush to speak to Emery. Had something happened? What could be so important that she had to see him this morning?

He warned himself, as he got out of his patrol SUV, that it might not have anything to do with his case. All his instincts, though, told him that there was a lot more going on with Olivia's old gang than it appeared. He couldn't shake the feeling that they all might have been in on it.

Jaden heard Krystal's raised voice even before he reached Emery's apartment at the back of the complex. He stood outside the apartment door for a moment, catching only snatches of the argument since she seemed to be the only one speaking and apparently moving around in an agitated state.

He knocked lightly, not surprised the occupants hadn't heard. Then he tried the knob. It turned in his hand and the door swung open. The apartment was small, cluttered, and smelled of stale pizza and beer. He stopped just inside the door where he could hear what was being said deeper in the apartment.

"You have to protect me," Krystal was saying. "I didn't want any part of this, and you know it." He couldn't hear Emery's reply. "This wasn't supposed to happen." She sounded close to tears. "Are you listening to me?"

Something hit the floor and shattered. Emery swore, and chair legs scraped across the flooring before there was another crash and his voice rose in anger. "Knock it off! Or so help me…"

From the kitchen doorway, Jaden saw a knocked-over chair and what appeared to be spilled coffee next to a shattered cup on the floor. Emery had Krystal backed up against the kitchen counter, his hands on her shoulders. He was saying, "Keep it together. Stop panicking. No one is going to find out unless you keep opening your big mouth." He shook her so hard, she banged her head against the kitchen cabinet.

"I hope I'm not interrupting anything," the deputy said, stepping into the kitchen.

Emery immediately let go of Krystal and moved back, his boots crunching on the broken glass glittering on the floor. Krystal moved deeper into the kitchen, her back to them as she hugged herself.

"Which one of you is going to tell me what's going on?"

the deputy asked. "No one is going to find out what? How about you, Krystal? Why don't you tell me why you're panicking?"

She turned slowly, her face flushed, eyes bright with unshed tears, but from the set of her jaw, she wasn't talking now.

"We can do this here or I can take you both down to the sheriff's office."

"On what charge?" Emery demanded.

"Assault, for starters."

Neither spoke for a moment. Emery began to clean up the mess on the floor. Jaden looked at Krystal, who had recovered and now looked defiant.

Jaden pulled up a chair and sat down. "I overheard enough to know that you're both involved in what happened out at Starling on Halloween. What I want to know is what the two of you are hiding. What was the plan that night? It was your idea to go out to Starling, Emery. Planning a murder?"

Krystal's expression changed to one of alarm. "Emery?" He had finished wiping up the floor and dumped the broken cup into the trash, clearly stalling for time.

"You've got it all wrong," he said and exchanged a look with Krystal before he righted the chair and sat down. "We were just going to play a prank. That's all it was supposed to be. Just scare some people."

So, Krystal had been in on it. Jaden turned to her. "How did you get to Starling without anyone noticing?"

When she didn't answer, Emery did for her. "She hid in the back of my van. With all the junk back there, no one was the wiser."

"Weren't Dean and Jenny still down where you parked?" Jaden asked.

There was pride in her voice when Krystal finally joined

in. "They were busy arguing, so they didn't notice when I opened the back and climbed out."

"What was the plan?" the deputy asked.

"She was dressed in all black, her hood up, and wearing a big, floppy dark hat," Emery said. "Anyone who saw her would think they were seeing—"

"Elden Rusk," Jaden said with a nod. "You said you wanted to scare *some* people? Cody and Olivia?" He looked at Krystal, then shifted his gaze to Emery when neither spoke. "Rob and the girls you were with? What about Dean and Jenny?" When neither answered, he said, "Who was it you really wanted to scare?" He watched the two exchange another look. "Rob Perkins," he guessed. "Why?"

Emery looked away for a moment, as if making up his mind, then said, "He owed me money. He promised to pay before he left town, but I didn't believe him. I knew that once he was gone, I'd never see a penny of it. All his big talk about his condo and his new job out there in Seattle…" He shook his head. "I didn't believe a word of it."

"Why would he lie?"

"Because it wasn't just me he owed money to," Emery said. "He'd gotten involved with the wrong people."

Jaden groaned inwardly, thinking this would have been nice to know from the get-go. "The wrong people? Drug people?"

Emery shrugged. "I just knew that he needed to get out of town. He said he wasn't planning to leave until after Saturday. But I found out that he'd already packed his truck in his garage and was planning to take off Halloween night. That's why he'd wanted to go out to Starling in my van. He hates my driving, so I knew something was up. I texted Krystal to check his house and garage."

"I looked through a crack in the blinds into his bedroom," she said. "The closets were empty, the bureau drawers dropped out on the bed and almost everything taken. I checked the garage, and just like Emery suspected, Rob was planning a quick getaway."

"He was going to miss the going-away party I was throwing for him Saturday night," Emery said bitterly. "Where he promised to pay me what he owed me with interest. Lying piece of—"

"So, the two of you decided to kill him," Jaden said, making Emery start.

"No! Not that I didn't want to, but…" He shook his head. "It's just money, right? He saved my life once. Sure, I was pissed, but I couldn't kill him. What would be the point? It wouldn't get my money back." He shrugged. "I just wanted him to think that Elden Rusk had come for him that night. My going-away present for the bastard."

Did Jaden believe Emery was telling the truth, that he'd just wanted to scare Rob by resurrecting Elden Rusk? After all, it had been Emery's idea to go out to Starling on Halloween night. Rob must have gone along with it because it would have been suspicious if he hadn't.

The deputy looked to Krystal, who was still standing at the other end of the table, her back to the wall. What was in it for her? "What did he owe you, Krystal?"

She seemed surprised by the question but recovered quickly. "Do I look like I had money to give him?" Her laugh didn't quite ring true.

"It wasn't money he wanted from you," Jaden said. "But he owed you something, didn't he?"

She chewed on her lower lip, her eyes shiny as she looked away.

"He'd promised to take her with him when he left," Emery said, getting an evil-eye glare from Krystal.

"But once you saw his loaded pickup, you knew different," Jaden said. He felt for her but wondered what that kind of humiliation could stir up in her. He recalled her chasing Livie out of town. Would she have run her off the road if she hadn't gone in the ditch?

"You were hiding in the back of the van when Rob and Emery picked up those underage girls Halloween night," Jaden said as he tried to work it out. "That had to make you angry. Angry enough that when you saw your chance, you took it?" But was she strong enough to push a concrete wall over on Rob? Only if Emery had helped her.

"Why would I care about Rob?" Krystal said. "I was with Cody. I never really believed Rob was serious."

"Only, Cody was with his old girlfriend down in a root cellar," Jaden said, trying to imagine how yet another betrayal that night could have been the straw that broke the camel's back. "You saw Olivia climb out and leave him to go for help. Save him or… You had to be furious by then. No one could blame you for picking up a rock and hurling it down at him. You just wanted him to hurt like he had made you. You didn't mean to almost kill him."

A tear escaped and ran down her cheek. She lifted her gaze to meet his. "I couldn't hurt Cody. I love him and he loves me," she said, making Emery look over at her in surprise. "It wasn't me. When you found him, wasn't Olivia the one standing over him? Maybe you should ask her what happened."

"Did you see anyone else?" the deputy asked, tending to believe at least part of her story. She shook her head. He thought she could have wanted to scare Cody, but he doubted she'd intended to put him in the hospital, let alone kill him. That was, if she had been the one to injure him.

Rising from the table, Jaden thought back to the argument

he'd overheard before coming into the apartment. "Any idea why Rob had insisted you all stay until midnight?"

"I didn't know then, but I do now," Emery said and swore. "He was killing time with us, using his old friends to shield him from the scary people he owed money to. Then, after midnight, he was skipping town."

"You know that for a fact?" Jaden asked, even though it certainly appeared that way.

Emery shook his head. But if right, Rob was leaving in the dead of night, running from debts and deceits, maybe even running for his life.

"Who are these scary people?" he asked Krystal.

"I heard him on the phone with them once," she said after exchanging a look with Emery. "It sounded like they would be crossing the border the next day. From what I could tell, they were threatening him. After he hung up, he went in the bathroom and threw up. I didn't ask."

"It had to be drugs," Emery said, pushing that theory. "I know he made a lot of trips up to the border." It was only sixty-five miles from Libby to the Canadian border, nothing to drive when you lived in a state as large as Montana.

"You never asked him why he made so many trips to the border?" the deputy asked.

Emery shook his head. "He told me he had a girlfriend up there. I knew he was lying. But, like Krystal, I didn't ask. I wanted nothing to do with it."

OLIVIA HAD SPENT all morning trying to shake off the terrifying dream she'd had the night before.

She'd been back out at Starling. Only, this time, Cody had climbed out of the root cellar first, leaving her to die. She'd screamed for help until her throat was raw before a dark shadow had fallen over her. She'd looked up and Elden

Rusk had been peering down at her. But then she'd seen who'd been standing next to Rusk and she'd gasped. Cody, smiling down at her, a rock in his hand.

She told herself it had just been a bad dream. It didn't mean anything. It didn't even make sense. Yet she found herself worrying about Cody. That really made no sense, given that she'd been the one in the hole, the one in danger, not Cody.

Still, she called his number. She'd tell him about the dream. They'd laugh about it. She'd put it behind her. His phone rang four times before voicemail picked up.

"You've reached Cody Ryan. Leave a message."

Olivia hesitated as she heard the beep. "Cody, it's Olivia. I had this crazy dream last night. I just wanted to make sure you were all right." She recalled their talk the evening before by the river, his need to remember what had happened Halloween night. He wouldn't go out to Starling, thinking it might help him remember, would he? "Please call me."

After she disconnected, she was more convinced than ever that he might have gone out there this morning. Hadn't people in the area been warned to stay away? Been told how dangerous it was because of all the debris left by the tornado? Like that would stop Cody.

She paused only a moment before she called the deputy. He picked up at once. Just the sound of his voice steadied her. He'd always had that effect on her. "Is the crime team done out at Starling?"

He instantly sounded suspicious. "Why are you asking me that?"

"Cody is determined to remember who attacked him. I couldn't reach him this morning. I think he might go out there."

Jaden swore. "Don't you go out there," he ordered, making her bristle.

"I didn't say I was going out there."

"It would be just like you. Do I have to remind you that there is still a killer on the loose, not to mention how dangerous it is out there?"

She was sorry she'd called him and said as much before disconnecting.

"That man knows you," her mother said from her bedroom doorway. "You're thinking about going to Starling because of that boy."

"Neither of you know me," Olivia snapped. "But it doesn't stop either of you from telling me what to do. Cody is my *friend*. He's hurting right now. I had this dream last night…" She waved a hand through the air. "I wouldn't expect either of you to understand."

Her mother just shook her head, turned around and disappeared back into the kitchen. Olivia could smell bacon cooking, which she realized was probably why her mother had come to her room, to offer her breakfast.

In the kitchen, she hugged her mom with one arm and said, "I'd love some bacon. Oh, and pancakes too? You're spoiling me." When her mother didn't respond, she added, "I'm sorry. I worry about my friends. Cody isn't doing very well right now."

"Cody's a big boy. He can take care of himself." Her mother plated bacon and pancakes and turned to hand it to her. "You chasin' after him sends mixed signals to the deputy—the one you say you're in love with."

"I'm not chasing after Cody. I need this whole investigation over. If Jaden and I stand any chance, I can't be one of the suspects."

Her mother shook her head. "Listen to your mother

for a change and let the man do his job. In the meantime, stay away from Cody Ryan."

JADEN HAD BEEN about to go inside Rob Perkins's house when Livie had called. He swore. She wouldn't go out to Starling looking for Cody, would she?

Probably, he thought with another curse. He used Perkins's keys to open the front door of the house. Just as Emery had described to Olivia, the place had been cleaned out. Only worn furniture remained and not a lot of that. In the bedroom, he saw the mess the man had left. Perkins had been in a hurry—just as Emery had thought.

Once Jaden stepped into the garage and saw the packed pickup, he had to agree. Definitely a man on the run. Perkins was leaving town.

He pulled on latex gloves and opened the passenger side of the vehicle. The first thing he saw was the automatic rifle wedged into the space between the seats. The serial number had been ground off. In the glove box, he found a handgun and ammunition. At the back of the space, he found an envelope stuffed with hundred-dollar bills.

Closing the glove box compartment, Jaden took a look in the backpack on the passenger seat. Another handgun. More ammunition. In a side pocket, more money. Zipping the pocket up, he closed the door and took a look in the back, not surprised to find more weapons and boxes of ammunition, as if expecting World War III.

Closing the door, he made the call to have the pickup taken into evidence by one of the state boys in the area. All his instincts told him this was bigger than some old friends getting in a drunken argument and one of them ending up dead and another injured.

He called Sheriff Brandt Parker and updated his boss on

the investigation, even though there wasn't much to tell. Then he called DCI and requested help to find out if Rob Perkins had a job in Seattle or not. "He'd allegedly purchased a condo out there and was going to work for a tech firm. From what I can tell, the man didn't even own a computer."

After hanging up, he locked the house and garage and waited for a state highway patrolman to arrive and secure the property until the pickup could be moved and the house processed.

He felt anxious, angry that all he could think about was Livie. She was just fool enough to go out to Starling. He tried Cody's number. It went to voicemail. He didn't leave a message. What could the man hope to find out there? All the evidence taken by the state boys had been bagged. Or was there another reason Cody had told Olivia he'd wanted to go back out there?

Either way, Jaden had no choice but to go back to that place he'd hoped to never see again.

On the way out to Starling, he got a call from the coroner. The autopsy results were pretty much as expected. But given what the deputy had since learned about Rob Perkins, he was surprised that the man had had no drugs in his system. There was also no indication that he was a drug user.

That didn't mean he hadn't been involved in the selling end. Still, it seemed unusual. But then, where had Perkins gotten all that money he'd had in his pickup? And why all the guns and ammunition? He was involved in something suspect, no doubt about that, and it had probably gotten him killed.

Ahead, Jaden could see the turnoff to Starling and began to slow. He told himself this was a wild-goose chase, driving out here. He had better things to do than chase down his ex-fiancée. It bothered him that she was so worried about

Cody. She'd said they weren't together. All indications were that Cody was now dating Krystal. Maybe they were just friends, as Livie'd kept saying. Jaden knew how she could be like a mama bear with her friends who were in trouble. He'd seen that in college.

What was left of Starling loomed ahead. He hadn't been out here since Halloween night. Driving up the road, he caught glimpses of the damage the tornado had done. Only a few structures remained standing against the skyline.

As he came over a rise, he saw Livie's vehicle and swore. Hadn't he known? He sighed as he pulled up next to her, cut his engine and got out. She had come alone, hadn't she? Cody Ryan wasn't with her, was he?

That was when he saw her trudging up the hill, avoiding the debris. He knew at once where she was headed and hurried after her. The dirt around the open root cellar was unstable. He hated to think what could happen to her.

He just hoped to get to her first. "Olivia!" he called. "Livie!"

OLIVIA STOPPED AND turned at the sound of her nickname. Jaden was the only one who called her that. Just the sound of it sent her heart pounding.

She saw him climbing up the hillside toward her. When she'd gotten here and seen all the destruction—and no Cody—she'd almost turned around and left. She couldn't imagine there was anything to find. Yet she understood why Cody might want to come back out here. It had been so dark and frightening Halloween night down in that hole with the house that had been over them ripped away.

Now, in broad daylight, she wanted to see it and possibly get a different perspective. She knew it had something to do with her nightmare that had made her start up the hillside.

The wind had been blowing, so she hadn't heard a vehicle approaching. She'd only stopped when she'd heard Jaden call her "Livie."

As he approached, winding a path through the destruction, she could tell he wasn't happy with her. Yet she was glad to see him. Even in bright sunshine, this place gave her the willies. Even almost completely destroyed.

Jaden said nothing at first when he reached her. He only looked at her before shaking his head. "What are you doing, Livie?" His voice was soft, caring, maybe even loving.

"Looking for answers," she said over the wind that whipped her hair. She started to brush it back, but Jaden was already reaching. He caught an errant lock and held it between his fingers. "You called me 'Livie.'"

He nodded as he tucked the errant lock of hair behind her ear. His hand seemed to move of its own accord to the nape of her neck. He dug his fingers deeper into her hair as he drew her closer. "What am I going to do with you?"

She shook her head. She couldn't speak. She could barely breathe. She looked into his eyes and saw desire burning there. He wanted her as much as she wanted him.

For a moment, she feared that he would draw away, release his hold on her and not go through with the kiss. She ached to feel his lips on hers. She could see him fighting a battle within himself. If he kissed her, he could no longer deny how he felt about her, about them.

The wind shrieked around them, whirling dust and dirt. She'd never felt more alone with him, as if they were the only two people left on earth, than she did in this moment. He pulled her closer. She leaned into him as they both fought the wind on the hillside, their lips only a breath away from touching.

"Livie," he said, making her pulse spike, and then his

mouth was on hers with an unbridled passion that made her weak with longing. He wrapped an arm around her, holding her up as the kiss deepened, and there was nothing but the two of them and their longing for each other.

Neither of them heard the sound of a vehicle approach, then turn around and leave. The wind was too loud, even if they hadn't been so lost in each other.

Chapter Fourteen

Shaken to his boots, Jaden drew back from the kiss. This was exactly what he hadn't meant to do. Yet he couldn't regret it as he looked in Livie's eyes. "We can't do this. I'm in the middle of an investigation and you're—"

"Still a suspect."

He nodded and tipped in to touch his forehead to hers for a moment before stepping back. "What are you doing out here? Cody's not here, is he?"

She shook her head. "I had this bad dream last night. It was so dark that night… I wanted to see the root cellar in daylight. I don't know what I'm hoping to find. Answers. Reassurance. Something, since I haven't been able to forget being in that hole and then seeing Cody lying down there." Her gaze locked with his again. "And seeing the doubt on your face, I didn't want you to suspect me anymore."

"I don't want to, either, but you know we can't take this any further until this investigation is over. That's if it's something we want to do."

"How can you even ask after that kiss?" she demanded. "I never stopped loving you. It's why I came back."

He hated to ask, especially after that kiss. "What about Cody?"

"Cody and I are just friends."

"Does he know that?" Jaden heard himself ask and wanted to kick himself.

"Yes, Cody knows that. We grew up together, shared a lot of things, but all we've ever really been is good friends. He'd thought we'd end up together and was upset when I left town, but he knows better now."

He knew she had a strong connection to Cody. Wasn't that the reason he'd called off the engagement? Livie had years of memories with Cody, something Jaden didn't have with her. Maybe what he'd picked up on was her longing for Montana and home more than her old high school boyfriend.

While he'd wanted to hear her say it, the kiss had convinced him even more than her words. She was right. Once his lips had touched hers, he'd felt his doubts dissolve and blow away like smoke on the breeze.

"If you're determined to see the root cellar…" He motioned toward the hillside. "Let me make sure it's safe to go over there."

OLIVIA GLADLY LET Jaden lead the way through the debris. They had to skirt around houses torn off their foundations and dropped at random on the hillside. Everywhere there were piles of lumber and pieces of twisted metal to traverse.

They hadn't gone far, though, when Jaden stopped to wait for her. She quickly caught up after finding herself gawking at the awesome power of what had been a small tornado by national standards. She saw that he was standing next to the hole in the ground.

"Don't get too close," he warned. "It's caved in some more."

The root cellar looked so much larger than it had seemed that night, even with more dirt having fallen in. She shivered, remembering being down there when the tornado hit, feeling it trying to suck them up and carry them away.

"Are you all right?" Jaden asked. The wind had picked up to a low howl, much like it had Halloween night before the real storm hit.

Pushing her hair back from her face, she looked down. "It doesn't seem as deep now," she said as her dream came back to her. In the dream, when she'd looked up and seen Cody standing over her, the hole had been so much deeper, so much more frightening.

"Have you seen enough?"

She glanced around and nodded. If Cody did come out here, she couldn't imagine that he would find any more answers than she had. "I'm done."

JADEN FOLLOWED LIVIE back to her turnoff to home. They'd stopped earlier when they'd reached their vehicles but kept their distance. He knew it wouldn't take a lot for him to cross the line with her during this investigation. He hadn't realized how much he'd missed her, how much he wanted her, that no matter what happened, he would always want her.

The kiss had sealed it. He felt even more determined to solve this case so he and Livie could see what happened next. He believed her about Cody Ryan. But he wondered if Cody had accepted that she'd moved on.

It all came back to Rob Perkins, he realized as he forced himself to concentrate on the case. Whatever Perkins had been up to, Jaden couldn't believe that his friends hadn't known, might even have been involved. He called the hospital, only to find out that Dean Marsh had been released.

He'd only just disconnected when he got a call from the Fortune Creek dispatcher. Dean Marsh had been trying to reach him. "He sounded upset and said he needed to talk to you right away."

On the outskirts of town, Jaden decided to swing by Dean's house, hoping to catch him at home. He doubted Dean would have returned to his job in construction yet, especially with a broken arm. He hit pay dirt when he saw Dean's car in the driveway. The vehicle had taken a beating during the tornado but apparently still ran after being brought into town when the state boys had finished with it.

Dean must have heard him coming up the steps, because he opened the door before the deputy could knock. "Thanks for coming by." He motioned Jaden inside. "I don't know if this is important," he said once they were seated in the living room, "but I overheard my wife on the phone planning to meet someone after Halloween. She didn't leave me because of what me and Jenny had going on. Apparently, she'd been planning this for some time."

Jaden had to admit he'd been surprised at how quickly Angie had bailed on the marriage—even before they'd known what had happened to her husband. "You have any idea who she was meeting?"

"No, but I got a call asking if I had made a reservation for a hotel in Spokane, Washington. I hadn't. The reservation had been made *two weeks ago*. Apparently, Angie hadn't checked in when she was supposed to—the night after Halloween—and she hadn't called to cancel, so they were going to have to charge me for the first night as per their policy. It was for a room with a king-size bed. Angie had told them there would be two people."

"Have you heard from your wife, Dean?" Jaden asked.

He shook his head. "I don't blame her for running off with someone, but I'm worried about her. Why hadn't she checked in? What if something has happened to her?"

"You should consult a lawyer," the deputy advised. "You might want to cancel your credit cards. That way, you'll probably be hearing from her. Let me know when you do."

"Can't you put out a BOLO on her car? Something. I just need to know she's all right."

Jaden hesitated. "I can do that. One more thing. Some of Rob's friends seem to think he might have been involved with the wrong people. Would you know anything about that?"

"Wrong people?"

"Drug dealers," Jaden said.

Dean blinked. "Rob? Seriously?" He sounded genuinely surprised.

"I can't seem to find anywhere he was employed for the past few years," Jaden said.

"He was working with Angie."

"Doing what?"

"She has a craft business she's been running out of an old barn in the country. Buys furniture and redoes it. Rob was helping her."

"Was it profitable?" Jaden asked.

"Seemed to be, but she wasn't paying enough taxes, you know?"

The deputy thought he did. "Where is this barn?"

Chapter Fifteen

"You're acting strange. Is it because I asked you to help me with the jelly?"

Olivia looked at her mother sitting across from her at the table. Each year, Sharon Brooks picked the crab apples from the huge trees in the backyard and froze the juice to make jelly once the weather got colder.

"I already told you that I'd be happy to help with the jelly."

"You're sure?" Her mother had insisted on making her lunch when she'd returned to the house. Beanie weenies, her mother's specialty.

"If I'm acting strangely, it's because I had an odd morning," she said, her gaze on the last few bites of her lunch. She could feel her mother waiting. Eventually, the woman would get it out of her. "I went out to Starling."

"Why would you do that?" Sharon demanded, making her wish she hadn't told her.

"I wanted to see the root cellar where we were trapped during the tornado." She shrugged. "I had a nightmare about it."

"I can't believe you'd go out there again and alone. What were you thinking?"

"I didn't go alone. Jaden followed me out there. He made sure it was safe." She could feel her mother's eyes on her.

The woman knew her too well. "He kissed me." She smiled and felt her face light up. "It was…amazing."

"I guess that answers all your doubts," her mother said and rose from the table to start clearing away the dishes.

"He's the one who had doubts," Olivia corrected her, only to have her mother huff. "I love Jaden. I want to marry him."

"And how does he feel about it?" her mother asked, turning to look at her daughter. "This kiss have the same effect on him?"

"Yes, I think so."

"You think so." She turned back to her dishes. "You think you're ready to marry a deputy sheriff and live in Fortune Creek, huh. What about Cody?"

"I told you. He's just a friend."

Her mother kept hand-washing the dishes in the sink.

Olivia rose to carry her dishes over. "Why don't you let me do that?" With a shock, she realized that her mother was crying.

"Mother?" No response. "Mom, what is it?"

Shaking the water off her hands, her mother reached for the dish towel and dried her hands before she looked at her. "Will I see more of you if you're living closer?"

"Yes, of course." She saw how much she'd hurt her mother the years she'd stayed away. "I'm so sorry that I didn't come home. It wasn't you." She reached out and her mother stepped into her arms. She held her close as her mom cried, reminded of all the times her mother had held her when she was growing up. It had just been the two of them. They'd been close. She hated how much she'd hurt her mother.

Her cell phone rang from where she'd left it on the table. She ignored it.

"You should get that," Sharon said, stepping from her

arms to reach for a paper towel to wipe her face. "It might be important. Go ahead."

Olivia picked up the phone, saw it was Cody and hesitated. Turning around, she saw that her mother was busy finishing up the dishes. "I need to take this," she said and stepped into the other room. "Hello?"

JADEN DROVE OUT of town on a road with no traffic, toward the mountains. Dean had said the barn where his wife and Rob worked together was out there.

He hadn't been driving long before a barn shape appeared ahead. The structure was small by barn standards, more like a large shed and surrounded by a barbed-wire fence. As he pulled off the road, stopping at the barbed-wire gate, he climbed out. He'd opened his share of Montana ranch gates. Shoving it aside, he drove in, pretty sure of what he was going to find.

The door to the small barn-shaped building had a large padlock on it. Jaden walked around the side to look for a window. He found one covered with what appeared to be black tar paper. Angie really didn't want anyone to see what she was working on with Rob, he thought as he circled the building to find all the windows blacked out.

Walking to his patrol SUV, he opened the rear and dug out what he needed from the tools he carried. Hesitating, he pulled out his phone and called Judge Nicholas Grand back upstate. "I'm going to need a warrant," he said.

"Heard you were working on a murder investigation down there."

"I'm pretty sure I'm about to find out why the victim was killed. But it means getting into a structure where he worked. The owner has left town in a rush."

The judge chuckled. "Could be a body in that structure. Who knows what you'll find. You'll get your warrant."

"Thanks, Judge." He disconnected, picked up his hacksaw and headed for the front door again. It took a few minutes to cut through the padlock. Leaning his hacksaw against the outside of the building, he started to open the door but stopped. He knew that if he was right, the place could be booby-trapped.

Picking up the saw again, he stepped back and pushed the door open with the blade end. Nothing happened. He looked past the doorway into the room, seeing pretty much what he'd expected. Several large tables. Scales. Baggies.

Dean had said that Angie had been restoring old furniture. *Restoring* didn't seem to be the right word. The old furniture was clearly being used to hide bagged drugs.

As he reached to close the door, he brushed something inside the room. An alarm went off. He slammed the door, the alarm still blaring—not that there was anyone around to hear it. Had the alarm been to scare people away?

Frowning, he shook his head. No. It had been to warn someone that the door had been breached. If he had worked here, he would know how to turn it off—or never set it off in the first place.

As he pulled out his phone to alert the DEA state boys, he wondered if the alarm was also set up to notify whoever was in charge of the operation. Angie? She apparently was long gone. Rob wasn't being notified of the alarm. Clearly, someone else was involved in the operation.

When there was no response on the other end of the phone line, Olivia asked, "Cody? Are you there?" She was beginning to wonder if he'd accidentally called her.

"Sorry, I had a customer," he said. She could hear the

sounds of the hardware store in the background. His father insisted on playing those old songs from the thirties and forties as background music.

"Is everything all right?" Cody sounded winded and she said as much.

"Just had to carry out a bunch of supplies to a pickup. I ran all the way back in. It's getting cold out. That wind is brutal," he said and seemed to catch his breath.

"I was surprised you called. What's going on?"

"I get off work in thirty minutes. I was hoping I could talk you into going with me out to Starling."

She glanced back toward the kitchen as she pushed out the front door, closing it behind her. Cody was right. It had gotten a lot colder, a sure sign that winter wasn't that far off. Often it snowed by Halloween. It hadn't this year, but now that it was November, the mountain peaks were snowcapped and there was a bite to the air.

Shivering, she said, "I was out there this morning. There's nothing to see, believe me."

"You went out there by yourself?" He sounded like her mother.

"No. The deputy went with me."

"Really? What were the two of you looking for?"

"We weren't looking for anything exactly," she said. "I just wanted to see it in the daylight. I was surprised that the hole wasn't as deep as it had seemed Halloween night."

"Then you have no interest in going with me."

"I'm sorry. I can't now anyway. I'm helping my mother put up crab apple jelly."

"You can't get out of it?"

She glanced back at the house. "No. Maybe you can get Emery to go with you."

"He's busy."

"Or Krystal."

He groaned. "I told you, we aren't together, not really."

"And I told you, I don't care."

"Yeah, you've made that clear. You and the deputy getting back together?"

"I hope so." Silence. "I should get back inside the house. It's freezing out here and—"

"You have to help your mother make jelly... Getting pretty domestic, aren't you. I remember when we were kids and you tried to make fudge."

She smiled. "Chocolate glue, you mean?"

He chuckled. "Good times."

She could hear the disappointment in his voice. "Want a jar of jelly?"

"Sure," he said. "Save me one."

Olivia heard something in his voice. "Don't go out to Starling alone. Promise me you won't go. It's too dangerous."

"Yet you and the deputy survived it."

"I'm serious. Promise me."

He sighed heavily. "I promise. It was silly. I doubt it would have jogged my memory anyway. Don't laugh, but I hate not being able to remember the last time you and I were together—even if it was during a tornado, down in an old root cellar."

She did laugh. "Trust me, it was far from romantic."

"I'll have to trust you on that. Got a customer. Gotta go. Take care of yourself, Olivia. I'm sure we'll see each other again."

She laughed again at his words. "Of course we will. We'll always be friends."

No response. Had he already disconnected? No, she could hear the hardware store music in the background. "Cody?" The phone went silent.

For a moment, she almost called him back and told him she'd go to Starling with him. He'd sounded so sad. But then the front door opened.

Her mother asked, "Is everything all right?"

Pocketing her phone, she turned and smiled. "Just getting ready to make some crab apple jelly with my mother. Just like old times. I need to start paying more attention to how it's done. Who knows—one of these days I might have a kitchen of my own. Though no one makes jelly as good as yours."

Her mother smiled and said, "You and your malarkey," but Olivia could tell that she was touched by the compliment as they both headed for the kitchen.

OUTSIDE TOWN, at the barn, Jaden pulled his coat tighter around him as he waited for the state DEA team to arrive. This case had been running them ragged. Knowing that Rob Perkins had been involved in this drug distribution business might be the key to solving his murder.

Rob could have been involved with dangerous people, as Emery had suggested. The question was, were they his friends? He thought about Dean. How could he not know what his wife and Rob were involved in? And if he had known, had Dean just thrown his wife under the bus to save himself?

His cell phone rang. Angie Marsh's car had been found in Spokane, abandoned on the street. "Looks like it's been looted," the police officer told him.

"Any sign of Angie Marsh?"

"Checked the surveillance camera in the area." He described the woman who'd gotten out of the car. Petite, dark-haired, wearing jeans and a hoodie. It hadn't captured much of her face, but she was young.

That definitely sounded like Angie. The officer said he

would get back to Jaden if he had anything to report about the woman. Like if her body was found. Or if another camera picked her up getting into someone's vehicle.

He thanked the officer and disconnected as a gust of wind out of the nearby mountains sent a chill through the air. What was it about this case? He felt as if he wasn't getting anywhere. It didn't help that Livie might be more involved than she realized.

Jaden squinted as dust blew past, reminding him of the hillside at Starling. Everything reminded him of Livie.

That thought didn't get a chance to go any further as he saw a van drive slowly by on the road, then speed up and disappear over the rise. He hadn't needed to see the van's license plate or to see him behind the wheel to know that it was Emery's gray van. What had he been doing out there, on this particular road, so far away from town?

The alarm. More than likely it was to warn those involved that someone had found out their secret—or already knew their secret and had come hoping to find drugs. Either way, whoever was running this operation now knew.

He waited, wondering if Emery would return this way. Not if he was guilty, in which case, he'd take another way back to town.

Even after the DEA boys arrived, Jaden kept an eye on the road.

The van hadn't come back.

Chapter Sixteen

Jaden wasn't surprised when he went to the bike shop and found it closed. No sign of Emery. He drove by his apartment. No van parked in the lot. No answer at Emery's apartment door. On impulse, he headed for Krystal's.

Still no sign of the van, but Cody's rig was parked next to Krystal's and the curtains were drawn in the living room window. He didn't bother to stop.

After driving around town and still not finding Emery or his van, Jaden thought about heading back out to the barn. But the state crew was still there processing the place. He told himself that Emery might have just been curious when he'd driven past earlier to see if the deputy had taken him up on checking it out.

What Jaden really wanted to do was to drive out and check on Livie. He felt antsy, like he always did when an investigation started coming together. It was the most dangerous time in any case, but especially in a murder investigation. He was getting close. Someone was getting nervous.

He pulled out his phone, opting to text Livie instead of showing up at her door.

You OK?

Making crab apple jelly with my mom.

My favorite, he texted back.

I remember. I'll save you a couple of jars!

Great. Tell your mom thank you.

At loose ends, he checked in with his boss in Fortune Creek, then drove down to the café. His growling stomach reminded him that he hadn't had anything since lunch.

Just the thought of Sharon Brooks's crab apple jelly had made him hungry. He thought about that one late night back in college when he and Livie had gotten into a care package her mom had sent. There was a jar of the jelly and peanut butter, along with homemade bread. He smiled at the memory. Best jelly he'd ever tasted.

Taking a seat in a booth facing the street, Jaden watched the sparse traffic as he waited for his meal order. This time of year, off season, things were usually quiet. He thought about everything he'd learned so far on the case. He had a pretty good idea why Rob Perkins had been killed. But it weighed on him that, while he had suspects, he still wasn't close to arresting the person who had committed the murder or the person who had assaulted Cody. Were they the same one?

His food came and he dug in, reminding himself that he'd solved one old murder at Starling, though, thanks to Rusk. He recalled the male remains. Make those two murders. Remembering that Evangeline might have still been pregnant, he amended the thought. Make those three murders. Solved, but he would never be able to prove it, let alone get justice. Or maybe Elden Rusk had already gotten justice since he was trapped in his own guilt until he died.

As Jaden was leaving the café, he spotted Emery driving by in his van. Once in his patrol SUV, he sped after him. He started to hit his lights and siren, but realized Emery was headed to his apartment. He followed, parking next to him in the lot.

Emery didn't seem happy to see him as Jaden climbed out and approached the van. The man's scared expression gave him hope that Emery was ready to tell him the truth.

"Would you mind if I took a couple of jars of jelly to share?" Olivia asked her mother. She'd been antsy after they'd completed their work. She needed fresh air. Mostly, she wanted an excuse to see Jaden.

Sharon Brooks sighed. "Is there a handsome deputy on your list?"

Olivia grinned. "There is." She told her mother about that night back in college when they'd opened her care package. At least, she told her the PG part. "He loved it. Said it was his favorite."

"You won't be late?" her mother asked, looking outside. It got dark earlier and earlier this time of year. The wind whistled through the bare branches of the trees. One limb scraped against the side of the house. "Something's blowing in," she warned. "Hate to see you get caught in a snowstorm."

"I'll be back long before that," she promised and loaded a couple of jars into her bag, thinking she'd drop one off at the hardware store before it closed.

"Thanks for helping with the jelly," her mother said as Olivia started for the door.

"It was fun," she called over her shoulder and was out the door, headed for her car. It had been fun making the jelly with her mother. She remembered the two of them working in the kitchen together when she was a girl. Her mother had sewn her a small apron to wear. She'd been so proud of it, she thought now as she swallowed the lump that rose in her throat.

Climbing behind the wheel, she hesitated as she looked back at the house. She could see the flicker of the television screen, the silhouette of her mother curled up in her chair to watch her stories. Olivia told herself that she wouldn't be gone that long. Maybe the two of them could watch a movie together when she got back.

That decided, she headed toward town, hoping to get there before the hardware store closed. Then she planned to go by the grocery store to pick up some peanut butter and bread before going to Jaden's motel. She knew it was risky. He might turn her away. Or even more risky, he might invite her in.

The jelly was just an excuse. He would realize that right away. Hopefully, he'd hear her out. She needed to tell him she wasn't leaving Montana. That she'd quit her job in California before she'd come home. That she loved him and was through running away—from being terrified that she would end up with her mother's life.

The lights were still on at the hardware store as she parked and, taking one of the jars of jelly, headed for the front door. The bell tinkled as the door closed behind her. She saw that some of the lights had already been turned off, but the music was still playing softly, so she knew someone was still there.

"Hello!" she called as she headed toward the back, where the office was. "Jelly delivery!" No answer. Her footsteps echoed on the worn wood floor as she moved deeper into the building.

The lights were on in the office, but she didn't see anyone. She caught a gust of wind coming down the hallway from the open back door to the alley. "Cody?"

"I THINK WE should talk," Jaden said as Emery climbed out of the van with obvious reluctance.

"I've had a rotten day, Deputy," the bike shop owner said. "Can't we do this in the morning?"

"I'm afraid not. We can talk in your apartment or go for a ride in my patrol car. Up to you."

Emery raked a hand through his hair. "I guess it's my apartment, then." He started in that direction, walking as if he had the weight of the world on his shoulders. Jaden suspected he did.

Once inside the apartment, Emery headed straight for the refrigerator, opening it and pulling out a beer. "Wanna join me?" When Jaden declined, he popped it open and chugged half of the can. Wiping his mouth, he said, "Let's get this over with. What do you want?"

"Why did you drive by the barn earlier in your van?"

Emery frowned. "What barn?"

"The one Rob and Angie worked out of." He saw the man tense.

"Sorry, but I have no idea what you're talking about."

"Are you saying you don't know what barn I'm talking about or that you didn't drive past earlier?" Jaden asked.

"Angie's restored furniture business? Yeah, I know where it is, but I didn't drive by it today. I didn't even have my van until an hour ago."

"Who had it?"

Emery finished the can of beer and, with a loud burp, tossed the can in the direction of the trash. His aim was off. The can hit the wall and clattered to the floor. He ignored it and reached for another beer. He took his time opening it before he looked up. "This is a small town. We're like family here."

Jaden saw the pain in his face. "I know it's a small town.

Hell, all of Montana is a small town. I understand local loyalty, but this is more than covering for a friend. This is murder and drugs."

Emery walked over to the secondhand-looking couch and dropped onto it. He cradled the beer in his large hands, his head down.

"Who had your van earlier? You know I'm going to find out. Are you covering for this person because you're also involved in the drug business or—"

"I had nothing to do with it. From the get-go, I told them to keep me out of it. I've got my bike business. That's all I need, all I want." He stared down at the beer for a moment before he said, "Cody borrowed my van. He said he had some things he needed to haul." He took a drink. When he looked up, there were tears in his eyes.

"I know Angie and Rob were involved in the drug business," Jaden said. "How is Cody involved?" Emery shook his head. "If you withhold what you know, it makes you an accessory. He just used your van and I suspect it wasn't the first time."

Emery dropped his head again. "I told you. I didn't want to be involved. I didn't ask. But Cody's been desperate to get out of that hardware store. He's worked there since he was a kid. His old man told him that if he left him to run it by himself, he'd sell it and wouldn't give him a dime. Cody had to stay, but he was at the point that he'd do *anything* to get out from under his father's thumb."

Jaden wondered how close Cody was getting to breaking free of his father, the hardware store and this town. "You told me that Rob owed a lot of people money," the deputy said as he took a chair across from Emery. "Did he owe Cody?" He took the man's silence as a yes. "How desperate was Cody? Was he desperate enough to murder Rob?"

The answer was written all over Emery's face, even as he refused to believe it. "Cody couldn't have killed him. He was trapped down in that root cellar. Someone attacked him. It had to be the dangerous people Rob did business with."

Some of those "dangerous people" appeared to be locals, including Cody, the deputy thought. But Emery had a point. How could Cody kill Rob? He would have had to find a way out of the root-cellar hole, find Rob, kill him and climb back into the hole and get seriously injured so he still had an alibi.

Yet something Livie had said earlier teased at his memory. Something about the root-cellar hole.

OLIVIA WAS HALFWAY down the hallway past the office when she heard voices in the alley. It sounded like boxes were being loaded in a vehicle. Cody or his father must have had a late order to fill. She started to turn back, thinking she would just leave the jar of jelly on the desk in the office. She was anxious to see Jaden. Her heart filled at the thought of their earlier kiss.

Before she could reach the office, she heard Cody's voice. "Olivia?" There was a tension in it that made her turn to look toward the dark alley and the man standing in the doorway. "What are you doing here?"

She held up the jar of jelly. "I was just dropping this off as promised. I was about to leave it on the desk in the office."

"How long have you been standing there?" he asked as he moved toward her.

"Just a few minutes. I could hear that you were busy. I didn't want to bother you." Why was he looking at her like that?

He glanced at the jelly, then at her. He seemed jumpy. "I was going to call you," he said, still moving toward her.

She fought the urge to take a step back. This was Cody, the boy she'd grown up with, her first real boyfriend back in high school.

She swallowed, her throat suddenly dry. Cody had left the back door of the shop open. She could feel the chill of the wind along the hallway as if it were a funnel. "Why were you going to call me?"

He reached her, stopping just inches away, his eyes dark in the dim light, his expression reminding her of Halloween night when they'd argued. From the alley, an engine started up, then another one, both pulling slowly away. She could see that the back of each pickup was filled with boxes and shiny new equipment.

"We should take a ride," Cody said.

Olivia shook her head. "I can't. I was just—"

He grabbed her arm hard, cutting off the rest of her words. "I insist."

She tried to pull free. "Cody, you're hurting me."

He jerked her to him, his body crashing into hers. She dropped the jar of jelly. It hit and broke, the smell of crab apple jelly filling the hallway. "Don't fight me, Olivia. I don't want to hurt you, but you are coming with me—one way or the other."

"Tell me why you're acting like this," she demanded and tried to pull away from him. She stepped into the jelly and felt herself slip, her feet sliding out from under her. Cody still had a firm grip on her arm, so he was going down with her unless he released her. He swung her around and slammed her against the wall as he struggled to stay on his feet. His grip released enough that she broke free. But as she tried to scramble away from him, he punched her, his fist connecting to the side of her head. She saw the floor come up fast to meet her as darkness closed in around her eyes.

The last thing she heard was "Damn it, Olivia. I didn't want it to end like this."

Chapter Seventeen

"Do yourself a favor," the deputy told Emery as he rose to leave. "Don't call Cody. Don't try to warn anyone involved. Unless you want to join them in prison."

"Don't worry. I'm not getting off this couch but to get another beer," the bike shop owner said. "I worried something like this would happen." He shook his head and took a gulp of his beer. "They were my friends. My brothers, man."

"I know. Any idea where I can find Cody?"

Emery hesitated, but only a moment. Maybe he was starting to realize that his friends, his brothers, had pulled him into their illegal activity knowing he didn't want to be involved. "Probably down at the hardware store. Whatever he had to move earlier is probably getting moved out the back door of the store as we speak."

Jaden left Emery on his couch and raced to the hardware store. He took the alley, hoping Emery had been right and he could catch them in the act. But the alley was empty.

The back door of the hardware store, though, was wide open.

He jumped out, weapon in hand, and moved quickly to the open doorway. His heart dropped to his boots as he caught the familiar scent of crab apple jelly.

OLIVIA BEGAN TO surface from what felt like a bottomless pitch-black pit. She became aware of movement, a blinding headache and the hum of a car engine. But what brought her out of the darkness was the memory of Cody in the alley and the realization that her wrists were bound.

She blinked, even though it hurt. Her eyes were the only thing she moved, knowing instinctively she had an advantage as long as her captor thought she was still out. She didn't have to look to her left to know who was behind the wheel. The smell of spilled crab apple jelly on her shoes brought back the memory of the hardware store hallway—and Cody.

Where was he taking her? She could hear him nervously tapping his fingers on the steering wheel. She didn't remember ever seeing him this jumpy, this…strung out? It heightened her fear—just like what she saw in the headlights. She caught glimpses of a landscape that sent her pulse pounding in her ears. This was the road to Starling. But why would he take her there?

She thought of the root cellar. The bones the tornado had uncovered. The crime scene team had finished. No one would look for her there—just as no one had thought to look for Evangeline buried down in the root cellar of an abandoned house.

"I know you're awake," Cody said with a chuckle. "You never could fool me, Olivia."

JADEN FELT TIME racing away from him as he stepped into the dimly lit hallway. He listened as he moved as soundlessly as possible. The closer he got to the front of the building, the scent of the jelly grew stronger—just like his dread and the faint sound of canned music.

Livie had been here. The realization was a scream in his

head. She'd been here and something had happened. Had she stumbled onto Cody moving product? Or robbing the place?

Pulling his flashlight out with his free hand, he flicked it on. The glow fell on something on the floor partway down the hall. Broken glass and a smear of red. Not blood, he told himself as he moved toward it.

It appeared that someone had dropped the jelly jar and then fallen? Or been dragged? His pulse thundered in his ears. Chest tight, he called out Olivia's name, even though he knew if she was there, she wasn't going to be able to answer.

He checked the building. No bodies. No Olivia. It gave him little relief, though. Where was Cody? He tried his number. It went straight to voicemail. Then he put in a call for backup.

He knew only two things. Cody was neck-deep in the drug operation and he had Olivia. Cody had driven by the barn earlier. He'd seen Jaden's patrol SUV. He would know that it was only a matter of time before he would be going down. He'd run. Was that what he'd been doing at the hardware store when Olivia showed up?

Had she seen something she shouldn't have? Caught him getting ready to skip town? What had he done to her?

Jaden thought of the broken jar on the floor, the drag marks in the jelly.

Cody had to have taken her. But where?

OLIVIA SAT UP and looked over at Cody. Her wrists were bound, but that wasn't all. He'd tied her bound wrists to the grab bar on the door so she couldn't jump out. Nor could she reach the steering wheel or attack him, both options she wished for right now as he slowed and made the turn down the road to Starling. Her stomach roiled as they rumbled along the road, the headlights giving her glimpses of the destruction ahead.

"What's going on, Cody?" she asked with a sigh as if bored by all this. Even as her heart raced, she told herself not to panic. She needed to keep all her senses sharp because she was going to get away from him. She had to.

"We're just going for a little ride," he said without looking at her.

"You were never a good liar."

His attention swung on her, his face contorting in anger. "Like you know anything about me. You left. You have no idea what I've had to do to keep from going stark raving mad." The venomous response alarmed her. "All I could think about was getting out of here, getting out from under that damn hardware store."

Her first instinct was to try to calm him down, to remind him that they were friends. "I'm sorry. I didn't know. I thought you didn't mind working with your dad."

Cory let out a bark of a laugh. "He had me over a barrel. Either I stayed and worked the store, or I walked away with nothing. Nothing. You think he would help me with college? With starting my own business? Not a chance. He started with nothing and made good, so he thought I should do the same." He seemed to grit his teeth. "He gave me no choice but to do what I did."

"No choice?" she asked almost in a whisper. He was driving slower now, but she could see what structures were still standing ahead getting closer against the skyline. As long as she could keep him talking…

The thought almost made her laugh out loud. No one knew where she was. No one was coming to save her. She was on her own. Her only chance to survive was to be ready. If he gave her an opening, she would take it to escape.

Cody looked over at her, and for a moment, he was the boy she'd grown up with. His gaze softened and the fury in his face dissolved. "I started my own drug business." She heard pride in his voice. "I made something out of myself."

Drugs? She tried not to show her revulsion as she listened to him talk about getting the supplies up on the Canadian border, hiring friends to bring them down and package them for distribution.

"It was a hell of an operation," he said proudly. "I should have done it sooner. Maybe you would have stayed."

She said nothing, gripping her hands together, her fingers white-knuckled. He'd never understood why she'd left to follow her dream. He'd just resented her for being able to do it. As it was, she'd learned that the grass wasn't greener. But it had made her figure out what she wanted. Montana, home and Jaden. And it had brought her back.

Cody looked lost in thought. She knew this wasn't about the two of them, no matter what he said. Nor about his father and the hardware store. This was about that night in Starling and Rob's murder. She didn't know how or why exactly, but she knew. "Who of the old gang work for you?"

He instantly perked up, anxious to talk about his enterprise. "Angie was my first hire. She'd rented this little barn outside of town to redo old furniture she found at garage sales." He scoffed. "I convinced her to use her skills and mine to make more money. She was like me. She wanted more. Her marrying Dean had been a mistake. He was still in love with Jenny. But as badly as she wanted to leave him, she couldn't until she had enough money to make it on her own. So I helped her."

They'd reached what was left of Starling. Even in the glow of the headlights, what the tornado had left looked more menacing than it had in daylight.

Olivia shuddered as if she could feel the violence, the death, the disappointment that had happened here. It had left a pall over the place and seemed to invite more of the same.

"Emery?" Olivia asked, afraid of what would happen once he stopped driving, once he stopped talking.

"Emery? That lily-livered SOB?" He shook his head. "He was too chicken to go into business with me. He likes being a deadbeat."

The pickup slowed to a crawl. Cody brought it to a stop and cut the engine.

There was one name she hadn't mentioned, afraid that once she did, the ride was over. "What went wrong?" she asked as Cody fell silent. "Sounds like you had a viable business going."

He looked over at her in the darkness of the pickup's cab. This far away from town, she could see stars and just enough moon to throw a silvery haze over the landscape. It gave Starling a ghostly presence, making what she knew was coming all the more frightening.

"I gave Rob a job. He was making good money. But apparently it wasn't enough. He got greedy," he said somberly.

She knew but was afraid to say it.

He reached for the driver's-side door handle.

"You killed him."

Cody froze for a moment. He drew back his hand and turned again to look at her. "He thought I didn't know. It wasn't so much that I could have let it slide. He was my best earner. He took the most risk, driving up to the border with the furniture he helped Angie redo so we could hide the drugs inside."

He looked out into the darkness. She wondered if he was seeing this Starling or the one from Halloween night. "It was all too perfect, things were going too well." He shook his head. "As my old man often says, best not to make waves when you're all in the same boat."

"I don't understand," she said. "I left you down in the root cellar."

He smiled over at her. "It wasn't that deep that I couldn't get out using some of the shelving. I had to move quickly. I knew you'd be back soon, and I was going to need an alibi. I saw Rob. He'd survived the tornado, the bastard. He was going to get away with all of it, ripping me off and, worse, taking Angie with him. The fool woman had fallen for another loser."

"Rob and Angie?" she asked in surprise.

"They worked together every day in that old building she'd bought." His shrug said that there was no accounting for taste. "She was skimming money too. She just wasn't as greedy as Rob. They were running away together. Rob thought I didn't know."

"He was killed when a wall fell on him," she said, still trying to buy herself time.

"That was a stroke of luck—just like the tornado. I was counting on getting my chance that night before midnight. I knew Rob was planning to take off at midnight. Take off with a lot of my money. I'd planned to pick up something I could use as a weapon. As it was, I caught him next to that rock foundation wall. I got lucky."

"But you must have had to move quickly to get back into the root cellar before I came back with the rescue workers." She realized that she didn't have to encourage him to talk about it. He seemed to relish finally being able to tell someone how smart he was.

"I wasn't even sure that the wall killed him. But I didn't have time to stick around to find out. I had to get back before you returned. Anyone could have seen me, but no one did. I hurriedly scrambled back down into the hole, but as I did, some of the dirt caved in." He let out a laugh. "For a minute there, I thought I'd be buried alive. Got to see the irony in that, huh? Especially after we'd found those bones."

"But when I came back, you'd been injured."

He nodded, chuckling. "I heard you coming back. I decided to make it look good. The cave-in had uncovered a large rock stuck in the dirt wall of the root cellar. I reached up and managed to dislodge it, thinking that I would move away before it came down. Got my feet tangled up. That was the last thing I remembered until I woke up in the hospital."

"You didn't have amnesia, did you?"

"Nope, I remembered *everything*." There was a sharpness back in his voice. "That night, you had pretty much spelled out how you felt about me. I was never good enough for you."

"That's not true. You were my best friend."

"*Were* your best friend," he repeated and opened his door.

BACK OUT IN the alley, Jaden's mind raced. Cody was a loose cannon on the run, and he had Livie. Where would he take her? He could feel the clock ticking. He had to find her before it was too late. If it wasn't already too late.

The moment the first law-enforcement vehicle pulled up, Jaden rushed to it. He told the officer everything he knew, including that Cody Ryan had Olivia Brooks. Leaving the officer to secure and wait for a team to come in to process the scene, he got behind the wheel of his patrol SUV.

For a moment, he didn't know where to go or what to do. Like Olivia, Cody had been born and raised here. He knew the country. He would know where to go to get rid of Livie's body, and that place could be anywhere.

The realization came to him like a bolt of lightning out of

the blue. The moment the thought surfaced, he knew where Cody had taken her.

Starling.

CODY CAME AROUND to Olivia's side of the pickup and opened the door. As long as her wrists were still bound and tied to the grab bar over her head, she couldn't try to get away. She reminded herself to wait until she had the advantage—if Cody ever gave her that.

He knew her, so he also knew how determined she could be. Backed in a corner, she would come out fighting. That meant he would also be waiting for her to try something.

"I don't understand why you're doing this," she said as he untied her from the grab bar and dragged her out into the darkness. "You got away with it. You fooled everyone!"

"Not everyone," he said under his breath. "Your boyfriend. He's coming for me."

"But what does that have to do with me?" she demanded.

"You're just collateral damage. You shouldn't have stopped by the hardware store tonight," he said with a shake of his head. "You caught me finishing up before I was skipping town. You and your damn crab apple jelly. I hate that crap and now it's all over the hallway at the shop. I couldn't leave you behind so you could tell the deputy what you'd overheard in the alley."

"I didn't hear anything," she cried as he dragged her by her tied wrists up the hillside.

"But the spilled jelly," he said like a curse. "Jaden will know you were there. He'll come looking for you. I can't take the chance that you'll tell him my plans."

"Cody, I swear I don't know your plans. I don't care about your plans. But if you kill me, Jaden will track you to the ends of the earth."

He stopped walking to turn on her. "It's like that between the two of you? But you weren't together."

"We had broken up, but I came home to see if he still felt the way I did," she said. After that kiss, she'd had hope. She'd been counting on Jaden finishing this investigation and then there wouldn't be any reason they couldn't find their way back together. At least, that had been her hope.

Cody seemed to think that Jaden knew about his drug business, that he would be coming after him. She could only wish. But Jaden wouldn't know Cody had her. He wouldn't know where Cody had taken her and now time was running out.

"Glad to hear this is going to break his deputy heart," Cody said, clearly taking satisfaction in that.

"You're going to kill me out of jealousy," she snapped, her anger overtaking her fear for a moment. She was furious with herself for thinking they could be friends and even more furious with him.

Cody smiled, the moonlight flashing on his teeth. "I wouldn't even venture a guess how many women have been murdered out of jealousy, but I bet it's a lot. No man wants to think he never mattered."

"You did matter. You still matter."

He laughed. "Not enough."

"Enough that I brought you jelly," she stressed.

"And signed your own death warrant." He jerked the binding on her wrists angrily as he continued to haul her up the hillside.

She could see the crime scene tape around the root-cellar hole ahead. It rustled in the breeze. Hadn't she known this was why he'd brought her here? Hadn't she known how it would end?

Unless she stopped him.

Chapter Eighteen

Jaden wanted to go after Livie lights and siren blaring. But he knew that would only warn Cody he was coming. *If* Cody had taken her to Starling, he reminded himself. The sooner he found out, the better. Better still if Cody didn't know he was coming for him until it was too late.

He tried not to second-guess himself as he tromped on the gas. There was little to no traffic on the road out of town. What he did encounter, he passed at high speed. Nothing would slow him down, given the urgency he felt to get to Livie.

The first time he'd seen her on the college campus his senior year, he'd fallen for her the moment he'd laid eyes on her. That moment in time was like a photo he'd snapped, a memory he could never forget. He'd never had that happen to him before. He'd known she was the woman he was going to marry.

He could find humor in that now since they hadn't married. Not yet, anyway, he mused as he drove. He'd lost hope for a while, but since that kiss... He smiled to himself, remembering that moment he knew.

She'd been coming out of one of the campus buildings with a couple of friends. Something one of them said had suddenly made her laugh. Just the sight of her had stopped him in his tracks, but it was the way she'd let herself laugh that had drawn him as if he'd lassoed and pulled her to him. She'd turned her face up to the sun, a joyous expression making her look radiant. Her long, silken blond hair seemed to float around her as she'd moved.

I'm going to marry that girl, he'd thought. But first he'd have to meet her, he'd amended, not in the least worried. It had felt meant to be. He still felt that way.

He looked at the highway through his headlights and couldn't bear the thought that something bad had already happened to her. He'd already called for backup to meet him at the abandoned community. It would take law enforcement from other towns too long to get there.

That meant he was on his own. All he could hope was that he got there soon enough. And that he wasn't wrong about where Cody had taken her. The backup hadn't been to help him anyway. It was so Cody didn't get away if things went south.

Jaden had no idea what to expect. Had it only been Cody who'd taken her? He hoped the man's friends wouldn't be involved. Either way, he had to assume that Cody would be armed. What worried him was why he'd take her back to Starling. Just to get rid of her body? Or was there something else Cody was planning to do out there?

The clock was ticking. He had no idea how long Cody had been gone from the hardware store with Livie. Nor did he know what the man had planned. Get rid of Livie's body and keep running?

Jaden just hoped there was time to get there, find him and stop him. He didn't want to think about what he would do if Cody hurt the woman he loved. He wouldn't need backup to take Cody to jail. If he let himself go, Cody would never see a cell. But then Jaden would never be in law enforcement again either. Right now, it seemed a fair trade-off.

He loved his career choice because he could find the bad guys and bring them to justice. Even as he reminded himself of that, he still feared what he would do when he got his hands on Cody Ryan.

It was his fear talking, he told himself.

With a curse, he shoved away the thought that he might be too late. She couldn't be gone. Wouldn't he feel that in his heart, if true?

CODY WAS THINKING about his future far from here as he worked his way through the debris toward what was left of the root cellar. It had been such an obvious place to get rid of Olivia's body. It felt meant to be. No one would look for her there because no one would know where she'd gone.

He liked the idea that some people—the deputy, for one—would think she'd run off with her high school boyfriend. Why not? It could have happened. If it wasn't for her being in love with the deputy. He cursed under his breath at the thought. Her loss. As his old man often said, there were a lot of fish in the sea.

Lost in dreams of how he'd spend all his money, he'd almost forgotten about Olivia.

Until she seemed to trip and stumble. He still had hold of her bound wrists, so, as she fell, it pulled him off balance—breaking his hold on her. As she hit the ground, he fell beside her.

Before he knew what was happening, she looped her bound arms around his throat and pulled, putting so much pressure on his windpipe that he couldn't breathe. She dug her heels in as she drove the rough rope of her bondage into his neck. He forced out a guttural sound as he clawed at the rope and fought for breath. It had happened so fast that she had him at a disadvantage, on the ground with her behind him. He couldn't breathe and the rope tore into his neck. If he didn't get her off of him soon, she was going to strangle him to death.

He quit trying to rip the rope from his throat. Stretching back, he clawed at her, trying to reach her face, her eyes. She managed to avoid his hands, but at least his attempts had forced her to let up on the pressure on his neck at little.

Getting a grip on one of her arms, he squeezed as hard as he could until she cried out. He wanted to call her names, but he didn't have enough air as he began to kick back at her legs while digging his fingers into the flesh of her arm.

He felt the pressure on him slacken, but then she jerked as hard as she could, slamming his head back into hers. The blow stunned him, but only for a moment. He swung an elbow around and caught her in the side of the head.

With relief, he felt her body go limp. Swearing, he grabbed her arms, the pressure off his throat, and tossed them back over his head. Through blurred vision, he rose awkwardly from the ground. Maybe she'd hurt him, but she'd hurt herself as well, he saw through his fury. Her eyes were unfocused from the blow to the head and her nose was bleeding, maybe even broken.

He was breathing hard as he rubbed his bruised and scraped throat and looked down at her. He wanted to kick her, beat her into the ground, to take out all his anger and frustration on her. He pulled the gun from his pocket, telling himself to save his energy and just shoot her. Her eyes must have focused enough that she saw how close she was to dying right here on the hillside.

She closed her eyes, expecting a bullet. He tried to catch his breath, tried to keep to his original plan. Killing her here would mean he'd have to carry her dead body up the rest of the way to the root cellar. Yet it felt impossible to rein in his wrath. She symbolized everything he couldn't have.

But then she opened her eyes and looked at him with raw defiance. Her gaze said that he'd have to look in her eyes as he killed her. He pointed the gun at her head and told himself she wouldn't be that heavy to carry up the hill. Seconds passed, his finger on the trigger, her gaze locked with his.

With a curse, he swallowed back his rage, reminding himself that he didn't have a lot of time. He needed to take care of her, then get what he'd left up on this hillside and clear out.

"Get up." His voice sounded rough. He coughed and swore again. "Get up or so help me…"

She rose slowly, looking dizzy and a little disoriented. Two blows to the head had probably left her with a raging headache. That made him feel a little bit better.

"Move," he said, motioning with the gun. "Try something again and I'll empty every bullet in this gun into you."

Olivia looked as if all the fight had gone out of her. She finally saw him for who he was, not some boy she would wrap around her finger. Not some teenager she'd left pining for her. That Cody was gone, replaced by a dangerous man she didn't know.

JADEN TURNED OFF his headlights as he reached the road into Starling. It was hard to drive slowly, but he wasn't going far. He pulled over and cut the engine in a stand of trees that had weathered the storm. With luck, his vehicle wouldn't be seen or heard from Starling. He took his shotgun. He was already wearing his sidearm. Both were loaded. He climbed out, closing his SUV door quietly.

He could see Cody's pickup with hardware store logo on

the side parked up the road. Taking long strides, he headed for it, all the time watching the hillside for any movement.

A thin layer of clouds muted the moon and starlight, but he could see well enough when he reached Cody's pickup. Empty. No sign of a struggle that he could see. What he really hadn't wanted to see was blood—and he didn't.

The chilly breeze stung his face but he welcomed the cold. It kept him alert and sharp, he told himself. If Cody had heard his vehicle engine coming up the road, he might be lying in wait somewhere up there to ambush him.

He slowed and listened hard. Voices. He waited, hoping to catch Livie's. When he did, he felt his heart soar. She was still alive. All he had to do was get to her quickly. He could think of only one reason Cody had brought her here.

When they spoke again, he realized that they weren't far from the open root cellar. He needed to get closer. His options weren't good, given the mountains of debris spread across this hillside. There would be no charging up the hill. They would hear him coming as he bounded over what was left of the community, only to get himself and Livie killed.

He began to work his way through the debris that separated them until he could get a decent shot at Cody.

OLIVIA HURT ALL over from her struggle with Cody. She wiped at her nose with her sleeve as she walked. She could feel him behind her. Earlier, she'd thought for sure he'd kill her right there on the side of the mountain. He'd certainly wanted to. She'd seen it in his eyes.

She'd hoped that the Cody she'd known was still in there and that all she had to do was reach him. She'd thought she could talk him down and stop him from doing what she knew he had planned for her.

But she no longer did. She stumbled up the rest of the hill, weaving her way through piles of splintered boards, piles of bricks and cement, portions of roofs and walls, to the spot where a small house had once stood.

Hadn't Jaden said his parents had lived there when he was a kid before they'd left Starling? It was gone now, leaving behind debris and a large dark hole in the ground that had once been a root cellar.

She feared she was about to suffer the same fate Evangeline had.

Feeling Cody directly behind her, Olivia moved slowly toward the open root-cellar chasm, knowing that once he got her down there it would be over. "This can't be the only reason we're here. Just to kill me?" she asked, surprised that she'd voiced her thoughts.

He shoved her forward. They were almost close enough that all he would have to do was give her a push and she'd tumble into the void.

She glanced down the hillside to where she'd heard Rob's body had been found and stopped abruptly. Cody jabbed her in the back with the barrel end of the gun. "Did you see that?"

"What?" He glanced down the hillside. But not long enough for her to take advantage of the misdirection, even if she felt strong enough to do so. The physical struggle with him had taken a lot out of her.

"I just saw someone," she said in a whisper. She pointed. "Down there. He went behind that house."

He looked at her, unsure, and she was afraid that she hadn't sold it well enough. "What are you trying to pull?" he demanded.

"I'm telling the truth. It was a man. He was...watching us." She opened her mouth and screamed "Help!" as loud as she could.

Cody grabbed Olivia's arm, dragged her to him and clamped his hand down hard over her mouth. He told himself it was time to finish this. Shove her into the hole, kick some dirt down on her and take care of the reason he had planned all along to come here tonight long before she'd shown up at the wrong time at the hardware store.

What stopped him was that he wasn't so sure she was lying. What if she had seen a man? But why would someone come out here tonight? Maybe for the same main reason he had. That was what really changed his mind. He realized he might need a human shield. As badly as he wanted to pitch her into the open root cellar, he realized it might benefit him to keep her with him.

He'd been so certain that no one had known what he'd been hiding up here. But Rob had. With a silent curse, he recalled that he'd foolishly brought Krystal with him on one of his late-night trips to Starling. He'd ordered her to stay in the pickup while he'd trudged up the hillside with his full backpack. But Krystal never did what she was told. He hadn't thought much of it, though. He never thought she'd tell anyone, knowing what he'd do to her if she did.

But she must have told Rob. And who else?

Holding Olivia by the back waistband of her jeans, he pushed her in front of him to the corner of one of the still-standing old houses. Pulling Olivia close, he peered around the corner.

No one. Yet he couldn't shake the feeling that they weren't alone. He told himself it was the drugs. They made him paranoid and anxious. He closed his eyes, only to have a flash of memory from Halloween night. He'd climbed out of the root cellar to kill Rob and found him digging in the debris. He'd known at once what Rob had been looking for—and why Rob had agreed to come to Starling that night. He knew about his boss's stash.

Cody had wanted to kill him for skimming from him. But once he'd realized that Rob knew about the money stashed here on this hillside, he wasn't about to let the man take everything he'd work so hard for. He'd known then that it was time to kill him.

That night, he'd felt a kind of fury like none he'd ever known. It still amazed him that he hadn't attacked Rob right then and there, blowing his alibi and any chance he would have had to get back in the root cellar in time. But he'd kept his cool. Finding Rob digging under the rock foundation wall, he'd realized that the man hadn't known exactly where the loot was hidden.

Moving swiftly, the clock ticking, Cody had slipped around the foundation wall and pushed with a strength that still boggled his mind. The wall toppled, but not before Rob had seen it coming and tried to scramble out of the way.

But the man hadn't been fast enough. Cody had stared at the body crushed beneath the wall. Only Rob's head and arms had managed to get free. He'd seen the shine of the man's eyes. Rob had been trying to say something, possibly beg for his life, mumbled words bubbling out in blood. It would have been so easy to finish him, but Cody hadn't had the time. He'd had to get back to the root cellar.

Reliving that night now, though, only made him more edgy. If Rob had survived, he would have turned on him. Good thing he hadn't. Like tonight. He couldn't leave Olivia alive. It was that simple.

But first he had to get to where he'd hidden the bags of money. He assured himself that if they'd been found by search and rescue or the state crime investigators, he would have heard about it.

Still, if someone else was really out here tonight with them, the person could already have found his stash and could be carrying it off right now.

He pushed Olivia ahead of him, keeping a strong grip on her to keep her from escaping as they descended the hillside. In the moonlight, he made out the old stone pump house below them. It didn't surprise him that it was still standing. The rock walls were thick, the space inside tight.

As they got closer, he saw that the door stood open, making his heart rabbit in his chest. Of course, it would have been searched. But had they found anything?

Too dark to tell if his secret hiding place had been discovered, he forced Olivia inside. She cried out when her hip connected with the rusted old-fashioned hand pump. He held her against it with his body as he took out his phone and used the flashlight to shine it on the stone wall. Relief made him weak. The loose large rock and the hiding space behind it that he'd discovered as a boy hadn't been found.

Putting away his phone, he worked the stone out, dropping it to the wooden floor with a thud. Then he reached in, still worried the bags wouldn't be there. Rescue and searchers had been all over Starling, not to mention law enforcement. Hurriedly, he reached deeper into the space between the stones, his panic growing until his hand brushed the canvas of a bag.

He let out a laugh as he began to pull out one bag after another. He still couldn't believe his luck. For a while tonight, things hadn't been going well. Olivia showing up at the hardware store had thrown him. But now he felt a lightness that reassured him it was all going to turn out just fine.

Or it would—once he took care of Olivia.

She hadn't seen anyone out here with them. She had just

been trying to throw him off. It had worked, but soon her time would be up.

"Is this why you killed Rob?" she asked as he opened one of the bags, half-afraid he'd been wrong and the bag would be filled with paper instead of hundred-dollar bills. With a laugh, he confirmed it was full of money. His money.

"There were a lot of reasons Rob had to go," Cody said, his relief warming him to the subject. Confession, it turned out, did feel good, especially when it didn't cost him anything. "I just got lucky Halloween night. I knew that if he got arrested, he'd take me down with him."

"Wasn't he leaving town for a job in Seattle?" she asked, sounding as if in pain with the old pump handle digging into her leg and hip.

"That bull about some great job out on the coast, buying a condo." Cody shook his head with disgust. "Who did Rob think he was kidding? It was no secret that he wanted out of the business. He was scared of getting caught. Emery treated Rob like he was some kind of hero, always saying that Rob had saved his life. What a joke, those two."

He froze to listen as he felt the hair quill on the back of his neck. He'd heard something. A footfall on loose rocks? The clang of twisted metal?

Olivia had been lying about seeing someone, hadn't she?

Chapter Nineteen

Jaden had cut across the lower part of the hillside, working his way through the debris, seeking cover where he could find it. He finally reached a spot where he could start up the hillside. They were standing next to the root-cellar hole. He feared that Cody would throw her down before he could get a shot at him and started to move toward them when he realized that he'd been seen.

In the moonlight, he could see them both looking in his direction. He froze, back pressed to the shadowed darkness of what was left of one of the houses. He cursed his luck. There was no way he could get a clear shot from this distance. On top of that, now Cody would be looking for him.

To his surprise, Cody seemed to change his mind. He pushed Livie ahead of him as they started down the hillside. Cody was keeping her where he could use her as a shield. Bastard. All Jaden could do was wait and hope for a shot. But that was going to be difficult since Cody had taken a path on the other side of the debris. Jaden was only getting glimpses of them.

Where was he taking her? To his surprise, they appeared headed for a small stone structure that was still standing farther down the hill. Jaden wanted to get closer but there was too much rubble. He watched as Cody and Livie disappeared into the tiny building.

He considered trying to get down there but realized that he stood a better chance once they emerged. He had no doubt that Cody would take Livie back up the hill as a shield until he felt he didn't need her anymore.

But why the little stone building? Because there was something he wanted to retrieve? Of course, he would have needed a place to hide his ill-gained money. Cody knew this place. But once he collected it, then what? Jaden waited, growing more anxious. What if he was wrong? He'd been so sure that if Cody planned to kill her, he wouldn't want her body to be found. Why else would he bring her here?

The waiting was killing him. He couldn't understand what was taking so long. What if he was wrong and Cody killed her inside that small building? There was probably a well in there. He could dispose of her body down the well if it was large enough, deep enough.

He couldn't take it any longer, even knowing that if he'd been wrong, then Livie was already dead. He started to step away from the side of the house, but as he did, the boards under him gave way and he dropped into darkness, coming down hard.

CODY FROZE. HE'D HEARD what Olivia had. She felt the change in him. He was scared. But so was she. What she'd heard sounded like boards breaking and then a duller crash followed by silence.

It was the silence that terrified her. Cody must have heard the same thing. But had it been someone out there? Or an animal? She'd been pretending she'd seen someone earlier, trying to buy time. As paranoid as Cody was acting, she was thankful it had helped. Otherwise, she would already be in that root cellar, probably under enough dirt that she would no longer be breathing.

The thought that it really might be someone gave her hope. If it was just her and Cody alone out here tonight, Olivia wasn't sure how she would survive. As jumpy as he was, he would be watching her closely. And he had a loaded gun. She felt as if he had reached a point where he had nothing to lose. Even if by chance someone tried to stop him, it would probably only get them killed. He was intent on getting rid of her and leaving.

That the law would eventually catch up to him didn't help. By then, she would have been dead for weeks, months or even years.

"Take these and don't drop them," Cody ordered as he shoved two of the bags at Olivia. "We're going to head back up the hill. I'll be right behind you with a gun at your back."

The bags of money were heavy as she stepped out of the pump room into the night. What was left of Starling appeared eerie in the thin light of the partial moon. She shivered against the cold breeze as she looked for movement. If someone was out there, she didn't see them. Because they'd fallen and either hurt or killed themselves.

Earlier in the day, her mother had predicted a snowstorm. Sharon hadn't been wrong. It had snowed in the mountains while she and her mother were making the jelly.

Yet there was no doubt that the temperature had dropped here in the valley. She could hear Cody behind her, almost feel his desperation. Several times, she glanced back to catch him looking around as if still not sure there wasn't someone out there in the shadows of the Starling skeletons.

Fortunately, he'd had to pocket the handgun he'd pulled earlier to carry the heavy canvas bags he'd retrieved. He seemed to be working himself up into a state as if afraid he'd come this far to lose everything.

Olivia knew the feeling. She'd come home to make amends for her bad decisions. She'd ended up alienating the two men she'd cared about. Was that why she hadn't noticed how much Cody had changed? He'd been angry on Halloween, but his whole demeanor had changed when she'd suggested they go back to the vehicles and leave.

Now she understood why. He'd planned to kill Rob Perkins that night. What he hadn't planned for was the tornado, but even that he'd used to his advantage.

That the boy next door had grown up to be a killer shocked her. She'd loved that young Cody. She could understand the pressure he was under with his father and the hardware store. He'd worked in that store from the time he was a boy, only to realize that he was trapped. He could have walked away, but without money and nowhere to go, he'd stayed and started his own lucrative but deadly business that would eventually get him killed.

It all seemed such a waste as she worked her way through the debris in the moon and starlight. Everywhere there were hazards. Splintered boards, broken glass, pieces of twisted, sharp metal. Something caught on her jeans. She heard it rip as she tried to pull free and felt whatever it was bite into her skin.

Her head still hurt from earlier, the dizziness making walking hard without worrying about what might attack her legs. The blows had weakened her. She didn't think she could get the better of Cody again—let alone fight him off.

JADEN HAD DROPPED a half dozen feet, landing hard and pulling broken boards down on him as he fell to his knees. As he'd tried to catch himself, he'd felt nails ripping through his flesh. Blood began to run down his arms as he fought to get to his feet in the broken boards around him. The moment he did, he knew his ankle was badly sprained. He could barely put weight on it.

Pulling out his flashlight, he shone it around. He'd fallen into a space with a dirt floor. He had no idea how large it was or if there was a way out. He looked up, afraid he might not be able to climb out and what that would mean for Livie.

Pushing aside the panic, he knelt to run his flashlight beam under the boards that had collapsed with his weight. If it was a basement, there had to be a way out. Dropping into an awkward crawl, his ankle aching in pain, he moved under the collapsed building until he found what he was looking for.

Ahead, he saw crumbling concrete stairs, but they, too, were blocked by debris. The feel of a breeze on his face gave him hope that there was an opening, and he was going to be able to get out. He moved some boards and other wreckage. Then he shone his flashlight into the darkness. It lit an opening a few steps above him. He began to climb, his only thought getting to Livie.

OLIVIA SLOWED AS ahead she saw the gaping black hole of the root cellar. Soon it would be over, she told herself. She rebelled at the thought, even as her mind raced for a way to save herself.

"Cody," she said, turning to look back at him. Out of the corner of her eye, she saw Jaden. He'd come out of a pile of rubble below them on the hillside. Her heart leaped, then fell. He was still too far away to help with a lot of tornado debris between them. She had to stall. Her life depended on it. Jaden was there. He was coming for her. "You don't want to do this."

In answer, he shoved her forward. *Stall*, she told herself. *Do whatever you have to do, but don't let him kill you. Jaden is trying to get to you.* She took a slow, tentative step and then another. Jaden had found her. She didn't know how, but she loved him for it. Ahead, the hole loomed black in the moonlight. A couple more steps and she would be down there in the dark.

"Stop right there," Cody said from behind her. "Drop the bags."

Olivia felt that spark of resistance that ran deep in her. With all her strength, she took another step and heaved both bags toward the open pit of the root cellar.

JADEN HAD LOST crucial time. He had dragged himself out. When he could finally stand, he realized how badly he was hurt. He wasn't sure how far he could walk on his ankle. It wasn't broken; at least, he hoped not. As badly as it hurt to put any weight on it, he ignored the pain and headed up the hillside. To keep from being seen, Jaden had previously been forced to stay on a winding path of tornado wreckage.

Now, though, he had no choice but to leave behind any cover and charge up the hillside as best he could with his ankle wanting to give out. He could see that Cody and Livie were almost to the dark abyss of the root cellar. If Cody saw him, Jaden had no doubt that the man would use Livie as a shield and start firing. All Jaden could hope was that Cody wasn't much of a marksman.

That was when he saw Livie turn and look in his direction. Earlier, he'd thought they'd both seen him. But this time, it was just Livie. There was no doubt that she saw him.

Cody shoved her toward the open pit. Jaden tried to run up the hill, but his ankle turned and he fell, crashing into more debris. He ground his teeth, the pain so intense he thought he would black out. The moment it passed, he was on his feet again.

Up on the hill, he saw Livie throw the large bags she'd been carrying into the old root cellar. There was no doubt that she would be next. Bleeding and limping, his leg apparently hurt worse than he'd thought, he kept moving toward them. He had to get to Livie before it was too late.

"No!" Cody let out a howl of anger and misery as he watched the bags filled with his money fly through the air over the opening—and then plummet. "You stubborn, impossible woman!"

Dropping the two bags he had carried up from the stone well house, he lunged forward to strike her in the back with his fist. His momentum shoved her forward. As his money hit the bottom of the root cellar's dirt floor, Olivia followed them down.

Propelled forward, Cody stumbled behind her, stopping so close to the unstable edge of the chasm that he almost went in after her. He teetered there, his anger feeling as if it were eating him up inside. If he could have gotten his hands on her neck, he would have choked the life out of her. What had ever made him think he could love this woman? Didn't he recall how stubborn she'd been as a kid? As a girlfriend? He'd told himself he liked a strong woman. Ha! he thought now.

For a moment, she didn't move. He stood waiting to see if she took a breath. Time seemed suspended. He breathed heavily, the exertion of his anger making his chest hurt. He really could use a little something to steady himself. Once he got to the pickup, he'd dig into his supply.

Not now, though. He just had to be sure that Olivia

wouldn't be getting out of that hole alive. She still hadn't moved. Maybe she'd hit her head. Maybe she was already dead.

Not that it mattered at this point. If she hadn't tossed his money down there, he had planned to cave in the side of the hole and bury her alive, if that was what it took. Then all he would have had to do was get out of Starling, get on the road, disappear before the law came after him. He'd known it was just a matter of time the moment he'd seen Jaden at Angie's barn. He'd known then that it was time to leave for good.

Earlier, it had seemed so simple. Just tie up some loose ends, starting at the hardware store. He'd made the calls to some of his associates. He couldn't just leave without letting his father know how he felt about him. It had taken four of them and a dolly to remove the old floor safe where his father kept his "retirement" money.

While they were at it, they'd loaded up everything they could haul of any value. If Olivia hadn't shown up when she had, they would have taken even more.

Now he just had to deal with this problem. He stared down at her and his bags of money and swore. "I can see that you're breathing," he said through gritted teeth. "Stand up."

She made no move to do so.

"I need you to stand up. You don't want me to come down there."

She let out a laugh and rolled to her side. "Come on down," she yelled as if she wanted the whole world to hear. She sounded as if the fall had knocked the breath out of her. But when she smiled up at him, he realized that the bags of money had broken her fall.

He cursed. He was pretty sure he could get back out of the old root-cellar hole, even though the rescue crew had broken a lot of the shelving in their attempt to get him out Halloween night. "Trust me, you don't want me to come down there," he said, raising his voice as well. He'd convinced himself that they were alone on the hillside. It didn't matter if she wanted to scream her head off.

"Oh, why not, Cody?" she shouted. "Afraid I might hurt you?"

He kicked dirt down on her, some of it hitting her in the face. That shut her up for the moment. She seemed to have forgotten that he was still in control. She sat up, wiping away the dirt and spitting a couple of times. He'd taught her how to spit like a boy one day in their tree house. She looked up at him again, defiance in her dirty face. "I'm waiting! Jump on down here!"

"Olivia, damn it, I never wanted it to end like this," he said, trying to sound as conciliatory as possible, yet still yelling too. "I would have let you be if you hadn't shown up at the store when you did."

"You mean when you were stealing your father blind?"

He doubled up his fists. "Just throw the bags up to me. I won't kill you. I'll just leave. Maybe you can even figure out a way to climb out. Or someone will find you. I could call anonymously once I'm down the road and tell your deputy where he can find you."

She laughed and shook her head. "Do you really expect me to believe that? What happened to you, Cody? You want everyone to feel sorry for you because you felt your father did you wrong. How about you stop making excuses for the decisions you've made? You broke the law. Now you're going to have to pay for it. Killing me isn't going to help. I don't think you're going to be able to live with the guilt." He gave her a smirk and kicked more dirt into the hole. This time she covered her face.

When she glanced up, he could see her eyes. They seemed

lit by the moonlight. He tried not to shudder at the look in those eyes, let alone her words. "I will come back and haunt you, Cody. I promise you. You'll never find peace for what you're about to do."

He took a step back. "Great speech, Olivia. Unfortunately, you're assuming I have a conscience." His laugh didn't ring true, even for him. "I don't. So come to me in my dreams all you want. You don't scare me." He pulled the gun from his pocket. "But if you don't throw those bags up to me right now," he raged, "I'm going to start shooting you—not kill you, just wound you so you can lie there bleeding to death, and no one will be able to save you."

"You don't think I know I'm dead no matter what? I just hope I don't bleed all over your money, Cody," she shouted as she pulled the closest bag to her chest, her look daring him to pull the trigger.

He took the dare.

Chapter Twenty

The loud argument between the two covered the sound of Jaden's footfalls as he scrambled up the hill as fast as he could, hurling himself forward with all his strength. His body took the stabs of splintered wood, glass shards and torn jagged metal as if no longer able to feel pain. He knew he was doing more damage, had already done damage to himself, but he couldn't let it stop him.

He was almost to Cody when he heard the report. The shot echoed across the hillside into the night. Breathing hard, weapon in his hand, he started to fire but was almost on the man. More than anything, he was afraid Cody would get off another shot at Livie trapped in the hole below him.

Jaden didn't stop. He launched himself. Cody, caught completely off guard, went down hard, Jaden landing on top of him. He started to grab for Cody's gun but realized it was no longer in the man's hand. He took a quick look for it around them. Those few seconds gave Cody a chance to catch his breath. Jaden took an elbow to his head that momentarily dazed him as Cody began to fight back as if his life depended on it.

He put an arm against the man's neck as he struggled to roll Cody to his stomach so he could handcuff him. "Livie!" he cried. "Livie?"

"I'm all right," she called back.

His heart soared at the sound of her voice as Cody kicked wildly, bucking and swinging his arms. A part of him wanted Cody to put up a fight, even relished the idea. But Cody was strong and desperate, and Jaden was becoming more aware of his injuries. It would be a fight to the finish of one of them. Jaden realized he had no choice as Cody fought wildly to throw him off—toward the black hole next to them.

Whatever drug the man was on, it had made him stronger. They were too close to the hole. Jaden tried to roll Cody away from it, fearing they would cave the dirt onto Livie. She was still alive. He hung on to that as he used everything he'd been taught in combat to restrain the man.

But Cody was a dirty fighter. That, added to his strength and desperation and Jaden's body's weakness, had the deputy feeling himself losing the battle.

OLIVIA HAD HEARD the gun drop down into the hole. It was too dark to see exactly where it had landed, but she was sure that was the sound she'd heard. She began to feel around for it, thankful that Cody had only fired a warning shot into the dirt inches from her head earlier. She'd been right about him not wanting to get blood on his money. Or maybe he hadn't wanted to kill her yet because it would mean he'd have to climb into the hole and dig his bags of money out from under her dead body.

She couldn't believe he'd still held out hope that he could talk her into throwing the bags up to him. The drugs he'd been taking must have addled his brain. Moving her hands palm-down across the dirt, she hunted as hurriedly as possible to find the gun. She could hear the struggle up on the ledge. Dirt came falling down, making her all the more frantic to find the gun before the wall of dirt caved in on her.

Her hand touched something cold as steel. She grabbed the gun, just as another chunk of the dirt wall collapsed. She barely had time to throw herself out of the way before it covered one of her legs. She quickly dug herself out, desperate to stop the fight that was about to bury her alive.

Gun tucked into her waistband, she hurried and grabbed the heavy bags of money, piling them on top of the dirt that had caved into the pit. Then she began to climb quickly upward, afraid the moving earth would cave in. She saw at once that she wouldn't be able to get out without help. But she could get high enough.

In the faint moonlight, she could see that Jaden had Cody down and was reaching for his handcuffs. Cody grabbed a handful of dirt and threw it into Jaden's eyes, then pushed him off and was going for Jaden's gun.

She could see that Jaden was hurt, his clothing torn and bloodstained. That sound she'd heard that had made her think someone had fallen through boards, she knew now it had to have been Jaden.

Olivia aimed the gun at Cody, trying not to see the boy she'd grown up with, her best friend, her high school sweetheart. He had wrenched the deputy's weapon, had it in his hand, started to point it at Jaden's head.

She pulled the trigger.

JADEN COULDN'T SEE, his eyes full of dirt. He'd been fighting Cody blindly when he'd felt his weapon being pulled from his holster. He lunged at where he thought the man was, heard the gunshot, felt the splatter of blood hit his face and thought he'd been hit. He wiped frantically at his eyes, expecting another shot and then another. All he could think about was Livie.

If he died here, she would too.

He heard her calling his name as his vision finally cleared enough to find Cody lying next to him. For a moment, he thought the man had taken his weapon to shoot himself. Then he looked up and saw Livie. She still held Cody's gun in her hand, resting it on the edge of the hole. She was crying as he crawled forward, stopping short of the edge to take the gun and hold her hand.

"Cody?" she whispered.

He shook his head as a wail of sirens filled the air. "Let's get you out of there."

Chapter Twenty-One

The rest of the night was a blur of sirens and lights. Jaden had managed to get Livie out of the root cellar by using all four of the canvas bags of money. She had climbed out into his arms as more of the unstable earth tumbled down into the hole.

With the arrival of help, EMTs saw to both his and Livie's injuries. He vaguely remembered them encouraging him to go to the hospital, but he was more worried about Livie and what she'd been through. Nor had he wanted to let her get out of his sight. The whole ordeal had left him afraid that he still might lose her.

There was so much he wanted to say to her. He worried that after everything she'd been through, the last place she'd want to be was in Montana—with him.

A state trooper arrived and took photographs and statements from them. When the coroner showed up to transport Cody's body to the morgue, he saw Jaden's injuries bandaged up temporarily by the EMTs and said, "Someone get this man to the hospital right now."

That was the last he remembered until he woke up in the hospital to find a doctor standing over him. "How are you feeling?"

He hurt all over, but he was alive. "Livie?" The doctor frowned. "Olivia Brooks?"

"Patched up and released."

"I have to see her," Jaden said and tried to sit up.

The doctor put a hand to his shoulder. "She's just fine. You, on the other hand, aren't going anywhere. You lost a lot of blood. We had to operate on your leg. Those were some nasty wounds. You're also not going anywhere on that other leg of yours."

He looked down to see a cast on his ankle. "Broken?"

The doctor shook his head. "Badly sprained. It's going to take some time for those tendons to heal. So just relax if you want to be able to walk again. You're going to be here for a while so we can make sure there isn't any infection."

He glanced around. No landline. "Can I at least get a phone to make a call?"

There was a twinkle in the doctor's eye. "To call Livie? Not necessary. She's right outside and very anxious to see you."

Jaden let out the breath he'd been holding and relaxed back on the bed.

"I'll tell her you're awake after your surgery. Remember what I said about taking it easy, Deputy." He smiled and left.

A moment later, Livie came in. She moved quickly to his bed and took his free hand. He hadn't even noticed how hooked up he was to machines. Had he looked, he could have seen his heart rate take off at the sight of her.

"I was so scared when I learned how injured you were." Tears filled her eyes. "All the time you were busy saving me… You had to be in so much pain."

He smiled. "I don't remember. All I could think about was getting to you and making sure you were safe."

She squeezed his hand. "Thanks to you, I am."

"Livie." His voice filled with emotion. "I was so afraid that I'd lost you. I've been such a fool—"

She touched her finger to his lips and shook her head. "You were right. I didn't know what I wanted. For years, I had this plan. Then you came along, and I didn't see how I could have both. I felt I had to stick to my plan."

He kissed her finger and took her hand. "I never wanted to keep you from it."

"I know. I thought a clean break was the best thing so neither of us got derailed on our plans."

He chuckled at that. "I was already derailed. I realized I didn't want to continue on to law school. When I got the opportunity to go to the academy, I took it. After we broke up and you left, I was lost without you. But becoming a deputy…" He grinned. "I think I found my calling."

She laughed. "I'd say so." She leaned down to give him a kiss.

He swallowed, his throat having gone dry. "What are your plans now?"

"If you're asking if I'm taking off again…" She shook her head. "I'm staying. You're going to need someone to look after you when you get out of here. That's if you—"

"Only if you'll marry me. You do have some idea of what it might be like being the wife of a deputy sheriff. Do you still want to?"

Livie nodded, her eyes filling with tears. She reached into her pocket and pulled out the engagement ring he'd given her not all that long ago.

He took it from her and met her gaze. "Remember the last time I asked you to marry me?"

"It was beautiful, but that was then. This is now. After everything we've been through, nothing can be more special than this moment."

He shook his head. "You're amazing. I want to spend the rest of my life with you, Olivia Brooks. Will you be my wife, my partner, my lover, my best friend?"

"I will," she said, her voice breaking as he slipped the ring onto her finger. Laughing and crying, she bent to kiss him.

He laughed but quickly grew serious again. "You *are* amazing. I mean that. You saved my life."

"And you saved mine. We make a pretty good team, don't you think?"

"I do, but let's not do anything like this again, okay?" he said as he drew her closer. "I promise that living in Fortune Creek, things will be much quieter and a whole lot less dangerous."

She laughed. "I guess we'll see about that."

Chapter Twenty-Two

For weeks, Olivia had stayed close to the rehab center after Jaden had been released from the hospital. They'd spent hours getting to know each other again—and silently coming to terms with what had happened that last night in Starling.

It was something they didn't talk about, but she suspected he was as haunted by it as she was. She'd killed Cody, her once neighbor, friend and high school sweetheart. He'd turned into a man she hadn't recognized. A killer. A drug dealer. A drug user. A man who was willing to kill again to save himself from capture.

When she'd told her mother about that night, Sharon Brooks had been shocked. "Do you realize what would have happened if not for your quick thinking?" she demanded. Tears had filled her eyes an instant before she'd grabbed her daughter and tugged her into a hug. "I've always thought I wasn't much of a mother to you. Better than my own, but that's not saying much." She'd pulled back to look at Olivia as if seeing her for the first time. "I must have done something right to have such an amazing daughter."

Now, as Olivia finished packing, she was glad she hadn't kept anything from her apartment. When she'd quit her job and moved out of her furnished apartment, she'd realized that she hadn't collected anything. Not even memories she'd wanted to pack.

"Is that it?" her mother asked, glancing around her daughter's old bedroom. It looked exactly like it had when Olivia had gone away to college all those year ago.

"You'll come up a few days before the wedding, right?" Her mother nodded. "Jaden has you a room at the hotel there."

"Where the wedding's going to be."

"Yes." She felt like she should say more. "Thank you for everything."

"I didn't do anything," her mother said with a shrug.

"You did." She stepped to her and hugged her, realizing how thin her mother seemed. "You'll come for dinner so I can fatten you up." Sharon huffed but Olivia could tell she liked the idea. "I'll come down to visit when I can, but you'll always be welcome. Did I tell you that Jaden and I are planning to start a family right away?" She saw her mother's eyes light up. "Well, I'd better get going."

Picking up her suitcase, she headed for the door.

"I've got something cooking on the stove, so I won't see you out."

Her mother had never liked goodbyes. "Then I'll see you before the wedding." She opened the door, glanced over her shoulder to see her mother in the kitchen, wiping her eyes. "Don't forget to bring some of your crab apple jelly," she called back and left.

Olivia felt teary-eyed herself as she walked away from the home where she'd been raised. But it wasn't goodbye. It was a new beginning. She would bring her children here. Her mother would teach them to cook and fuss over them.

She put her suitcase in the back of the car and climbed in behind the wheel. But she hadn't gotten very far down the road when she saw a rig coming toward her that she recognized. The vehicle slowed, an arm coming out the window to flag her over.

Slowing, she put down her window and pulled alongside in the middle of the road. This was rural Montana; there was no traffic. "Hi, Dean." She'd wondered how he was doing after all of this. He'd lost his wife, still hadn't completely recovered from the injuries he'd sustained during the tornado and seemed a sad figure with so many of his friends gone. "You all right?" she asked when he said nothing.

"I heard you were leaving for Fortune Creek. The deputy already up there?"

She nodded. "I'm on my way now. Something wrong?"

"I just wanted to offer best wishes on your engagement."

"Thank you, but won't I see you at the wedding?" she asked.

"I'll have to get back to you on that." He looked down the highway. Still no traffic. "Well, I should get going. You take care of yourself."

"You too." He drove off. She watched him go in her side mirror for a moment before putting up her window and continuing along the road toward the turnoff to Fortune Creek.

It wasn't until she'd made the turn and was headed north on the way to her new home, her new life and her soon-to-be husband that a thought nudged her.

Where had Dean been heading before he'd seen her? This road didn't really go anywhere except the mountains. Unless he'd been using it as a shortcut to his wife's barn. Wasn't that property off-limits until after the trial?

Chapter Twenty-Three

Olivia had never been to Fortune Creek. Jaden had told her it was small, but *tiny* might have been closer to the truth. The town was in the northwest corner of the state, a rock's throw from the Canadian border. That whole part of the state was lawless except for the small sheriff's office where her husband-to-be worked.

She saw at once that the town was wild country, set in the mountains surrounded by pines, lots of pines, and rocky cliffs. The closest place of any size was Eureka, miles away, across the narrow Lake Koocanusa that crossed the border into Canada. It made the small Montana town she'd grown up in seem metropolitan.

Jaden, once healed enough to return home, had gone on ahead. She'd taken a few days to pack and spend time with her mother before hitting the road. The first thing she saw when she drove into town was the historic Fortune Creek Hotel with its wide porch across the front.

She'd done a little research on the place she would soon be living in. The all-wood structure had been built in the 1930s by a wealthy Easterner who'd wanted a hunting lodge for his many friends. Since then, it had changed little structurally. A tall, rather skinny building, it rose to four floors with only four large rooms per floor.

The rest of the town was a series of small, narrow buildings. There was a convenience store/gas station, a café and a few empty buildings. But what caught her eye was a boutique with a bright display in the front window. Jaden had told her that the sheriff's wife, Molly, had opened it. She collected unique things from all over the world to sell there.

It was definitely somewhere Olivia planned to explore, but first she wanted to see her fiancé. She drove only a little farther to find the town ended at a stream. Turning around, she drove back to the sheriff's office.

Like the rest of the town, it also was small and narrow, with an apartment upstairs where she and Jaden would be living until the wedding. Getting out, she breathed in the mountain air ripe with pine scent. Jaden had already warned her about Helen Graves, the sixtysomething dispatcher.

As she pushed open the door, she spotted the gray-haired Helen behind a desk, knitting something large with variegated yarn. "Hello," she said as she let the door close behind her.

The woman looked up, eyes squinting. "So, you're the fiancée, huh?"

"That would be me," she said with a nod.

Helen looked her up and down for a moment before she smiled. "You'll do. He's in the office with the sheriff. You can go in." With that, she went back to her knitting.

Jaden was sitting in the small sheriff's office. He rose when he saw her and introduced her to his boss, Sheriff Brandt Parker. They exchanged a few niceties. Then Jaden suggested he help her unload her car and see the apartment upstairs.

"So, what do you think?" he asked, looking anxious as he waved an arm toward Fortune Creek.

"I think it's charming."

He grinned and pulled her to him for a kiss right there on the town's main street. Then he led her upstairs to the apartment. He still had a limp from his injuries at Starling, but the doctor had said he was healing nicely.

Later, Olivia wouldn't remember much about the small apartment over the sheriff's office. The moment the door had closed, she was in his arms and he was kissing her, and she'd felt as if she'd finally found her way home.

They hadn't been together like this since they'd broken off their engagement a year ago. Desire spiked through her, a wildfire of emotions. Her body tingled with expectation as he began to slowly unbutton her blouse, his gaze locked with hers. Her blouse dropped to the floor. He gave her an appreciative look as he took in her black lace bra, passion burning in his eyes.

She could feel her hard nipples straining against the lace as he dipped his head to take one aching tip in his mouth and then the other. Her bra dropped to the floor as she opened his shirt, pressing her palms against his muscled chest and then her breasts to the warmth and strength of him.

Jaden let out a groan of pleasure and the next moment they were tearing off the rest of their clothing. Laughing, they stumbled back to fall on the bed. Naked bodies melting together, they made love without restraint—at least, the first time.

It was late by the time they got around to unloading her car and walked down to the café for dinner. Jaden introduced her to everyone they came across. She felt her face flush with appreciation as the town seemed to welcome her with open arms.

Everyone wanted to know about the upcoming wedding and seemed delighted to hear it would be in Fortune Creek at the hotel—and they were all invited.

Olivia felt a glow of warmth like none she'd ever known. She was excited and full of joy, so much so that she completely forgot about mentioning to Jaden that she'd seen Dean.

JADEN FELT AS if he were dreaming as he and Olivia walked back to the apartment after dinner. He hadn't let himself believe this was possible in the time the two of them were apart. But now here they were, together, engaged and planning their life in Fortune Creek.

He stopped to point out the full moon lolling over the top of the pines and pulled Livie close. "Do you think you could be happy here?"

She nodded and smiled up at him. "I'd be happy anywhere with you, but I'm already falling in love with this town. The people are so friendly. Even Helen, kind of."

He laughed at that as they continued down the street. It wasn't until later that night, the two of them lying in bed together, that they talked about Starling and the case. He was still working to tie up the loose ends, but basically, it was over.

Angie had been picked up in Washington and was being brought back to stand trial. Rob and Cody were dead. The town was still grieving. Emery had closed up his shop, getting on one of his motorcycles, Krystal on the back, and taking a trip down to California. Both were required to come back for the trial.

During the weeks Jaden and Livie had been healing from the ordeal they'd barely lived through, they hadn't talked about it. Instead, they had talked about the future. There was the upcoming wedding, the move to Fortune Creek and where they would live.

Olivia said she was looking forward to being a wife.

They'd both agreed that they wanted to start a family, buy a house and put down roots.

Now, though, in the darkness of their small apartment over the sheriff's office, they talked about the case and their near-death experiences.

"It's a miracle I lived through the tornado," Livie said.

"Cody saved your life that night."

She nodded. "Only because he needed an alibi."

"I think there was more to it than that. He loved you. How could he not?"

"We both loved each other growing up, but that boy I knew was gone. Some of it was the drugs, but a lot of it was his bitterness. He'd never really been trapped at the hardware store. He'd used that as an excuse. Such a waste."

Jaden agreed. "He was looking for an easy way out, though I don't think he would have ever left town if he hadn't been forced to run. For a lot of people, leaving the safety and security of what you know is just too hard." He looked over at Livie. "But not for you. That's another reason Cody resented you. You were a lot braver than him, and he knew it."

"I'm not sure how brave I was. But I was determined—to a fault."

"Well, now you have your business degree."

"Molly was impressed," she said with a laugh. "She seems excited for me to be working with her since she spends so much time on the road looking for more product for the store. I like her."

"I thought you would." He pulled her close. "We're going to be okay here, aren't we?"

She nodded. "About that night when you found me in Starling. I can't believe as injured as you were…" Her voice broke.

"At one point I thought I was going to have to crawl up

that hill," he said. "But nothing could keep me from getting to you." He kissed her. "I love you, Livie. Always have. Is your mother going to be all right with you marrying me?"

She laughed, brushing at tears. "She's excited that I'm closer to home. And, of course, she's excited about the wedding. She never had one of her own. She can be…prickly, but she'll grow on you, I promise." He chuckled. "She really is excited about us giving her grandbabies."

"Me, too," he whispered. "Maybe we should work on that right now? What do you think?" She answered with a kiss.

It amazed Olivia what a small town the whole state of Montana felt like. She and Jaden had posted their wedding announcement in the local shopper. It was what was done in small-town Montana since everyone in the community was invited.

On Thanksgiving, her mother had come up for the local feast down at the café. Alice, the café owner, put it on every year. Olivia couldn't believe how warm and welcoming everyone was. It was clear that they all loved Jaden and were happy for the two of them.

Ash Hamilton, over at the hotel, had told them not to worry. He had plenty of room. Local café owner Alice Weatherbee was to cater the affair and promised there would be plenty of food. The local bar would be furnishing the booze.

"Are you sure about an open bar?" Olivia had asked.

"Don't worry. Anyone who drinks too much will be put up at the hotel," Jaden had assured her.

Sharon Brooks had arrived two days early for the wedding to help. "This place is really nice," her mother had said of the hotel room Jaden had gotten for her. She'd sounded surprised. "The town, though, seems a little…small."

Olivia had laughed, surprised she wasn't more nervous as the wedding loomed. She couldn't wait to become Mrs. Olivia Montgomery. She and Jaden had waited until they were both settled in to have the wedding. During those weeks, when he wasn't working, they'd spent their days looking for a house in the area and making love.

With the wedding only days away, she wanted to pinch herself. She and Jaden had found a cute house that overlooked the stream on the edge of town. It had plenty of room inside and out for the family they were planning. Olivia had spent hours painting and decorating their new home. They'd stayed in the apartment over the sheriff's department, planning to spend their first night as husband and wife in their new house.

Olivia couldn't wait to start her future with Jaden—and put the past behind her. Especially Starling. Unfortunately, that part wasn't that easy. She found herself thinking about all of it.

Jaden had filled in some of the blanks. She now knew why she'd thought she'd seen Elden Rusk the night of the tornado. Emery had put Krystal up to it to scare Rob. Apparently, he owed everyone in town. That he was running away with Angie had come as a surprise.

"He'd been busy keeping his affair with Jenny Lee from her," Jaden had said. "But I wouldn't be surprised if he'd suspected more was going on out at the barn than she'd told him."

Had Dean really not known what his wife was up to? "That reminds me," she said. "It completely slipped my mind until just now. I saw Dean as I was leaving home. He flagged me down on the road. He said he just wanted to give his best wishes to my engagement to you, but after he drove away,

I thought it was strange since he hadn't seemed that glad to see me."

"But he flagged you down."

"Maybe only because it was just the two of us on the road," she said. "It would have looked strange if he'd just driven by." Jaden didn't look convinced. "At first, I thought he was on his way to my house, but wouldn't he have turned around and gone back to town?"

"Where did he go?"

"On down the road. It seemed odd until I remembered there was a shortcut back to town."

"Shortcut?"

"It connects to the road to the south." She saw his expression change.

"The road out to Angie's barn," he said.

"Is there any reason he'd want to go out there?" she asked and saw him frown.

She shouldn't have been surprised the next morning when he announced he was going back down south on deputy business. It was a miserable late-November day, the mountains socked in, a mist of rain and snow peppering the windows.

"This is about Dean, isn't it?" Livie said. "I thought the case was over?" He didn't have to answer; she saw the answer on his face. "Jaden, we're getting married tomorrow," she cried. "The rehearsal dinner is tonight!"

Chapter Twenty-Four

Jaden stepped to her, taking her in his arms. "This is what it is going to be like married to a deputy. You can still get out of it."

She sighed and shook her head. "Not this time. I'm in it for the long haul. But please don't make me have to rehearse my wedding alone."

He kissed her. "I'll be back in plenty of time. But it might help if you had the dinner first, then the rehearsal," he said sheepishly. "This is probably just a wild-goose chase, but I've got to check it out."

She gave him the side-eye. "Just be careful."

"I always am."

ALL THE WAY on the drive, he kept trying to put the pieces together. He hadn't told Livie, but the investigation had felt unfinished, as if he'd missed something important.

When she'd told him about Dean, he'd known at least why he'd been feeling that way. Everything about Dean Marsh's story had felt off. But then, the entire Halloween night and the days after the tornado had made it hard to pin it down. So many relationships, so many lies.

He kept thinking about the one question that had bothered him. What if they were all lying?

It had begun to snow by the time Jaden reached the barn property. There was no sign of anyone around. The crime scene tape had been removed, except for a small piece that flapped in the wind by the front door.

He reminded himself that this could end up being all for naught. Yet his instincts told him there was something here to find. He parked and pulled on his coat, drawing up the hood and reaching for his bolt cutters as he stepped out into the weather. These kinds of days were the worst. Wet snow hit his jacket and ran in rivulets.

As he walked toward the barn, he felt the hair rise on his neck. Dean wasn't there, but he'd been here. Not that he'd left tracks in the freezing earth. A new padlock had been placed on the door. It took a little longer to snap this one since it was thicker than the last. It finally gave with a loud snap.

Putting down the bolt cutters, he opened the door. No alarm went off. The crime team had disconnected it so it no longer alerted Cody Ryan of a break-in.

The electricity had been cut off, the barn abandoned, until Angie Marsh could be found and arrested.

He pulled out his flashlight and shone it around the room. He wasn't sure what he expected to find. The interior looked as it had the last time he'd seen it before the crime team had closed up the place. Dean hadn't been in here, he realized. He wouldn't have been able to get past the large padlock on the door.

Still, he'd had to look. Dean could have forced a window. But why would he? He had to have known that the investigators would have found anything of interest to the drug operation. What would Dean have been looking for? The DCI would have taken any drugs, any money, so what else was there? Maybe he'd just wanted to look around, though that seemed unlikely.

Stepping back out into the storm, Jaden closed the door. He still couldn't shake off the eerie feeling Marsh had been out here. Something was wrong. Livie had seen Dean headed this way with a shovel in the back of his pickup.

The wind whirled the snow around him, giving him glimpses of the mountains. It felt too quiet, but then, snow did that. At the sound of flapping of wings, he looked up to see a bald eagle fly past. He followed its flight path with his eyes as it disappeared behind the barn.

He felt an icy chill rush up his spine as another eagle flew by, headed in the same direction. Moving toward the back of the barn, he told himself whatever the birds were feeding on could be the carcass of an animal that had died back there.

But he knew better. His stomach lurched at the scent of rotting flesh as he came around the corner. One of the eagles took flight. The other kept picking at the flesh of the body now only partially buried.

He shooed away the eagle and stepped closer to the body. It appeared a burrowing animal had dug up what had been buried in the shallow grave before the ground had frozen solid. He could see where someone had tried in vain to dig up the body with a shovel with no success.

It would have been impossible to identify the woman's body as Angie Marsh's except for her dark hair. She'd had it pulled up in a ponytail the day she'd been frantically packing to leave her husband. Jaden recognized what was left of the T-shirt she'd been wearing that day. Turning away, he fought the nausea that rose in his throat. Nothing about this case had been easy. He had wanted to believe it was over, everything explained, all the loose ends tied up. But that nagging feeling that he'd missed something had continued to haunt him.

Pulling out his phone, he made the call. He would have

loved to have arrested Dean himself, but there was somewhere he had to be.

"Going to also need Dean Marsh picked up for questioning in the murder of his wife."

"Aren't you getting married soon?" the officer asked after Jaden told him what he'd found.

"I sure hope so." He thought of Livie waiting for him back in Fortune Creek. No way was he standing her up. "Send a state trooper as quickly as possible to secure the scene. I have a rehearsal dinner to get to."

Jaden remembered the surveillance camera that had picked up a woman abandoning Angie Marsh's vehicle in Spokane. Dark hair, pulled back in a ponytail, sweatshirt, dark glasses, same build as Angie Marsh.

Then he thought about the rotting corpse. Angie Marsh had never left the valley. Dean had made sure of that.

"Also, you need to pick up Jenny Lee for aiding and abetting a criminal," he said. "She's possibly an accomplice in Angie Marsh's murder. I'll write up my report after I get married."

If he got married, he thought, looking at the time. He was calling it close.

Chapter Twenty-Five

Olivia refused to look out the window one more time. Jaden was right. This was what she had to look forward to being married to a deputy. Wondering if he was all right or if he was dead, killed by one of the bad guys he was so determined to capture. Was she sure she could do this?

"What do you want to do?" her mother whispered. They were seated at the large table in the café. "Alice is ready to serve the meal. Should we wait?"

Shaking her head, Olivia said, "No, we'll go ahead and eat. He'll be here soon."

The sheriff's wife, Molly, reached over and squeezed her hand. "He'll be here. I'm sure he's fine. I've been here before," she said, glancing at her husband. "You just have to think positive."

Olivia nodded. Unfortunately, she couldn't right now. It wasn't even about the wedding. She wanted to see Jaden come through that door. She couldn't bear the thought that she might not see him alive again. Her hand went to her stomach as she thought of the news she hadn't yet told him. She'd been saving it for their wedding night. She was pregnant. They had started their family.

Her eyes burned with tears. She fought them back, lifting her chin. "Yes, let's eat," she said to the small gathering. "Jaden is out saving the world, but we don't have to starve while he does it." Her voice sounded much stronger than she felt.

JADEN SLIPPED IN the back of the café just as Alice started to serve the rehearsal-dinner meal. He'd cut it close, all the way thinking of his beautiful bride-to-be. He hated to let her down tonight. Not that he didn't know there would be other nights. He was an officer of the law. It wasn't a nine-to-five job, especially in Fortune Creek with so much area of the state to cover.

If she didn't realize that, he feared she had tonight as he slipped into the seat next to her. A round of applause went up. He saw the relief on Livie's face and knew he would see that a million times in the years ahead. His job was dangerous and unpredictable and often ran overtime. He'd found his calling after he'd lost her the first time. He hoped the job wouldn't cost him her now.

Her eyes filled with tears as he met her gaze. She smiled, her relief palpable. He smiled back. The group at the table began to clink a utensil against their glasses.

"Kiss! Kiss!" they chanted.

They didn't have to tell him twice. He leaned in and kissed the woman he loved. She put her arm around his neck, drawing him closer. They lost themselves in the kiss for a moment, pulling back when the crowd at the table got rowdy and Alice announced, "Let's eat. We have a rehearsal to get to!"

OLIVIA SPENT THE night in her mother's large two-bed hotel room across the street from the sheriff's office and the apartment over it. It had been their plan to spend the night before their wedding apart, but after her fears yesterday, she wished she was curled up in his arms.

Her mother had already fallen asleep and Olivia found herself at loose ends. After the dinner and the rehearsal, Jaden had told her what he'd discovered.

"You think Dean killed her?"

He'd nodded. "I don't think she ever left for Spokane."

"But I thought you said she was caught on a surveillance camera?"

"I now believe it was Jenny Lee, pretending to be her. It made no sense that she would leave her car to be vandalized, her belongings stolen," he said. "I think he either found her out at the barn or managed to get her out there."

"And killed her." Olivia had frowned. "You're saying this happened when he was allegedly missing after the tornado."

"Angie said he would turn up, and he did. But he must have come back sooner than when he was found walking down the road saying he didn't remember anything."

"Like Cody," she'd said.

Now, as she looked out the hotel room window, she could see the light on in the sheriff's office. Her husband-to-be was busy the night before his wedding writing up his report. Olivia sighed and told herself that Jaden had said there were hardly ever tornadoes, let alone murders, around Fortune Creek.

She could only hope, she thought as she crawled into bed. She was getting married tomorrow. Unless there was another murder.

JADEN HADN'T REALIZED how long he'd been waiting for this moment as he stood at the altar in the church, his best man the sheriff beside him.

"Nervous?" Brandt asked. Jaden shook his head. "Liar."

The music began. He stared down the aisle, waiting for that moment when he would see his bride. Molly Parker came in first, and moments later, there Livie was. He tried to swallow the lump in his throat at the sight of her. She'd always been beautiful, but today she took his breath away as she walked toward him.

He tried to breathe, his heart racing. This was the moment. He looked into her eyes as she joined him. He thought he might see doubts or at least nervousness, but he saw none of it. This woman was going to marry him.

The weight of that didn't help his breathing. Somehow, he got through the ceremony. They'd agreed to keep it short and sweet, and it was.

The next thing he knew, the pastor told him he could kiss his wife. He pulled her to him, their gazes locked, and he knew in his heart that this was the real thing. The kiss drew applause. People in this small town would applaud anything, he told himself as he stepped back, smiling.

Livie was smiling, too, her face aglow. He reached for her hand as the pastor announced them as husband and wife.

For Olivia, the wedding was a blur of people Jaden had often talked about from his hometown. All of Fortune Creek had turned out for the wedding. The sheriff's department's elderly dispatcher/receptionist, Helen Graves, had brought her knitting bag, working on a project as she waited in the pew. There was Jaden's good friend Ash Holland, from the hotel, and Cora Green, who owned the convenience mart and gas station, and, of course, Alice Weatherbee, who was catering the reception in the hotel lobby. Even the local coroner, J. D. Brown, attended.

There was a huge wedding cake as well as Alice's signature dessert, her famous huckleberry pie. Olivia couldn't believe what a warm welcome everyone gave her. After the stories Jaden had told her, she'd felt as if she already knew them all. But over the weeks preceding the wedding, they'd become like family.

Her mother had cried during the ceremony and again at the reception. "I'm so happy for you," she'd said, hugging her. "Did you know Ash said there is a hotel room open for me, no charge, anytime I come up to visit?"

"You can also stay with us," Olivia told her. "We have an extra room with your name on it."

"That's nice, but the two of you will be honeymooning for the first year," Sharon Brooks said.

"Maybe for quite a few months," she agreed. "After that, the baby might make it harder."

"Baby?" Her mother's face lit up. "Does Jaden know?"

"I'm telling him later tonight," Olivia said and pretended to lock her lips and then her mother's, since she looked as if she might burst with the news.

"I'm so happy for you," her mother said, her voice breaking with emotion. "All I've ever wanted was for you to be happy."

"I am happy," she told her as Jaden approached and a familiar song began to play.

She'd planned to wait until they were alone to tell him about the baby, but the moment she looked at him, heard their song begin and stepped into his arms, she knew she couldn't keep it to herself any longer.

"Having fun?" he asked, pulling her closer.

"It's incredible, isn't it?" she said of the love she felt in the room, saw in his eyes.

His gaze held hers. "Mrs. Montgomery, you're glowing. I've never seen you look more beautiful."

She smiled up at him, then moved closer to whisper, "We're pregnant." She hadn't meant to just blurt it out, but she couldn't stand it any longer.

Jaden jerked back, surprise and delight in his expression. "You're sure?"

"It's early, but yes. We're going to be a family."

"Oh, Livie," he said, tugging her close. "We're going to be a family."

She shook her head and looked around the room at everyone who'd helped make this day so special before settling her gaze on his again. "We already are a family."

* * * * *

HER BABY, HER BADGE

DELORES FOSSEN

Chapter One

The rain was washing away the blood.

That was Sheriff Grace Granger's second thought as she panned her flashlight over the scene. Her first thought had put ice in every vein in her body—the woman was dead.

Correction: the *cop* was dead.

The female officer was wearing a khaki-colored uniform, which meant she worked for the county sheriff and wasn't one of Grace's deputies in the Renegade Canyon Police Department. Still, that didn't lessen the overwhelming grief and the sickening feeling of dread that Grace felt.

"Get the tower lights set up here," Grace told her team of deputies, who'd responded to the 911 call with her. She pointed to two spots that were to the sides of the victim and far enough away from her that they wouldn't destroy any potential evidence.

The generator-powered lights were necessary to illuminate the scene so it could be examined. However, Grace needed no such illumination to see the dead woman. Her flashlight and the headlights of the responding vehicles were doing an effective job of that.

"Another one," Deputy Livvy Walsh muttered as she stepped shoulder-to-shoulder with Grace. She had no trouble hearing the slight tremble in her deputy's voice.

"Yes," Grace agreed. Her voice wasn't especially steady, either. Hard to be steady when taking in the scene in front of them.

The dead cop had been tied to a fence post in such a way that her head stayed upright, thanks to the thick rope around her neck. The killer had left her in her uniform, but he or she had shredded it so that parts of the fabric flapped in the stormy wind.

Although Grace didn't have any proof yet, the woman likely hadn't died on the post. Not if her manner of death was the same MO the killer had employed on another officer who'd been murdered a month earlier.

In that murder, San Antonio Detective Andrea Selby had been stabbed repeatedly, and then her killer had tied her to another fence post that was about a quarter of a mile from this particular one. And even though there was no evidence to link Detective Selby to Renegade Canyon, her body had been left just outside the grounds of the McClennan family's Towering Oaks Ranch. Which was in Grace's jurisdiction.

And she had personal ties to the ranch.

Very personal ties these days, she reminded herself as she thought of the baby bump that her high-visibility raincoat was concealing. Yes, her unborn child was about as personal as it got.

Unfortunately, every personal tie she had was also mixed with some bad blood that extended back to three generations of the McClennans and her own family. If there'd been only one murder, Grace might have been able to consider the location of the body a coincidence. But with two, this was a message. Exactly what message, Grace didn't know, but she needed to find out before another officer died.

"You okay?" Livvy asked her.

"No," Grace admitted. She blinked away the rain that was

slapping at her. "And I figure you aren't, either." It was impossible to look at the cop's dead face and not see their own. Or future victims. "But we'll do our jobs."

Livvy made a sound of agreement that Grace knew wasn't merely lip service. They would indeed do their jobs and hopefully stop this killer from claiming anyone else.

"Any idea who she is?" Grace asked, tipping her head to the dead woman.

"No. She doesn't look familiar."

Grace was about to agree, but the slash of more headlights and the sounds of engines behind her had Grace looking over her shoulder. When she saw who'd arrived, she silently muttered a thanks.

And then a groan.

The thanks was for the CSI team who had just arrived, and they began to scramble from their van. Grace had contacted them immediately after she'd gotten the 911 call that there was a dead body, because she'd known this would be a race against the elements to preserve the scene. The spring storm was hitting hard and fast, and what the wind didn't destroy, the rain probably would.

Grace's groan was for the two men who exited a shiny silver truck with the Towering Oaks Ranch logo on the door. The family patriarch and all-around thorn in her side, Ike McClennan. And Dutton, his son. Except Dutton was more than just that. He was the reason for those "very personal ties" to his family ranch.

Since she didn't want any civilians trampling on the crime scene, Grace began to make her way to Ike and Dutton. With the glare of the headlights, it was hard for her to see Dutton's expression, but she figured he'd be concerned. One of his ranch hands had no doubt alerted him to the cop activity outside the fence, and not only would he want to know what was going on, but he would also want to make sure she was alright.

"What the hell happened?" Ike snarled. His rough voice thundered through the night.

He charged toward Grace, his gestures and sounds reminding her of a snorting bull. Ike might be approaching the seventy-year mark, but he still looked plenty strong and formidable with his six-foot, three-inch height and beefy build.

While Ike continued to move toward her, Grace stared him down. Or rather glared him down. She'd had plenty of practice doing it, and though this situation shouldn't be a confrontation, Ike usually managed to turn it into one any time she was involved.

"Well? What the hell is going on?" Ike persisted.

Dutton didn't move in front of his father and didn't do anything obvious to try to rein in the man. Grace hoped it stayed that way. Dutton, she knew, had a protective streak inside him. For their unborn baby. For Grace, too. But Grace didn't want him acting on that. Tonight, she was the badge, and not his ex-lover and the mother of his child.

"You can't be here," Grace told Ike. "This is a crime scene."

Of course, that didn't set well with Ike, who looked ready to implode, so Grace just hiked her thumb in the direction of the fence post. And the body.

That stopped Ike in his tracks, and when his attention landed on the dead woman, he cursed. "Another one," he said on a groan.

Dutton cursed, too, but his profanity stayed under his breath. He looked at her, combing his intense brown eyes over her face, no doubt checking for any signs of injury. Or stress. The stress would be there. Nothing she could do about that. But there wasn't a mark on her.

"I didn't find the body," she told him. "An anonymous call came in through Dispatch. The caller said we'd find the body tied to a fence post outside the west side of the ranch."

And since a nearly identical call had come in with the first murder a month earlier, that's how Grace had known it was almost certainly the real deal. Still, she had hoped for the best. Obviously, though, the best hadn't happened.

"You haven't done a good job of stopping this, have you?" Ike muttered, shaking his head in disgust.

"No, I haven't," Grace admitted, and that sickened her.

It didn't matter that the killer hadn't left any traceable forensic evidence and there'd been no witnesses to either the murder or the body dump. It was her job to keep the community safe, and she was failing at that, big-time.

She shoved aside the pity party that threatened, but this felt like a serious jab at her professionalism, while her private life had had its own jabs. Including the "jab" standing in front of her.

Dutton.

He was still staring at her with those intense eyes. Ironic, since the rest of Dutton was the opposite of intense. Everything else about him was normally laid-back. The easy stride of his lanky body. That quick smile that only made his face even hotter than usual. The smooth drawl that she was certain had worked in his favor too many times to count.

"No wonder you can't solve this," Ike went on. "You need better hired help."

The venom in his voice went up a notch, and Grace didn't have to guess why. She followed his narrowed gaze to his other son, Deputy Rory McClennan, who had just finished setting up one of the lights. Grace wasn't the only one who had to deal with bad blood with Ike. Rory did as well, by basically turning his back on his dad and becoming a cop.

"Mr. McClennan," Grace said, "as I've already informed you, this is a crime scene, and you should just go home."

Of course, that earned her a huff from the man, but he finally moved away from her and back toward the truck. What he didn't do was get in. Despite the storm taking swipes at him, he leaned against the hood and stared out at the responders and cops.

Dutton didn't leave, either. Nor did he go to the truck, as his father had done. He stayed right by Grace's side, and Livvy must've decided to give them a moment, because she stepped away.

"This is the same as the other one," Dutton said. Not a question, and he could certainly see the similarities for himself. "What kind of precautions are you going to take?" he asked. "And I know I'm making you plenty mad just by asking that, but I'd like to know."

She sighed. "I'll be as careful as I can be. But I'll also do my job," she said, certain that he'd known that was how she would respond.

Dutton didn't say anything about that not being enough. And that had to be hard for him. Because he was just as invested in this baby as she was.

"If I can help, let me," he muttered.

Not a pushy demand. Again, that had to be difficult for him since Dutton was a man used to being in charge. Not a growling-bear kind of in charge like his father, but the real deal. These days, Ike was just a figurehead on the ranch. Dutton owned it and ran it his way despite what seemed to be constant criticism and interference from Ike.

Grace made eye contact with him. A mistake. Whenever she was this close to Dutton, she was flooded with memories. And not all were bad, just unwanted. Of course, the heat she felt for him was unwanted, too, but she just couldn't seem to make it go away.

That heat had made life a whole lot more difficult for both of them, and sometimes it felt as if the two of them were caught up in a feud, like the Hatfields and McCoys. Or rather, they would have been caught up if they hadn't decided years ago to keep their distance from each other. And that had worked.

Until five months ago.

That's when things had gone south after what had essentially been a shootout at the ranch between the McClennans and thieves who'd tried to steal some champion horses. Grace and several of her deputies had been involved in the gunfight. Dutton, too. And after surviving a near-death experience, the adrenaline and heat had landed a double punch that had in turn landed them in bed.

Grace hadn't looked up the stats of getting pregnant from what was essentially a one-night stand, but it had happened. And now here she was. Both she and her baby caught in the cross fire between the McClennans and pretty much everyone else in Renegade Canyon.

Dutton glanced over his shoulder and muttered some profanity under his breath. At first, she thought his father was heading back their way, but Ike was still by the truck. Still glaring. A new visitor had arrived in a county cruiser and had parked next to the McClennan truck.

County Sheriff Wilson Finney.

Grace knew the man better than she wanted to. Dutton likely could say the same. Wilson had been born and raised in Renegade Canyon, but when he'd lost the sheriff's election to Grace six years earlier, he'd moved and had eventually become the county sheriff.

Wilson donned a raincoat over his toned and heavily muscled body and made his way toward her. Or rather, toward the dead cop. He stopped right outside the crime-scene tape that the CSIs had already set up, and stared at the woman who'd once been his deputy. Wilson cursed, too, and it wasn't under his breath. He stood there several more moments before he turned toward Grace.

And scowled.

Grace wasn't sure if the facial expression was for her or Dutton. Maybe both. But Wilson didn't even attempt to rein it in.

"Sleeping with the enemy," Wilson growled. His gaze dropped to her stomach, and even though he couldn't see her baby bump under her raincoat, he knew it was there. Grace suspected everyone in the county did. "Why haven't you arrested him yet?" he demanded.

By *him*, Grace had no doubts whom he meant. "Dutton doesn't have a criminal record."

"Only because he hasn't been caught." Wilson stopped directly in front of them and propped his hands on his hips. The glare was still firmly in place. "That whole family should be locked up, and you should be fired for sleeping with him."

Even though Dutton wasn't touching her, Grace could practically feel every muscle in his body tense. Not because of the insult to him. But because of the insult to her.

Grace decided to try to nip this in the bud. "Sheriff Finney," she said, purposely addressing him by his title and surname to remind him this was work and not some free-for-all at a bar, "since you're probably in shock and grieving for your fallen deputy, I'll give you some leeway on that. *Some*," Grace emphasized.

"I won't," Dutton snarled, and there was a lethal edge to his voice. An apparently effective one.

Wilson stared at him and must have decided this was not a fight he needed to launch into tonight, because the county sheriff shook his head, cursed and then pinned his attention back on the murdered deputy. Grace gave Wilson a few more moments before she said anything.

"Tell me about her," Grace began.

Judging from the long pause, Wilson wanted to hang on to his temper a bit longer, but he finally spoke. "Deputy Elaine Sneed. She's been on the job for less than a year."

Grace waited, expecting more, but more didn't come. She sighed and took out her phone. Now that she had a name, she tapped into the database to retrieve what info she could.

"Sneed," Dutton repeated. "Is she Frank Sneed's daughter?"

"You know her?" Grace asked, and as the deputy's bio loaded, she could confirm that Elaine was indeed the daughter of Frank and Marion Sneed from Carson, a town about twenty miles away.

"Frank recently bought some horses from me," Dutton explained. "And he brought his daughter with him to pick them up." He, too, had another look at the dead woman. "That looks like her."

"It is," Grace confirmed, since Elaine was the Sneeds' only child. "She was twenty-four and had been a county deputy for eighteen months." So slightly longer than Wilson had guessed. Strange that he wouldn't have known that about one of his people, but then, maybe he wasn't a hands-on boss.

"She was young. I didn't give her any of the hard cases," Wilson volunteered, but Grace had the feeling he just wanted to contribute something that wouldn't make him seem so clueless when it came to someone who'd worked for him for a year and a half.

"She's engaged," Dutton informed them. "Or maybe already married. Frank mentioned that."

"She's not married," Grace said, referring to the bio. "Or if she is, she didn't update it in her records." She paused, looked at Wilson. "I need to be at the death notification of her next of kin, but I'm assuming you'll want to be the one to deliver the actual news?"

"Why do you need to be there?" Wilson snapped. "She worked for me."

"And she was killed, or at least her body was left in my jurisdiction," Grace quickly pointed out. "This is my investigation, and you know the protocol. I need to talk to her next of kin."

Sadly, that was because the killer was often someone close to the victim. Grace didn't think that was the situation here, but she had to go by the book.

Wilson looked ready to argue with her, but the head CSI, Larry Crandall, called out before Wilson could launch into anything.

"Sheriff Granger," Larry said. "There's a note on the body."

That got Grace's attention, but she didn't charge forward to take a look. She had to hold out her arm, though, to stop Wilson from doing just that.

Grace moved her flashlight over the body and saw the edge of a plastic bag that was tucked in the deputy's shirt. The CSI eased it out, then held it up for Grace to see. Yes, it was a note alright. A handwritten one. And whoever had put it there had no doubt encased it in that bag to make sure it didn't get soaked.

"What does it say?" Grace asked, since she wasn't able to make out the words from where she was standing.

The CSI turned it toward him, and started to scan it, then muttered something she didn't catch before he read it aloud.

"'Two down. Sheriff Grace Granger, you're on the list, too, and your time is coming. Or should I say ending? And for you, I'll add a bonus. Two for the price of one. You and Dutton McClennan. Soon, you'll both be dead.'"

Chapter Two

While Dutton waited in Grace's office, he paced and continued to read through reports from his ranch hands and his PI that were coming in on his phone. Something he'd been doing for the past two hours as he waited for Grace to return from notifying Deputy Elaine Sneed's family that she was dead.

Dutton knew he wouldn't be included in that tough job, but he wished he'd been allowed to go, anyway. And not just so he would have been close to Grace to make sure she was safe. That was a huge concern. However, he also needed answers as to why Grace and he were now targets of a killer.

Well, maybe they were.

Thanks to a copy of the threatening note now pinned to Grace's board in her office, Dutton could see the words, the threat, every time he paced in front of it. Which was often. Even though Grace was the sheriff and therefore the top cop, her office wasn't huge by anyone's standards. More of a barebones kind of place, designed for work and not much else.

He suspected that over the fifty or so years that the office of the Renegade Canyon PD had been here at this particular location, there'd been plenty of work done in this space. At the very desk that had once been occupied by Grace's mother, Aileen, and before that, Grace's grandfather, Chet. Before that, there'd been cousins at the helm at the original police station. A string of Granger sheriffs going back over a century.

A law-enforcement legacy that Grace had continued.

Normally, thinking of her as the sheriff didn't put a knot in Dutton's gut. It was simply who she was and had been for six years.

Of course, *simply* hadn't always been, well, simple.

Not with his own family legacy that was often at odds with Grace and her family. Still, he had always thought Grace as capable of balancing that feud, this forbidden attraction they had for each other and anything to do with the badge.

But that note changed things.

Two down. Sheriff Grace Granger, you're on the list, too, and your time is coming. Or should I say ending? And for you, I'll add a bonus. Two for the price of one. You and Dutton McClennan. Soon, you'll both be dead.

Yeah, no way could Dutton be unaffected by that. Grace and he might not be an actual couple, but in four months or so, they'd become parents. And if Grace's life was in danger, then so was the baby's. That more than tightened his gut. It twisted at everything inside him.

It twisted even more when he had to mentally spell out something he already knew. That Grace wouldn't want him to play protector in this. In fact, she'd want to protect *him*. Not because of their past, but because he was now the job to her.

Dutton would need to figure out a way around that. He wanted Grace focusing on her own safety. On the baby's. And that would involve shoving aside their past so they could work together.

Which wouldn't be easy.

Especially since the past was front and center between them. Not only the baby, but also the scalding attraction they'd fought for years. A fight they'd lost just twice. Once when they'd been teenagers and had become each other's "firsts." Then again, five months ago, when she'd gotten pregnant. It was easier to fight the attraction when they weren't around each other, but that note would make any distancing impossible.

But they needed some emotional barriers.

Their families would make it next to impossible for them to be together and still live and work in this small town. The bickering and conflicts would escalate, and Ike would make Grace's life as miserable as possible.

Dutton glanced at the movement in the doorway. Not Grace or one of the deputies, who had likely been instructed to babysit him and make sure he didn't go anywhere. This was a black cat that strolled in as if he owned the place. With only the arrogance that a cat and a Greek god could have managed, the cat eyed Dutton and then sauntered past him to leap into Grace's chair.

He knew the cat's name was Sherlock. Knew, too, that the police department had more or less adopted him after he'd been found standing guard over his late owner's body.

Not a murder but a heart attack.

The plan had been for Grace to take Sherlock to the county animal shelter, but since that'd been four months ago, Dutton figured the feline was here to stay. Especially since he'd noticed that someone had added an automated litter box and feeding area in the break room.

Dutton stopped pacing at the sound of approaching footsteps, and turned to see his brother, Deputy Rory McClennan, step into the doorway. Genetically, they looked like twins, with their black hair, dark brown eyes and nearly identical McClennan DNA, but Rory was five years younger than Dutton and therefore the baby of the family.

Rory handed Dutton a cup of coffee and sipped his own while his cop's eyes studied his big brother. He didn't ask Dutton if he was okay. No need. He wasn't. He was shaken to the core, and while that wouldn't have been obvious to most people, Rory would have seen it.

"Grace is on her way back," Rory said. "She'll be here in a couple of minutes."

"Any idea how the notification went?" Dutton asked.

Rory shrugged, which was apparently all the info he was going to dole out. They were brothers, but Dutton knew that Rory was a solid cop, one who was loyal to his boss, and he would want any info about the notification to come not from him, but from Grace herself.

Rory tipped his head to Dutton's phone and then the note on the board. "How exactly are you looking into that?" his brother asked.

"The same way I've been looking into it for the past month." Since the first body had been left just outside the ranch.

Even though there'd been no threatening note left on that victim, Dutton had had to consider that the location of the body hadn't been random. That the death of San Antonio Detective Andrea Selby was somehow linked to his family, and the ranch.

Or to him specifically.

After all, Towering Oaks might be considered the McClennan family ranch, but Dutton was the owner and had been since he'd turned twenty-one.

Despite the tensions it had created with his dad, his mother had transferred ownership to Dutton as a birthday gift. It had been a nasty little twist in their family littered with nasty twists, and Ike hadn't been able to stop it because Dutton's mom had never given any portion of the ranch to Ike when he'd moved there after they'd married.

The Towering Oaks had belonged to Dutton's mom's parents, and when they'd passed, they had made her the sole owner of the place, an ownership that his mom hadn't tried to change to include her husband. That, and many other things in their marriage, had created a rift that still existed when his mother had died six months ago.

Dutton hadn't found any connections to the first murder victim, and he'd looked. Hard. So had Grace and all of her deputies, including Rory. After all, his father had made plenty of enemies over the years. Dutton had, too. Ditto for Grace and her own family of cops. But so far, there wasn't anything to link Detective Selby to Grace or them.

Now this new murder had to be factored into what they already knew. And judging from the note, the two dead cops were indeed connected in some way. In exactly what way, Dutton didn't know, but he'd instructed the PI, Jake Winters, whom he kept on retainer to dig deep into Elaine Sneed's life, and look for any association she might have had with the first murdered woman.

The PI had gotten right on the assignment and for the past two hours had been sending Dutton info he was gathering. So far, Dutton didn't see anything in those updates that gave him the answers he needed.

Rory stepped out of the doorway moments after Dutton heard the approaching footsteps. He felt his body automatically rev up. Cursed his reaction and saw the same mental cursing on Grace's face when she came into her office. Even though their gazes only held for a couple of seconds, the usual intensity was there.

And the blasted heat.

Of course, there was something else in the mix now. That razor-sharp concern for each other and their child.

"The parents aren't suspects," Grace said right off the bat. "Airtight alibis and no motive. Learning about Elaine's death crushed them," she added in a murmur.

Dutton hadn't thought for one minute that the parents had murdered their daughter, but it was good to have them ruled out. Especially since their suspect pool included anyone who had a beef with Grace, him or the two dead cops.

"Did County Sheriff Finney come back with you?" Rory asked.

"No," she answered.

A muscle flickered in Grace's jaw, and Dutton suspected Wilson Finney had continued to act like the jerk that he could be when it came to Grace. Everyone knew the jerk behavior was because Grace had beaten him in the election for the town sheriff, and because of it, Grace and Wilson usually gave each other a wide berth. Just as she and Dutton did. But again, that couldn't happen in this investigation.

"You and I need to talk," she said to Dutton.

It wasn't his imagination that she sounded all cop. She clearly wanted to draw some lines here. Those lines, for the time being, were that she wasn't viewing him as her baby's father, but as the target of a killer. Her goal would no doubt be to do what she could to ensure his safety and then get him out of her office.

Dutton was going to have something to say about that, though.

Grace peeled off her rain gear, hanging it on the wall pegs. Despite the gear, the storm had gotten to her, and her dark blond hair was wet and pressed to her head and neck. She wasn't pale, not exactly, but Dutton could see the unsteadiness on her face and in her cool green eyes.

Eyes that she pinned to the board.

She studied it. The note that'd been added. Elaine's photo, too. Not one from the crime scene. This was a picture taken from the county sheriff's webpage, where the fresh-faced deputy was in uniform and trying to look stern. She hadn't quite accomplished that, in Dutton's opinion.

There was another photo pinned to the other side of the board. This one was of the first murdered cop, San Antonio Detective Andrea Selby. Beneath the pictures, the names of about two dozen suspects had been written in.

And all crossed off except for two.

Dutton was familiar with both of them. They were men whom Detective Selby had arrested, and they had recently been released from prison. Even though they were still on the board, it was because they didn't have alibis and not because there was any evidence to link them to her death.

Now Grace and the deputies would need to add suspect names beneath Elaine's photo. Dutton had already started the process. Not on a board, but mentally, with the info his PI was gathering for him.

"I'll see if I can get an update from the CSIs," Rory said, no doubt heading back to his desk in the bullpen.

Dutton figured his brother would indeed check for updates, but Rory was also likely giving him some time alone with Grace. Time she wouldn't want, but Dutton needed it.

"So why leave us a note?" Dutton asked. "Did the killer warn or threaten the SAPD detective before she was murdered?"

When Sherlock bounded out of the chair and went to rub against her legs, Grace shook her head and bent down to scratch the cat's head. "Nothing has come up about that, and considering how visible the killer made this note, I think if there had been some kind of premurder threat, then we would have found it."

That was what Dutton figured. "So this is meant to scare us," he concluded. "To make us keep watch over our shoulders and lose sleep."

Which it would do. But Dutton had no intention of running scared. No. He had every intention of finding this snake and making him pay for the hell this was causing the families of the victims, Grace and everyone else involved.

"Sheriff Finney suggested you and I were the reason his deputy was murdered," Grace said, standing upright again, and he could tell from her tone that the suggestion had hit her hard.

Because there could possibly be some truth to it.

Neither Grace nor he had done anything intentional to provoke these deaths, and they certainly weren't to blame. But the guilt was there, rolling right through them. Someone might be killing female cops to get back at them for something. Then again, maybe it was to get back at someone else and the two of them were simply targets on a killer's list.

"How much did *Sheriff* Wilson Finney hassle you tonight?" Dutton asked, and he added some venom to the man's title. Venom that Wilson aimed at them every chance he got.

Grace dragged in a long breath. "He thinks I should be fired." She slid her hand over her baby bump. "Then again, so do a lot of people."

Dutton sighed and did some silent cursing. What he didn't do was touch her even though that's what he wanted to do. He wanted to try to ease some of that tension he saw on her face, but touching her would do the opposite of that.

He couldn't argue with Grace about a lot of people wanting her fired. Plenty of people in town hated him and his family, which meant they hated Grace being pregnant with his child.

Thankfully, though, there were enough members of the town council who were staving off a recall election that would oust Grace. Maybe because those members thought the pregnancy had nothing to do with the excellent job Grace had done. Maybe, too, Grace's mother, Aileen, still had enough influence to keep her daughter where she was. That despite Aileen not approving of Dutton, his family or the pregnancy.

Since there was no way either of them wanted to dwell on the opinions of the town or the county sheriff, Dutton moved on to something she needed to know. "After the first murder, I had more security cameras installed."

Grace's head whipped up. "I didn't see any cameras."

"Long-range ones with night vision that are motion-activated. They're mounted on trees along the fence line. But before you get your hopes up, the angles of the cameras in that area might not be right to capture who did this. Or the person might not have gotten in range to trigger the motion activation. The security company is downloading any feed now and will send it to both of us as soon as they have it."

Though he'd said that part about not getting her hopes up, the news seemed to do just that. Some of the tension in her face eased just a little. Capturing the killer on camera was a long shot, but it was better than what they had now—which was pretty much nothing.

Dutton's phone dinged with a text. "From my PI," he muttered, reading through the latest bit of info. "According to what he told his boss, Elaine's fiancé has been in El Paso on business for the past three days. He's a real-estate agent, and he went there to meet with some bigwig client. FYI, he works for Elaine's parents. They own the real-estate agency."

Grace didn't ask if that alibi was confirmed. She'd want to do that herself, but she went to the board and wrote "Brian Waterman, fiancé, person of interest." Since Dutton hadn't told her the man's name, she had obviously already run her own background check.

"I spoke to Brian Waterman on the phone on the drive back here," she volunteered. "If he killed Elaine, then he did a top-notch job of covering up his guilt. He sounded just as broken as her parents. *Sounded*. But he stays on the list until we can confirm his alibi." She paused a heartbeat. "Tell me who you believe killed her and who's coming after us."

"I don't know," he admitted, and that brought on more silent cursing. "I'm having my PI look for broader connections. Those with possible grudges against female cops. Those with grudges against us." Dutton handed her his phone, and he felt the trickle of heat when his fingers brushed against hers.

Yeah, this was why touching her was a bad idea.

"So far, this is what the PI has come up with," Dutton explained.

It was a list, a very long one, of known criminals in the state who'd made public threats against cops—specifically female ones. Threats either posted on social media or actually made during arrests and court proceedings.

"Dozens," she said on a sigh.

There were indeed dozens, and Dutton suspected other names would be added to the list as the PI continued to dig. Grace and her deputies would no doubt tack on even more potentials. Which meant there had to be a way to narrow it down.

"You'll be stretching your resources thin if you try to investigate every single one of them," Dutton pointed out. "My PI can help, though, if you're willing to let a civilian in on this."

If Grace heard his offer, she didn't respond. Something had obviously grabbed her attention.

"Avery Kenney," she said, and she hurried behind her desk to boot up her laptop. "His name came up in the first investigation…"

Her voice trailed off while her gaze flew over the screen. Dutton had figured that many of the names on his PI's list had also been on Grace's, and he went to stand next to her so he could see the info she was accessing.

"Yes, Avery Kenney, a bartender from San Antonio." She highlighted the name. "He was shot by a female officer who mistook him for a burglar. Lots of angry posts on social media about how the officer should have never been given a badge since she was overly emotional and clearly 'not ready for duty.'" She put that last part in quotes.

"You interviewed him?" Dutton asked.

She scrolled farther down the screen. "Yes. But it was a phone interview since Kenney was out of state at the time. His boss vouched for his alibi, but I got a bad feeling about him. Enough so that I drove to San Antonio to see him. He said in a not-so-friendly way that he'd already answered my questions and that if I wanted to talk to him again, I'd have to go through his lawyer."

"I'm guessing since he had already given you those answers, you didn't have enough to force him to come in for further questioning?" Dutton asked.

Grace nodded and she tapped the two former prisoners' names beneath Detective Selby's photo. Charlie Salvetti and Teddy Gonzales. "Because of their criminal records, I did bring them in." She sighed, shook her head. "And I got absolutely no hint of guilt. Maybe they're just good at hiding it."

She didn't sound convinced of that last possibility. Neither was Dutton. He hadn't interviewed the pair, but he'd had his

PI research them. Dutton had ruled out Salvetti because he was five feet, two inches tall and weighed 120 pounds. He likely wouldn't have been able to lift the dead women and stage them against the fence posts. The second man, Teddy Gonzales, was nearly seventy, and while he had the size, Dutton didn't think he had the strength. Added to that, there was no proof that either man was familiar with Renegade Canyon or the ranch.

Dutton's phone dinged again just as Grace got the signal for an incoming email. "It's the video from the security cameras," he pointed out, and he stayed right by Grace's side while she downloaded it to her computer.

The dark footage appeared on her screen. Emphasis on *dark*. And the rain certainly didn't help. It was like looking through a gray gauzy curtain. But the fact there was footage meant something or someone had activated it, and Dutton was hoping that was a good sign they'd managed to film the killer.

Grace scrolled through the first part of the feed, zooming in on what had triggered the motion-activation feature. A deer with its eyes casting an eerie glow in the night. Dutton checked to see the location of this specific camera, and he guessed it was a good thousand yards from the part of the fence where the body had been left.

She moved on to the next camera feed. And zoomed in when there was some motion. Not a deer this time. This was a person. Specifically, a person dragging something.

The killer with the body.

Grace made a soft sound, a moan that she obviously had tried to silence, but Dutton heard it. Felt it, too, since he was experiencing that same sense of dread that Grace no doubt was.

She slowed the footage, continuing to zoom in as much

as she could. The killer was wearing what appeared to be a long dark raincoat with a large hood that completely concealed his or her head and face. It reminded Dutton of the images of the grim reaper, and it was grim alright, since the camera had managed to capture the dead body.

It was definitely Deputy Elaine Sneed.

"Move so I can see your face," Grace muttered, obviously speaking to the killer.

But the person didn't cooperate and kept his or her head angled down. It was also possible the person was wearing a balaclava, which had created a black-hole effect.

"Based on the size, I can't tell if it's a man or woman," Grace added.

"Neither can I, and the fact the killer is dragging rather than carrying means it doesn't have to be a big person." He mentally shrugged. "Still, dragging takes some strength, especially since this point is about hundred yards or so from the road."

This time the sound Grace made was one of agreement, and they continued to watch as the killer stopped by the fence post and hoisted up the body. And it was indeed a body and not an unconscious deputy. There was already blood all over the uniform.

Dutton tried to keep his breathing level as they saw the killer coil the rope around the dead cop. Despite the rain, it took less than a minute to secure it in place before the killer stepped back as if to admire the work.

And then, the murderer looked up.

Directly at the camera.

Hell. That gave Dutton a jolt, and he'd been right about the balaclava, or maybe it was a mask, because the only part of the face that was visible was the strip that exposed the eyes. Definitely not enough to make any kind of identification.

While still looking up at the camera, the killer reached into the raincoat pocket and extracted something. Exactly what, Dutton couldn't tell, because it was wrapped in what appeared to be black cloth. The person used it to point at the camera in a threatening gesture that seemed to say "you're next" and then flung it over the fence and onto the ranch.

Grace whipped out her phone, and Dutton didn't have to guess whom she was calling. The CSIs.

"Check over the fence now, in the area behind the fence post," she said to the person who answered. "The killer left something for us."

Chapter Three

Grace stared at her phone, willing it to ring so the CSIs could tell her what they'd found. She had thought it would only take them a couple of minutes.

Apparently not, since it was going on a half hour now.

She had used the time to continue viewing the security-camera footage to make sure the killer hadn't returned to the scene to retrieve whatever had been tossed. But she didn't see anything. In fact, there were no signs of anyone other than what Dutton and she had already viewed. So they'd watched and rewatched frame by frame as the killer had dragged and posed the body.

The crime lab would view the footage, too, and Grace was hoping they'd see something that the two of them had missed. While she was hoping, she added that maybe there'd be some usable forensic evidence left on the body. Or in the bag that'd been tossed onto the ranch. Because right now, she essentially had nothing that could help her prevent another murder.

Including Dutton's. And her own.

Yes, that was weighing heavily on her mind, and she was certain it was the same for Dutton. After all, these were the highest stakes, since their precious baby could be at risk.

"The killer seemed to know the location of the security camera," Grace pointed out.

Dutton's quick agreement let her know he'd already considered that, and he took out his phone. "I'm forwarding you the contact info of the security company I used in case an employee there is the killer. Not likely since the employees are heavily vetted." He fired off the text to her and started another one. "I'm also sending you a list of all my ranch hands. Again, they're heavily vetted."

She doubted they'd find the killer's name on the lists, but again, she'd check. "How many people knew you had the cameras installed?" she asked.

"Plenty," he admitted. "The security company had a big truck with their logo, and the installers would have parked in that part of the pasture. So basically, anyone driving by could have seen it."

True, and gossip about the cameras would have gotten around. It hadn't gotten back to Grace, but then people usually shied away from talking to her about Dutton.

"Are the cameras visible from the road during the day?" she asked.

His forehead bunched up while he gave that question some thought. "Probably. The idea wasn't to conceal them. It was to record the killer if there was a return visit."

Which there obviously had been. And maybe the killer had worn that bulky raincoat because of the storm, but it had served double duty of concealing the killer's body and face.

"There has to be a reason the killer threw that bag onto the ranch," Dutton said a moment later. "Maybe to extend the crime scene? To put you in the position of having to deal with my dad and question us about it?"

Grace had already gone there and had to agree it was a possibility. A way of adding one more thing to an already complex situation. And part of that complexity was she would indeed have to investigate Dutton and his family. Heck, she already had after the first murder.

"Still," Dutton went on, "the bodies were practically on the ranch grounds, anyway."

"Yes," she agreed. "But there's a subtle difference between practically and actually on it. This is an escalation of sorts."

She tapped a name that had been crossed off on the board. The name of the person who actually owned the land where the bodies had been dragged and staged. Elmer Dawson. He was in his nineties and in assisted living. Grace suspected that once Elmer passed away, his next of kin would be selling the acres, and Dutton would buy them.

"I couldn't find a single connection between Elmer Dawson and the first murdered woman," Grace revealed. "And I suspect there won't be one between him and the second woman, either. Still, I'll check," she added on a heavy sigh.

Before she could add more to that, her phone rang. "It's the CSIs," she announced and immediately answered it. She didn't put the call on speaker, but she figured Dutton was standing close enough to her that he could hear Larry Crandall's voice.

"We got the bag," Larry said. "It took us a while to find it because the rain had caused some mud and grass to cover it." He paused. "It's a knife, and there's some blood on the blade and in the bag itself."

Grace drew in a sharp breath. "The murder weapon."

"Possibly," Larry admitted. "We've got it bagged, but I'll take a picture of it and send it to you. It's not an ordinary knife. It's got some fancy carvings on the handle."

Maybe that meant it'd be easier to trace. But if so, Grace had to wonder why the killer would have left it behind. This could be part of the cat-and-mouse game that the killer seemed to be playing.

"I'll send you a picture in a couple of minutes," Larry added, then ended the call.

Grace didn't even have time to put her phone in her pocket before someone stepped into her office doorway, and it wasn't one of her deputies. However, it was a familiar face.

Cassie Darnell.

Not exactly a welcome visitor. Along with owning several businesses, including the town's only fitness center, she was also on the town council. The very council that had considered trying to oust Grace when word had gotten around that she was pregnant with Dutton's baby. But Cassie was more than that.

The woman was also Dutton's ex-girlfriend.

Even though Dutton and Cassie had broken up nearly a year ago, months before Grace had gotten pregnant, it was still awkward for Grace to be around her. It was probably the same for Dutton, too, since Grace had heard the breakup hadn't been Cassie's idea.

Cassie had already opened her mouth to say something, but she froze in the doorway with her gaze fixed on Dutton and Grace. And Cassie had no doubt noticed that the two of them were standing close, arm to arm. Grace refrained from stepping away from him. It would only make them look even more guilty of some PDA at the police station.

"Oh," Cassie said, her voice filled with the surprise already on her face.

A classically beautiful face, Grace noted, to go along with her golden blond hair and blue eyes. A striking set of features that explained why Dutton had likely been attracted to the woman in the first place. That and Cassie's perfectly toned, athletic body. Cassie looked as if she could have been a model for the posters hanging in the fitness center.

"Dutton," Cassie began, "I didn't know you'd be here."

Now Grace did move, but it was to cover the board. Cassie might be on the town council, but that didn't make her privy to the details of an investigation. The same could be said for Dutton even though he did have more than a personal interest in this case.

"I'm giving the sheriff some info," Dutton replied.

It wasn't a lie. He had indeed given her those lists, and Grace welcomed picking his brain for possibilities as to the identity of the killer.

But it wasn't the full truth, either.

Grace knew he was there because he was worried about the baby and her.

"Good," Cassie said. "I hope you catch the killer soon." She paused. "That's why I'm here. I got a call from Wilson."

Grace held back a groan. Dutton didn't. "Was he whining to you about how Grace is handling the investigation?" Dutton asked.

Cassie nodded, and her face flushed a little. "He asked me to press the rest of the town council not only to oust Grace from the case, but also to push for the recall vote to try to get rid of her as sheriff. I reminded him that the town council doesn't get involved in the day-to-day dealings of police business, but Wilson insisted this was a conflict of interest for you. He feels he should take over since it was his deputy who was murdered."

"If you use that logic, then the lieutenant at SAPD should take over since his detective was the first death," Grace quickly pointed out. She tried to keep any anger out of her tone. Hard to do, though. "Both bodies were in my jurisdiction. I'm staying on the case." Grace didn't bother to address the part about Wilson pressing her to be ousted.

Cassie nodded again. "I figured you'd say that. But I thought you should know he insisted he'd be calling other members of the council. And the Texas Rangers."

"The Rangers?" Dutton asked.

"Wilson thinks Grace is out of her depth and that she should have already asked them for assistance."

"I'm considering it," Grace admitted. "But until two hours ago, it was a single murder that might or might not be connected to Dutton, me or the town. Once the current crime scene has been processed, I'll consider whether or not to bring in the Rangers."

The Texas Rangers were similar to the FBI, but on a state level. The Rangers only assisted when requested. Now that she had two bodies and the threatening note, Grace almost certainly would ask for support in processing the evidence. The Ranger crime lab could likely do that much faster than the county one.

"I hate to say this," Cassie went on, "but Wilson sounded… enraged. He really despises you, Grace. You, too, Dutton. He still blames you for firing his father as ranch foreman."

"I fired him because I caught him stealing supplies," Dutton reminded her.

That'd been years ago, when Grace had been a deputy, and Wilson was indeed still sporting a grudge about that. Wilson felt as if that'd played into him not winning the election. Played into his father's death, too, since he'd died a broken man about six months ago. His cause of death was a heart attack, but Wilson insisted it'd been brought on by stress caused by Dutton.

"I think Wilson's going to push and push to make things harder for you," Cassie said, aiming that comment at Grace.

Great. Just what she didn't need, with a double-homicide investigation and with the town council breathing down her neck. Every move and decision she made would be scrutinized to the hilt. Then again, that had been happening, anyway.

Cassie checked her watch and then glanced out the window at the rain that was continuing to pelt against the glass. "Well, I should be getting home."

"Late night for you," Grace commented.

Cassie attempted a smile that didn't quite succeed. "I was catching up on some paperwork. That's where I was when Wilson called me."

Grace didn't ask why Cassie had decided to deliver the news of that call tonight, when it was already going on midnight, but she didn't miss the longing glance Cassie gave Dutton. Yes, longing. Apparently, the woman still had feelings for him and wasn't doing a good job of hiding it.

"Good night," Cassie added and headed out.

Dutton waited until Cassie was out of earshot before he whispered, "Could Wilson have murdered those two cops?" he asked. "Cassie was right about him despising both of us."

"He does indeed," Grace agreed. She shook her head, though. "But it'd be beyond extreme for him to kill just to make our lives miserable."

The moment she said the words, Grace realized there could be more to it than that. Wilson wanted her job, period. And he wanted to get back at Dutton for firing his father. So if Wilson had gone off the deep end—and that was a massive *if*—he could be masterminding these murders to make Grace look bad while also dragging Dutton into the investigation.

"I think you should at least consider Wilson a possible suspect," Dutton commented.

Oh, she would. Grace just wouldn't put his name on the board, but she intended to look into the possibility that she was dealing with a dirty cop. Of course, that was just one thing she had to deal with. Another was standing right next to her.

She turned toward the board and tapped the note the killer had left. Specifically, she pointed to his name. "Because of that, I should put you in protective custody. *Should*," Grace stressed.

"My house on the ranch is more secure than any place you could arrange for me," Dutton quickly pointed out. "In fact, it'd be safer for you and the baby to be there, too."

"Probably," she admitted. "But there's no way I'm staying at your ranch."

"You wouldn't be staying with my family," he insisted. "You'd be staying in a guestroom at my house on the ranch."

She was well aware of that and knew that Ike lived in the main house, even though it, too, belonged to Dutton. Dutton had basically given it to him after he'd had his own place built when he'd been in his early twenties.

Ike didn't live alone in the massive mansion, though, but resided with his much younger brother, Asher, and his wife, Kitty. They had an adopted twelve-year-old daughter, Jamie, who, because of the big age difference, was more of a niece to Dutton than a cousin.

"It's still *your* house, on *your* ranch," Grace pointed out.

Dutton opened his mouth, probably to launch into a lecture about her not letting the gossip play into where she stayed, but he closed his mouth just as fast. He knew what a complicated situation this was for both of them.

"So you'll go back to your place, turn on any and all

security systems you have and shut your gate to visitors," she stated.

He gave her a flat look. "Will you do all those things at your place? Wait," he continued. "You don't have a gate to keep out killers, and you live out in the middle of nowhere with no neighbor in sight."

That was true. No gate. She lived on what had once been her grandparents' horse ranch, and her nearest neighbor was over a half mile away. Normally, that suited her just fine, but this was the first time she had a killer targeting her. Still, she wasn't going to let this SOB run her out of her own home.

"I have a security system," she said. "And I'll use it."

Dutton muttered some profanity under his breath. "Then I'll be there to keep watch to make sure the killer doesn't get to you."

She muttered her own profanity. "Dutton, there is no way I can let you stay with me in my house."

"I'll stay in my truck, which will be parked in front of your house," he argued.

He would have no doubt continued to argue if her phone hadn't dinged with a text, and she saw it was from Larry. As promised, the CSI had sent her a photo of the knife they'd found. It was now encased in a clear plastic evidence bag, but she could see the smears of blood on the blade, and Grace felt the fresh punch of dread since this was the blood of a fallen fellow cop.

"Enlarge the handle," Dutton insisted.

Of course, she was aware he'd moved back to her side. It was impossible not to realize that since…well, this was Dutton. But Grace heard something in his voice that was more than a request.

She used her fingers to enlarge the photo, zooming in on the handle. It was ornate, alright, and made of something white. Maybe a special kind of wood or bone. An eagle had been carved into it.

"Hell," Dutton said, and he groaned, then cursed some more.

Grace snapped toward him to see why he'd had that reaction. "What's wrong?" she demanded.

Dutton groaned again before he answered. "That knife belongs to my father."

Chapter Four

"Won't this be fun?" Dutton muttered, the sarcasm heavy in his voice. He was in the doorway of Grace's office and had an unobstructed view of his father as Ike came into the police station.

Grace, who was right beside Dutton, didn't say anything, but her sigh told him she wasn't looking forward to this, either. Her sigh turned to a raised eyebrow though when an unexpected *visitor* came in behind Ike. Dutton cursed under his breath at the sight of the dark-haired girl.

His twelve-year-old cousin, Jamie.

The girl's arrival obviously grabbed the attention of his brother, too, because Rory got up from his desk. He was talking to someone on the phone, but he pinned a questioning look at Ike and Jamie.

Dutton did more than give her a look. "What are you doing here, Jamie?" Dutton demanded. He checked his watch. It was one-fifteen in the morning, which was way past the girl's bedtime.

Jamie gave a dramatic roll of her eyes. "Dutton, Sheriff Granger," she greeted, and her attention lowered to Grace's baby bump.

The girl smiled a little. For some reason, Jamie was

one of the few people in town who seemed happy about the pregnancy.

"Well?" Dutton persisted. "Why are you here?"

"I heard when the sheriff called and told Uncle Ike to come into the station. I insisted on coming with him."

"Insisted," Ike snarled, not sounding too pleased at having a companion for this. Then again, his father was likely just riled at pretty much everything that had gone on tonight.

Dutton ignored Ike for the time being and focused on Jamie. "Does your nanny know you're here?" he asked.

"No, she's asleep, and please don't call her," Jamie was quick to say. When Dutton took out his phone to do just that, the girl added, "Sheriff Granger, I can help with the investigation."

Grace pulled back her shoulders, and Dutton moved to the side so that Grace could come out of her office and walk closer to Jamie. Dutton followed her. "What investigation?" she asked, aiming a glare at Ike for spilling any info about a murder to a child.

"I didn't say a word," Ike protested.

"He didn't have to," Jamie explained. "It's all over social media about the woman who was left by the fence."

Of course, it was, and Dutton didn't press to know why Jamie would have read such things. He already knew. Jamie's own parents had been murdered when she was a baby, and it was how she'd ended up in foster care and then adopted by his aunt and uncle.

Jamie's tragic family history had given her a fascination with police investigations. So much so that she'd applied to do a summer internship of sorts here at the police station. Grace might approve it, too, in a limited-scope kind of way with Jamie only getting schooled on procedures for nonserious cases.

Grace was clearly more tolerant of Jamie than she was the rest of his family. Including him. And it was easy to see that Jamie idolized Grace.

"It's awful what happened to her," Jamie went on. "And it's like that other murder, isn't it?"

"I can't discuss that with you," Grace said, probably hoping that was the last of the conversation about murder. "You really shouldn't be here."

"But I had to come. Like I said, I can help," Jamie insisted, and she was no doubt about to add more when her eyes lit up. "Sherlock," she called out as the cat waltzed toward her.

Dutton knew that Jamie was familiar with the cat because she'd gone with Rory when he'd taken Sherlock in for a checkup with the vet. Jamie scooped him up, and the often standoffish cat consented to some cuddles.

"Help how?" Grace pressed the girl.

"I know about the knife," Jamie stated.

Everything inside Dutton went still. Hell. He didn't want Jamie involved in this in any way, but if what she said was true, then her involvement was already there.

"Like I said, I heard when Sheriff Granger called Uncle Ike," Jamie continued a moment later. "He didn't put the call on speaker or anything, but I could tell from the way he was answering that the sheriff was asking him about that knife with the white handle he keeps in his office. Not locked up," she added. "But sitting in a little wooden holder on the top of the big bookshelf behind his desk."

That was indeed where his father had kept it, and it had been there for as long as Dutton could remember. It was way out of reach of kids and was surrounded by other antique memorabilia. Dutton hadn't been in that office in more than a year, and even if he had had a more recent visit, he likely wouldn't have noticed it was missing.

"A knife that isn't there because someone stole it," Ike snapped, his ire aimed at Grace, not Jamie. "And then that someone used it to try to set me up. I didn't kill that woman."

Grace sighed, obviously not comfortable discussing a murder in front of a child. "You said you knew something about the knife?" she reminded Jamie.

Jamie nodded. "Last month when I was home on spring break, this electrician came. He claimed that he needed to check some wiring, and he had some kind of ID from the electrical company that must have been convincing enough because Miss Diane let him in."

Diane McGrath was the current head housekeeper at the ranch, and while Dutton didn't have daily contact with the woman, this was the first he was hearing about an electrician.

"I wasn't home when this happened," Ike said, taking up the explanation. "I was at a meeting in San Antonio. And Asher and Kitty were away on one of their usual trips."

He grumbled *usual* as if it was a profanity. Which it sort of was, in this case. Jamie's parents were gone far more than they were home and rarely took their daughter with them on their travels to tropical adults-only resorts. There were times Dutton wondered why they had adopted a child only to leave her in the care of a nanny.

"Was there something about this electrician that was suspicious?" Grace asked, aiming the question at Jamie.

"Definitely suspicious," Jamie said quickly. "I mean, he did more looking at the stuff in the house than he did the outlets and such. I thought he was casing the place. I was about to call Uncle Ike so he could check and make sure this guy was for real, but he up and left."

"Did you get his name and confirm he was actually with the electric company? And do you believe he stole the knife?" Grace pressed.

Ike shook his head and grumbled something under his breath. "Diane doesn't remember the man's name. She said the ID looked real, though, and that she personally didn't follow him around to see where he went. She definitely didn't notice him going into my office. But he must have. He must have gone in and stolen it."

Grace stayed quiet a moment. "Alright, I'll contact the electric company and see if they sent anyone out."

"I'll do that," Rory volunteered. "Though there probably won't be anyone in their office for hours."

Grace muttered a thanks for Rory taking that chore, then turned back to Jamie. "Describe this man."

The girl's forehead bunched up as she continued to stroke a now purring Sherlock. "Reddish brown hair, but most of it was covered up by a cap. It had the electric company logo on it. I didn't get close enough to him to see the color of his eyes, but I think his beard might have been fake. It didn't look like it belonged on his face, if you know what I mean."

Jamie was certainly observant. And maybe overly suspicious as well. Since she'd said this had happened during her spring break, she might have been bored enough for her imagination to go way overboard. Dutton almost hoped that was the case because the alternative sickened him.

It meant the killer could have been in the house with Jamie.

Grace turned to Ike. "Is it possible your security system recorded the visit?" she asked.

Ike shook his head and looked at Dutton for the answer, but Jamie responded before he could. "Yes, but the feed records over itself after a week."

The sound Grace made indicated that was what she'd expected. "How tall was this man? And how was he built?" Grace continued.

"Shorter than Dutton and Rory." Jamie paused, obviously giving that more thought. "So maybe five-ten-ish. And he was on the skinny side." Her eyes brightened again. "Maybe I can work with a sketch artist."

"Possibly," Grace said. "But if he actually is or was an employee of the electric company, we should be able to get his name. Then, he can be brought in for questioning." And Grace would have another person of interest to add to her murder board.

"Questioning?" Ike said, using more of the irritated tone. "Like what you're doing to me right now. I didn't kill that woman," he stressed.

Grace drew in a long breath. "For the time being, I believe you," she stated, cutting off what would have no doubt been a continued tirade from him.

Dutton didn't know who was more surprised by Grace's comment, but he thought Ike won that particular prize. Still, he didn't seem willing to soften the hard look he was giving Grace.

"It's possible this is some kind of reverse psychology," she continued, ignoring Ike's expression. "But if you had committed this crime, I don't believe you would have used a knife that could be so easily traced back to you. And you wouldn't have left the bodies by the ranch. Everything points to someone setting you up. Or setting up someone in your family." She glanced at Rory and Jamie, and then Dutton.

Ike muttered something under his breath again. Probably a profanity that Dutton hoped Jamie hadn't heard. "Plenty of folks dislike me and my kin. But I see this going back to you." At the sound of the front door opening, they all turned and looked in that direction. "Or back to your kin," Ike snarled.

And Grace's mother, Aileen, came in.

Even though the woman was in her sixties now, she looked just as formidable as she did when she'd worn the badge, and she seemed to take in the entire room with her cop eyes. Eyes that were nearly identical to Grace's own. In fact, the two shared enough features that it was no mistaking they were related.

"Sorry for the interruption," Aileen said, settling her attention on her daughter. The apology seemed heartfelt. So was the look she gave Grace.

And Dutton.

Hell. What now?

Unlike many people in town, Aileen didn't seem to despise him simply because he was a McClennan. Though there wasn't exactly a warm, fuzzy feeling between them, either. Especially since he'd gotten Grace pregnant. But Dutton hadn't recalled Aileen ever giving him that sort of look. An apology mixed with something else.

Worry.

Aileen walked past Jamie and Ike, giving them a nod of greeting that conveyed zero warmth. Well, for Ike, anyway. Aileen's expression softened a little when she glanced at Jamie.

"I wouldn't have come if it weren't necessary," Aileen said to her daughter. "But someone sent me this." She held out her phone for Grace.

Grace took it and read what was on the screen. Dutton read it, too, and barely managed to bite off the profanity in front of Jamie.

"Your daughter and her lover will be dead soon," he read aloud.

"Unknown sender," Aileen explained. "Which means it'll likely be impossible to trace, but I figured you'd want to try."

Grace nodded, and while most people would have thought

she appeared composed, Dutton saw the nerves in the slight tightening of her mouth. "Yes, I definitely want to try. I'll have it sent to the tech guys at the lab."

Rory whipped out an evidence bag and took Aileen's phone to get that process started. Dutton wasn't an expert on such things, but he was the brother of a cop and figured that an unknown sender would cover his or her tracks well enough so it couldn't be traced. Still, Grace might get lucky.

"Why would the killer want to involve you in this?" Dutton asked Aileen.

Aileen lifted her shoulder, and he saw the nerves in her expression, too. "Maybe because it'll put Grace under more pressure. Because now she's probably wondering if the killer will try to use me in some way to make her suffer even more." She locked eyes with Grace. "I'm retired, but I'm not careless. I'm taking precautions just as I'm sure you're doing. You, too," she added to Dutton.

"Precautions will be taken," Grace assured her.

Her mother studied her. And sighed. "You're going back to your place. Alone."

Grace nodded.

"And you can't talk her out of it," Aileen said to Dutton.

"I can't," he verified.

Aileen sighed again. "Alright, you can both stay at my place if you want. You could consider it Switzerland. Neutral territory."

There was nothing neutral about it because it belonged to a woman who had a feud going on with his family. Added to that, Dutton wasn't sure Aileen's house would be any safer than Grace's. It probably had a security system, but it, too, was out in the country and far away from any backup.

"Thank you for the offer, but no," Grace said. "I won't let the killer run me out of my own home."

Aileen looked at him, maybe to see if she thought there was anything he could do to change Grace's mind. There wasn't. And the look he gave Aileen must have conveyed that because she didn't press.

"Alright," Aileen said on a sigh. "Let me know when I can get my phone back." She handed Grace a yellow sticky note she took from her pocket. "That's the number of the burner I'll be using in the meantime."

Aileen muttered a goodbye, but didn't hug Grace. Though it looked as if that's what she wanted to do. But Aileen probably felt like any show of affection like that wasn't appropriate for the workplace. She gave all of them one last look before she headed back out into the night.

"Am I free to go, too?" his father snarled at Grace. "Or do you need to pester me with more questions?"

"You're free to go," she said. "And I'll see about getting the sketch artist," she added to Jamie.

Jamie smiled as if this was some grand adventure, but the smile quickly faded. "You two are going to be careful, right?" Jamie asked Grace and him. "I mean, you're not going to like make yourselves bait or anything like that?"

"We aren't," Grace and he said in unison.

That relieved a little of the fresh worry on the girl's face, and she set down the cat after giving him one last cuddle. Unlike Aileen, Jamie went with some PDA, first hugging Dutton, then Rory.

Then Grace.

Dutton had to hand it to Grace. She didn't protest the gesture. She just went with it, and murmured, "Everything will be alright."

Of course, there was no way Grace could be sure. The killer didn't seem to be backing off, and that text to Aileen proved it.

"You need to be careful," Dutton told his father.

Ike opened his mouth as if to argue that but then closed it. Nodded. "You, too. I'll change the codes on the security system just in case that so-called electrician tries to get back in."

Dutton nodded in approval and then watched as his dad and Jamie headed out. He glanced at his brother, who was still on the phone, probably trying to get in touch with someone from the electric company. Then, Dutton turned to Grace to try once again to convince her to stay either with him or at her mother's. However, her landline rang before he had a chance to say a word.

"It's Dispatch," she muttered when she saw the blinking light on the base of the phone. She immediately went into her office to answer it.

And Dutton held his breath. Hell. He hoped there hadn't already been another murder. Rory must have thought that was a possibility, too, because he ended his call and joined Dutton in the office doorway.

"Sheriff Granger," she answered, and thankfully she put the call on speaker.

"You have a call from a Felicity Martinez," the dispatcher informed Grace. "She says she has information about the murder."

Grace looked up at Dutton and Rory to see if they recognized the name, but they both shook their heads. His brother and he also started searches on their phones.

"Put the call through," Grace instructed, and moments later, Dutton heard the woman come onto the line.

"Sheriff Granger," she said, and there was a tremble in her voice.

"Yes. How can I help you, Miss Martinez?" Grace asked.

"I, uh…" She stopped, and Dutton heard the woman's sob. "I've been seeing Brian Waterman."

Dutton had no trouble recalling who that was. Elaine's fiancé.

"Seeing?" Grace queried.

Another sob. "I've been having an affair with him. And, yes, I know he's engaged. He was up-front about that but said he couldn't break up with her, that it'd crush her parents if he didn't go through with it, that they would probably even fire him since he works for them."

Dutton figured that Grace had only scratched the surface of her research on Brian, and an affair might not have come out in the usual background checks.

"I'm the other woman," Felicity muttered. "I know it was wrong, but I'm in love with him. Was in love with him," she amended.

Grace jumped right on that. "Was? What happened to change your feelings about him?"

Felicity couldn't answer for a couple of seconds because she was sobbing more now. "Brian called me about an hour ago and said he needed for me to tell the cops that he was with me tonight. He said I was to say we're old friends and we were just catching up and that he was telling me all about his wonderful fiancée."

Grace's expression went hard. "Was Brian with you tonight?"

"No," Felicity said on another sob. "I haven't seen him in two weeks." She paused. "And then I heard on the news about the woman who was murdered. It was her, wasn't it? Brian's fiancée?"

Grace didn't answer those questions. "Where was Brian when he called you?"

"He wouldn't say, but I assumed he was at his house in

San Antonio. I'm in Austin, and it's not storming here, but I could hear thundering in the background when I was talking to him."

Or the man could have been in Renegade Canyon, since San Antonio was less than an hour away.

"Has Brian been to El Paso any time over the past week?" Grace asked, obviously following up on what the man had told the police.

"No. Not that I know of." She stopped, and Dutton could hear her trying to slow down her breathing. She failed. "And he wouldn't explain why he needed me to lie to the cops." Felicity broke down again. "Sheriff Granger, I just have to know. Did Brian murder his fiancée?"

Chapter Five

Did Brian murder his fiancée?

That was the question that kept repeating through Grace's head. Too bad she didn't have an answer, but she hoped to remedy that soon.

First, though, she had to locate Brian, and so far she wasn't having any luck. He hadn't responded to a knock on the door when officers from San Antonio PD had gone to his house. So Grace had left messages for him not only on his personal phone, but also with his employer. If she didn't hear from the man soon, she would need to issue an APB. With Brian's alibi in question and asking his lover to lie for him, Grace had grounds to force him to come in for questioning.

The second thing going through her mind was Dutton. Even when the man was out of sight, it was hard to keep her thoughts off him. It was impossible now that he was following her in his truck.

She had no doubts—none—that he'd stick to his "threat" of sleeping outside her house. Sadly, part of her actually welcomed that for the sake of their baby's safety, but she also didn't want Dutton sitting in his vehicle if the killer just decided to gun him down. She doubted he'd agree to sleep in the bullet-resistant cruiser, either.

And that left Grace with a huge dilemma.

She could back down on her insistence that he not stay with her. Or she could just accept it for what was left of this night. Then, after a few hours of sleep, she might be able to work out a better arrangement.

She turned onto the road that led to her place, and while she was always aware of her surroundings, she was more so right now. The rain had stopped, but there were still plenty of clouds to block out the moon, making it pitch-black. The headlights of her cruiser created some spooky-looking shadows as she drove past the trees and shrubs that lined the road. She hoped one of those shadows wasn't the killer, but she had to be prepared just in case.

The house came into view, and she used the voice command on her phone app to turn on not only the porch lights, but also the ones on both floors of her house. Gone was the absolute darkness, but not the shadows, and she slowed, looking for any signs of an attack.

Nothing.

Since the house was well over a hundred years old, there was no garage, but she pulled beneath the covered part of her driveway that was only steps away from the door that led into the kitchen. Of course, Dutton pulled in right behind her, and he was darn fast at getting out of his truck.

"I want to check the house," he insisted. "To make sure no one got in."

She didn't remind him that she had a security system that would have alerted her to an intruder. That's because Grace knew systems could be hacked.

So far, the killer hadn't used something like that to get to the victims. There'd been no break-ins at either woman's residence. Instead, they'd likely been snatched shortly after leaving work and incapacitated in some way. In the case of the first murder, that had been with a stun gun, and Grace was betting the same had happened to Deputy Elaine Sneed.

And that brought her to a big question.

How had the killer gotten so close to two cops to use a stun gun on them? If Brian was indeed responsible, then getting close to Elaine wouldn't have been a problem since they were engaged. But what about the first cop? Grace needed to look for a possible connection there. First, though, she had to do some looking around her house.

Again, using the app, she unlocked her kitchen door and moved quickly inside. Dutton was right behind her, and it didn't surprise her when he drew a gun from the back waist of his jeans. He had a permit to carry a concealed weapon and Grace knew he wouldn't hesitate to use the weapon to protect her. Even if she was capable of protecting herself.

She drew her own gun, and without speaking, they started the room-to-room search. First, the bottom floor. The kitchen, then the living area, her office and the small bathroom that she'd had added after she'd moved in a decade earlier.

Dutton made it to the stairs a split second ahead of her, which meant she ended up following him. Something she didn't care for on several levels. First, she didn't want him in the lead here, and second, she didn't appreciate the view she had of his rather superior backside.

Well, she actually did appreciate it.

Her body did, anyway. But it was a reminder and a distraction she didn't need. It didn't help that the rest of his body fell into that superior category as well, and once again, she silently cursed this need for him that just wouldn't go away.

They searched the three upstairs bedrooms, including the empty one she'd had cleared out for the nursery. Soon, it would be painted a pale yellow, since Grace hadn't planned on learning the gender of the baby before delivery. Some considered that an old-fashioned notion, but she was trying to savor every moment of this pregnancy since it would likely be her one and only.

And it was somewhat of a miracle.

Over the years, doctors had told her it would be hard for her to conceive because of irregular ovulation, but Grace had figured she would still try if she fell in love and married. That hadn't happened, and now with her thirty-eighth birthday on the horizon, she had all but given up on the possibility of motherhood.

That one night with Dutton had changed everything.

And Grace was fighting to hold on to some kind of control and normalcy in her life. This murder investigation and the close contact with Dutton weren't going to help with that. But somehow, she had to keep her feelings for him at bay. If not, they could both pay a very high price by giving the killer a window to get to them.

After finishing the room search, he went to the top of the stairs and frowned when he looked out the massive window over the front door. Dutton quickly switched off the lights. Grace didn't have to ask why. Usually, that window gave her an amazing view of the pastures and the six horses she owned. But now, she was very much aware that it would give the killer a clear line of sight of her whenever she went up or down the stairs.

"Is anything out of place?" Dutton asked, drawing her attention back to him. Not that it'd strayed too far. "Any sense that anyone has been in here?"

"No." And that was the truth. Still, her nerves were far from being steady. "I can keep the lights off up here on the stairwell and in the hall. Or I can sleep downstairs. My office has a pullout sofa."

Still frowning, Dutton turned to her. "You've dug in your heels about me not staying here with you?"

She nodded, though Grace had to admit her heels didn't feel as firmly dug in as they had earlier. That wasn't just for her sake, either. Or the baby's. "You've dug in your heels about keeping watch of the place?"

His nod was a lot firmer than hers had been.

Grace sighed. "Then will you at least stay in the cruiser?"

The corners of his mouth lifted in a smile that made his face even hotter than usual. "Yes." Their gazes connected and held for a few moments before the smile faded. "And will you stay away from the windows?"

She made a sound of agreement. No security system would prevent someone from shooting through the glass. And that brought her right back to Dutton. The windows of the cruiser were bullet-resistant, but that didn't mean it was a safe place to spend the night. Grace was about to press him once again to return home to his ranch when she saw the movement out the large window.

"Hell," Dutton muttered, and he'd obviously seen it, too.

A woman wearing a billowing white dress was staggering through the darkness toward Grace's house. Once again, Dutton beat her to the punch and hurried down the stairs ahead of her. She was about to warn him not to open the door, but that wasn't necessary. Dutton slapped off the lights in the entry and went to the front window instead. He kept to the side and peered out.

She turned off some lights, too, on her way to the window to join him, but she kept the porch light on so they'd be able to see if the approaching woman was armed. Grace took up position on the opposite side of the window from Dutton, and both of them kept their guns drawn and ready.

"She's got blood on her dress," Dutton muttered.

Grace could see that. Not a lot of it, but there were streaks running down the sides of her dress.

"But I don't know who she is. Do you?" he asked.

"No." The woman with the long, dark brown hair, a lanky body and an ashen face was a stranger.

Grace felt that punch of dread that went well beyond just worry and concern. Was this another potential victim who'd managed to escape?

Or was this a trap?

The woman truly did appear to be injured, but that could all be a facade meant to draw them out. In fact, this could be the killer, someone who hadn't even been a suspect in the investigation.

"Help me," Grace heard the woman yell as she neared the house.

"Don't open the door yet," Grace instructed Dutton, even though he didn't look anywhere ready to do that. No doubt because he, too, was concerned this might be some kind of ploy to kill them.

Grace took out her phone to call for both backup and an ambulance. If the woman was truly hurt, then she would need help. And if she was the killer, then Grace wanted at least one of her deputies here to assist with the takedown and the arrest. Also, in case this turned into a full-fledged attack.

They watched as the woman made it to the porch steps. She didn't look in the window, where she might have spotted Dutton and Grace. Her eyes seemed unfocused, but her attention remained on the door.

She didn't make it.

The woman stumbled and fell face-first onto the porch. Her head hit hard, loud enough for the sound of the thud to carry into the house, and she didn't move. She just lay there, sprawled out over the steps.

"Backup and the ambulance are ten minutes out," Grace reported when she got the text of the update. Considering she lived six miles out of town and on a rural road, that was fast.

But maybe not fast enough.

Grace felt an overwhelming sense of dread as she stood there and saw the blood begin to pool around the woman's head. "I have to go out there," she said.

"I'll go," Dutton quickly volunteered. "I can carry her inside—"

She was shaking her head before he finished. "And while you're carrying her, you wouldn't be able to return fire if someone tries to kill you. There's a real possibility of that," she added. "The killer could have drugged the woman and pointed her here toward my house just to get us to open the door."

In a perfect scenario, Grace would be able to handle this on her own. But this wasn't perfect. She couldn't lift the woman by herself. So she either had to wait the fifteen minutes for the ambulance and backup...

Or she had to accept Dutton's help.

She glanced at the bleeding, unconscious woman again and knew what she had to do. "Please feel free to say no to any part of this rescue plan," she stated.

"Depends on the plan," he replied right back. "If it involves putting the baby at risk, then the plan isn't going to happen."

Grace figured he'd said "the baby" instead of "you" on purpose, to remind her of just how dangerous this could be. "I can't make this risk-free," she argued. She tapped her badge. "But I can't stand by and not offer someone assistance when she could be out there dying."

Dutton stared at her. And then he cursed. His groan told her what she already knew. Even without a badge, Dutton would help someone in need, and at the moment, the need was there. If it turned out the woman was the killer, then an arrest could put an end to the danger. No more female cops would die, and she and Dutton could get back to their normal lives.

Well, as normal as things could be for them, anyway.

"We need to do this fast," Grace said, hoping that by spelling it out, she would figure out a way to make this safer for both of them. "We both stay down and go out on the porch. We'll check to make sure she isn't armed. If she is, I disarm her. If she isn't, you can bring her inside while I cover you."

She could tell Dutton wasn't a fan of what she was proposing, but he nodded. "Any chance you have a Kevlar vest around you can use?"

"There's one in the trunk of the cruiser." Which meant trying to get it was out of the question since it would mean going outside to retrieve it. It would be faster just to rescue the woman.

Dutton cursed again and met her gaze head-on for a couple of seconds before he headed toward the door. "Stay down, and on the count of three…"

Grace nodded and temporarily disarmed her security system while she went to the door. Dutton didn't hesitate on doing the countdown. Nor did he wait once he'd reached three. He unlocked the door and threw it open.

The night air rushed in. It was damp and earthy from the storm. But there was also the smell of blood. Grace prayed the woman wasn't already dead. Even if she was the killer, Grace wanted her alive so she could answer so many questions.

Grace glanced around the yard and the road. No sign of anyone. Of course, that didn't mean someone wasn't there, waiting to try to get the best shot possible at Dutton and her.

Together, they rushed onto the porch, and both of them kept watch while Dutton frisked the woman as best he could. "I can't find a weapon," he said, scooping her up into his arms.

The woman moaned, the sound of someone in pain. Or perhaps someone pretending to be. But one thing was for certain—the blood was real. So was the injury on her head, probably from where she'd fallen.

Moving the woman was risky. However, staying put was riskier. If the murderer was indeed out there, the woman could be killed.

"In the house," Dutton insisted, firing a quick glance at Grace.

But Grace held her ground and waited so she could continue to cover him until he was inside. Grace's lungs were aching, but she finally released the breath she'd been holding once she was in the foyer and had locked the door.

"Search her again for weapons," she instructed once Dutton had laid the woman on the floor. Grace watched him do that while she rearmed the security system.

Dutton patted her down, and then Grace repeated the procedure once she'd put away her phone. Not just a pat-down, but she also checked to see the source of the bleeding. The woman wasn't armed. And those injuries were very much real. Not just the fresh one on her head, but now that Grace had gotten a closer look, she could see the cuts in the fabric on the front of the woman's dress.

She'd been stabbed.

Grace handed Dutton her phone. "Check on the status of the ambulance." Now that her hands were free, she balled up the front of the woman's dress and used it to apply pressure to the wounds. There were at least two cuts, maybe more. It didn't appear she was on the verge of bleeding out, but there could be serious or even fatal internal injuries.

Beside her, Dutton called Dispatch, and he'd just gotten through when a crashing sound tore through the house. Breaking glass.

Mercy. The noise caused Grace's heart to drop to her knees. What had happened? It sounded like a window had been broken, which meant that someone could be trying to break in.

Before Grace could try to pinpoint the location of the sound, the alarm kicked on. Not a warning beep, either. This was a full-blown blaring that drowned out all other sounds.

And then, Grace caught a whiff of something in the air.

A whiff that caused her eyes and throat to burn like fire. She couldn't breathe, and her instinct was to run. She didn't. Instead, she somehow managed to take her phone from Dutton and disable the alarm. A necessity to be able to hear someone approaching.

"Pepper spray," Dutton said, and he began to cough. So did Grace, and the woman on the floor was gasping for air as well.

Yes, this was most likely pepper spray, and while Grace had never been personally exposed to it, she had gone through training on how to deal with it. The spray hadn't actually come in contact with their skin, but it was obviously airborne, which meant it had likely been tossed or shot through the window.

It was next to impossible for Grace to see with her eyes watering and burning, but she tried to think of what to do. Opening the door would allow in some fresh air. It could also allow the killer easy access.

"The bathroom," she blurted in between the coughs that were robbing her of every bit of her breath.

The door to that particular room was closed, and while it didn't have an exterior window, it did have a shower, and right now, she thought that was their best bet in washing the pepper spray from their eyes.

Despite the coughing, Dutton managed to pick up the woman, and they stumbled their way to the bathroom. They got inside as fast as they could and locked the door.

Grace tried to drag in as much of the fresh air as she could while groping toward the shower. She tried not to think of what this might be doing to her baby. Or if the killer was about to break down the door and come after them. She just focused on turning on the shower.

Dutton lay the woman on the floor and shoved the bath mat against the bottom of the door to stop the pepper spray from seeping in. He also wet the hand towel in the sink and placed it over the woman's eyes.

Grace dropped her phone and her gun on the closed toilet lid, where they would hopefully be easy to reach if someone did try to knock down the door, and she stepped into the shower. Dutton didn't follow her, maybe because he wanted to be able to hold on to his gun. Instead, he ducked his head beneath the running faucet in the sink. Hopefully, they'd be able to get their vision cleared before the killer could come after them.

Well, maybe that was the killer's plan.

Grace didn't know if that was it, or if this wounded woman somehow played into things. She hoped she got the chance to find out before any more damage was done.

She kept her eyes closed but held her face up to the spray of water. Within seconds, Grace felt some relief, though her eyes weren't anywhere near normal just yet. So she stayed under the water, blinking hard, trying to wash away the burning sensations caused by the pepper spray.

Outside, Grace heard the welcome sound of sirens, and she prayed the EMTs and her deputies weren't walking into a trap. Dutton must have considered the same thing because he came out from beneath the running water long enough to call Dispatch.

"This is Dutton McClennan," he said. "Alert the responders to the sheriff's house that there could be an attacker lying in wait."

Grace immediately had a sickening thought. She had two female deputies, and if one of them was a responder, then she could be the target. This could have all been set up to kill another cop.

She came out of the shower, the water still sliding down her face and the rest of her. She was soaked to the bone, but she took her phone from Dutton and ended the call with the dispatcher, then called Rory, since she knew he was on duty and would no doubt be in the cruiser that was approaching her house.

"What happened?" Rory asked the moment he was on the line, and Grace put the call on speaker so Dutton could hear what was being said.

"An injured woman came to the house, and then someone fired pepper spray through the window," Grace explained. "Who's with you?" she quickly asked.

Rory was equally quick with his answer. "Livvy."

Grace groaned. No. Not this. Not one of her own. "Livvy stays in the cruiser, understand?"

"No—" Rory began, but then he stopped. "Livvy's the target?"

"Possibly. Is anyone else responding?"

"Judson and Bennie," he said, referring to Deputies Judson Docherty and Bennie Whitt.

Grace's next breath was one of relief. Until she considered something else. "Call Eden and make sure she's okay."

Rory cursed, and the alarm deepened in his voice. With good reason. Deputy Eden Gallagher was Rory's ex, and she was also the mother of his son. And Eden could be the target, not Livvy or her. The best way to torture and punish Grace would be to go after one of her people.

Grace ended the call with Rory so he could contact Eden, and while she waited, she looked at Dutton. His eyes were red and his skin was flushed, but he seemed to be able to focus. He also had his gun drawn and was keeping watch of the door. Grace picked up her gun and did the same while she also checked on the woman.

Still alive, but there was a lot of blood on her dress.

"Sheriff Granger?" someone called out. It was Judson, which meant Bennie was close behind.

"Here," she answered.

She heard both the deputies coughing, no doubt reacting to the still lingering pepper spray, and a moment later there was a knock at the bathroom door. Dutton opened it, slowly and cautiously. Maybe because he thought there was a possibility the killer had taken the deputies hostage.

Thankfully, that hadn't happened, and the moment Dutton had the door fully open, she saw Judson do a sweeping glance around the bathroom while Bennie kept watch behind him.

"Are you all okay?" Judson asked.

No. Grace was far from okay, but she nodded, anyway. She wasn't injured, but there was still the fear of the effects this was having on the baby. The fear, too, that this attack wasn't over.

"The ambulance just arrived," Judson explained. "I'll get the EMTs in here." He fired off a quick text to do that, and then he looked at Grace. It was the kind of look that told her something else was wrong.

"What is it?" she asked. "What happened?" And she forced herself to tamp down the worst-case scenarios flying through her head.

"There's a note on the front door," Judson explained, and then he paused. "I think it's written in blood."

Chapter Six

Look how easy it is to get to you, Grace. This was a trial run. Next time, it'll be the real thing.

Dutton had an image of the note fixed in his head. The note that had been taped to the front door, right here at Grace's house. And Judson had indeed been right.

It'd been written in blood.

Whose blood was still to be determined, but it'd been sent to the lab for analysis. Dutton assumed it belonged to the injured woman who had collapsed on Grace's porch. A woman who, the last he heard, was clinging to life.

All of that—the pepper-spray attack, the injured woman, the threatening note, the other two dead cops—hadn't allowed him to get much sleep. Then again, he hadn't expected to get much sleep, anyway.

Not since he was staying under the same roof with Grace.

They weren't at her house, though, since it would need to be processed as a crime scene as well as have the window replaced. That's why they had ended up at Rory's house with Grace and Dutton in guestrooms directly across from each other. And sharing a bathroom. His body hadn't let him forget that.

At least the pepper spray hadn't harmed the baby. Grace and he knew that because she'd gone to the hospital shortly after the attack and had a checkup along with an ultrasound. All was well with their child. In the grand scheme of things, that was a top priority, and now Dutton had to figure out how to keep them safe when Grace was trying to do the same to him.

He checked the time—almost seven, which meant he'd been taking catnaps on and off for the past four hours. Maybe Grace was faring better across the hall, and that's why Dutton stayed as quiet as possible when he made his way to the bathroom. He took a quick shower and changed into the clean clothes that he'd had one of his ranch hands bring over shortly after they'd arrived at Rory's. Dutton was still zipping up his jeans as he came out of the bathroom.

And ran right into Grace.

Thankfully, not a hard slam, but there was body-to-body contact. Contact he was even more aware of since he hadn't buttoned his shirt. She'd put up her hand on impact, and it landed against his bare chest.

"Sorry," she said and stepped back as if he'd scalded her.

Dutton instantly felt the loss of the contact. Probably because he'd instantly felt it in every inch of his body. Not good. He didn't need this physical ache for her playing into, well, anything. Still, the ache came, anyway. So did the worry. Along with still managing to look amazing, the fatigue was there in her eyes.

"I was hoping you'd sleep in," he said.

She shook her head. "The baby's kicking."

That shifted his focus, and he wanted to put his hand on her stomach, wanted to feel those kicks. He didn't, though. And Grace didn't invite him to do it, so he stepped out of the bathroom to let her enter.

"Rory's in the kitchen," she informed him. "There have been a few updates, and he can fill you in."

Since Dutton very much wanted to hear any updates, he finished dressing, put on his boots, holstered his gun and made his way downstairs.

Unlike Grace's house, his brother's was only a few years old, and it had that new, modern feel to it. It was also closer to town, even though it was still out in the country, and like Dutton and the rest of the McClennans, Rory kept up the family tradition of raising horses. Rory had obviously shucked another tradition, though, by becoming a cop.

Dutton spotted two palominos out the side window that faced the pasture. He also spotted plenty of toys and a mesh playpen, a reminder that Rory was the father of a baby boy, Tyler, who wasn't quite one year old. Rory and the baby's mother, Eden, were estranged, but apparently they were managing to co-parent. Dutton was hoping Grace and he would be able to manage the same.

He followed the scent of coffee and found Rory in the kitchen, scrambling some eggs and frying some bacon. Rory took one look at Dutton and poured him a huge cup of the coffee. "Good thing you take it black because I'm out of sugar and milk."

"Thanks," Dutton said and took a sip. It was too hot, but he needed the caffeine hit. Needed to say something to his brother as well. "Thanks for letting us stay here last night."

His brother shrugged. "Anytime." He studied Dutton from over the rim of his own mug. "But I'm guessing you would have preferred to take Grace to your place at the ranch?"

Dutton made a sound of agreement. "This was a good compromise."

Rory's home had a security system along with a reserve deputy sitting in a cruiser out front. Dutton figured the killer wasn't bold enough to try to tape any notes written in blood on Rory's door with a cop watching and two more cops inside.

"Grace said you have some updates," Dutton prompted while he continued to gulp more coffee.

"Lots," Rory acknowledged. Some toast popped up from the toaster, and he put the two slices on a plate and set them on the counter next to Dutton. "The injured woman has been identified as Georgia Tate. She's in critical condition and unconscious so we haven't been able to question her."

"How'd you get an ID so fast?" Dutton asked while he ate some toast. He wasn't hungry, but his body needed fuel, and that was probably why his brother added some of the eggs and bacon to the plate. "Did she have a police record?"

"No, her sister filed a missing-person report on her. Georgia works in San Antonio, but she shares a house with her sister about ten miles from here, in Comanche Creek. She's employed as a cocktail waitress, and when she didn't come home after work, her sister filed the report. Good thing, too. Since there's no minimum period for filing a report in Texas, it helped us make a quick ID."

Dutton took a moment to process that. "Does Georgia have any obvious connection to Renegade Canyon or to Grace?"

"None that we've found so far, but Eden's working on it."

At the mention of the deputy's name, Dutton had to ask. "Are Eden and Tyler alright?"

A muscle flickered in Rory's jaw. "They're safe. Eden wouldn't stay here," he added. "But Livvy is at her place, and they have a reserve deputy outside in a cruiser as well."

Good. Livvy was a solid deputy. And possibly a target, too, since she was female. This way, Eden and Livvy could look after each other. But Dutton totally understood his brother's tight-jawed reaction. Rory would have preferred having his ex and son with him.

"A rep for the electric company came in early to check their records," Rory continued a moment later, obviously returning to the updates. "And they didn't send anyone to the ranch."

So that was bogus, which could mean a couple of things. Either the person was the actual killer, and the ploy was to steal the knife. Or the killer could have hired someone to go in. Either was possible, but it still didn't make sense to Dutton that the killer would use Ike's knife.

"Yeah," Rory said, and he was watching Dutton. "You're trying to work out what's going on with that knife. Maybe the killer didn't think Dad would have alibis?"

Dutton nodded. "Or else this is a way of creating bad publicity. Some stress, too. Because now the ranch and the family are part of the investigation."

Which pointed right back to Grace and him being the primary targets. It was possible the other murders had simply been meant to create more of that stress Dutton had just mentioned. But there was another possibility.

"What about the lying, cheating fiancé, Brian Waterman?" Dutton asked. "Any sign of him yet?"

"None, but there's an APB out on him now."

That was the right call because it was possible Brian was the person killing the female cops. Maybe all in an effort to cover up the murder of his own fiancée and to take the focus off him. But as far as Dutton was concerned, the focus was there, especially since Brian had seemingly dropped off the radar.

Dutton turned at the sound of footsteps, and as expected, Grace came in. Somehow, she'd managed to make herself look rested and ready for work. If he didn't look her straight in the eyes, that is. But he did, and saw the fatigue and the pressure this investigation had caused. Yet even that didn't lessen the reminder that she was a beautiful woman, and once again, he felt that usual kick of heat.

"Can your stomach handle some food?" Rory asked, fortunately interrupting the fantasy that Dutton was starting to spin about Grace.

She nodded. "Thankfully, the morning sickness passed a few weeks ago."

Dutton had known about the morning sickness, and he'd wished it was an ailment he could have taken on for her. Grace was bearing a lot of the downsides from this pregnancy. Then again, she was also getting the upside of feeling those kicks.

Rory dished her up a plate of the eggs, bacon and toast, but instead of coffee, she had a glass of water. Dutton wasn't sure how she managed to get through a morning without coffee, another downside to being pregnant.

"Thanks," she told Rory, and she sat at the counter to eat. "I just got an update from the CSIs," she said, tipping her head to her phone, which she set next to her plate. "There were no prints on the pepper-spray canister that was shot through the kitchen window. They believe it was probably launched with something like a paintball gun."

Dutton shook his head. "I didn't know that was possible."

"Neither did I," Grace admitted. "But this means almost anyone could have obtained a paintball gun and fired the shot. And apparently the shooter didn't even have to be that accurate, since there was a second canister that must have missed the window because the CSIs found it on the ground. It hit the side of the house."

So not a marksman. Well, maybe not. A lot of things could cause a person to miss a single shot. The other one had certainly been effective enough in getting them to take cover in the bathroom, which had likely been when their attacker had put that bloody note on the door.

"How about the note itself?" Dutton asked. "Anything on that yet?"

She nodded. "It's Elaine Sneed's blood."

Dutton silently cursed. What a sick SOB to hold on to one of the victim's blood to use it to write a message to Grace. This wasn't exactly breakfast conversation, but Grace continued with both the explanation and her breakfast.

"The paper is from a standard notebook you can buy anywhere, and the handwriting likely won't be able to be analyzed because it's smeared block lettering. Still, they'll send it to the lab."

"What about the tape?" Dutton asked. "Were there any fibers or prints on it? Any way to trace it to the source? And there must have been footprints or tire tracks somewhere because the ground was muddy."

Grace looked at him, lifted an eyebrow. "Have I told you before that you can sometimes sound like a cop?" Her mouth quivered in what might have been a suppressed smile.

Since this was probably as light of a moment as Grace and he were likely to have for a while, Dutton made a show of being insulted. "A momentary lapse." And he did smile. But as expected, it was short-lived.

Grace sighed. "No fibers or prints on the tape, and like the paper, it's the stuff you can buy pretty much anywhere." She sipped some water before she went on. "No tire tracks, which means the person either parked on the road or a trail and then walked to the house."

Dutton was going with option two. There were plenty of trails threading off the roads and into the woods, and even some of the pastures. Since these murders had started a month ago, that would have given the killer time to case Grace's house and property and know where to park in order to remain out of sight.

"There are some footprints," Grace confirmed, "but the person dragged their feet, no doubt to obscure them. It worked," she added in a disappointed mutter.

This was more proof they were dealing with someone who'd planned this to a *T*. And it'd worked. Well, maybe it had if the goal had been to terrorize them and put that note on the door. But if the killer had hoped to get into the house and go after them directly, then that had failed.

"Eden and I are digging into Georgia's background," Rory volunteered. "If we find out how and why she was taken, we might be able to figure out the who."

Grace made a sound of agreement. "Her doctor is supposed to contact us the moment she wakes up."

None of them voiced the worst-case scenario here. That Georgia might never wake up. That she could die from her injuries. If so, that would be three deaths, which would make the snake after them a serial killer.

"Any indications that Georgia was ever a cop or was maybe married to one?" Grace asked Rory.

Rory shook his head. "The best I could find was her brother-in-law was once a security specialist in the military."

Grace made another of those disappointed sighs, and Dutton decided he'd get his PI to do some digging on Georgia as well. It was possible the attack against her had been random, but there could be a reason the killer had chosen her. But then something occurred to Dutton.

Something that had him making one of those disappointed sighs.

"Georgia is alive," Dutton stated. "Yes, she was barely

conscious when she made it to the house, but she had the chance to say something to help rat out the killer. She didn't."

Grace obviously knew where he was going with this. "So the killer probably concealed his or her identity. We might still be able to get something from Georgia, though. Height, weight, that sort of thing." But she didn't sound especially hopeful about that.

Dutton had to agree. Georgia had likely been drugged or stunned before she'd been taken, and then stabbed. He was still considering that when the sound of Grace's phone ringing shot through the room.

"It's Livvy," she told them, then she answered the call on speaker.

"Eden and I are at the station," Livvy immediately said. "And we have Tyler and his nanny here in the break room," she added, no doubt for Rory's benefit. "But someone just walked in and demanded to see you."

"Who?" Grace asked.

"Brian Waterman," Livvy replied. "And judging from his appearance, he's got a story to tell."

Grace was already getting to her feet. "What about his appearance?"

"There's blood all over the front of his shirt and on his hands," Livvy explained. "Lots and lots of blood."

Chapter Seven

With Rory in a second cruiser right behind her, Grace pulled into the parking lot of the police station. The reserve deputy was no longer with them and wouldn't return until night if needed.

Grace was very much hoping that it wouldn't be needed.

But she steeled herself for that possibility, just in case.

She silently sighed because she'd already spent the last ten hours of her life in steeling-herself mode. First, for having Dutton so close to her at every waking moment—as he was at this very moment. Then, for dealing with the aftermath of the attack and murders. But now, the bracing herself and mental prep was for the man she was about to question.

Brian Waterman.

After Livvy had called to tell her that Brian had arrived at the police station, and that he was covered in blood, Grace hadn't pressed for any details other than to make sure Brian hadn't needed medical attention. Livvy had informed her that he had refused and had insisted on talking to her. Now that talk was about to happen, and it was possible she'd soon be making an arrest for the murders.

If Brian was here to confess, that is.

Grace hoped that was the reason for this impromptu visit and that his confession would explain why he had the blood on his clothes and hands. Maybe the explanation would include a lot of things, so it would put an end to the danger and this investigation. Then, there'd be a lot less *steeling up* required. For the threat of more murders.

For Dutton being around her.

Since threats included him, though, Grace intended to keep him in this pseudoprotective custody until the danger had passed. Of course, he was likely thinking the same thing about her. She knew he wanted her close so he could protect the baby and her, and at the moment, Grace had no intention of trying to talk him out of that.

"You could deputize me," Dutton said out of the blue.

She'd already reached for the handle of the cruiser door, but that stopped her. And for some reason, it made her smile. "Despite what I said about you sounding like a cop, you're not really cop material."

He smiled as well, causing dimples to flash in his cheeks. Yes, dimples. And somehow, they only managed to make that hot face of his even hotter. "True, but I could be in on the interviews if I had a badge. I could play bad cop and maybe get Brian to own up to the murders."

"I play bad cop." Or rather she had often taken on the tougher role in interviews before she'd gotten pregnant. The baby bump, though, had reduced any menacing presence she could bring into the room. "And I can't let you in interview. Everything I do has to hold up in case this goes to trial."

Dutton sighed, then nodded. And she saw the frustration in both actions. Frustration she understood because he wanted a quick end to this.

"I can let you observe," she conceded. "I can justify that by putting in my report that I wanted you to listen for anything that would connect you to the victims. Something that could explain why you were named as a target in the threatening note left on Elaine Sneed's body."

He nodded, accepting the compromise, and they got out of the cruiser and entered the building through the side entrance that led directly into her office. Rory was right behind them and went straight to his desk, where he no doubt had plenty of work waiting for him.

Grace immediately glanced around the bullpen and saw Livvy already making her way toward her. No sign of Brian, but Jamie, Eden and a woman whom Grace assumed was the sketch artist were huddled together around Eden's desk.

Jamie spotted them, too, and the girl gave a perky wave and smiled. Grace attempted a friendlier expression as well, but was sure she failed big-time. That's because of the somber look on Livvy's face.

"Where's Brian?" Grace asked the moment Livvy stepped into the office, and Grace noticed that the deputy looked both tired and wired. A common combination when an investigation was heating up.

"Interview room *A*," Livvy answered. "I stashed him there when I saw Jamie coming in to work with the sketch artist. I figured the kid didn't need to see someone in that state."

That was a good call. Jamie seemed much older than her years, but she was still just a child. A child who'd hopefully be able to give them a good enough likeness that they could use to identify the killer. If the sketch matched Brian, then that was even more evidence they'd have for an arrest.

"Brian refused medical treatment when I offered it again," Livvy went on, "but once I had him in the interview room and had read him his rights, he decided to do a little talking after all. He claimed he blacked out after drinking too much, and he woke up in a ditch. He let me take samples of the blood on his clothes, so I'm guessing it's actually his."

Dutton muttered some profanity, and Grace knew it was from disappointment. She was feeling it, too, because Livvy was right. Brian likely wouldn't have offered the sample if it had the potential to incriminate him.

The same could be said of his showing up at the police station like this. Then again, he might have done that to try to convince them that he'd been too drunk to kill his fiancée. It'd take more than that, though, to convince Grace of it.

"Observation," Grace reminded Dutton. "Livvy, you're with me in interview." And Grace was about to head that way when the front door opened, and Ike came in.

Her first instinct was to groan, that he was there to give her some grief, but then she realized he had come for Jamie. He made a beeline to the girl, and when he saw she was still working with the sketch artist, Ike turned his attention to Dutton and her.

"I need to tell you something," Ike said, aiming his statement at Grace.

So he might just dole out that grief after all.

Ike had his usual stony expression as he made his way toward them, but as he got closer, some of that look eased away. Grace thought he seemed almost hesitant. She was probably wrong about that, though. Ike McClennan wasn't the hesitating sort.

"I thought of something," he said, dodging Dutton's gaze and fixing his attention on Grace. "It's probably not important. But Cassie came to the ranch about two months ago."

Of all the things Grace had expected him to say, that wasn't one of them. And she latched right on to the timing. Two months ago was when her pregnancy had become public knowledge.

"What'd she want?" Dutton quickly asked.

"She wanted me to help her get back together with you,"

Ike admitted after a long pause, and he kept his voice at a whisper.

Dutton groaned and scrubbed his hand over his face. "I broke things off with Cassie a year ago," he said, and then he paused as well. And added some under-the-breath profanity. "Cassie was riled about me getting Grace pregnant."

Ike nodded. "Though riled is putting it mildly." He shifted his gaze to Dutton. "She was spitting mad and thought Grace had tricked you. She said it would ruin you financially if you two got together."

"We aren't together," Grace muttered just as Dutton insisted, "No trickery involved."

Dutton opened his mouth to say more but then stopped. Maybe because he was about to say the culprit was lust or something along those lines. Yes, best not to spell that out loud, especially since the lust was still lingering around.

"So what did she expect you to do to help her get back together with Dutton?" Grace asked Ike.

"She was short on specifics and long on ranting." Ike shook his head. "I think she just wanted to vent. She went on about how she'd always wanted kids and that Dutton didn't and that's why they broke up."

Dutton's next groan was laced with frustration. "I didn't want kids with her," he said and then sort of froze. Maybe because it sounded as if he didn't mind Grace being the mother of his child.

But Grace understood what he meant. She'd wanted kids, too, but she'd never found the right relationship for it. Then, when she'd gotten pregnant, she realized she could have the baby with no relationship commitment. Well, there was the whole co-parenting side, but that didn't mean she and Dutton had to be a couple.

"The reason I'm telling you all of this," Ike went on, "is because I'm thinking the knife could have been taken then."

Grace's heart rate revved up. "What do you mean?"

Ike huffed. "I mean Cassie could have taken it. We had the meeting in my office, and I had to step out for a couple of minutes to take an important call. When I came back in, Cassie was acting funny. Nervous and rattled, and she said a quick goodbye and hurried off."

"But you can't say for sure she took the knife," Grace concluded. It wasn't a question.

"No," Ike responded. "But she went from ranting to acting strange all within a matter of a couple of minutes. It's possible she took the knife, figuring she could use it somehow to get back at Dutton and you."

Grace played that all through. And felt a new wave of dread wash over her. Two months ago could have possibly been when the killer was plotting the murders. Of course, the plans could have happened well before that. And it didn't mean Cassie was the one doing the planning, or that she'd even been the one to take the knife, but Dutton's ex had to be questioned.

Feeling even more of that dread, she took out her phone and called Cassie's office. Almost immediately, Cassie's PA answered to say that Cassie wasn't in yet, so Grace left a message for the woman to come into the police station for a chat.

If Cassie didn't show soon, Grace would get the number for the woman's personal phone and try to contact her that way. She didn't think the woman was any kind of flight risk, so she wouldn't go full throttle on this now, especially since there was no proof that Cassie had taken the knife, only that she'd had the opportunity to do so.

"Thank you for letting me know," Grace told Ike.

He muttered something she didn't catch, but it definitely wasn't "you're welcome." There was still too much bitterness for that. It was possible Ike had held out hope of Dutton and Cassie getting back together, since Cassie was a much more palatable choice for Dutton than Grace would ever be. But Ike had come forward with this because he was also worried about Dutton's safety. If Cassie had indeed taken the knife, and was the killer, then Dutton was on her hit list.

And the woman had motive.

Even though Cassie had never ranted to Grace about her being pregnant with Dutton's baby, it was possible that Cassie was so enraged that she had crossed a very big line. She could be killing female cops to cover up that it was only one cop she wanted dead.

Grace.

She forced aside that troubling possibility and got back to work. She glanced at Jamie. Still busy with the sketch artist. So she motioned for Livvy and Dutton to follow her toward the interview with Brian. She showed Dutton into the observation area—not a room with a two-way mirror, but rather a computer where he'd be able to hear and see the interview.

Even though his observing was somewhat of a concession, Grace truly hoped he did hear something that would give them a clue as to why Brian might have targeted them. Of their two top suspects, she preferred Brian to be the killer, rather than Cassie. It was harder to accept when it was someone she knew who wanted Dutton and her dead.

Grace took in a couple of deep breaths before she stepped into the interview room, and she got her first look at Brian. He was seated, his elbows on the metal table, and his hands bracketing the sides of his head. There was indeed blood on the front of his shirt, his hands, his jaw and even in his pale blond hair. She also saw a deep cut on his forehead and some scrapes and bruises on his arms and hands.

He immediately looked up, spearing her with eyes that were bloodshot. "Sheriff Granger?" he asked, getting to his feet.

She nodded and motioned for him to stay seated. "Were you read your rights, Mr. Waterman?" Grace asked.

She was certain he had been. However, she wanted both the question and his response on the recording that Livvy had started the moment they'd stepped into the room. Ditto for activating the camera mounted on the wall. A reminder that Dutton was watching every bit of this.

Brian pointed to Livvy. "She Mirandized me. But it wasn't necessary. There's been a big misunderstanding."

Grace had been a cop long enough to know that some suspects clammed up and some couldn't stop talking. She figured Brian was the latter because he continued as they took seats across from him.

"After I got the horrible news about Elaine, I got drunk." He shook his head as if disgusted with himself. "It's what I do. I drink when I'm stressed and when I can't deal. I just couldn't deal," he added, his voice cracking.

"Were you drinking at a bar or at home?" Grace asked. Because a bar would likely have security footage.

"Home," he said, dashing any notion of security footage. "When I got the call about Elaine, I walked around in a haze for a while. I was probably in shock. By the time I needed a drink, it was too late to go to a bar."

Grace kept her face blank. "Was anyone with you?"

"No. I was alone." He groaned and pressed his hands to his head again. "I'm not sure how much I drank, but I'm sure it was a lot. And then I heard something on my back porch. Or at least I thought I did. So I went outside to see."

Now Grace added some skepticism to her expression. "You'd just learned someone had murdered your fiancée, and you weren't concerned the killer might have come to your place? Your instincts weren't to call the cops?"

"No." Brian's eyes widened, and he seemed stunned at that possibility. "It never occurred to me, but I was pretty drunk by then."

Her skepticism went up a notch, though Grace silently had to admit that being drunk didn't lead to clear thinking. "What happened next?"

"I fell off the porch," he readily admitted. He pointed toward the gash on his head. "That's when I got this. Man, it started bleeding, and the blood got in my eyes. I couldn't see so I was staggering around, trying to find my way back inside."

Livvy jotted something down on a notepad, no doubt a reminder to ask SAPD to check the back porch for any blood. Grace wanted more than that, though. She believed that she had enough to get a search warrant for Brian's place, and she'd press for one once this interview was over. But that would be much easier if she could actually arrest the man, so she continued with her questions.

"Did you call out to any of your neighbors? Or try to use your phone to ask someone for help?"

"No and no." His tone was a little sharp now, and Grace hoped his annoyance, and possible anger, paid off. Angry people sometimes vented. "It was late, and I didn't want to wake anyone. And I'd left my phone inside."

"So you staggered around," Grace continued, upping her own sharp, skeptical tone, "and then what?"

Brian seemed ready to snap out a response, but then Grace could see the man visibly making an attempt to rein in his emotions. "Like I said, I tried to get back to the porch, but

I guess I went the wrong way, because this morning I woke up, and I was in the drainage ditch behind my house. I must have passed out from the cut on my head and the alcohol and fallen in there."

Grace knew that could be the truth. *Could be.* But there was a reason this man was her top suspect, and she played that particular card.

"You told the cops that you were in El Paso when your fiancée was murdered," Grace stated.

There was no panic on his face, which meant he'd already known he'd be questioned about this. Of course, he had. It would have been next to impossible for him to travel all the way from El Paso, which was an eleven-hour drive. And Brian hadn't flown since Livvy had checked airline records and the man hadn't been on any flight that would have fit the timing of his drunken account.

"Yes, that," Brian muttered, and he took a moment. "I fudged the truth about that."

"You lied," Grace snapped. And she saw that flash of temper again. His jaw muscles tightened.

"Yes," he admitted. "I love my fiancée. *Loved,*" he amended, "but I needed some time away from her. I felt smothered, and I didn't think she'd understand, so I made up the work story. I told it to her and her parents, and then booked a hotel in El Paso under my name. I did a digital check-in on my phone so it would look as if I'd actually been there."

Brian hadn't mentioned the possible reason he felt smothered—because he was seeing another woman. And since he hadn't mentioned his chat with Felicity to beg her to give him an alibi, it meant Felicity had thankfully followed Grace's instructions and hadn't told Brian about her phone call to the cops.

"Felicity Martinez," Grace said simply, and she waited.

The effect was instant. Brian groaned and squeezed his eyes shut. He didn't say anything for several moments. "I'd like a lawyer," he muttered.

And that made Grace want to groan. Of course, she had known he might play the lawyer card when cornered, but there was nothing she could have done to prevent it.

Grace and Livvy stood. "If you don't have a lawyer, one can be appointed for you," Livvy reminded him.

Brian took out his phone. "I have someone," he assured them, and then stared up at her and Livvy, clearly waiting for them to leave so he could make the call.

She and the deputy did just that. They left, and Grace hoped it wouldn't be too long before the lawyer showed up. She was betting though once that happened, the attorney would demand Brian see a doctor. Which meant it would give them plenty of time to come up with a story that wouldn't paint Brian as a killer.

There was no law against being a lying, cheating scumbag, so Brian would no doubt own up to that and hope it was enough to keep his sorry butt from being arrested.

"I want you to try to get a search warrant for Brian's place," Grace whispered to Livvy the moment they were in the hall.

"I'll get right on that," Livvy assured her, and she headed in the direction of the bullpen just as Dutton came out of the observation area.

"You believe him?" Dutton immediately asked her.

Grace had to shrug because she wasn't sure. That's why she needed the warrant. Before she could fill in Dutton on that, though, she saw Rory making his way toward them. He was carrying a tablet, and judging from the look on his face, he had something important to tell them.

Or rather, show them.

"This is the artist's rendering of the man who posed as an electrician and possibly stole the knife," Rory explained.

Grace hoped it was a close enough resemblance to Brian. However, when Rory turned the tablet toward her, she didn't see any features matching their top suspect. The person was wearing what appeared to be a fake beard, just as Jamie had said, but the face was all wrong to belong to Brian.

"Is that…?" Dutton muttered, staring at the sketch.

Dutton didn't finish. Didn't need to, because Grace had seen the same thing. The sketch bore an uncanny resemblance to someone they knew.

County Sheriff Wilson Finney.

Chapter Eight

Dutton saw the dread take over Grace's expression. And he totally understood it. That sketch artist's image meant she had to question a fellow cop. A cop who already loathed her.

It was understandable why neither Jamie nor Diane had recognized Wilson. By the time Jamie had moved to the ranch, Wilson had left town to become county sheriff. As for Diane, she had moved to Renegade Canyon only two years earlier, so it was likely her and Wilson's paths had never crossed.

Grace sighed but didn't waste any time taking out her phone to call the county sheriff's office, and she put it on speaker. Moments later, a cop who identified himself as Deputy Mendoza answered.

"Sheriff Granger calling for Sheriff Finney," she said.

"He's not here. In fact, he's on his way to see you. He said he…" The deputy stopped and muttered an apology. "That he wanted to light a fire under you so you'd work harder to find Elaine's killer."

That erased some of the dread on Grace's face, and Dutton saw the flicker of anger.

"Sorry," the deputy continued. "But those were his exact words. Look, I know you and Sheriff Finney have a bad history, but that won't stop you from finding this SOB, will it?"

"It won't," Grace assured him.

"Good, because we're all ripped apart by what happened to her. She didn't deserve that. No one does."

"I agree," Grace replied. "Any idea when Sheriff Finney will be here?"

"Should be soon. He left here well over an hour ago."

That was more than enough time for the county sheriff to have made the trip, and Dutton had to hope the man wasn't setting in motion another murder or attack along the way.

Grace thanked Deputy Mendoza, ended the call and then turned to Rory. "I'll interview Sheriff Finney in my office. The location won't lessen any of his anger when he realizes why I want to talk to him, but I don't want to treat this like an official interview until I see how he reacts to the sketch. I'll also need to find out if he has an alibi for that visit to the McClennan ranch. For that, I'll need to narrow down the time that fake electrician showed up."

"Jamie is still here so I can ask her about that," Rory volunteered.

"Good," Grace muttered. "Move Jamie to the break room. I don't want her in the bullpen when Sheriff Finney arrives."

Hell. That hadn't even occurred to Dutton, that Jamie could possibly be at risk for witnessing the "electrician's" visit.

"I can arrange protective custody for her," Grace said, clearly picking up on Dutton's concern.

"Do that," Dutton insisted. He didn't want to take any chances with her safety. Then, he looked at Rory. "Ask Diane, too, about the timing of that visit," Dutton instructed him. "And the ranch hands. One of them might be able to help you pinpoint the exact time."

If several of the hands or the house staff could verify Jamie's account, then that would help Grace narrow down whether or not Wilson could have done this.

Grace nodded her thanks for his suggestion and shifted back to Rory. "In the meantime, Livvy is working on securing a warrant for Brian's house. I also want his clothes bagged for processing and for him to be examined by a doctor or an EMT. I don't want him to use any possible injuries to get out of anything he's already said in a statement."

Rory muttered an agreement and handed her the tablet. "After I get Jamie into the break room, I'll go in and tell Brian that. He's waiting on a lawyer?"

"Yes," she confirmed. "And Brian might insist on not being examined until he talks to his lawyer. That's fine as long as he's given medical clearance before any more questions."

That was a cover-your-butt sort of move for Grace, but Dutton was glad she was taking it. Yes, the image of the fake electrician might resemble Wilson, but Brian still had to be her number-one suspect. Then again, Wilson and Brian could be working together.

But why?

Dutton could understand Brian's motive. He could have wanted Elaine out of the way so he could pursue a relationship with Felicity. The man might have felt it was the better path for him rather than merely breaking up with her. However, what was Wilson's motive?

"Do they know each other?" Dutton asked. "Wilson and Brian? I mean, Brian's fiancée did work for Wilson, so it's possible they've met."

"I'm not sure," Grace answered. She motioned for Dutton to follow her to her office while Rory went into the interview room, where she'd left Brian. "So let me try to find that out before Wilson arrives."

They went into her office, and while Grace didn't shut the door, she partially closed it, then she sank down into her chair. He saw what he already knew. The toll this was taking on her. She looked exhausted and stressed. Definitely not good.

Cursing under his breath, Dutton went to the fridge in the corner to get her a bottle of water. What he found instead were little cartons of milk.

"This doesn't seem like comfort food," he said, setting a box in front of her. "But consider it a substitute for a shot of single malt. Or in your case, a glass of wine, since that's the only thing I've ever seen you drink."

She didn't smile at his attempt to keep things light. But she did thank him and drank the milk as if chugging some much-needed wine. Dutton considered it somewhat of a miracle that it seemed to steady her. Or maybe Grace was so deep in cop mode now that she was pulling from a deep well of mental reserves. Either way, she opened her laptop and started typing.

"I'm searching for any connection between Brian and Wilson," Grace told him.

Dutton took out his phone, sent a text to the PI to check for the same thing and then began his own searches on Google and social media.

"Well, I'm not seeing anything obvious in the thumbnails of their backgrounds," she said after a couple of minutes. "Brian was born in San Antonio, and Wilson was born here. Wilson is thirty-six. Brian, twenty-seven. Brian went to college. Wilson didn't. Let me go deeper...." Her voice trailed off. "Wilson is engaged to a rookie cop at SAPD, Bailey Hannon. Now she might have a connection to Brian since they live just a couple of streets from each other."

"Check Facebook," Dutton said, turning his phone screen

so Grace could see it. "That's Elaine's page, and she posted this picture eighteen months ago when she became a deputy."

He watched as Grace studied the photo of the young deputy with her boss, Wilson, on one side of her, and Brian on the other. It was clearly a posed shot and in no way proved that the men had teamed up to kill, but they did know each other. That was a start.

"Any other photos?" she asked, and he saw her start her own social-media search.

"Maybe. This is the one that came up in the results because Elaine had tagged both Wilson and Brian." He added Bailey Hannon's name to the mix to see if there were any connections.

There was a tap at the door, and a moment later, Livvy stuck her head in. "Fastest warrant ever," Livvy said. "I sent a request to the judge, listing all the circumstantial evidence we have against Brian, and he immediately issued the warrant. SAPD will send someone out to go through Brian's house and yard," Livvy added after Grace responded with a sound of approval.

"Make sure Officer Bailey Hannon's not on the search team," Grace insisted, earning her a raised eyebrow from Livvy. "She's Wilson's fiancée."

"Ah," Livvy said. "I'll work that out with SAPD. Discreetly work it out," she added. "I'm guessing you don't want to send up a red flag about Wilson."

"You're right. So maybe just phrase the request as experienced officers to conduct the search. And that's not unreasonable. If Brian is the killer, then he might have all kinds of evidence hidden away at his place."

Livvy nodded and headed back to the bullpen, no doubt to get started on Grace's request. Grace didn't continue her computer search, though. She just sat there a moment as if processing all of this.

"If Brian's the killer, he's probably removed anything we could use against him," she said. "Well, unless he had so much faith in Felicity that he thought she'd never turn on him."

Dutton shrugged. "He did seem shocked when you brought up her name. And he did ask her to lie for him about his alibi. Not sure if that's faith or stupidity."

"Yes," Grace muttered, and she took out her phone. "I need to have another conversation with Felicity. It's possible Brian said something else to her that would help add to the circumstantial evidence."

However, before Grace could make that call, her phone dinged with a text. "It's from Rory," she said to him. "It's the time and date Jamie gave him for the visit from the fake electrician."

Good. That was a start. "I could call some of the hands to ask them. It'd take some of the workload off Rory and the rest of you."

She didn't exactly jump at the offer. Probably because he was already involved more than she wanted. But she finally nodded and said thanks under her breath. However, Dutton didn't get a chance to get started on those calls because there was a knock at the door. Rory opened it, but he didn't manage to say anything before their visitor stormed in.

Wilson.

Dutton wasn't the least bit surprised to see that Wilson was already past the stage of being merely angry. There was rage in the hardened muscles on the man's face.

"You've got Elaine's fiancé in custody for her murder, and you didn't bother to tell me?" Wilson demanded. "I always knew you were incompetent. And your word means nothing. You said you'd keep me in the loop on this investigation, and then you go behind my back."

Dutton got to his feet and had to rein in his own temper. He wanted to dole out some venom of his own, but that would only escalate an already tense situation. Wilson had obviously come in here gunning for a fight, and that anger was going to soar once he realized what Grace was about to show him.

In contrast, Grace stayed seated, and she looked way calmer than Dutton could have ever managed to appear. He figured it was a facade, that she was fuming inside, but she was clearly holding it together.

"How did you know Brian Waterman was here?" she asked.

Wilson seemed ready to spew out his response, but he hesitated. "Cassie."

Dutton hadn't expected that, and obviously neither had Grace. "How did Cassie know he was here, and why did she call you about it?"

Again, he hesitated, but there was still enough anger brewing inside him that he snapped out a response. "She was at the diner when she saw a man with blood on his shirt come in here. She asked around, and someone told her it was Brian."

Grace glanced at Rory, who was still in the doorway behind Wilson, and the look she gave him had Rory stepping away, no doubt to find out who'd given that info to Cassie. It wasn't a secret, but no one should be blabbing about it, either.

"I don't have Brian Waterman in custody," she stated to Wilson, her still calm voice matching her expression. "He came in voluntarily and is waiting on his lawyer so I can continue to interview him. He lied about his alibi."

She didn't add the whole story about Felicity, and Dutton

wondered if she would. Maybe she'd wait until she had ruled out Wilson as a suspect. If she could rule him out, that is.

"Why did he have blood on him?" Wilson snarled.

"He said he got drunk and fell." She never took her eyes off Wilson, so she was obviously watching to see the man's reaction. And she got a reaction alright.

"Is he lying?" Wilson demanded. "Was it Elaine's blood?"

"I'm not sure. We've taken a sample, and it's at the lab."

Wilson huffed. "You should be pressing to get those results ASAP," he stormed. "You should be on the phone with the lab right now, demanding—"

She stopped him by holding up the tablet. At first, Wilson just looked confused, and then he went in for a closer look. Dutton moved, too, putting himself at an angle so he could see Wilson's face. There didn't seem to be any shock, though the man might just be good at concealing his emotions. He was a cop, after all.

"What is that?" Wilson asked.

"A sketch of a man wearing a disguise who lied his way into the main house at the McClennan ranch," Grace answered, and then she waited.

Wilson studied it some more. "What did he do?"

"He likely stole the knife and used it to murder Elaine," Grace explained.

That caused Wilson to stare at the screen several moments longer. And then he cursed. When his gaze went back to Grace, there was a new wave of fury in his eyes. "You think that's me."

"It looks like you," Dutton volunteered, earning him a glare.

Wilson exploded with profanities and went on for several seconds. "This proves you're lousy at your job, Sheriff Granger." He tapped his badge. "I'm a cop, not a killer."

Again, Grace managed to look unfazed by that. "Is that you in the sketch?" she asked. "And would you be willing to stand in a lineup so I can eliminate you as a suspect?"

If looks could have killed, Grace would have been dead. "No and no," Wilson stated through clenched teeth. "It's not me and I won't be in a lineup that you've arranged to try to set me up." He put his hands on his hips and his glare turned mocking. "You're really scraping the bottom of the barrel with this theory. I didn't know you could be so petty."

"I need to eliminate you as a suspect," Grace returned, sounding not petty but like the solid cop she was.

"This eliminates me." Wilson tapped his badge again and started pacing. Not that he could go far in the small office, but he attempted it, all the while continuing to mutter profanities.

Grace jotted down a time and date on a note and slid it across the desk for Wilson to see. Dutton could see it was the info Jamie had given them. "I also need to know if you have an alibi for then."

That definitely didn't improve Wilson's mood, but he whipped out his phone as if he'd declared war. He opened an app and scrolled through it. "I was at work that day. If you don't believe me, you can call my dispatcher and ask for the duty rosters."

"Did you leave work at any time?" Grace pressed.

Wilson attempted an answer, but his anger got the best of him, and he had to take a moment to settle. "Probably. That was two months ago, so I can't say for certain, but I normally go out for lunch." He stopped and surprised Dutton by not cursing, but sighing. "I didn't kill two cops," he insisted. "And I didn't put on a fake beard and steal a knife."

Grace didn't say anything. She just sat there, waiting, with her eyes drilling into Wilson.

The man sighed again. "I'm going to give you some leeway here because you're pregnant and hormonal," Wilson said.

Again, Grace didn't respond with venom. Though that's what Dutton wanted to do. He suspected she did, too, but Grace merely sat and waited for Wilson to continue.

"I'm going to give you leeway," he repeated. "Because we're all on edge about these murders. Hell, my fiancée is a cop. I'm scared for her. Scared that the next time I kiss her goodbye before work, that'll be the last time I see her. And then I come in here and you show me that." He flung his index finger at the tablet. "It's disgusting you think I could do any of this."

"Yet I had to ask because this is part of the job," Grace reminded him. She didn't add more. Again, she just waited, and she didn't have to wait long before Wilson pointed to the sketch again.

"The real killer wants you to think that's me so you'll go on a wild-goose chase and waste time. Time he or she will use to kill again. *She*," he said with emphasis, staring at Grace.

For a moment, Dutton thought Wilson was about to accuse Grace of being the killer, but then he added something that had Dutton's stomach twisting.

"Is Cassie a suspect?" Wilson pressed.

Grace didn't alter her expression one bit. "Why do you ask that?"

"Because she sure as hell should be." Wilson shifted his attention to Dutton now. "Hell hath no fury like a woman scorned."

"So you're saying because Cassie is upset with our breakup that she's gone on a killing spree?" Dutton countered. Though that very idea had occurred to him, especially since Ike had admitted that Cassie could have stolen the knife.

Wilson hesitated. Then he huffed. "I'm just saying that I hope Sheriff Granger is looking at this from all angles. That's what good cops do."

"Which is why she wanted to question you about the sketch," Dutton quickly pointed out.

Oh, Wilson didn't care for that, but he seemed to put a choke hold on spouting out any more profanities. "I like Cassie," Wilson said. "I think she's probably not the killer, but she has motive in spades. And I don't want that motive spilling over to my fiancée just so a scorned woman can cover her tracks."

"I don't want that, either," Grace assured him, and now she stood. "Trust me when I say the stakes are the highest for Dutton and me. It isn't just our lives at risk, but also our child's. I'll investigate anyone who might be the killer or anyone helping them."

Wilson stared at her a long time as if looking for a way to punch holes in what she'd just said. He didn't try that, though. "Call me the second you get lab results back on that blood you took from Elaine's fiancé," he demanded. And with that, he turned and walked out, slamming the door behind him.

Grace stood there a moment before she blew out a long breath. Dutton saw the tremble in her hand then, but didn't go to her. Though that's exactly what he wanted to do.

"So much anger in him," she muttered. "And, yes, I believe he's capable of murder because he hates the two of us that much."

Dutton wished he could disagree with that, but he couldn't. As far as he was concerned, Wilson, Cassie and Brian were all suspects.

Grace winced a little and slid her hand over her stomach. "The baby kicked during that entire conversation."

"And yet you didn't show any signs of it," Dutton remarked, watching her hand move over their baby. "No sign of hormones and pregnancy," he joked, repeating Wilson's childish insult.

One corner of her mouth lifted, just as he'd hoped it would. Dutton wanted to lighten this moment for her and wished he could take all of her stress onto his own shoulders.

Grace reached out, took his hand and placed it on her stomach. It felt odd to touch her, especially since they'd spent the last five months making sure there was no physical contact between them. But there was contact now, not just with Grace and him. Dutton also felt the slight thumps of the baby.

His breath went thin, and he got a surge of…well, he wasn't sure, but it felt good. For something so small, it certainly packed a punch, and in that moment, Dutton understood why parents gushed about their kids.

He looked at Grace and saw that she was smiling. He got that. She was able to feel these little miracle kicks even when dealing with a pain like Wilson. Even when things seemed so dangerous and uncertain.

His gaze automatically dropped to her mouth, and Dutton had to fight the overwhelming urge to kiss her. It was an urge he might not have been able to suppress had her phone not rang.

Grace sighed but then also seemed a little relieved. He got that. A kiss would feel amazing, but it would skyrocket the uncertainty and maybe cause them to lose focus.

She took out her phone and glanced at the screen before she answered it. "It's Larry Crandall," she said.

He was the head CSI who'd been working the crime scenes

by the ranch, so Dutton was very much interested in this call. Thankfully, Grace put it on speaker.

"Sheriff Granger, this is Larry," the CSI greeted her. "We found something."

Chapter Nine

Grace realized she was holding her breath. And hoping. Because she really wanted the CSI to tell her that they'd just gotten a huge break in the investigation and could now find the killer.

"What did you find?" Grace asked.

"Fibers caught on a splinter in the fence post. They haven't been here long and don't match the rope or anything the victim was wearing," Larry said. "It's possible it's from the killer or maybe the carpet or floor mats in the killer's vehicle. They're gray," he added.

Grace's mind began to whirl with possibilities. She didn't need a search warrant to glance through the windows of the suspects' vehicles and see the color of the carpet.

"Obviously, I'll get these to the lab right away," Larry assured her. "And while I've got you on the phone, the team out at your house found some tire tracks in the mud on the trail behind your house."

She knew which one he meant. It was only about twenty yards away and was hidden in some trees. But Grace had to mentally shake her head.

"The stabbed woman came from the front of the house," Grace said.

"Yes, and there are no unusual tracks there. Just the ones

from the cruisers. I guess it's possible the killer dropped her off toward the front of your house and then parked on the trail."

That made sense, but it also meant the woman's blood would likely be in the vehicle the killer was driving.

Grace thanked Larry for the info, and the moment she hung up, she fired off a text to Eden to ask her to have Brian's car impounded and examined. That was the easiest of the three since it was in the parking lot. Checking the carpet in Cassie's vehicle wouldn't be that hard, either. Wilson's, though, would be tricky.

"You want me to have my PI check and see if any of our suspects rented a vehicle?" Dutton asked.

She nearly smiled but didn't repeat her comment about him sounding like a cop. Because she was stretching her deputies thin, she nearly took him up on his offer, but she had a different task in mind.

"Could your PI go to the county sheriff's office and take a discreet look at the carpet inside Wilson's vehicle?" she asked. "And maybe a glance inside the other cruisers as well? Discreet," she repeated. "Nothing illegal. If I send a deputy, someone there might recognize them and report back to Wilson."

"Let sleeping dogs lie," he muttered while he composed a text, no doubt to his PI. "Or maybe this is more like not poking a rattlesnake with a short stick."

Grace nodded. "If Wilson is the killer, then enraging him might provoke him into committing another murder. He has a very short fuse, and I'd rather not set it off."

Dutton gave his own nod and was finishing up the text when there was a knock at the door. A moment later, Rory came in.

"Just wanted you to know that the EMTs are here with Brian," Rory said. "He didn't refuse the exam."

"Good. And the lawyer?" she asked.

"Not here yet, but I did just call the hospital to see if there was any change in Georgia's condition. She had to go in for a second round of surgery for internal bleeding."

That definitely didn't sound good. "And there's still nothing to connect Georgia with Renegade Canyon, the other two victims, Dutton or me?"

"Nothing. But her sister is at the hospital, and I was about to head there to have a chat with her."

"Good idea." Because it was possible the sister might know something that hadn't turned up in any searches.

Rory stepped back, but then had to stop from bumping into Cassie, who'd come up behind him. Grace was thankful she hadn't had to jump through hoops to get Cassie in for questioning, but it took Grace a couple of seconds to mentally switch gears. And to steel herself for what would possibly turn into an ugly situation. She could tell from Cassie's expression that the woman was already riled.

"My PA said you called and that you wanted to see me?" Cassie said, the words sounding like an accusation. She spared Dutton a glance and then huffed as if to say "of course, you're still here with Grace."

"Yes, I need to ask you some questions about a visit you paid to Ike two months ago," Grace explained.

"A visit..." Cassie's words trailed off, and her eyes widened. "Why would Ike tell you about that?"

Dutton stood. "I'll be in the break room," he muttered.

Cassie huffed again and folded her arms over her chest. "Wait." She moved in front of Dutton. "Did you put your father up to this, whatever *this* is?"

Dutton looked her straight in the eyes. "I don't put Ike

up to anything," he told Cassie. There was just a smidge of cockiness in that statement.

Cassie's attention flew back to Grace, and for a moment it seemed as if she was about to accuse her of the same thing, but then she must have remembered that Ike would never be swayed by anything Grace said. Just the opposite.

"So what is this?" Cassie demanded, and once again, she moved in front of Dutton to stop him from leaving.

Dutton huffed and glanced at Grace to get her take on this. She motioned for him to stay put. Technically, this wasn't an official interview and couldn't be. Not without something with more "teeth" than Ike's account. So Grace just went ahead and laid it out there for Cassie.

"Ike told me that you'd visited the ranch two months ago and that means you had the opportunity to take a knife that went missing."

Cassie seemed to do some kind of mental double take, making Grace wonder what the woman had thought this meeting was about. Had Cassie thought she was going to be questioned about something else?

If so, what?

The woman quickly regrouped, though, and the anger came back into her eyes. "No, I didn't steal a knife and then use it to murder a woman I never met. I'm not a psychopathic killer. I'm a respected businesswoman who shouldn't be treated like a criminal."

Grace didn't point out that this wasn't criminal treatment. If it was, she would have Mirandized Cassie and had this chat on the record in an interview room, probably with the woman's lawyer present.

"I was merely asking," Grace replied instead. "I have to either verify or eliminate any and all possible evidence, and sometimes I have to do that by asking hard questions."

"Well, you should have known the answer because you know I'm not capable of something like that." Cassie gave a dry laugh. "And if I were going to kill someone, why in the name of heaven would I have used Ike's knife to do it? That makes no sense."

"It does if you wanted to get back at me," Dutton pointed out.

Cassie gave him a withering look. "You no longer mean enough to me for me to do that. If I wanted to get back at you, I'd pressure the town council for that recall vote to get Grace out of office."

She stopped again, shifting her attention to Grace, and in that stare Grace saw that was indeed Cassie's intention. Pressure just might work, too. But she couldn't think about that now. The murder investigation had to be her focus.

"Is that all, Sheriff?" Cassie snarled.

Grace didn't respond but instead sent a quick text to Rory to make sure he'd gotten a look at the carpeting in Cassie's car. Rory was equally quick with his reply.

I did, Rory texted. It's gray.

Grace looked at Cassie again. "Would you be willing to let us examine your car?" she asked, purposely not mentioning the carpet.

Cassie looked as if Grace had just asked her for her firstborn, and the woman aimed a look at Dutton that seemed a mix of both outrage and confusion. "I know we aren't together any longer, but I can't believe you'd stand there and let her treat me like this."

"She's doing her job," Dutton said.

"Well, she can do it without snooping in my car when she has no right." Judging from the increasing volume of Cassie's voice, Grace thought the woman's tirade would just continue.

It didn't.

Cassie stopped, then shifted back to Grace. "Are you doing this because of what the CSIs found at the crime scene?"

Grace tried very hard not to blink. It was poker-face time. "What do you mean?"

Cassie huffed. "I heard that the CSIs are back at the fence."

So maybe Cassie was fishing, but Grace wasn't playing. "A CSI will often examine the scene several times. It's routine."

"No," Cassie argued. "This wasn't routine."

Grace merely lifted an eyebrow, an invitation for Cassie to continue.

Once again, Cassie huffed. "A friend was driving by and saw the CSIs and stopped. She said they looked excited, and that one of them made a call. That doesn't sound routine."

Grace considered the possibility that the "friend" was actually Cassie. But there was nothing criminal about observing CSIs unless the person actually trespassed or went onto the crime scene. If that had happened, Larry would have let her know.

"Anything found at the scene will be processed and evaluated," Grace finally said. "And I can't discuss the details of an active investigation with you."

Oh, that statement didn't please Cassie. She aimed a glare at Dutton. "But you've discussed it with him."

Grace didn't mention that Dutton was a potential target and not a suspect, and thankfully her silence let Cassie fill in the blanks. "You'll regret this," Cassie warned them and then stormed out.

Well, that was two people she'd managed to rile in the past hour. Three, if she counted Brian. And while this was part of the job, Grace felt at the moment that being sheriff was taking a serious toll on her. Dutton must have seen that on her face, because on a sigh, he shut the door and went to her.

And pulled her into his arms.

Grace nearly went with the knee-jerk reaction of pushing him away. But she didn't. It was ironic, but Dutton was the one person who truly knew the fear she felt over the baby being in danger. That shared camaraderie, though, was a dangerous thing.

Still, she didn't move away.

Didn't stop him from easing her closer to him until they were body-to-body. Breath-to-breath. She purposely didn't look up at him. No way could she resist him if she did that. So she just stood there and took everything he was giving her. And he was giving her plenty. Not just comfort, but that swirl of heat that seemed to make her forget the urgency of their current situation.

"I can't do this," she muttered, but still didn't move away.

He did, though. Despite his bad-boy reputation, Grace knew a statement like that from her was as good as a no. "I, uh, just hate to see you like this," he said.

"I hate to be like this," she confirmed. Now she risked looking at him and saw the traces of heat still in his eyes. "Mercy," she muttered. "I wish I could take a pill or a vaccine to stop this heat."

Dutton smiled, that damnable smile that made him look so hot. "Trust me, I've wished the same thing about you." Then, he lifted his shoulder in a shrug. "Well, I did before I got you pregnant, and after that, well, let's just say I need a pill to stop spinning certain fantasies."

Grace felt what she thought might be a shiver of fear, excitement and worry all rolled into one. Dutton hadn't meant *that*. Had he? He must be talking about sex and not some fantasy about them riding off into the sunset together with their baby. For once, she hoped it was the sex. The attraction was a lot easier to deal with than a lifetime commitment with the one man who could shake the very core of her world.

Thankfully, Grace didn't have to respond because Dutton's phone rang, and when he looked at the screen, he muttered, "It's the PI."

"Jake, you're on speaker," Dutton told the man. "And Sheriff Grace Granger is listening."

"Good," the PI said, "because she'll want to hear this. Eleven years ago, Grace's mother arrested two teenagers. Delaney Moreland and Keith Cassaine. They were sixteen."

Grace didn't have to press her memory to recall the names despite it being over a decade ago. "Underage drinking. Delaney choked on her own vomit in the back seat of the cruiser while my mother was bringing them in."

"Bingo," Jake confirmed. "And you were one of the deputies who assisted in the arrest. Delaney's parents filed a lawsuit against your mother and the entire police department, but they lost."

"Yes, because the ME stated that Delaney likely would have died from alcohol poisoning if she hadn't choked."

Still, that hadn't lessened the guilt her mother and she had felt. A girl had died, and they hadn't been able to prevent that.

"Do you think this is connected to the murders of two cops?" Grace asked.

"A strong possibility, because shortly after Delaney's death, Keith Cassaine changed his name." The PI paused a heartbeat. "These days, he goes by Brian Waterman."

Chapter Ten

Dutton forwarded Grace the email of the report that Jake had just sent him, and then he moved a chair next to hers so they could read the arrest report on Keith Cassaine, aka Brian Waterman.

The man who was probably now at the top of Grace's suspect list.

He'd never read an actual police report and saw that it was broken into four sections. The first contained the names and photos of those involved, the date and the arresting officer, Sheriff Aileen Granger. Below that were sections labeled Details of the Event, Actions Taken and Summary. Grace skipped to the summary that her mother had written eleven years ago.

On her way home from work around ten on a Friday night, Aileen had witnessed a car driving erratically, so she'd pulled it over. Brian had been driving and Delaney was the passenger. There was an open bottle of tequila on the console, and both teens were visibly intoxicated. They both failed breathalyzers. Aileen had called for backup, and when Grace had arrived, they'd taken the pair into custody, putting them in the back of Aileen's cruiser.

On that fateful night, Grace had followed Aileen in her own vehicle to the police station, but along the way, Aileen had stopped to try to resuscitate Delaney. Grace had been the one to call the ambulance, but by the time it arrived, Delaney was already dead.

Maybe out of shock and grief and fueled by the alcohol, Brian had become violent and had attempted to assault Aileen. He'd failed, though, because Grace had managed to restrain him. After they'd returned to the police station, it'd been Grace who'd actually arrested him because Aileen had likely been dealing with the aftermath of Delaney's death.

"I need to talk to my mother about this," Grace said. "Give her a heads-up that this old case could be linked to the current murders." She paused. "She'll realize right away that she could be the motive for the killer and that she could also be the actual target."

Yeah, Aileen would understand that. "Any chance your mother will let you put her in protective custody?"

"None," Grace quickly responded, and she sent a text to her mother to give her the basics. "This is better than a phone call since she won't want to discuss it until she's had a chance to refresh her memory."

That didn't surprise him about not nixing the protective custody. In fact, it would likely feel like an insult to the woman who'd been a sheriff for three decades.

"There's a separate report on Delaney," Grace continued once she finished the text. She pulled up that report as well and put it side by side with the one they'd been reading.

It was all there. More details of Aileen's attempts to revive the teenager, along with toxicology reports. Delaney's blood alcohol content, BLC, had been 0.40 percent. Since anything higher than 0.08 would be legally over the limit, Delaney had obviously had way too much to drink. Brian was over the limit, too, but nowhere as high as Delaney.

Dutton switched his attention to the mug shot of the then

sixteen-year-old Brian. Obviously, he wasn't looking his best in the photo. He was probably still drunk and in shock, and he was well past the disheveled stage. What stood out about him was his mop of ginger hair. It fell in shaggy chunks all around his acne-scarred face.

"Brian looks nothing like he did when he was a teenager," Dutton pointed out.

Grace made a sound of agreement. "Different hair color, and he's at least fifty pounds heavier now than he was back then. He must have had some cosmetic procedure to get rid of those acne scars. And he legally changed his name when he was eighteen." She stopped, then sighed. "Still, I should have recognized him."

"Yeah, because you should have special cop powers that allow you to recall every feature of every face you've seen over the past eleven years."

Dutton added a smile and enjoyed both the roll of her eyes and that sliver of heat he saw when their gazes met. He was tired of cursing that heat. Tired of having to fight it. But even the heat couldn't override that Grace and he should keep fighting it for no other reason than to focus on the here and now. On this investigation, that might just save some lives.

"I'll question him about this when I've got him back in interview," she said, obviously moving the conversation in the right direction.

No smiles now. Minimal heat as well. And she kept the focus on the job as she downloaded the report from the PI. Still sitting side by side, they read it together, but they'd barely gotten started before Grace got a text.

"It's from Rory," she said as she continued to scan the report. "Brian's lawyer is here. I'll give them a few minutes before going in. That'll give me time to get a better picture of what Brian's been doing for the past eleven years. Wow,"

Grace said when something obviously caught her attention. "He had a second arrest a year after the one here."

Yeah, he had. And it had been for assault on his sister. So Brian had a temper and could be violent. First, the attempted attack on Aileen and then this. "But no jail time," Dutton pointed out.

"No, because he was charged as a juvenile. A surprise because of his previous conviction for what happened here. I'm guessing either he had a very lenient judge or a very good lawyer. Maybe both."

"His family comes from some money," Dutton said, referring to the man's parents' net worth, which Jake had included in the report. They were worth nearly a million. However, the same couldn't be said for Brian, who seemed to be living paycheck to paycheck.

"Yes," she muttered. "It'll be worth the time to have a quick chat with his parents to see if they've cut him off financially." She paused. "I'd better let Livvy or Eden handle that, though. They weren't deputies eleven years ago, and Brian's parents might not want to speak to anyone who'd been involved in his arrest."

Good idea, and he continued to read the PI's report while Grace texted Eden to contact the parents. Maybe they'd be able to give Eden some insight about their son. Since Brian had changed his name, it was possible there'd been a rift.

"So Keith changed his name to Brian during his first year of college," Grace stated, continuing with the report. "I'm guessing because he might have wanted a fresh start. And there are no more arrests. He got a degree in business and works for a real-estate company. SAPD has agreed to send someone to get a statement from Brian's boss. Austin PD is getting a statement from Felicity."

Dutton figured Grace must have requested that, with

two of the many texts and calls she'd made in the past twelve hours.

"And you've got Brian's vehicle," Dutton reminded her. "So if the carpet fibers are a match to those the CSIs found, then you can make an arrest this morning."

Dutton knew that was a long shot, though. So did Grace.

"I doubt it's a match or he wouldn't have driven it here and risked the possibility of it being scrutinized by cops," she said, voicing what Dutton was thinking.

If Brian was the killer, then this visit was all some kind of ploy, maybe to try to convince Grace that he was innocent. Or to continue a sick cat-and-mouse game with her.

"What are the chances you'll get warrants to search Cassie's and Wilson's vehicles?" he asked.

"Zero." She gave a weary sigh. "Everything I have against them is circumstantial, and unlike Brian, I can't even prove they've lied to me. At least a lie could be construed as obstruction of justice. Added to that, a warrant likely wouldn't produce anything, anyway."

"Because they probably wouldn't have used their own vehicles," he muttered. And he thought of something else. "I can have my PI look into rental-car records for the area. Maybe the killer used one and left some kind of paper trail."

Grace made a sound of agreement and took a moment, obviously processing that possibility. "Let me do that search through official channels, though. I don't want anything questioned or thrown out if there are any doubts about the chain of custody if this turns out to be evidence we need for a trial."

Dutton understood, but he hated that he couldn't do something to speed things along. Grace and her deputies were already stretched thin, and he was betting that neither Cassie nor Wilson would be forthcoming to help Grace if it turned out one of them was the killer.

That brought Dutton to another question. "Would Cassie have been able to lift the two dead cops?"

Grace shrugged. "Both dead women had slight builds, and Cassie could have used the over-the-shoulder fireman's carry to get them from the vehicle to the fence. It wouldn't have been easy, but she could have managed it. Plus, she's familiar with the area and has motive."

"Yeah, motive because of me," he said under his breath.

Grace met his gaze, and for a moment he thought she was about to lecture him on not taking on that kind of blame. She didn't. She stunned him by brushing her mouth over his. Apparently, she'd stunned herself, too, because she immediately jerked away from him.

"Sorry," she blurted at the same time he insisted, "Don't you dare apologize."

Dutton didn't add more. Something like it barely qualified as a kiss, anyway. Or that maybe it'd helped relieve a little stress. It certainly had for him, anyway. But for Grace, she probably saw this as a serious lapse in concentration.

She got to her feet. "I'll go in and interview Brian now. You can watch on the video feed."

It seemed to Dutton that she couldn't get out of the office fast enough. Yep, that kiss was weighing on her. It was weighing on him, too, but in a totally different kind of way. It'd been a reminder of just how intense his need was for her.

Her phone dinged with a text, and he saw Aileen's name on the screen. "'I'm sorry the past has come back on you like this,'" Grace said, reading aloud. "'Sorry about the whole damn mess of it. And, no, I won't go into protective custody. Keep me posted about any developments and do what you need to do to get this pathetic excuse for a human off the streets.'"

Grace sighed, no doubt because her mother had indeed denied the protection. Which she just might need. In fact, it was possible that Grace and he were the decoy targets and that the person Brian wanted to punish was Aileen. That theory only worked, though, if Brian was the actual killer.

"Ready for the interview?" Grace asked Livvy when she went out into the bullpen.

Livvy immediately nodded and got up. "SAPD is at Brian's place now," Livvy explained as they walked down the hall. "Fingers crossed they find something we can use to get him to confess."

"Fingers crossed," Grace agreed in a mutter, but she didn't sound especially hopeful. Again, that was probably because this particular killer wouldn't have left something incriminating for the cops to find.

Grace made eye contact with Dutton before he went into the observation area, and he saw that the laptop was still on the table. The screen was blank, but Grace or Livvy must have activated the camera because soon he saw the feed of them in the room with Brian and a smartly dressed woman who must be his attorney. Brian was sporting a bandage on his forehead and a clean T-shirt and jogging pants.

"Sheriff Granger and Deputy Walsh resuming interview with Brian Waterman," Grace stated. "Also present is his attorney. Please state your name for the record."

"Cecily Monroe," the woman said.

Grace pinned her gaze to Brian. "You didn't mention earlier that you knew me. Why not?"

Because Dutton could see their faces, he noted that neither Brian nor his lawyer showed any surprise over the comment and question, which likely meant Brian had told the lawyer about it.

"I don't like talking about my past," Brian replied. "It was a painful time for me, and I worked hard to put it all behind me."

"But you did recognize me," Grace pressed.

"Yes. You were a deputy when my girlfriend died," he said.

Dutton listened for any venom in those words, but didn't hear any. It was possibly there, though, and Brian was managing to keep it under wraps. After all, the anger over Delaney's death could be motive.

"I was," Grace said. "Your fiancée's murder must have triggered some memories of your girlfriend's death."

Again, nothing obvious flashed on Brian's face. "It did, but like I said, I've tried to put all of that behind me."

"Is that why you changed your name and appearance?" Grace asked.

"In part," he readily admitted. "But my parents disinherited me after my arrest, and I thought it best if I didn't have any association with them. Name included, since Keith is also my father's name. As for the hair color, well, that's just a personal preference. I wasn't fond of the ginger and thought this better suited me."

Grace stared at him for several moments. *"Arrests,"* she said.

It seemed to take Brian a moment to realize she was correcting his use of the singular. "Yes, arrests." Now his voice did tighten a little. "That happened so long ago that I don't even think about it. But I suppose I should. It made me turn my life around." There was some cockiness to his tone now.

It was short-lived, though.

Because he must have recalled what had prompted him to end the earlier interview and call in a lawyer.

"You'll want to know about Felicity," Brian volunteered. He glanced at his lawyer. "I've made a full disclosure to her, and now I'll do the same for you. I had an affair with Felicity Martinez. *Had*," he repeated. "I ended things with her two weeks ago, and she was very upset. I suspect she had some not-so-pleasant things to say about me."

So Brian was trying to get ahead of this, probably by lying, since Felicity hadn't mentioned a breakup. It was possible it had happened, and maybe that would come out when she was interviewed by Austin PD.

"You broke up with the woman you were cheating with?" Grace asked.

The lawyer huffed and looked ready to object, but Brian touched her arm to silence her. "Yes, I broke up with her because I realized just how much I loved Elaine. I wanted to marry her and start a family." His voice cracked. "And now, I've lost her."

Grace gave him a moment, but Dutton figured she was thinking this could all be an act. He wished suspects were equipped with a built-in lie detector that would go off during questioning.

He stopped, replayed that notion and nearly smiled. Yeah, sometimes he did think like a cop.

"Is it true that Elaine was on the verge of breaking up with you?" Grace asked. And she asked it with a straight face, too. Dutton knew it was a bluff, that she hadn't gotten even a whiff of that so far in the investigation.

Brian's eyes widened. "No. What? No," he repeated and was visibly flustered. "Did Felicity tell you that, because if so, it's a lie."

"That didn't come from Felicity," Grace assured him, maybe so Brian wouldn't take aim at his former lover.

"Then, who?" Brian demanded. Now it was his lawyer who touched his arm as if to settle and silence him.

Grace fixed her hard stare on Brian. "I'm not at liberty to divulge that."

Oh, that didn't please the man, and Brian looked on the verge of a verbal explosion before he seemed to rein it all in.

"Well, whoever told you lied," Brian concluded. "Or maybe you're the liar. Cops can do that. They can lie through their teeth and try to entrap innocent people." He rammed his thumb against his chest. "I'm innocent, and I won't be railroaded by some cop who clearly doesn't have a clue how to investigate my fiancée's murder."

Grace didn't appear fazed by the insult. "Shortly after Delaney's death, you made threats against the Renegade Canyon Police Department."

Dutton didn't know that for sure, but it was a good guess on Grace's part. Brian had been a hotheaded teenager and had probably done some threatening. Maybe even on social media. And since that might be an avenue to explore, Dutton sent another text to Jake so he could add the search to his to-do list. He also told the PI to employ as many other investigators as needed to get the job done quickly.

"I was upset," Brian responded after a whispered conversation with his lawyer. "So I possibly said some things I shouldn't have."

"You made threats," Grace repeated. "You attempted to assault the sheriff during the lawful arrest she made on you. Obviously, you have quite a temper, so I have to wonder if that temper ignited when Elaine wanted to end the engagement."

There. Dutton saw it in Brian's expression. The anger,

yes, but there was something more. Maybe the truth. And in that moment, Dutton realized this was a man who could kill.

But had Brian done that?

It was possible, but he could say the same thing about Cassie or Wilson. And both of them had motive to include Dutton in the death threat. Brian didn't. As far as Dutton knew, he'd never crossed paths with the man. He made a mental note to check that. It was possible they'd had an encounter that he didn't recall.

He was about to do a Google search with both Brian's name and his own when his phone rang, and he saw Jamie's name on the screen. Dutton instantly got a bad feeling, since the girl rarely called him.

"Anything wrong?" Dutton asked the moment he answered.

"Yes," the girl said, and her voice was filled with fear. "Uncle Ike brought me home to get my backpack before he dropped me off at school. He was waiting in his truck. But when I came back out, he wasn't there."

Even though there could be a reasonable explanation for this, Dutton's stomach stayed in a hard knot. "Maybe he went inside, too. Did you look for him?"

"Yes, I looked," Jamie insisted, her words coming out quickly. "And he didn't come in. The alarm is set to chime when a door opens, and I would have heard it. I didn't." A sob tore from her throat. "Dutton, his truck door is open, and there's blood on the seat."

Chapter Eleven

Grace tried not to do a mental worst-case scenario as she and Dutton drove to the McClennan ranch. Hard not to think the worst, though, when there was a killer on the loose.

A killer she thought she might have in an interview room.

But if this was an attack, then Brian couldn't have possibly done it, since she'd been grilling him with questions at the time of Jamie's call. Still, it was possible the man had an accomplice or had hired someone to do this.

Whatever this was.

Jamie had said there was blood, but Grace was hoping that maybe Ike had somehow injured himself and had left his vehicle to get help. Though that didn't explain why he wouldn't have stayed put and called for help. Or simply gone inside, where Jamie would have seen and heard him.

"Keep looking," Dutton told his head ranch hand that he'd called as Grace and he had been hurrying out of the police station.

Hurrying with caution... After all, this could be some kind of ploy by the killer to lure them out, so that's why they were in the bullet-resistant cruiser with Rory and Livvy in another cruiser directly behind them.

"Nearly all the ranch hands are searching for Ike," Dutton said to her the moment he finished the call. "The house staff and two other hands are inside the house with Jamie, in case…well, just in case."

Apparently, he didn't want to spell out the worst, either, and Grace was glad Dutton had been so quick to organize a search for his father and an immediate fix to protect Jamie. It sickened her to think the girl could be in danger.

Because if the killer had taken Ike, or if a hired gun had done that, then he or she could still be at the ranch, ready to attack. Grace didn't want Jamie caught in the middle of a gunfight.

During her frantic call with Dutton, Jamie had mentioned that there'd been a big truck by the bunkhouse, and while she hadn't known exactly why it was there, Dutton had been able to provide that info. It'd been a scheduled delivery of some new equipment for the stables. Dutton had vetted the driver, the helper he'd brought with him and the company itself. However, that didn't mean someone hadn't snuck into the truck and then onto the ranch.

"You're sure Jamie didn't see anyone lurking around when she went inside for the backpack?" Grace asked Dutton.

As expected, he shook his head, and Grace knew he had indeed asked the girl that specific question. Jamie hadn't seen anyone or anything unusual. Dutton hadn't pressed her, probably because he'd wanted to get off the line and contact the ranch hands. But it was something Grace would need to question her about.

"I'll call her back now that we're on the way," Dutton muttered.

"Hold off on that," Grace said. "It's a long shot, a bad one, but I don't want anyone to use the sound of her phone ringing to pinpoint her location in the house. You told her to keep away from the windows and to lock herself in her bedroom with her nanny, the cook and one of the housekeepers. And she reactivated the security system. That's the best we can do for right now."

Also, Jamie would no doubt call them if she did hear anyone, or if someone tried to break into the house. For that to happen, the intruder would apparently have to get past several ranch hands. With a house that size, it was possible for someone to do that, but then the alarm would go off to let those inside know what was going on.

"Maybe Eden will see something on the security camera feed," Dutton muttered.

Yes, maybe. Dutton had given Eden the access codes to the feed, so she could study it while they were at the ranch. Even though she figured the cameras were top-notch, that didn't mean someone hadn't managed to evade them. They hoped, though, there hadn't been any evasion and that the person had been captured in the footage.

"I won't suggest you staying in the cruiser while the hands finish checking for a gunman," Dutton said. "But just know, that's what I wish you could do. Hell, I wish I could wrap you in bulletproof bubble wrap instead of just that Kevlar vest."

Yes, she was wearing a vest. All of them were, except Dutton, who'd turned down the offer since his ranch hands wouldn't have that particular safety measure. And while Grace appreciated his concern about her, he was right. She had to do her job, and right now, the job was finding his father and maybe catching a killer in the process. Even if this was a hired gun, if they managed to catch the person, then that might lead them straight to the killer.

Even though it took less than ten minutes to get to the ranch, it felt like an eternity before Grace took the final turn to get there. Of course, she had to pass the fence line along the way, the very part where two bodies had been left. She automatically checked, just to make sure there wasn't another one. But no one was there. Even the CSIs had apparently already left.

They passed the pastures, where horses were grazing by a shady pond. It seemed like much too serene of a scene, considering what might be happening at the ranch. She imagined the frantic search that had to be going on. And she was right. The moment she drove through the wrought-iron gates, she saw several ranch hands hurrying between two of the massive barns on the grounds. There were two smaller barns and another outbuilding.

Plenty of places for a killer to be lying in wait.

She stopped the cruiser right at the porch steps and turned to Dutton. "I need to go in and talk to Jamie and the housekeeper," she explained. "They might have seen something."

He nodded and used his phone to pause the security system so it wouldn't go off when she entered.

Part of her wanted to tell him that she wished she had bulletproof bubble wrap for him, too, but she knew he would have to look for his father. She looked at him, their gazes locking.

"Be careful," they said to each other at the same time.

Grace held the eye contact a few seconds longer, needing it, and also needing the unspoken assurance they'd all make it out of this alive. Then, they bolted from the cruiser with her heading to the front door and him running to the barn to join the search for his father.

Obviously, one of the ranch hands standing guard inside the house had seen Grace coming and knew who she was, because he opened the door to let her in. She recognized him as well. Cooper O'Malley. Like her, he'd been born and raised here in Renegade Canyon, and she was certain that Dutton had vetted him as well.

"Jamie, her nanny, the cook and the housekeeper have

moved from her bedroom and into her bathroom," Cooper said, motioning toward the stairs. "It's the second room on the right."

She nodded but didn't budge until Cooper had shut the door, locked it and reactivated the security system.

Grace could count on one hand how many times she'd been to the palatial house. Definitely a mansion, but the furnishings weren't what she'd call fancy. It was more classic cowboy, with its leather furniture and artwork of the prized horses and cattle that had been raised on the ranch over the years.

When she made it up the stairs and to the hall, she saw yet another hand, Taylor O'Malley, Cooper's brother, and he opened the bedroom door for her. No cowboy vibe here. It was the decor of a girl caught somewhere between childhood and teens, since there were at least a dozen stuffed animals on the pale pink bed along with posters of some K-pop singers.

"Jamie, it's me," Grace said, and almost immediately the en suite bathroom door opened. Jamie rushed out and into Grace's arms.

"Did you find Uncle Ike? Is he alright?" Jamie blurted.

Grace held her for a moment, silently curing the terror she could practically feel coming off the girl. "Not yet. Lots of people are looking, though, and we'll find him," she added as she led Jamie back into the bathroom, where there were no windows, thankfully.

The cook, Jeannie Ingram, the nanny, Millie Roberts, and one of the housekeepers, Ruby Bilbo, were near the tiled shower, and they all looked as frightened and concerned as Jamie.

"Tell me what happened," Grace said to the girl. Yes, Jamie had already spilled the basics to Dutton, but often people remembered small but important things when they repeated the account.

"Start from the beginning," Grace instructed. She kept her voice calm, hard to do, knowing the search was going on outside. Outside, where Dutton, her deputies, Ike and the hands could become targets.

Jamie nodded and drew in a long breath. "Uncle Ike and I came back here after we left the police station. He stayed in the truck, and I went inside to get my backpack."

"Was the delivery truck you saw earlier still here?" Grace asked when the girl paused.

"No. But a few of the hands were down by the corral. No one was near the house, though."

Well, someone likely was, but Jamie just hadn't seen them. Grace figured Ike's attacker could have been waiting by the side of the house, or even behind the perfectly manicured shrubs and hedges that threaded through the grounds.

"I went straight to my room once I was inside," Jamie went on. "And I didn't see or hear anyone. I got my backpack and then stopped to answer a text from my friend, who wanted to know when I'd be at school. Oh, and I went to the bathroom."

Grace tallied up the time, and all of that should have only taken about five minutes or so. Not much time, so Ike's abductor must have been close.

"And then what?" Grace prompted.

"When I went outside, the truck was still running, but Uncle Ike wasn't in it. So I looked around, thinking that maybe he'd gone down to the corral where I saw the ranch hands. But they weren't there, either. No one was." Jamie stopped, swallowed hard. "Then, I saw the blood on the seat. Did someone hurt Uncle Ike?"

Grace dodged that question. No way did she want to spell out the possibilities. So she went with a question. "Did you hear anything when you were looking around for Ike? Maybe footsteps? Or did you sense anyone moving nearby?"

Jamie shook her head, and the tears welled in her eyes. "Is this my fault?" she asked.

"No," Grace was quick to say. "Why would it be?"

"Well, if I hadn't forgotten my backpack, Uncle Ike and I wouldn't have been here." She went into Grace's arms again, and Grace held on to her, wishing she had the time to soothe her.

She didn't.

Grace eased Jamie back and met her gaze. "I need the four of you to stay here so I can go help look for Ike. As soon as we find him, I'll let you know. In the meantime, don't go anywhere near the windows."

"Because someone could shoot at us," Jamie muttered.

The girl's raw emotion felt like a fist squeezing Grace's heart, and she found herself brushing a kiss on Jamie's forehead before she hurried away. The sooner she got out there looking, the sooner they could maybe put an end to this. However, she'd barely made it back to the stairs when she heard someone shout something that she definitely hadn't wanted to hear.

"Fire!"

DUTTON HEARD THE shout from one of the ranch hands a split second after he smelled the smoke. It was coming from one of the storage buildings behind the barn, and Dutton ran as fast as he could in that direction. Ran but kept watch. Because this very well could be a ploy by the killer to lure him away from the house, farther from Grace.

Or it could be just a way of making him an easier target.

Still, Dutton had to go in. He had to make sure his father wasn't inside.

Dutton rounded the corner of the barn and saw the smoke billowing from the storage building, where they normally kept tractors, ATVs, a hay baler and other large equipment. There were no windows, but the smoke was coming out from around the large garage-style door.

Two of the hands reached the storage ahead of him and began trying to lift the door. Not easy, not with the smoke coming right at them, so Dutton drew in a deep breath and hurried to help. If the killer was going to strike, this would be a darn good time since it would take him precious seconds to draw his gun or to dive to the ground away from gunfire. He hoped the killer didn't just start shooting to try to take out as many of them as possible.

Dutton soon saw the reason the door wasn't budging. Someone had jammed a piece of wood on the side, and it was acting like a wedge to prevent it from opening. Blinking back the sting of the smoke in his eyes, Dutton yanked out the wedge, and the three of them lifted the door.

The smoke charged out at them.

He had to fight the coughing spell that overtook him, and despite his burning eyes, he fired glances around the building. It was one large area with no windows and no other exits. No working overhead lights, either, he realized, when he tried to turn them on. It was possible the fire had damaged them or else someone had tampered with them.

His gut told him it'd been the latter.

Hell. If so, then a lot of planning had gone into this. And his father could end up dying in whatever sick game the killer was playing.

Dutton drew his gun and then covered his mouth and nose with the crook of his arm. And he stepped inside. He couldn't see any actual flames, only the thick white smoke, but he heard something. A thud, as if someone had kicked the wall, and he was pretty sure someone inside was coughing, too.

"Wait," someone called out to him.

Grace.

Dutton cursed again because he'd been hoping she was still inside the house. Apparently not. Here she was, right in the thick of things, and it's where she'd no doubt stay until the situation was resolved. One way or another. Dutton decided to try to put a faster end to it by hurrying into the cloud of smoke toward the sound he'd heard by the back wall.

As he got closer, he heard other sounds, too. Definitely coughing, and he doubted it was the killer. With all the planning, the killer would have likely been wearing a gas mask. And if the killer was, then he or she was almost certainly waiting for Dutton to be in a better position to kill him.

"Dutton," someone said. Not Grace this time. He was pretty sure it was his father.

That got him moving even faster, and then he realized someone was right behind him. Thankfully, it wasn't Grace. It was the two hands and Rory. The four of them continued to fight through the smoke to reach the back wall.

And that's when Dutton saw the figure on the ground.

There was blood on his head, and his hands and feet were tied. But he was moving and trying to speak, which meant he was alive. Dutton needed to make sure he stayed that way and that meant getting all of them out of there.

"Get him," Rory said. "I'll cover us."

Good thing, because the killer could be right there. Or on the way out to go after Grace. Dutton had to shove aside that thought and just do what was necessary. He scooped up his father, hoping he wasn't making his injuries even worse, and he started running toward the door.

His lungs felt ready to burst, and each step felt like an

eternity, but he finally made it outside and into the fresh air. And he saw Grace. She, too, was coughing and trying to bat away the smoke while she kept watch around them, looking for any signs they were about to be attacked again.

Dutton didn't stop running. He moved his father away from the storage building and to the side of the nearby barn that was about ten yards away. It wasn't ideal cover, but it was better than being out in the open. And it had the bonus effect of getting Grace, Rory and the hands there, too.

"I'll call an ambulance," Rory said, taking out his phone. "And the fire department."

Yeah, the EMTs were definitely going to be needed. Ike's head was bleeding, and it looked as if someone had clubbed him. There were also marks on his neck that looked as if they'd been caused by a stun gun. Added to that, Grace had inhaled enough smoke that she needed to be checked as well. Hell, they all probably did.

"What happened?" Dutton asked his father while he untied him.

They were all still coughing, and Ike was shaking his head. That only caused the bleeding to get worse, so Dutton tried to stop him. Tried and failed.

"An ambulance will be here soon," Dutton said to try to soothe him.

His father's eyes were wild, pleading, and the headshaking continued. He tried to speak but couldn't get out any intelligible words.

"Not a fire," Ike finally managed to say, and even though the ropes were still on his hands, he tried to latch on to Dutton to pull him to the ground.

Obviously, Ike was trying to tell him about some kind of

threat, but Dutton didn't know what. Until his father said one word that made it all clear.

"Bomb."

And just then, the storage building exploded.

Chapter Twelve

Grace sat on the examining table in the ER and waited for the nurse to finish stitching up the cut she'd gotten on her arm. A cut from a sliver of wood that had shot through the air when the building exploded. In the grand scheme of things, it was a very minor injury and could have been worse.

A whole lot worse.

If the blast had happened just seconds earlier, when Dutton, Ike, Rory and the hands had still been in the building, they likely would have been killed. She could have possibly been, too, since she'd been standing right by the door. It was somewhat of a miracle they'd all survived.

Of course, Dutton and she had been plenty worried about the effects the blast might have had on their baby so they'd skipped waiting for a second ambulance, and instead Dutton had driven her in the cruiser to the ER.

Thankfully, no one inside the house, including Jamie, had been hurt in any way and now the girl and the house staff were safely tucked away at the police station, where they were giving Livvy and Eden their statements about the incident.

Grace looked at Dutton, who was getting his own stitches on his forehead. He was in the chair next to her, not an ideal place for the nurse who was doing his stitching, but he'd refused to leave the room. She was actually thankful for that, but not because she wanted his protection. She didn't want him out of her sight.

Ike had been the one assaulted and put in that building with a bomb, but she was certain this had all been planned to draw Dutton, and probably her, too, inside so they could be blown to bits. That wasn't the MO the killer had used for the other two murders. However, he or she had maybe been willing to stray from the MO just to accomplish the task of killing them.

Her phone buzzed again, and she tried to read the text that Rory had just sent her. Hard to do that with the nurse right in her face. Still, she saw the message and relayed it to Dutton.

"Your father has two cracked ribs and a concussion. They're taking him down for more tests now."

Grace hoped those tests didn't reveal any more serious internal injuries, and while she was hoping, she added that maybe Ike would remember something that would help them figure out who was responsible for what happened. She hadn't been able to question him yet, and so far, all Ike had said was that his attacker had been wearing a ski mask. Grace figured that once he was thinking clearer, he might be able to recall some critical details.

Dutton's own phone dinged twice, and as Grace had done, he relayed the text to her. "All the hands have been treated and released. No one other than Ike required an ambulance. The other text is from Rory and a repeat of what he told you."

So Rory was keeping them in the loop. Good. Because at that moment it felt as if she and Dutton were trapped here in this ER room. First, she'd had an ultrasound, to confirm the baby was alright. Then, they'd both been examined to determine how much smoke they'd inhaled. Even a small amount was worrisome, since anything that affected her also affected the baby.

"Alright," the nurse working on her said. "Finished for now. Just wait here for the doctor to come back in and go over any test results."

More waiting, but Grace knew there was nothing she could do to hurry things along. Besides, she could still work while she was here. She could continue to get updates not only on the injuries, but also from the CSIs, who were now at the McClennan ranch, pouring over what was their new crime scene.

Grace sent off some texts to both Austin and San Antonio police departments to ask them about the statement from Brian's lover, Felicity, and the search of Brian's house. Both could be crucial reports since they could add to the circumstantial case against Brian.

Since that case wasn't anywhere near solid enough, she'd been forced to allow him to leave the police station after his lawyer had filed a complaint about being held for so long. She hadn't wanted anything like a legitimate complaint to allow Brian to wiggle out of any charges that might eventually be filed against him.

The nurse with Dutton finished his stitches, repeated a similar comment about staying put until they see the doctor, and she headed out of the room. Grace looked at Dutton then, at the fresh bandage on his forehead, and she felt the emotions flood through her. He was safe. The three of them were all safe.

For now.

Dutton stood and went to her, and he might have pulled her into his arms if there hadn't been a tap at the door.

"It's me," Rory said, and he opened it to peer inside at

them. No stitches for him, but he had several bruises on his jaw, where a board had smacked into him.

One look at his face, and Grace knew something was wrong. "What happened?" she asked at the exact moment she got a text. A text from the doctor who'd been attending the unconscious woman, Georgia Tate.

"Georgia died," Grace muttered, and Rory confirmed that with a weary nod. She finished reading the text from the doctor. "She didn't regain consciousness before she passed away."

Which meant she was taking to the grave any details she might have known about her killer.

"Three women," Dutton said, and then he groaned and cursed. He scrubbed his hand over his face and then cursed again when his fingers raked across the fresh bandage.

Even though Dutton hadn't known Georgia, she totally understood his reaction. It wasn't just the loss of life. Or the loss of potential critical information. It was the fact that the killer had murdered three women…and for what? For revenge? A warped vigilante justice to right old wrongs that could never be made right?

"You want me to notify Georgia's next of kin?" Rory asked. "Her sister went to her place to get some things, but she should be back here at the hospital any minute now, and I can tell her then."

Grace nodded. She didn't have the mental bandwidth to do that right now, and it had to be done before the woman's sister learned about it through some other means.

"Are you two alright?" Rory pressed, volleying glances at both of them. He added a third glance at her stomach.

"Right enough," Grace assured him, and Dutton echoed much the same. It was a lie. They were far from alright, but then everyone involved in this investigation could say the same thing.

Rory made a sound of agreement and then left, closing the door behind him. Dutton immediately moved toward her again, doing what he'd no doubt intended to do before his brother's arrival.

He drew her into his arms, being very careful not to touch her wounded arm.

This was a bad idea. Every part of Grace knew it, too. But that didn't stop her. She melted right into the embrace as if she belonged there. And felt the instant soothing comfort that only Dutton could provide. Even when she didn't want him to.

She braced herself for him to ask how she truly was, and she'd have to repeat the lie she'd just told Rory. Instead, he brushed a kiss on her forehead and then eased back to lock gazes with her.

"I saw something I shouldn't have," he said. That gave her a fresh jolt of alarm before he smiled and added, "On the ultrasound. The gender is no longer a secret."

Just like that, she relaxed. And smiled. "Since I've heard ultrasounds look very grainy, I'm guessing what you saw was a part of a body that's…obvious."

"Obvious," he confirmed. "We could just run with this newfound knowledge and start testing out names."

"Boy names," she muttered, knowing that would have been the *obvious*.

Again, this was wrong, but so much of it felt right, too. The baby was a boy, and Dutton was the one person who would understand this was one of the pregnancy moments. They were going to be the parents of a little boy.

"Mordecai," Dutton joked. "That's an old family name."

Grace shook her head, but she was still smiling. Yes, it

was good to think of something that didn't involve murder and attacks. Leave it to Dutton to come up with something that could ease this weight on her shoulders.

"Thank you," she whispered.

"You're welcome." He paused, keeping his gaze locked with hers. "You don't mind knowing the gender?"

She shook her head. "The timing is good. Like an unexpected gift. Though I would have been equally pleased had you seen nothing obvious and the baby was a girl."

"Yes," he quickly agreed. "Part of my dad fantasies involved old stereotypes of teddy-bear tea parties and me fending off boys who'd want to date her once she reached her teens."

It was odd to think of him having fantasies like that, but Grace didn't push for any other details of what his dreams for the future would include. In fact, it was probably time for her to move out of his arms and send off texts to try to get any updates.

She didn't do that, though.

Grace stayed put, and made things a whole lot worse by moving even closer. And closer. Until her mouth met his. It was just a touch, but it packed a punch alright. The heat didn't come in slow, gentle waves. This was more like a tsunami.

Dutton reacted. Of course, he did. He eased her even closer and deepened the kiss. In a flash, it turned into something much more. Hot and filled with need. Until it felt like foreplay.

Still, Grace stayed put, and she did her own share of deepening. Her own share of fantasizing, too, and this had nothing to do with tea parties and teenage dates. It was about this ache she'd had for Dutton for as long as she could remember. It was about the single time she'd made love with him. That's where her mind went. To the bed. To the sex. To those incredible moments when they'd forgotten about their pasts and given in to the need.

She slid her hand around the back of his neck, urging him to take more. He did. He took and moved his hand down to the small of her back, moving her forward until their centers met. Well, as much as they could with the baby bump. It was that reminder of the baby that finally forced Grace to come to here senses.

Gasping for air, she let go of him and stepped back. Way back. But even the space between them didn't cool the heat. It was right there, zinging between them, and willing her to go back into his arms. She might have done that, too, if there hadn't been another tap at the door.

Good. It was probably the doctor, who could give them the all clear to leave. They could go back to the police station, where they'd be surrounded by people and wouldn't be able to give in to the temptation of kissing again.

Or doing more than kissing.

Her body was all for that notion, but Grace forced aside those thoughts and called, "Come in," to the person who'd tapped on the door.

But it wasn't the doctor. Her mother took one step inside and then sort of froze, her attention sliding between them. Aileen's sigh told Grace that her mom had no doubt figured out what had just happened.

"I've interrupted you," Aileen said, and it wasn't an apology. "I came to see how badly you're hurt."

"Not bad. Just this." Grace motioned toward her arm and Dutton's forehead. "We were lucky," she added.

Aileen sighed again. "You were. You were damn lucky." She turned to Dutton. "I'm about to lecture the sheriff. I'd ask you to step outside while I do that, but considering you've got a killer breathing down your neck, that's probably not a smart idea. So you get to listen, too."

Grace stood there, more than a little stunned. Her mother wasn't prone to lectures, and in the time Grace had been sheriff, Aileen had never interfered in an investigation.

"You should be on desk duty, and you know it," Aileen said to her. "It's policy, and I know this because it's a policy I wrote."

"Policy isn't strictly mandatory," Grace said, but then she immediately waved off that comment rather than get into the interpretation of the department's guidelines with her mother.

The policy spelled out that officers should be put on desk duty unless there was a critical operational reason for them not to be. A triple murder investigation was the very definition of a critical operational reason, but the truth was, there were other cops who could have filled in for Grace in the field.

But Grace had opted against that.

"As soon as the killer is caught, I'll go on desk duty," Grace said. That'd been her plan all along.

Clearly, that wasn't enough for Aileen, though, and Grace knew Aileen wasn't a former sheriff at the moment. She was Grace's mother. And she was worried about her safety.

Aileen looked at Dutton. "I'm guessing you tried to talk her out of doing anything dangerous." She sighed. "Of course, you did. I might not like you, Dutton, but you're not an SOB. You're trying to keep the baby and her safe, and it's putting you at risk."

"I'm at risk no matter what I do or don't do," Dutton was quick to say. "The killer named both Grace and me in that threatening note."

It was a bad time for it, but Grace nearly smiled. Aileen had wanted to play the guilt card to get Grace to consider putting both Dutton and her "behind a desk" and out of reach of a killer. But backing off wasn't going to fix this. Not for Dutton and her. Maybe not for her mother, either.

"The killer didn't name you in the threat that was left at the last crime scene," Grace said to Aileen. "But if the killer is Brian, you know you could be the main target. Heck, you could be a target even if it's not him, since we aren't sure of the killer's motive. I'll ask you again to consider protective custody."

A muscle flickered in Aileen's jaw. "No protective custody. Because if I'm truly the endgame target, then I want to make myself available. Not so he or she can kill me," she added when both Grace and Dutton opened their mouths to object. "But because I believe I'll be able to stop it."

Grace groaned, and she went closer, meeting her mother eye-to-eye. "I don't want you in danger. But I understand that you are," she acknowledged before Aileen could object. "It's the same for Dutton and me. I want the killer caught, and that means we all need to take more precautions than we're comfortable taking."

"Like Dutton and you sharing the same air space," Aileen muttered.

Grace pulled back her shoulders, waiting for her mother to snap out a reminder of how much she disapproved of Dutton and his family. That didn't happen.

"Is the baby okay?" Aileen asked. "I figured you had some kind of tests and an ultrasound."

"Both," Grace verified, relaxing her stance just a little. She thought of what Dutton had seen on the ultrasound, though, and automatically placed her hand on her stomach. "It's a boy," she told her mother.

Aileen flexed her eyebrows. And then sighed. "A grandson," she muttered, sounding almost happy about that. It didn't last because her gaze volleyed between them again. "I don't have to say that all this time you two are spending together will fire up the gossips. Yes, I know gossip doesn't mean squat. Not usually. But in this case, it does." She fixed her attention on Dutton. "I've heard this baby has cost you plenty of business."

Grace turned to him, expecting him to deny it. But he didn't. "How much business?" she asked.

"Some," he admitted, but she suspected *some* was minimizing it and that her mother's *plenty* was more accurate.

Even though she hadn't huffed or done any of the cursing aloud, Dutton clearly picked up on what she was thinking because he locked gazes with her. "I don't need local business to keep my finances solid. If locals don't buy the livestock, others will."

Grace would have questioned him more about that, but there was another blasted knock at the door.

"Probably the doctor," Dutton said and went to open it.

Again, it wasn't the doctor, but rather Wilson Finney, and the county sheriff gave Dutton and Grace a look similar to the one Aileen had aimed at them moments earlier. Of course, now there was no lingering heat from the kiss in the room.

At least Grace hoped there wasn't, anyway.

Wilson shifted his attention to Aileen, and she, too, earned a cool glance from him. Probably because he blamed her for not doing more to get him elected sheriff. He probably thought Aileen had shown Grace some favoritism over the years, but if she had, Grace certainly hadn't been aware of it.

"I heard about what happened at the ranch," Wilson said, aiming his comment at Dutton. "Is your father alright?"

"He was injured, but he should be fine." Dutton didn't add more even when Wilson gave him a blank stare.

Wilson shifted to Grace. "I read the report you had Livvy send me about this Brian Waterson, aka Keith Cassaine."

Good. Grace had asked Livvy to send it to him in case he had anything to add to the original reports. Wilson hadn't been involved in the arrests, but he'd been a deputy then, and Grace had had Livvy contact all former deputies in case they recalled something that would help with the investigation.

"I have some vague memories of him and the teenage girl who died." Wilson went on. "And I heard him threaten Aileen. But I haven't had any contact with him in the past eleven years." He paused. "You didn't think I'd teamed up with him to kill those female cops, did you?"

There it was, that snark that had become Wilson's default reaction when it came to her, and as Dutton had done, Grace went with a blank-stare response. Yes, she had to consider that Wilson might have joined forces with Brian, but that was a long shot. She figured either the killer was working alone, or had hired a henchman to do some of the dirty work.

Like assaulting Ike and blowing up a storage building in an attempt to murder Dutton and her.

Wilson huffed. "I'm not a killer, and while you're obviously having trouble wrapping your head around that, I want you to know that I came here to help."

"Help?" she asked, and Grace wished she'd toned down a smidge of the shocked tone. "How?"

"By letting one of your deputies take a sample of the carpet from my cruiser and my personal vehicle," Wilson said. "That'll rule me out as a suspect."

It wouldn't. The only thing it would absolutely rule out was that the fibers either did or didn't match the ones taken from the fence post. It definitely wouldn't prove Wilson's innocence. He still had means, motive and opportunity. It was his image on the sketch the police artist had done. And he could have been the one who'd orchestrated the attack at the ranch.

But Grace didn't spell out any of that.

However, her expression must have conveyed her suspicions about him because Wilson huffed again. "I had a second reason for coming here. I got a call from Cassie about a half hour ago, and she told me that the town council is meeting in the morning to discuss the recall process."

Grace managed to get her cop face on in time before Wilson could see the gut punch that'd given her. "Oh?" she said, trying to sound nonchalant.

Wilson attempted to hide a smile, but he obviously wanted her to see how pleased he was. "Yes. It's possible that by morning, a recall election will be approved and you'll finally be on your way to being ousted as sheriff."

Chapter Thirteen

Dutton hated the smug look Wilson was giving Grace. Hell, he hated pretty much everything about this jerk, whose pettiness over losing an election had caused him to launch this vendetta against Grace.

A vendetta that had caused Wilson to murder three women?

Maybe. There was plenty enough hatred for Wilson to do that and more. But Dutton recalled something. A little dig he could fire back at the jerk.

"I've heard you've got some serious opposition running against you in the upcoming county-sheriff election," Dutton commented. "And you're way down in the polls. I mean, it's not looking good."

As he'd hoped, that got Wilson turning his gloating face away from Grace and pinning his eyes on Dutton. "Serious opposition that I heard you funded."

Dutton shrugged. "I know Jacob Morales," he said, referring to the opposing candidate. "I've done business with him for years, and he's honest and not prone to pettiness and grudges." The remark hit home and caused Wilson's eyes to narrow. "I haven't kept my donations to his campaign a secret, but it's not common knowledge, either. How'd you find out about it?"

Of course, it wasn't just a simple question, and there was a whole lot of insinuation in it. Well, one big insinuation, anyway. That campaign contribution could be Wilson's motive for including Dutton in the death threat. Added to that, Wilson could have murdered his own deputy as a warped way of garnering some sympathy, which he might believe would help him in the election. Of course, if Wilson, Cassie and their cronies managed to oust Grace, then Wilson probably thought he could step into her job.

Dutton would do everything within his power to make sure that didn't happen.

It was bad enough that Grace was facing this moronic recall threat because he'd gotten her pregnant. Bad enough that she was having to deal with that while also trying to stay alive and find a killer. It would be just one more layer of nastiness if Wilson somehow managed to take her badge.

"FYI, I contributed to Morales's campaign, too," Aileen said. "And I plan to officially endorse him."

Dutton really enjoyed the flash of anger those words stirred in Wilson's expression. But his enjoyment was short-lived. Because it was way too easy to fire up Wilson's temper, but the man usually took that anger and aimed it at Grace. He didn't get a chance to do that this time, though, because his phone rang. So did Grace's.

Grace and Wilson took out their phones at the same time, and even though neither put the calls on speaker, Dutton could immediately tell that something was wrong.

"What? When?" Wilson demanded, and shock replaced the anger on his face.

"Read the note to me," Grace said to the person who'd called her, and she was experiencing plenty of shock, too.

Hell, had there been another murder?

"I'm on my way," Wilson blurted, and he headed for the door.

Grace stepped in front of him, blocking the door, and told the caller, "I'll get right back to you. Go ahead and text me a copy of the note and assemble a team. We also need to make sure no one is inside the church, so call the pastor and check that," she added before she ended the call and looked at Wilson. "Just stop and listen. You can't go charging out there."

Even though Dutton had no idea what was going on, he stepped in when Wilson tried to move Grace away from the door. He took hold of the man and hauled him back. But it wasn't easy. Wilson was strong, and he was hell-bent on getting out of there. Dutton was equally hell-bent on keeping him in place, at least until he learned what the heck was going on.

"I'm going to Bailey," Wilson shouted. "I have to save her."

"Then save her by thinking this through," Grace said, her voice level and calm, the exact opposite of Wilson's. She glanced at Dutton and her mother. "Officer Bailey Hannon has been kidnapped."

Dutton didn't have to ask who that was. Bailey was a cop in San Antonio. And she was also Wilson's fiancée.

Damn.

Did the killer have her? Was she dead? Was she the murderer's fourth victim?

He hadn't asked those questions aloud, but Grace obviously knew what he was thinking. "Kidnapped," she repeated. "This isn't like the murders. The killer didn't contact us for those, but for this one, he left a message taped to the front door of her house, where she was likely taken. Then, he or she made an anonymous call to SAPD so they could get the note and let us know what's going on."

"Kidnapped," Dutton muttered, and despite still struggling with Wilson, he forced himself to think this through. "What's the ransom demand?" Because there likely was one, and Dutton had a bad feeling he knew what it was.

Grace looked him straight in the eye. "The kidnapper has demands," she began just as her phone dinged with a text. She stopped, read it and lifted the screen to show Dutton and Wilson.

Wilson immediately stopped struggling. Good thing, too, because Dutton's main focus now was on that image. A copy of the note Grace had already mentioned.

"'Grace, here's what you need to do to save Officer Hannon,'" Dutton said, reading. "'Dutton and you get in a cruiser. I know you have one handy. And just the two of you come to the Hilltop Church. I've left the cop in the cemetery. Come alone. If you bring Hannon's boyfriend with you or anyone else, she dies.'"

So, a note from the killer.

"You can't go there," Dutton immediately told Grace. "It's a trap."

"I know," she confirmed on a sigh.

"You can't let her die," Wilson said. "You have to go. You have to save her."

No shout this time. It was barely a whisper, and it was filled with emotion. Well, it seemed to be, anyway. But at the back of Dutton's mind, he wondered if Wilson was putting on an act.

Because Wilson could have arranged this whole mess to kill Grace and him.

Yeah, that sounded extreme, to use his own fiancée, but everything about this situation was extreme. And potentially deadly.

"I told Rory to assemble a team," Grace said. "And he will.

You and I will go in a cruiser to the cemetery, and Rory and at least two other deputies will be behind us. They'll stay out of sight until we can figure out how the killer intends to handle this."

"He'll handle it by killing Bailey if you two don't get there now," Wilson insisted.

Grace shifted her attention to Wilson. "The killer will have to communicate with us somehow. Maybe a phone call or text. Maybe another note, since that seems to be the preferred method. But unless he's an idiot, he won't expect Dutton and me to speed up there and bolt from the cruiser so we can be gunned down."

"I can go to the cemetery and park my truck on a trail," Aileen offered. "I can be backup to your backup."

Grace sighed. "And that could be exactly what the killer wants. Remember, you could be the primary target."

Dutton could tell Aileen wanted to argue that. She was a cop to the bone, and she wanted to help. She wanted to try to protect her daughter and unborn grandchild. But Aileen didn't push. She gave a confirming nod.

"I'll go to the police station and wait there for news," Aileen conceded. "I'm guessing you'd rather me be there than drive back to my place?"

"Yes," Grace quickly agreed, and she reached out and gave her mother's hand a gentle squeeze. "Dutton and I will be as careful as we can be." With that assurance, she turned to Wilson. "And I want you to go to the station, too. Use your own car," she added, but didn't spell out that she didn't want him in the same vehicle with Aileen. "Don't go near that cemetery, understand?"

Wilson nodded, but Dutton was nowhere near convinced the man would stay put. Maybe because he was out of his mind with worry over his fiancée. Or the man might go if he was the killer. Dutton just wished he knew which.

And that he could figure out how to stop this nightmare.

When Grace's phone rang, Dutton was close enough to see Rory's name on the screen, and she motioned for him to follow her. "Please make sure Wilson goes to the police station," she said to her mother, and Grace added a hard look at Wilson, no doubt to convince him to comply.

Grace and Dutton went out and into a hall that led to the ER itself, and she didn't answer the call until she was out of Wilson's earshot. She didn't put the call on speaker but held it close to both of them so Dutton would be able to hear.

"Made it back to the station about five minutes ago, and the team is assembled," Rory said, and he could hear the concern in his brother's voice. "Livvy and me in one vehicle. Judson and Eden in another. We're leaving now, so we should make it to the church ahead of you. What's the next step?" he asked. "And please don't say it's you and Dutton going to the cemetery."

"We're going," Grace confirmed. "But we're not getting out of the cruiser until I'm sure we aren't going to be gunned down. We'll try to get a visual of Bailey, evaluate the situation and wait for the killer to contact us. In the meantime, I want you and the rest of the team to park on the dirt road behind the church. Obviously, stay out of sight and look for any signs of trouble."

"There'll be trouble," Rory protested. "The cruisers are bullet-resistant, but Dutton and you can still be shot."

"We'll put on the Kevlar," she said. *"We,"* she emphasized. "Dutton won't refuse it this time."

He wouldn't. It was the smart thing to do in this situation, and Dutton also wanted to reduce any worry Grace had about him.

"Once the team is parked," Grace went on, "try to get into a position to cover Dutton and me if it becomes necessary."

"Of course," Rory muttered. His brother said something Dutton didn't catch. Profanity probably. "Just be careful."

"You and the team do the same," she said and then ended the call.

They started toward the exit where Grace had left the cruiser, but they didn't just bolt outside. After all, this could be the plan, to kill them as they were hurrying from the hospital. They stopped at the sliding glass doors and glanced around the parking lot. Dutton didn't see anything out of the ordinary, but that didn't mean someone wasn't out there, waiting.

Grace looked at him, but not with the harsh expression she'd aimed at Wilson. This look was loaded with worry. With regret, too. "I hate that you've been pulled into things like this. I wanted the badge. You never did."

"Never. I'm a cowboy to the core," he agreed. "But you might have been pulled into this because of me," he reminded her.

She certainly didn't latch on to that. "Either way, just swear to me you'll do everything humanly possible to stay safe."

"I will if you promise me the same thing," he countered.

Grace nodded, held his gaze a moment longer and then glanced around the parking lot again before she motioned for them to move. They did. Both of them drew their guns, hurrying to the cruiser, and they climbed inside as fast as they could.

Dutton had held his breath during the short dash to the vehicle, and he'd also braced himself for the sound of gunfire. But there was nothing. Apparently, the killer hadn't planned for the showdown here but at the cemetery.

She started the engine but then reached across the back seat to retrieve the Kevlar vests she'd left there. They put them on before Grace drove away.

"My mom is buried at that cemetery, and I've been there many times," Dutton told her as he kept watch of their surroundings. "There are plenty of places to hide."

"Yes," she muttered.

Like him, she had probably been there many times, too, and was probably trying to picture the place so she could calculate the best spot for the killer to lie in wait for them. The limestone exterior church was old, built over a hundred years ago, and wasn't huge by any standards.

The grounds were a different matter, though.

The cemetery spread out over at least three acres. Not a wide-open space, either. There were massive trees mixed in among the tombstones and yet more trees and shrubs encircling it. That's likely where the killer would be.

"Can you pull up a photo of Bailey on your phone?" Grace asked him. "There might be one on the SAPD website."

While still volleying glances around him, Dutton typed in the woman's name and almost immediately got a lot of hits. Since one of the top hits was an engagement announcement, he tapped on that one and saw a smiling Wilson with a tall willowy blonde who was sporting the same expression. It was strange to see Wilson like this, since the man was usually snarling, but the couple looked very much in love.

Looked.

Dutton hadn't ruled out the possibility that Wilson was a cold-blooded killer who might harm female cops to get back at Grace. However, would Wilson actually murder his fiancée? Maybe. But then there were a lot of maybes in this investigation.

He showed her the photo, and Grace made several quick

glances at it, as if committing the image to memory. The hope was they'd find Bailey looking pretty much the same as she was here. Almost certainly not smiling, but perhaps she hadn't been harmed. Or worse.

Grace's phone rang, and he saw Livvy's name pop up on the dashboard screen. She took the call hands-free, and immediately the deputy's voice began to sound through the cruiser.

"The church is supposed to be empty," Livvy explained. "I called Reverend Michaels, and he said no one was scheduled to be there today, that he was working from home. They have a security system, and he insists it would have gotten an alert had anyone tried to get in."

Dutton knew security systems could be compromised, but he still doubted that's where the killer was. It was just far easier to hide in the woods. Added to that, if things went wrong for the killer, it'd be harder to escape from the church. Dutton was betting the SOB had a vehicle stashed nearby. A vehicle that hopefully the deputies would see and disable so the killer couldn't use it to make a getaway.

"We just pulled onto the dirt road," Livvy added. "Nothing out of the ordinary so far. What about you? What's your location?"

"Nearly there, about a half mile out," Grace answered and then paused. "I want Judson and Eden to stay in their cruiser so they can watch the road. Rory and you should put on Kevlar and ease your way through the woods, so you'll have a visual of the church. Watch every step, though. Remember, this guy's already used explosives and pepper spray. So far, he hasn't fired any shots, but that doesn't mean he won't this time."

Livvy made a sound of agreement, and they ended the call just as Grace took the turn onto the main road that led to the church. It didn't take long before the church itself came into view, since it was perched on a hill. Grace had to take the final turn before he saw the cemetery.

And he cursed.

Dutton had known there were a lot of graves here, but it suddenly seemed like hundreds and hundreds. And they weren't all low headstones, either. Some were actual mausoleums that would be the perfect place for launching an attack.

Grace slowed the cruiser as they approached the church, and both of them started combing the area, looking for both Bailey and the person who'd taken her. The driveway between the church and cemetery was gravel, and the rocks and dirt crunched under the tires of the cruiser. Not a deafening sound, but a distracting one that Dutton hoped wasn't drowning out other noises they should be hearing.

Such as Bailey calling for help. If she was alive, that is.

Or a killer moving toward them.

Hard not to react to that, but Dutton tried to keep his breathing and heartbeat level. He hoped Grace was able to do the same.

Grace continued the slow speed, inching the cruiser past the church, where they examined both the doors and the windows. Nothing was open, and nothing seemed out of place.

"He might have tied her to a tree," Grace muttered, a reminder that it wasn't just the church and cemetery they had to check, but also the woods.

Dutton looked there, too, while Grace stayed on the narrow, rough road that threaded between the headstones in the center and to the far back of the cemetery. Most people didn't use the road when they visited a departed loved one. They parked by the church and walked, but he suspected the road was for maintenance vehicles and gravediggers.

As the cruiser crept along, it meant a new area to search,

and with each passing moment, the adrenaline just kept revving up. His body was obviously preparing for a fight that Dutton hoped didn't happen. He didn't want Grace and their baby in the middle of a gunfight.

He looked up and saw they were approaching the end of the road ahead. Once they reached it, Dutton suspected Grace would just turn around and keep driving through the cemetery until the killer made contact with them.

Or attacked.

The SOB sure wasn't going to make this easy, and Dutton was about to curse again when he saw something. A flutter of movement at the end of the road and on the right. Grace obviously saw it, too, because she hit the brakes and motioned toward the blond-haired woman.

Bailey.

Not tied to a tree but rather a tall column headstone. Her captor had used thick rope that coiled around her body twice and was no doubt tied in the back, where she couldn't reach it. Her hands were cuffed in front of her, probably with her own handcuffs, and for good measure, her feet were tied as well.

She was gagged but very much alive because she was struggling to get loose while she had her wild-eyed gaze fixed on the cruiser. That eased the knot just a little in Dutton's gut, but he knew the woman was far from being safe.

He had to fight his instincts to bolt from the cruiser and rescue her. Which was no doubt what her captor hoped he'd do, with Grace in tow, so all of them could die.

Grace used the hands-free to send a text to Livvy. *We found her at the far back of the cemetery. She's alive.*

Maybe they would relay that to Wilson. Of course, if Wilson had orchestrated this, then he already knew.

"Why not put her in the middle of the graves, where it'd be harder for us to get to her?" Dutton muttered.

Grace made a sound of agreement. "Because this is both a trap and a way to torture all three of us," she answered almost idly and then made some quick glances over her shoulder. "Keep watch because I'm going to back up and try to get closer to Bailey. I'll have to run over some graves to do it, but I don't think the dead will object if it can save a life."

She threw the cruiser into Reverse, which caused some even more frantic movements from Bailey. Probably because she thought they were leaving. But Grace merely backed up a few yards and then drove forward, the right bumper of the cruiser scraping against a marble headstone while the tires crushed several artificial-flower arrangements.

"We're not getting out of the cruiser," Grace said while she got closer to Bailey. "What are the chances you can untie her and pull her through your window?"

"I'll make it work." He had to because there weren't a lot of options here. And it had to be done fast. Because he was certain that time wasn't on their side.

Dutton kept hold of his gun, kept watch around them, too, but he fumbled in his jeans and came up with a pocketknife. The moment Grace was level with Bailey, she stopped the cruiser. So close that the passenger-side door was only a couple of inches from the woman.

He lowered the window and had to put his gun on the dash. Grace would cover him, but it would still be possible for a gunman to shoot through the now-open window and hit both Grace and him. That's why Dutton worked as fast as he could.

Since Bailey was frantically trying to tell them something, he yanked down her gag and got to work cutting the ropes.

"The man who took me ran that way," Bailey blurted, tipping her head to the woods.

That gave Dutton a punch of hope. And dread. Maybe the deputies would be able to catch him and not get shot or killed in the process.

"Who took you?" Grace asked.

Sobbing, Bailey shook her head. "I didn't see his face. He wore a mask and used a stun gun on me."

That was similar to what had been done to the other victims, and Dutton was sure Grace would question Bailey about it further once they were away from this place.

Dutton continued to hack away at the ropes until he'd cut through them, and he immediately latched on to Bailey. This was likely going to give her some bruises, but it was better than dying.

Despite her hands and feet being restrained, Bailey helped by moving forward. Or rather staggering. She would have bashed her head against his had Dutton not caught her.

Grace didn't actually say "hurry," but he could practically hear the word repeating in her head. And he did hurry. Unfortunately, he also had to lean out of the window to be able to grip Bailey. Dutton steeled himself for gunshots.

But they didn't come.

He wanted to believe that was because the deputies had managed to apprehend the killer, but Dutton knew they weren't that lucky. In fact, that sense of dread went up a whole bunch of notches when he heard a sort of hissing sound.

Around them, the ground ignited into flames. Lots of them. They shot up hot and high in a circle around them.

Hell. The killer had set this up, and within seconds, the fire surrounded them. It wasn't actually touching the cruiser, but was so close that the heat felt like it was scalding him.

The temperature was skyrocketing, and if they didn't move, they'd be burned to death.

Dutton gave Bailey a hard yank to get her all the way through and into his lap so he could close the window. The moment he did that, Grace gunned the engine, and the cruiser shot through the wall of fire and thick black smoke.

She couldn't see, of course, and that was a risk, but the biggest risk would be staying put and having the fire ignite the gas tank.

The tires kicked up the gravel, the rocks ramming against the undercarriage and the sides of the vehicle. And even though Bailey was blocking his view, Dutton saw the moment Grace managed to get them out of the fire. He had just a split second of relief.

Before the cruiser slammed into a tree.

Chapter Fourteen

Now that Grace was back in her office, she had given up on mentally complaining about having had to make yet another trip to the hospital. Because needing to go there for a checkup was a far better outcome than what could have happened.

Bailey, Dutton and she could have all been seriously hurt. Killed even, since they'd barely escaped that firetrap mere seconds before it could have gotten a whole lot worse. Yes, Grace had then crashed the cruiser because she hadn't been able to see what was right in front of her. But thankfully, the airbags had deployed, and none of them had been hurt other than a few nicks and bruises.

Still, it'd meant another visit to the hospital, and this time, Grace had looked at the ultrasound screen when the nurse had been moving the wand over her stomach. She'd seen her precious little boy kicking around inside her, and it had given her so much peace. The spent adrenaline had likely contributed to that peaceful feeling, as well as bone-weary fatigue doing its best to take over.

"As soon as you talk to Bailey, you should get some rest," Dutton told her. He was seated across from her in her office, and both of them were reading through reports from the CSIs and the deputies.

Or rather trying to do that.

Grace just couldn't focus and that's why she didn't argue with Dutton. He was right. She needed rest, and she wanted to be home. Only minutes earlier, she'd gotten a text from Judson, who'd let her know that her window had been repaired and her security system upgraded. And the work had been done by someone they trusted, the same handyman who'd been doing repairs for both her mother and the police station for decades. She hadn't wanted to take any chances with the killer or a hired gun getting into her house and waiting to attack them again.

The team of deputies that had been in the woods behind the church hadn't seen anyone running from the scene, but it was possible the killer or a hired gun had been there, watching, waiting for them to die.

Then again, he or she could have set the firetrap on a timer even before Bailey had been brought to the cemetery and tied to the headstone. It was something the CSIs were investigating, and hopefully, they'd soon have some answers.

Grace looked up when there was movement in the doorway, and because she was still on edge from the latest attempt to kill them, her body automatically braced. She had to stop herself from reaching for her weapon. Because this wasn't a threat.

It was Jamie, Ike and Rory.

Jamie immediately came into the room, and as Dutton stood, she threw herself into his arms. She wasn't crying, but it didn't look as if she could hold herself together much longer.

"I'd like to take Jamie and Dad home if that's okay," Rory said to Grace. "I can come back as soon as I drop them off."

"I've hired two bodyguards," Ike quickly explained. "And Dutton's canceled all deliveries and has posted one of the hands at the gate to make sure no one comes in. Another hand is monitoring the camera in case someone tries to sneak onto the ranch."

Grace nodded. Those were all good security measures, but she could add one more. "I can also arrange for a reserve deputy to stay with you."

Ike opened his mouth as if he might say something ugly about the offer. No doubt a knee-jerk reaction for him. But then he glanced at Jamie, and he must have seen the fear and weariness on the girl's face. Jamie had been through way too much. Ike, too. And the man must have realized that.

"Thanks," Ike muttered.

Grace muttered, "You're welcome," and texted Dispatch to send out a reserve deputy. She didn't have a lot of personnel who weren't already working the case. But there was a retired deputy, Mack Henderson, who would be able to fill in. Maybe, though, his services wouldn't be needed and the killer wouldn't go after Ike again.

Dutton held on to Jamie several more moments and brushed a kiss on the top of her head. "Text me when you make it home."

Jamie stepped back and looked up at him. "I will. And you'll stay safe?" she asked, glancing at both Dutton and Grace.

"We will," Dutton assured her. And they would indeed try to do that, but the killer was definitely hell-bent on killing them.

Well, maybe.

So far, the attacks had been life-threatening, but either they'd gotten lucky or else the attempts hadn't been designed to kill. They could be just ways of stringing out the torture. And that took Grace to the theory of Wilson being the killer. If the town was being terrorized, and made people believe she wasn't doing her job, then that would perhaps get the town council to vote for a recall election.

A recall that could cost her the badge.

The thought of that added a sickening dread to the rest of what she was feeling. All her life, she'd only wanted to be a cop, and now that might be taken from her.

Jamie said her goodbyes to Dutton and Grace, and the girl left with Rory and Ike. Grace started to turn back to the reports, but then Livvy tapped on the still open door.

"We might have something," Livvy said, and while she wasn't exactly smiling, she did look hopeful. "The church has two security cameras. Apparently, after some break-ins at other churches in the county, the pastor had them installed less than a month ago, so a lot of people don't even know they're there. Neither of the cameras face the cemetery," she quickly added. "But they cover both the front and back doors so they might have captured the attacker coming and going."

Grace felt some hope over that, too. "Please tell me the cameras save footage."

"They do," Livvy confirmed. "They're motion-activated so if a vehicle or anyone moved within their range, the cameras would have kicked in, and that would have been sent to the company that monitors it. We should be getting copies of that feed within the next hour or so."

"Good," Grace muttered. "When you get it, go through it, and if you need help, just let me know." She paused. "Are Wilson and Bailey still in the break room?" She hadn't seen them leave, but considering Wilson was a suspect, Grace hadn't wanted the man to try to sneak out with or without his fiancée.

"They are. I was just in there to get a cup of coffee, and they were on the sofa. Bailey said she'd come in here soon and give her statement. She just wanted a little more time to settle her nerves."

Grace totally understood that, but she wondered just how settled Bailey's nerves would be if she learned that her boyfriend was a murder suspect.

"One more thing," Livvy said, and this time, there was no silver-lining look in her expression. "Brian's lawyer is filing a harassment suit against you. I figure it won't go anywhere. We had more than enough to bring him in what with him lying to us and his boss about his alibi."

They had indeed had just cause. Still did. But Brian had likely wanted to do this in an attempt to make himself look innocent. It was too bad the SAPD cops hadn't found anything incriminating when they'd conducted a search of his house and the yard. According to the report Grace had been trying to read, everything the cops had seen meshed with the story Brian had given them.

"I'll let you know if I see anything on the church security cameras," Livvy said, and she turned to leave. She stopped, though, and sighed when she looked at Grace and Dutton. "You two are in some serious need of rest. Want me to shut the door so you can catch a catnap?"

It was tempting, but Grace shook her head, and on another sigh, Livvy walked away.

A closed door would likely mean she'd end up in Dutton's arms. And she might be the one to initiate it, too. Grace knew she'd find comfort there. But she'd find trouble as well. Because the barriers between the two of them no longer seemed to exist, and something as comforting as a hug could turn into a whole lot more.

"Security gate," Dutton said, holding up one finger. "Ranch hand guarding the gate." A second finger went up. "Cameras that are being monitored." A third finger lifted.

"And five other hands on the grounds who have licenses to carry and know how to use a firearm."

She didn't give him the flat look she would have doled out to him just twenty-four hours earlier. "My security system has been upgraded," she reminded him, but then Grace immediately waved that off.

An upgrade and the gossip it'd cause if she stayed with him—and it would generate lots and lots of gossip—was paltry compared to the security measures and backup that'd be available at Dutton's ranch. They'd both be safer there and so would their baby.

"FYI, if we're worried about us ending up in bed together, it could happen just as easily at my place as yours," he said. Except he didn't just say it. The words came out in that easy drawl that soothed and aroused.

Yes, even now he could remind her of the heat.

"Alright," she said. "We'll go to your ranch."

She didn't get a chance to see his reaction to that statement, though, because at that exact moment Wilson and Bailey walked in. And it was obvious from the slight smirk on Wilson's face that he'd heard what she had said. Despite the ordeal his fiancée had just gone through, Wilson seemed pleased that he might have more fodder he could use against her in a recall.

Bailey, however, wasn't smirking. Just the opposite. She was pale, and her eyes were red from crying. This ordeal had clearly shaken her to the core.

Dutton moved to the side so she could take the seat he'd been using, and the woman sank down onto it as if her legs were too weak to stand. Wilson dragged the other chair over to sit beside her.

"Have you caught the SOB who did this to Bailey?" Wilson snapped, aiming a hefty dose of anger at Grace.

"I'm working on it," Grace assured him and then turned all of her attention to his fiancée. "Bailey, for now, let's just chat in here. Later, you can make your formal statement. Is that okay?"

"Okay," Bailey muttered, and she practically folded herself into Wilson.

No way could Grace ask the man to leave or Bailey just might clam up, but Wilson couldn't be present during the formal statement process.

"I know this is hard," Grace continued, "but can you tell me what happened? Start with how you were taken."

Bailey gave a shaky nod and swallowed hard. "I was home, getting ready for work, and I heard something in my backyard. It sounded like a wounded cat or something, so I went out my kitchen door to check, and someone must have been waiting there. He immediately stunned me."

"He?" Grace pressed.

Another nod from Bailey. "Definitely a man, but he was wearing a ski mask so I didn't see his face."

Grace so wanted to ask if the man could possibly be Wilson, but she went in a different direction for now and hoped the woman was truly an observant cop. "Any sense of his height or weight?"

"I think he was about six feet, maybe slightly shorter, and had an average build. He was solid but not bulky and didn't have any trouble throwing me over his shoulder after he stunned me."

Bailey had answered that quickly, letting Grace know she'd given this some thought. Grace only hoped Wilson hadn't planted anything in the woman's head that would skew the guilt away from him.

Both Wilson and Brian were right at six feet tall, and both men had what she'd call average builds, so the description didn't rule them out. But Grace was betting this had been the work of a henchman. It would have been too risky for either Wilson or Brian to kidnap a cop in broad daylight.

"Anything about the man stand out?" Grace went on. "Did he say anything to you?"

Bailey shook her head. "He didn't speak, and he was wearing gloves so I couldn't see his hands. He was wearing black steel-toed boots, though." She stopped and shook her head. "I know that's not much. Lots of people wear boots like that. But there was nothing about him that told me who he was."

"Alright," Grace said, trying to keep her voice soothing despite the steely stare Wilson was giving her. "What happened after he used the stun gun and picked you up?"

This time, there was no quick answer. "I'm not sure," Bailey admitted. "Right after he had me, he jabbed me with a needle." She pointed to her arm, but Grace couldn't actually see the puncture mark because of the bruises and scrapes she'd gotten from being pulled through the window of the cruiser, and then the crash.

"The tox results aren't back yet," Wilson said, and even that was a snarl. "And don't you dare say I don't have the right to call the lab about that. Bailey's my fiancée. That gives me the right."

It didn't. Not legally. And especially since he was a suspect, but as long as Grace got the results, she couldn't see the harm in Wilson knowing them. Besides, if he'd been the one to arrange this attack, then he likely already knew what had been used to drug her.

"When I regained consciousness," Bailey went on a moment later, "I was tied to that tombstone, and I saw Mr. McClennan and you driving up." She turned to Dutton then. "Thank you for getting me into the cruiser. You saved my life. You both did," she added to Grace.

"They wouldn't have had to save your life if she'd done her job in the first place and caught the killer," Wilson snapped, and it seemed as if he was geared up to do more lashing out, but Bailey gave his hand a gentle squeeze.

Grace was surprised that the gesture worked and Wilson seemed to throttle back a couple of notches.

"Why didn't he just stab me?" Bailey asked. She tried, and failed, to blink back tears. "That's the MO. Why did he let me live?"

"I'm not sure," Grace answered honestly. "This attack does break the pattern from the first two murders."

"But then there's the attack on his father," Wilson said, tipping his head to Dutton. "And the one at your house that left another woman dead. No pattern in those two."

"No," she replied. "But both of those attacks were likely meant to get to Dutton and me."

What she didn't voice was that the pepper spray could have been shot with a paintball gun that many people knew how to use, but using explosives and setting up a firetrap required some kind of expertise. Wilson might have that knowledge, but there were no indications that Cassie or Brian did. Then again, it might be something that could be learned from the internet.

"Pattern," Wilson grumbled. "That's the problem. You're looking for a pattern, and it's not there. That's because all this has to do with you. I think it's happening because the people of this town don't want you wearing that badge."

Grace lifted an eyebrow. "You think the killer is someone from Renegade Canyon? Someone who hates me? Someone who has a skill set that allows him or her to plan attacks like these?" She pinned her gaze to Wilson, letting him know that he fit that criteria to a *T*.

Wilson cursed, but before he could lash out, Bailey spoke.

"Wilson told me you consider him a suspect because of the drawing the sketch artist did. The drawing based on what a little girl said."

"His cousin." Wilson jabbed his index finger at Dutton.

"Jamie," Dutton stated. "She's a good kid with an excellent memory and attention to detail. She wants to be a cop," he added.

That caused Bailey to smile just a little, but it was very short-lived, because Wilson went into anger overdrive.

"And the man she described just happened to look like me," Wilson growled at Dutton. "It reeks of a setup. If you get rid of me, then your girlfriend gets to keep her job. Well, I won't let you railroad me." He shifted his attention back to Grace. "This little chat is over. And you won't be the one interviewing her. Get one of the deputies to do that, but it'll have to wait. I'm calling a lawyer to sit in when Bailey gives her account of this nightmare you let happen to her."

With that, Wilson stood and practically hauled Bailey to her feet. Bailey's eyes widened in surprise, and for a moment Grace thought she might protest. She didn't. It seemed she had little fight left in her. Bailey allowed Wilson to lead her back in the direction of the break room.

Grace dragged in a long breath and got up to get a bottle of water from the fridge and take a moment to calm down. That didn't happen, though, because as Bailey and Wilson moved out of Grace's line of sight, someone else moved into it.

Cassie.

Great. Another round of what had been a hellish day. Cassie was probably there to gloat about getting the town council to consider a recall vote.

"You have a minute?" Cassie asked.

Much to Grace's surprise, there wasn't any gloating or anger in her tone. Not even after Cassie got Grace's nod to enter and she stepped into the office, where she obviously spotted Dutton. Normally, Cassie's expression and mood turned sour when she saw them together, but apparently, the woman had something else on her mind.

"I heard about what happened at the church," Cassie said, easing the door shut behind her.

"I can't discuss the details of an investigation with you," Grace told her.

Cassie made a sound to indicate that's what she was expecting—that Grace wouldn't be sharing that kind of info. "Reverend Michaels said you were going to review the church's security cameras."

Grace didn't quite manage to suppress a groan, and wished the pastor hadn't revealed any information. Of course, it wasn't possible to keep something like that secret in a small town. Still, Grace didn't confirm that they would indeed be looking at the footage.

"I'll be on it," Cassie blurted. "On the security feed, I mean. I'll probably be on it."

That got Grace's attention, and she automatically adjusted her stance in case she had to draw her gun. From the corner of her eye, she saw Dutton do the same. Was Cassie here to confess to the murders? And was she about to launch into some last-ditch attack?

Grace prepared herself for just that.

Cassie would have had to go through the metal detector when she entered the building and likely wouldn't have been able to bring in a gun, but there were other weapons that could possibly be concealed.

"Why are you on the security feed?" Grace asked when the woman didn't continue.

Cassie huffed, but again, she didn't seem to be angry. "Because I was visiting my grandmother's grave. It's something I do on her birthday. Her birthday's not for another two weeks," she added quickly. "But I had some free time in my schedule so I went." She paused to draw breath. "I just wanted you to know in case you saw my car on the feed and, well, thought the worst."

Grace did think the worst, but then she was doing that about all of the suspects. This could be a clever move on Cassie's part—to dismiss why she was in the very location where an attack had occurred.

"When were you there?" Grace asked, though she would verify it once they had the footage.

Cassie checked her watch. "About four hours ago."

That could have been about the time the killer was setting up the firetrap and tying Bailey to a tombstone. But Bailey had said a man had taken her. One who was about six feet tall. Cassie was on the tall side, but she wasn't built like a man. It was possible, though, that Cassie had been there to assist someone she'd hired to help. Grace really needed to try to get a better timeline of events from Bailey once the woman was ready for a full interview.

"Did you see anyone or anything suspicious when you were at the cemetery?" Grace pressed.

"Of course not. With the murders going on, I would have reported it right away. It was just a routine visit to my grandmother's grave, and I had no idea about the cameras until the reverend mentioned them."

Grace considered all of that for a moment. If Cassie was the killer, then there might be something on the footage that would indicate she had been there to help her henchman set up an attack. It was even possible the henchman had been with her in the vehicle.

"Alright," Grace said. "We should have the security footage soon, and I'll review it." And she wondered if it was just her imagination, but Cassie seemed very uncomfortable when Grace said that.

Cassie nodded and glanced at Dutton, who was scrolling through something on his phone. She opened her mouth as if she might say something else. Maybe about the town-council meeting that would be held tomorrow morning. But then, Cassie just muttered a terse goodbye and walked out.

Dutton reached over and eased the door shut. "Her grandmother's birthday is indeed in two weeks, but she has a lot of family buried there. In other words, Cassie could have used a variety of birth dates and anniversaries of deaths as an excuse to be at the cemetery."

Grace made a sound of agreement. "She could have had Bailey in the trunk of her car. Or maybe some of the equipment used to set up the firetrap." She stopped, considered that and wanted to curse. "There's no chance of me getting a search warrant for her car. It'd be seen as harassment for her part in pushing the recall. And, yes, I could just ask Cassie to allow a search, but the only way she'd agree to that is if she's got nothing to hide."

Dutton made his own sound of agreement just as his phone rang. "It's the PI," he told her as he put the call on speaker.

"Just got an interesting tip from a cop friend at SAPD," Jake immediately said. "Apparently, Elaine's parents realized a lot of money is missing from her savings account. About twenty grand."

"That'd be enough to hire someone to do some work," Dutton commented. "Did Brian have access to the account?"

"You bet he did," Jake confirmed. "My cop friend says they've got security footage of Brian making the withdrawal three weeks ago. They'll be sending the report over to the sheriff there once it's ready."

Good. It was yet more circumstantial evidence, but it was

a legit reason to bring Brian back in to question him about it. Tomorrow morning, though, because Grace didn't think she had the bandwidth to conduct another interview with Brian until she'd gotten some rest. Of course, in the morning she might also have to deal with the fallout from any decision the town council made about the recall.

"There's more," the PI went on. "The camera footage doesn't stop there. The bank is near other businesses with cameras, and SAPD was able to follow the footage of Brian leaving the building. Once outside in the parking lot, Brian met with this man and handed him at least some of the money he'd just withdrawn. I'm texting you the picture of the guy he paid."

Within seconds, Dutton's phone dinged, and he cursed when he saw the image. Grace hurried over to him to see it for herself. The image was grainy, as most were from security cameras, but it was clear enough.

The man receiving the money looked like Wilson.

Chapter Fifteen

Despite trying not to think about it, one thought kept racing through Dutton's head. Grace was in his bed.

Or rather, she was in a bed in his house on the ranch.

He'd argued to get her here, and while Dutton still believed that was the right call, it wasn't easy. Because he wanted to be in that bed with her. Hell, he wanted to try to burn off some of this heat between them with sex. That wasn't going to happen, though, not tonight, anyway. Even if his body kept suggesting it.

Since Grace had left the guest room door open and Dutton had set up a makeshift office on the floor outside the room, he could hear her if she moved around. So far, she hadn't. She'd fallen asleep seemingly seconds after she'd muttered good night and gotten into bed. Dutton was thankful she was finally getting some much-needed rest, but he just couldn't seem to turn off his mind so he could do the same.

Not that he'd planned on a whole lot of sleep, anyway.

No.

He wasn't just listening for Grace moving around, but was concerned about anything that could be a sign of trouble. The gate was shut, the security system was on and ranch hands were patrolling both the grounds and the perimeters of Dutton's place and the main house, where Jamie and Ike were. He had his laptop and was getting a continuous feed from the cameras by the fence.

Added to that, Ike had the two bodyguards inside with them, which was even more protection if the killer decided to go after Ike again. But Dutton thought the threat was over for his father. Not for Grace and him, though. He didn't believe the killer would stop until he or she got their primary targets—Grace and him.

Dutton intended to make sure that didn't happen.

He tried to get his mind off death and danger. Off Grace in his bed, too. And once again, he attempted to read the reports that Grace had shared with him. The SAPD one on Brian's withdrawal was thorough. The man had indeed taken money from his fiancée's savings, but there was nothing illegal about that, since Elaine had added his name to the account. Had Elaine been alive, she might have said she hadn't given Brian permission to take the cash. However, she was dead, so they only had Brian's side of the story.

Or rather, they would when Brian told it.

So far, the man was dodging another interview with his lawyer filing what seemed to Dutton to be delay tactics. Since Brian was a solid suspect, that strategy wouldn't last for long, though. Eventually, Grace would get him back into the police station to answer some hard questions. Like what had he used the money for. And who the man was that was with him in the parking lot.

The man who'd been the spitting image of Wilson.

Wilson's response to that was in another report. He'd insisted the person in the photo wasn't him. There'd been lots of cursing to go along with the denial and the accusation that Grace had a vendetta against him. Ironic, since someone had a deadly vendetta against her. Maybe Wilson. Maybe Brian or Cassie.

Of course, that led Dutton to another possibility, that the killer's crusade to kill them was because of him. And that led right back to Cassie. It was hard for him to imagine a woman he'd once had a relationship with now wanted him dead, but Cassie had seemingly been devastated when he'd ended things with her. But he'd done that after coming to the realization that he'd never love her.

Couldn't.

Because a part of him would always be in love with Grace. He'd felt that way about her since high school, and even though he'd thought the feelings would fade, they hadn't. They'd gotten stronger and hotter. Until they'd landed in bed five months ago. Now they were going to be parents.

Dutton wished though they could be a whole lot more.

But that might not be in the cards for them. If Grace lost her badge, it was possible she wouldn't be able to get past it, that a part of her would resent him for his part in making that happen. Dutton got that. He had plenty of resentment for the people who were trying to force her out of office. However, his feelings for Grace and their baby wouldn't change, whether or not she was a cop.

"Hell," he muttered under his breath. And he groaned. Why not just admit to himself that he was in love with Grace? Because that could lead to a Texas-size heart crushing, that's why.

He might have done some pity wallowing about that if he hadn't heard Grace moving in the bed. Dutton peered into the dark room and wanted to curse again. She wasn't just moving. She was awake and sitting up, and her gaze went straight to him.

"You said you'd sleep," she muttered.

"I will. I was just catching up on a few things."

She sighed and pushed her tousled hair from her face.

"You're working, listening for any kind of break-in and keeping an eye on me. On the floor, no less."

Guilty on all counts, but he didn't want to explain that he hadn't been able to sleep because of thoughts of her. No, she didn't need to hear that.

Yawning, she got out of bed, causing him to groan. "You should try to go back to sleep."

"I will. Once the baby stops playing soccer with my kidneys." Grace headed to the en suite bathroom, but a few minutes later when she came out, she didn't go back to bed. She came toward him.

And Dutton felt his heart go into overdrive.

The rest of his body followed suit and began to rev up. Dutton hated to disappoint that part of him behind the zipper of his jeans, but he was still adamant that sex wasn't going to happen. He was still holding out hope that he could coax Grace back to bed so she could get more sleep.

"It's barely eleven o'clock," Dutton told her. "You've only been asleep three hours."

Grace nodded, retrieved her phone from the nightstand and continued to make her way toward him. There was nothing remotely sexy about the loose sleep pants and T-shirt she had on, but she managed to make everything look hot.

She sank down beside him, landing with her shoulder pressed against his, and she had a look at his laptop screen. "You're so much like a cop," she muttered as she read. "You keep this up, and you're going to lose some of that bad-boy shine."

"I haven't *shined* as a bad boy in a long time," he assured her.

"In this town, that never goes away," she said, and much of the lightness faded from her voice.

She was no doubt thinking of other things that remained

in place, like the gossip about them. And the possibility of losing her badge. Of course, the thing that had to be weighing on her the most was the killer on the loose.

Dutton decided to try for some lightheartedness. "Yeah, gossips still mention the time I got drunk when I was a teenager, climbed on top of the roof at town hall and used red paint to scrawl pretty much every curse word I knew."

As he hoped, she did smile a little. "My mother took you into custody and made you clean up every syllable. You're lucky she didn't arrest you."

"I am," he concurred. "She probably wishes she had." He paused. "As for the other reasons for my bad-boy reputation, some events were greatly exaggerated."

"Only some. You went through that whole love-'em-and-leave-'em phase with many, many women. And then there are the business deals. All legal," she quickly added when he opened his mouth. "But some were cutthroat."

"Some," he admitted. "And others simply got enough attention to make me look ruthless. Like firing Wilson's father, for example." He paused again. "Or breaking Cassie's heart."

She looked at him. Not a good idea since they were sitting so close. It put her mouth much too close to his. Not good if he was truly going through with resisting her tonight.

"If the killer turns out to be one of them, this isn't your fault," she said. "It's theirs, and none of it is on you."

He wanted to believe her, but Dutton could still feel the guilt. That must have shown on his face, too, because she leaned in and kissed her. Nothing hot and hungry. This was a kiss meant to heal. And it worked, but just a little.

Of course, it also worked to kick up that heat.

The heat that was always there. Always.

And that led him to do something stupid and he deepened the kiss. Despite the lecture he'd given himself earlier, he probably wouldn't have done more than just dive into the kiss. He would have pulled Grace into his arms and gone from there.

But her phone rang.

The sound shot through the hall and was so unexpected, Grace let out a soft gasp. "The phone," she muttered. "Not the security system."

No, not that, but Dutton instantly got a bad feeling when he saw Rory's name on the screen. Grace must have as well because she answered it on speaker and blurted, "Did something happen?"

Dutton knew she was steeling herself to hear there'd been another murder, but that wasn't what his brother said.

"Yes, something happened," Rory confirmed, and there was a helluva lot of gloom and doom in his voice. "It's your mother. She's missing."

Missing.

That wasn't a word any cop wanted to hear. Especially with everything else going on. Grace had to fight hard to tamp down the horrible thoughts that immediately flew through her head.

"Explain that," she choked out to Rory, though her throat had seemingly clamped shut.

She heard Rory take a deep breath. "About thirty minutes ago, your mother called Dispatch to ask for a deputy to come out to her place for backup. She said someone had just broken in."

Grace had to calm her own breathing, and beside her, Dutton cursed. And she knew why. It wasn't solely because of her mother's call and being missing. He no doubt knew the question Grace was about to ask.

"Why didn't she call me?" Grace demanded.

"You mother told Dispatch that you weren't to be contacted, that she wanted a deputy only." There was an apology in Rory's tone even though he'd had nothing to do with her mother's insistence. "I suspect that's because Aileen didn't want you to respond to her place this late at night, and she persuaded the dispatcher to do as she said."

Grace knew Rory was right, but her mother had been wrong to put Grace's safety over an active murder investigation. "Who did Dispatch send out to her house?"

"Bennie, but Ellie went with him," Rory explained, referring to Ellie Trainor, one of the night deputies who'd been on the job for nearly two decades. "I had already gone home, but after Bennie and Ellie arrived at your mother's house and found the door wide open, Bennie called me."

"And not me," Grace muttered. She was going to have a chat with her deputies and the dispatcher about following protocol for such things. Her mother, too.

If her mother was alive, that is.

Grace had to shut down any other possibility. Otherwise, she wouldn't be able to do her job. And right now, she had to focus on finding her mother.

She got up from the floor, and with Dutton right behind her, she went into the bedroom to change back into her work clothes. She didn't even care that she was undressing in front of him. Grace just wanted to be ready to get out the door as soon as she had all the details from Rory.

"Bennie and Ellie went into Aileen's house to search it," Rory went on. "When I arrived, they'd already figured out that someone had bashed through the back door and a window on the side of the house."

So possibly a two-pronged attack, maybe done at the same time to gain access and close in on her mother. It made her wonder which of their suspects and a henchman had done this. Or maybe they were both hired thugs.

"The security alarm didn't go off?" Grace asked as she yanked on her pants and then her boots.

"Not that we could tell," Rory answered. "There was a gun on the floor. A white-handled Smith and Wesson. And there were signs of a struggle."

The gun was likely her mother's since Grace knew she had one like that. What she couldn't understand was how the two attackers had gotten to Aileen without her being able to take at least one of them out. Her mother didn't have the physical strength to fight them off, but she had solid aim.

"Any blood?" Grace asked.

"None that I could see," Rory answered.

That was something to be thankful for. If the killer used the same MO, her mother could have been stabbed. Of course, it was possible the killer still had plans to do that.

"I called your mom's neighbors to ask if they saw anything," Rory went on, and that's when Grace realized he was driving. But where? Did that mean he had a lead, or was he coming to get her? "Mr. Henry said he saw headlights and that the car was moving fast. He didn't get the plates or a description of the vehicle, but he said it was heading south."

South would take them in the direction of the ranch. Specifically to the pasture where the other two bodies had been dumped.

"Yeah," Rory said as if he'd read her mind. "Maybe returning to the scene of the crime, so to speak. I'm heading to the ranch now, and Bennie and Ellie are in their cruiser right behind me."

"We'll meet you," Grace said, and she knew that Dutton was about to protest and remind her that this could be a trap to lure her out. It most likely was. "She's my mother," Grace muttered, and that cooled the argument she saw in his eyes.

"Will you wear Kevlar and stay in the cruiser?" he asked as they hurried down the stairs.

"Yes to the first, and I'll try to do the second."

That was the best she could give him right now, and Dutton didn't push her. Probably because he knew she was frantic to find Aileen. Just as he had been when Ike had been taken.

They went to the garage, where Grace had left the cruiser, but before Dutton opened the garage door, he used his phone to access the cameras around the perimeter of the house.

"It's clear," he told her. "The two men you'll see are ranch hands."

Grace did indeed see the men the moment she backed the cruiser out of the garage. In fact, they weren't the only ones standing guard. She saw more scattered throughout the grounds all the way to the gate.

Dutton used his remote to open it, and Grace drove through, but she made herself wait until the gate was closed again before she sped away. She hadn't wanted the killer to be able to sneak in the moment they were out of sight.

There were no other vehicles on the private road, but like the cemetery, there were so many places for someone to hide and ambush them. Which could be the point of all of this. Her mother could be the lure just as Ike had been, and Grace hoped that meant Aileen hadn't been harmed, that she was being held as a bargaining tool or bait for Dutton and her.

Of course, Aileen would be furious about being used like that, and Grace knew her mother would do everything humanly possible to prevent Dutton and her from being attacked.

But humanly possible wasn't always enough.

Grace threaded the cruiser through the deep curves of the narrow road, wishing there'd been a full moon to give better illumination to the sides, where there were trees and trails. However, she did see different kind of lights ahead. The whirling blue lights of the cruisers. The two sets of responding deputies had obviously already made it to the fence.

Her chest tightened, and Grace realized she was holding her breath, waiting for the worst. A call to tell her that there was yet another body tied to the fence post. But none came, and that gave her hope. Hope that she had to clasp on to because she couldn't deal with the worst right now.

When they approached the fence, Grace pulled her cruiser behind the two others and tried to pick through the darkness to determine what was happening. All four deputies were out of their vehicles and had flashlights they were panning over the posts and the nearby trees.

Rory shook his head and started toward her. "Nothing," he said.

That gave her a jolt of sickening dread. She hadn't wanted to find her mother here, tied to a post and bleeding out. But if Aileen wasn't here, then where the heck was she? If this was a sick game meant to draw out Dutton and her, why hadn't the killer led them straight to him or her.

She lowered her window as Rory approached. "You got a look inside my mother's house," she said. "How much of a struggle had there been?"

The tightening of a jaw muscle let her know it'd been bad. But she hoped he wouldn't sugarcoat it. "Lots of things toppled over. Some broken glass." He paused. "It looks like someone shot into the wall. But no blood," he disclosed.

Both of them were well aware that sometimes blood wasn't in abundance if a cop-killer bullet was used. The

Teflon coating on a bullet like that created all sorts of internal injuries, though.

"The killer's yet to shoot anyone," Dutton reminded her.

That didn't mean there hadn't been a gunfight this time. And if her mother had won that particular fight, she wouldn't be missing right now.

"Rory," Bennie called out. "You need to see this."

Grace's attention raced to Bennie, who was in a cluster of trees about fifteen yards from the fence. He had his flashlight aimed at something on the ground.

"What is it?" Grace asked as Rory hurried toward his fellow deputy.

Bennie shook his head, and it took Grace a moment to realize he wasn't doing that because he didn't know what he was looking at, but because it wasn't something he wanted to say. Finally, though, he spoke, and the words slammed into Grace like gunshots.

"We have a dead body."

DUTTON CURSED, and he automatically reached for Grace, who was in turn reaching to open the door of the cruiser. He figured she was in shock.

Which was no doubt what the killer had planned.

This way, Grace could be attacked when she bolted from the cruiser, something Dutton couldn't let happen. He took hold of her arm and turned her to look at him. She struggled to get away, to run to her mother, and Dutton had to do something to stop her.

"Just wait a second," he insisted.

She did. With her breath gusting and panic in her eyes, she looked at him just as Bennie called out to them again.

"It's not Aileen," the deputy shouted.

The relief was instant in everyone at the scene but especially for Grace. The fight in her body drained away, and on a hoarse sob, she dropped her head onto his shoulder. Dutton felt her trembling when his arms closed around her.

Because she was no longer looking out the window, she didn't see the double takes Bennie and the other deputies seemed to have when Bennie inched a little closer to the body, fanning his flashlight over it.

"It's Wilson Finney," he said, causing Grace's head to whip up and snap back toward Bennie. "A gunshot wound to the head."

"Wilson?" Grace muttered, and Dutton knew her mind was whirling with the reasons for him to be murdered.

"No," Bennie amended a moment later. "He sure as hell looks a lot like Wilson, but it's not. Should I glove up and see if he's got an ID on him?"

Grace hesitated, probably because touching the body could destroy possible evidence. But there was a bigger picture here. The identity of this man might lead them to Aileen because Dutton wasn't buying that this guy wasn't connected to Aileen's abduction.

"Do that," Grace instructed. "Just be careful and make sure there aren't explosives or some kind of firetrap rigged around the body."

That put some alarm in all the deputies, and Rory went to join them in using their flashlights to search the area. While they did that, Dutton eased his door open so he could be ready to assist Bennie, Ellie and Rory because this would be the perfect time for the killer to attack. Across from him, Grace did the same thing.

"I don't see anything," Rory relayed to her.

With that go-ahead, Bennie handed his flashlight to Ellie and put on a pair of latex gloves he took from his pocket. Dutton glanced at the deputy as he went closer to the body.

His steps were slow and cautious, and like Dutton, Bennie and everyone else were volleying looks around the pasture and the trees.

It didn't take long for Bennie to ease a wallet from the dead guy's pants, and he opened it. Ellie turned the flashlight on what had to be a driver's license.

"His name is Teddy Lunsford," Bennie declared. "Thirty-one. His address is in San Antonio."

Grace yanked out her phone and did a search on the man. Dutton watched as Lunsford's photo popped up. Oh, yeah. He looked like Wilson. Maybe not an identical-twin kind of thing, but this guy could be Wilson's cousin.

"He's got a record," Grace added, and she cursed under her breath. "Eight years ago he was arrested for blowing up his ex-girlfriend's car and setting a fire ring around her house. She escaped, and there were no injuries, which explains why Lunsford only served six years in prison."

Well, that explained two of the attacks. Lunsford had likely done the one at the ranch and the cemetery. But there was something Dutton wasn't seeing in the report Grace had accessed.

"He doesn't have any obvious connection to our suspects," Dutton muttered. "Or to your mother."

Aileen hadn't been the one to arrest him. Cops in SAPD had. And Lunsford had served his time in prison hours from Renegade Canyon.

"No, nothing obvious," Grace agreed. "But there could be something."

She stopped, and he could feel the hope draining away. She had needed there to be something to help them find Aileen.

"Keep searching him," Grace told Bennie. "See if he has

car keys because he could have a vehicle parked nearby. My mother could be in it."

That was possible, but it led Dutton to a whole bunch of questions. Would Aileen still be alive and had Lunsford been the one to take her? Also, why had Lunsford been killed? Was he a loose end that the killer had wanted to eliminate? If the last was true, then Aileen would likely be considered a loose end as well.

Bennie resumed his search of the body while Grace continued to go through Lunsford's background. Dutton was reading it as well, while throwing glances out the windows.

"Keys," Bennie called out. He held them up and pressed the keypad, no doubt to try to figure out if the vehicle was nearby.

It was.

The short beep sounded through the night. And it was close.

"I think it's on the trail just across the road," Dutton said, pointing in that direction.

Bennie double-tapped the keypad again and got the same beep from the same location Dutton had pointed out. Grace started the cruiser but then stopped. Dutton soon saw why when he spotted the movement in the rearview mirror.

A man.

He was behind the cruiser and coming straight toward them.

The adrenaline shot through Dutton, and getting off the seat, he stepped out and turned his gun in the direction of the man. Grace looked up from her phone, then tossing it aside, she got out also and took aim at him as well. The guy wasn't running, but he was hurrying.

And he had a gun.

"Everyone get down," Grace shouted.

That caused the man to stop in his tracks. "Is Aileen dead?" he called out.

Both Dutton and Grace cursed, saying nearly identical profanities, because they recognized the voice.

Wilson.

Dutton didn't ask himself why the county sheriff was here. He just kept his gun trained on him. Wilson had to know if he shot Grace that the deputies would open fire on him, but if the man was filled with enough hate and desperation, that might not matter.

"It's me, Wilson," he said after looking at the stances of the deputies, Grace and Dutton.

He had five guns trained on him.

Wilson did some cursing as well, and he shook his head in what seemed to be disgust. "You think I'm here to kill someone?" But he didn't wait for a response. "Well, I'm not."

"Then, holster your gun," Grace snapped. "And then you can tell me what you're doing here."

That amped up Wilson's disgust. However, he did put away his weapon. "Because I want to catch the person who nearly killed Bailey. I want to do your job for you since you're not doing it."

Grace ignored him and looked at Rory. It seemed to Dutton that she was debating with herself as to how to handle this. "We need to check out Lunsford's vehicle and deal with Wilson," she said, keeping her voice low, probably so that Wilson wouldn't be able to hear. "Dutton and I can take Lunsford's vehicle—"

"No," Rory and Dutton said in unison. Dutton held back and let his brother take over his particular argument.

"Ellie and I can go across the road in a cruiser," Rory insisted. "We'll be careful, and yes, we'll look for any traps.

If your mother's there, we'll find her." He tipped his head to Wilson. "Bennie, Dutton and you can deal with him."

"Take Bennie with you," Grace told Rory. "All three of you should go."

Rory shook his head. "If Wilson's the killer, you'll need backup."

"Dutton is my backup." She glanced at him for a confirming nod.

But Dutton wasn't sure he wanted to give her a confirmation. He would have preferred Grace had an entire team of cops around her, but he understood it was important for her to find out if her mother was in that vehicle. Important, too, to get to her fast before she could be murdered like the other female cops.

So Dutton nodded.

"Go," Grace told Rory.

Rory groaned, but did as he was told, eventually. He hesitated a couple of seconds, probably hoping Grace would change her mind. When she didn't, he muttered some profanity under his breath, and he hurried to the other deputies to get them moving to the cruiser.

"What the hell is going on?" Wilson demanded. "They're leaving?" he asked when Bennie, Rory and Ellie hurried to a cruiser. "Do they have a lead on the killer?"

Dutton huffed and was glad Grace ignored Wilson's questions and fired off some of her own. "Who told you about my mother, and how did you know to come to this spot on the ranch? While you're at it, you can explain why you're walking and not in your vehicle."

Wilson was slow to answer. "I have my police radio tuned to Renegade Canyon PD Dispatch. And before you say I don't have a right, I do. Bailey is going through hell and had to be sedated. Her folks are with her now, but they're a mess, too. All because you can't catch this killer."

"And you came here to catch him," Grace said with a whole lot of sarcasm in her voice.

The man shrugged. "Well, this was where he left the first two victims. So I parked up the road and walked here. I wanted to see what you were doing, and I figured my best shot at that was sneaking up on you and having a look for myself." He glanced at the fence. "Is Aileen here? Is she dead?"

Dutton shot Wilson a glare for the callous tone, and he so wished he could take the man down a notch. But now wasn't the time. Not when they were sitting ducks. Best for Grace to finish up what she needed to do, so they could go back inside the ranch gates.

"No, Aileen isn't here," Grace said, and her tone matched the icy feelings Dutton was having about Wilson. "Tell me about Teddy Lunsford," she demanded.

Wilson shook his head. "Who? I've never heard of him."

Dutton couldn't tell if the man was lying, but at this point, he was going to assume everything that came out of his mouth was meant to cover up his guilt in the murders and attacks. If Wilson turned out to be innocent, then Dutton would owe him an apology.

"Teddy Lunsford," Grace repeated, and she would have no doubt added more if they hadn't heard the revving of an engine.

A loud one.

Loud enough for Dutton to motion for Grace to get back in the cruiser. They did, both practically diving inside.

Dutton didn't spot any headlights, but there was definitely a vehicle coming from the road in front of them. There was a hill, and he didn't see the semitruck until it was coming right at them.

Chapter Sixteen

Grace couldn't throw the cruiser into reverse since Wilson was right behind it. Besides, she didn't have time to do anything before the crash came.

The huge black truck slammed into them.

It wasn't the kind of truck that was usually on the rural roads. This was a commercial vehicle that was double the size of the cruiser, and the driver was using it like a lethal weapon.

The impact jolted her back just as the airbag deployed and slammed into her face. It knocked the gun from her hand. Knocked the breath from her, too, and she immediately thought of her precious baby. Thought of what her OB doctor had told her as well, that an airbag wouldn't hurt an unborn child.

Still, the fear was there.

So was the fear of them being killed.

Grace started batting down the airbag, looking for Dutton. She had to make sure he was okay, and to check and see if the driver of the truck, or Wilson, was coming after them. She saw he was doing the same thing. He was frantically punching down the airbag so he could glance over to make sure she was alright. Then, he turned both his gaze and his gun in the direction of the truck.

"No cargo trailer, which makes it easy for the driver to maneuver," Dutton muttered. "He'll try to come at us again."

Mercy. Dutton was probably right, and Grace tried to put the cruiser into gear so she could at least try to get out of the path of the truck before it immobilized them. If it hadn't already. The engine was on, but she wasn't sure if the vehicle was still capable of being driven.

She heard Wilson yelling, but she had no idea if he'd been hurt. Since he'd been standing behind the cruiser, it was possible he was hit. It was equally possible though that he was calling out some orders to his henchman, who was behind the wheel of that semi.

A henchman who could be hell-bent on trying to kill them.

The driver of the truck reversed, the massive tires sending up billows of smoke on the asphalt, and he sped back a few yards. Then, as Dutton had predicted, he came at them again. The first collision had taken out the cruiser headlights, and because of the height of the semi, Grace couldn't see the driver.

But she saw he was about to crash into them for a second time.

There'd be no airbag this time, but Grace was still wearing her seat belt. She prayed that was enough to keep her baby unharmed.

The semi rammed into them again, and the night was filled with the sound of metal crushing against metal. The front end of the cruiser crumpled, taking out the engine and mangling it as if it was an accordion. A part of the hood flew off, slamming into the windshield and cracking it.

Now they were trapped. And their attacker knew that. He continued the forward momentum of the truck, pushing them back.

And back.

The driver didn't reverse, didn't crash into them again. He just continued to push them backward. Grace stomped her foot on the brakes, hoping that would at least put up some resistance, but the brakes weren't working, either.

"He's trying to push us into a ditch," Dutton said. "And it's filled with water from the storms."

She glanced at her side mirror and realized that was exactly what the driver was trying to do. And once they were jammed into the ditch, killing them would be easy. Grace couldn't see Wilson and wondered if he'd be the shooter once they were trapped. If so, she didn't intend to make this easy for him.

Grace felt around on the seat and console for her gun, and for several heart-stopping moments, she couldn't find it. Finally, her fingers raked across it, and she snatched it up.

She glanced in the side mirror and saw the ditch was way too close. They'd be in it within seconds, and if the cruiser went in at the wrong angle and the ditch was deep enough, water could get inside and drown them. Added to that, they might not be able to get the doors open if the semi wedged them in.

"We have to move," Dutton said at the exact moment she was about to say the same thing. "Stay low, run to the back end of the cruiser and use it for cover. Keep a lookout for Wilson, too."

"You do the same," Grace insisted.

That was all they had time to say because the semi driver revved his engine again, and Grace knew it was now or never. She threw open her door, which thankfully hadn't been damaged, but her heart dropped when she saw that Dutton was struggling to get out.

She glanced at the truck, then at Dutton, and Grace knew if she didn't do something, he'd be in the cruiser if the truck's tires managed to roll over the top of it. Or crushed it with Dutton inside.

Grace bolted out of the cruiser, then took aim at the truck's windshield.

And fired.

It was a risk since the bullet could ricochet off the metal. A risk, too, because she still didn't know where Wilson was, and at the moment she was an easy target, especially if he was still behind her. He could just shoot her in the back. But Grace refused to think about that right now. She only focused on getting Dutton out of the cruiser.

Dutton gave up on opening his door and scrambled across the driver's seat. Not easily. The now deflated airbags were in the way so he had to fight through those. And the driver just kept coming at them.

Grace took aim at the truck's windshield again, specifically targeting the driver's side of the vehicle, and this time she didn't fire just one shot. She aimed three in rapid succession. The bullets all slammed into the glass, shattering it. Maybe hitting the driver, too.

Because the truck finally stopped.

Dutton bolted out beside her, but he didn't stop. He took hold of her arm and got her moving away from the cruiser, away from the truck. And hopefully away from any bullets that the truck driver might send their way.

With each step, Grace steeled herself for gunfire.

But it didn't come.

There was only the menacing roar of the truck's engine and the sound of sirens. The deputies had no doubt heard the gunfire and were responding. She prayed that didn't end up costing her mother her life, but she had no idea if Aileen was even anywhere near here. The truck driver could be another hired thug doing the killer's bidding, and her mother and the killer could be anywhere.

They ducked behind some wild shrubs that weren't much cover but were better than nothing. Dutton immediately started shifting his gaze between the truck and their surroundings. Grace did the same. It was too dark for her to see the driver or anyone else who might be inside the truck, but she spotted a cluster of trees not far from a narrow portion of the ditch.

"There," she said, tipping her head in that direction. Moving there could get them farther away from the truck in case it came at them again. Plus, the trees would be better cover.

Dutton nodded and met her eyes for a split second. "Try to stay behind me," he muttered. "Think of it as desk duty."

Grace didn't especially want to take him up on the offer, but she didn't want to argue with him about this. She just wanted them both in a safer position so they could protect their child and maybe catch a killer in the process. The location by the trees might give them a better angle to see exactly who was in the truck.

Dutton sprang up from the shrubs, taking aim at the truck, and he started to move the moment Grace was in place behind him. She kept watch, ready for an attack. She didn't see anything, but she heard something just as they darted behind the trees.

Maybe a door opening?

Her gaze fired to the truck, but the passenger-side door was shut. She couldn't see the driver's side, though, and she was pretty sure Dutton couldn't, either.

They stooped there, with their breaths gusting, waiting for something, *anything*, that would help them pinpoint a killer. The seconds crawled by, the sounds of the siren getting closer. But even over the blare of that, Grace heard something else.

Running footsteps.

"I think someone just got out of the truck," Dutton whispered.

Grace agreed, though she still couldn't see anyone. Well, not by the truck, anyway, but she could definitely hear those running footsteps. Then, she caught a blur of motion from the corner of her eye and pivoted in that direction with her gun ready.

And then she saw something.

"Wilson," she muttered.

Dutton followed her gaze and no doubt also saw Wilson doing some running of his own. He was sprinting toward the tree line, where they'd found Teddy Lunsford's body. Was Wilson trying to retrieve some possible evidence that could be on the dead man? Or worse. Was there some kind of firetrap that Wilson was about to unleash?

"Wilson?" she called out.

He stopped and turned, and she thought he was trying to pick through the darkness to find her. "I have to go," Wilson said, tipping his head to deeper within the woods. "It's your mother. I just spotted Aileen."

DUTTON TOOK HOLD of Grace's arm when she started to bolt from the trees. He knew it was an automatic response for her, a desperate need to save her mother. But he couldn't let her run out into the open, where she could be gunned down.

Because Wilson could have just told a huge lie to make that happen.

They didn't know if Wilson was the killer, but the man was certainly on the short list of suspects, and if Wilson had indeed orchestrated this nightmare, then he likely wouldn't hesitate to use Aileen to get what he wanted.

But what the heck did he want?

That was a question that had kept going through Dutton's mind since the start of these attacks, but this all seemed extreme for someone jealous of Grace's badge. Still, people had killed for less than that, and maybe Wilson had as well. If so, that could mean he intended to use Aileen to draw out Grace and then murder both women.

Dutton wouldn't let that happen.

However, he also wasn't going to be able to keep Grace in place much longer. Both the cop and daughter in her were obviously urging her to do something and to do it now, now, now.

The deputies pulled to a stop near what was left of Grace's cruiser, and Rory, Bennie and Ellie barreled out. All of them had their guns ready. All fired glances around to try to figure out what was happening.

"Call for more backup and then check the truck," Grace told them. "But be careful. The killer could still be inside."

That was true, but Dutton figured those running footsteps they'd heard belonged to the killer. Maybe to Aileen, too, if the killer had forced her out of the truck and into the woods. Still, there was a chance that Aileen had managed to escape and was trying to put some distance between herself and the person who'd taken her.

Dutton watched while Bennie and Ellie kept watch and Rory went to the truck. And Dutton got a jolt of worry for his brother that Grace had almost certainly gotten for Aileen. But no gunshots came, and the truck didn't roar to life again to try to run them all down.

"It's empty," Rory said moments later. "But there's blood on the seat."

Grace made a sound, part gasp, part groan, and Dutton could feel the battle she was having with herself. Dutton wanted to remind her that Wilson had said he'd seen Aileen. Alive. But he had no way of knowing if that was the truth.

Not yet, anyway.

"You could stay here with two of the deputies," Dutton told Grace. "And the other deputy could go with me to look for Aileen."

She shook her head and stood, remaining hidden behind the tree. Grace motioned for the deputies to come to them. They kept the whirling blue lights of the cruiser on and made their way toward her. "We'll all go," she insisted.

Dutton had no way of knowing if that was the right call. After all, if she had stayed behind with a deputy, the killer might use that opportunity to sneak up on Grace and kill her. Or use Aileen to draw her out. At least this way, Grace would be with him, and he could do whatever it took to protect the baby and her.

"Wilson?" Grace called out once the deputies reached the trees.

No answer.

Dutton didn't hear any sounds of movement, either.

"How thick are these woods?" Grace asked him.

"Thick," he assured her. "But there are some trails and a few streams." Whether or not the killer knew about them was anyone's guess.

Grace nodded and motioned for them to get moving. They did, and Dutton figured there was no way for five people to stay quiet as they trudged through the trees and underbrush. The killer could be counting on that, too. He or she could be lying in wait for them.

The night air was heavy and damp. Almost smothering. It only added to the desperation and worry they were likely all feeling. Still, they kept moving and continued watching and listening.

Once they were away from the cruiser and were beneath the canopy of the thick trees, it became impossible to see, so Bennie turned on his flashlight to illuminate the way for them. The light would be another beacon for the killer, and if he or she wasn't on the run, then it would make them easy targets.

And it was indeed possible that the killer was running.

He thought of the blood Rory had seen in the truck. It could have belonged to the killer. Aileen was an experienced cop, after all, and she might have been able to injure the person who'd taken her. Maybe not a big enough injury to incapacitate, but it could give the five of them the upper hand.

While they moved, Dutton kept glancing behind them, checking for both Wilson and the killer. Who, of course, could be one and the same. But there was no sign of him. No sign of blood, either, as Bennie panned his flashlight on the ground in front of them. However, there were indentations in the ground to indicate that someone had recently gone this way.

They all came to a quick stop when a sound cracked through the woods. Not gunfire. Dutton thought this might be someone stepping on a tree branch. And it had sounded close.

Hell, was it the killer?

Was he or she getting into position to shoot them?

Dutton wanted to move in front of Grace, to try to protect her, but they were all jammed too close together for him to do that. Still, he tried to prepare himself in case he had to pull Grace to the ground.

"There," Rory whispered, and his brother pointed to a small clearing to their right.

Bennie immediately shifted the flashlight in that direction, and Dutton caught just a glimpse of the movement. A person wearing all black ducked out of sight and into some thick bushes and undergrowth.

And the person wasn't alone.

Dutton also spotted Aileen. Her hands were tied in front of her, and judging from the way she was walking, her feet were tied as well. She was gagged. Her captor latched on to her hair with a gloved hand and dragged Aileen out of sight.

Grace opened her mouth as if she might call out, but she reconsidered that, and snapped toward the deputies instead. "Rory, you, Bennie and Ellie try to sneak around on the right side. I didn't see a gun, but it's possible the killer is armed." She looked at Dutton. "You and I will take the left side."

To keep Grace as protected as possible, Dutton nearly argued for a deputy to be with them. But it was hard for a trio of people to sneak up on someone. Maybe the deputies would make enough noise to distract the killer, so that he and Grace could move in for the capture.

Or the kill.

Dutton wouldn't hesitate to end this SOB if it came down to it. He only hoped that the killer didn't manage to use Aileen as a human shield to try to draw out Grace. But that was likely the plan.

Maybe the truck had been damaged enough so it couldn't be used for an escape. That was the only reason Dutton could think of for taking this fight on foot. That, or maybe Aileen had managed to hurt her captor. That blood had come from someone, and he was hoping it was the killer.

Bennie turned off the flashlight, plunging them into darkness again, but that didn't stop them from moving. The deputies went to the right. Grace and Dutton, to the left.

Thankfully, after walking a few feet, Dutton's eyes began

to adjust to the darkness, and he could at least make out where he was stepping. He couldn't hear anything, though, not over the pounding thud of his own heart.

His heart thundered even more when there was a slash of blue light that knifed through the trees. The cruiser. Maybe that was another distraction for the killer, too. Dutton just didn't want this snake focusing in on the deputies, Aileen or them so they'd be easier targets.

Dutton stopped when he reached the area where he was pretty sure there was a stream. Or at least there had been when he'd played here as a kid. And it was there, alright. The water coiled and snaked right in front of them. Not especially wide, but they had to jump to get to the other side. He prayed that this physical activity and stress wasn't taking a toll on the baby.

He and Grace landed together on the stream's bank, their boots sinking into the mud and soft dirt. They didn't stop. They just kept moving. Kept working their way past the trees and shrubs toward that clearing, where they'd last seen Aileen and her captor.

A sound stopped them. Not the snap of a tree branch but more like someone moving around on some twigs or dried leaves. They stood there, heads lifted, trying to pinpoint the direction. They both pointed to a massive oak at the same time.

Someone was there.

They didn't move directly toward the person. Staying low and walking as quietly as they could, they continued to go left so they could come up from behind.

Each step caused the knot in his stomach to tighten even more. Caused his fear about Grace and the baby to skyrocket. But they kept moving.

Until he saw something.

Aileen.

It was definitely her. She was wearing jeans and a shirt, and he'd been right about both her hands and feet being tied. She was standing by the tree right next to the person wearing all dark clothes and a half mask that covered the bottom portion of the face. The hooded jacket concealed the hair as well.

But not the knife.

Dutton saw it then.

The cruiser light caught the blade just right so there was a flash of a reflection. Enough for him to see that the person had it pressed right to Aileen's throat.

Was this Brian? Or Cassie?

Or some hired thug?

It was impossible to tell, what with the bulky outfit that reminded him of a grim-reaper costume. It could even be Wilson, if the man had managed to change when he'd run into the woods. It was possible he'd left clothes there just to pull this off. A disguise so he wouldn't be identified. Then, he could kill Grace and Dutton, maybe Aileen, too, and get away.

Dutton looked at Grace, and even in the darkness, they managed to connect gazes. She took a long, slow breath before she gave the nod for them to get moving again. They hadn't spelled out what the plan was here, but he was hoping Grace would let him tackle Aileen's captor. If Dutton got the chance to do that. He'd have to time it so Aileen wouldn't get her throat cut.

Their steps were even more cautious now, but Dutton knew they were still making some noise. Noise that the person in black must have heard because his head whipped up, and he dragged Aileen against him.

Dutton couldn't be sure, but he didn't think the person had actually pinpointed Grace and him. The killer seemed to be firing gazes all around, not just in their direction, but the side from where the deputies were no doubt approaching.

Grace stopped, reached down and picked up a rock. She hurled it toward the clearing. It got the captor's attention, and he whirled in that direction, causing the hood of his jacket to fall off his head.

Except it wasn't a *he*.

Dutton saw enough of the person's hair and forehead then. Enough to know who the killer was.

Cassie.

His heart dropped, and the sickening dread washed over him. Cassie was killing because of him. He was the reason that Grace, their baby and everyone else in Cassie's path were in danger.

And now he had to stop her.

Chapter Seventeen

Cassie spat out a string of profanities when the hood slipped off her head. She was wearing a stocking cap beneath it, but there was enough of her blond hair exposed that it was easy enough to tell who she was.

The killer.

Grace had no doubts about that now. Not with Cassie pressing the knife to Aileen's throat.

Cassie yanked Aileen even harder against her, but while she was glancing around, clearly spooked, she didn't seem to pinpoint Dutton and her. Maybe it was the deputies, though, since her attention seemed to be lingering in the direction they should be coming from.

"I don't see a gun," Dutton whispered.

"No," Grace agreed. "But she could have a hired thug nearby."

So very true. Lunsford was dead, but that didn't mean there weren't others. So this was either a standoff or a trap. Either way, people could be killed.

"Distract Cassie, and I'll sneak up behind her," Dutton muttered. "And please don't argue with me about this. I don't want you to end up having to tackle a killer with a knife."

Grace looked at him, and she mouthed a single curse word under her breath. Then, she nodded. "Don't you dare let her turn that knife on you," she whispered. "And save my mother," she added, brushing a quick kiss on his mouth.

Dutton didn't linger with the kiss, though Grace would have liked holding on to him for a moment or two. Even a couple of moments could end up being fatal for her mother.

"Keep watch for any hired guns," he said as his parting words, and Dutton began to make his way toward Cassie. He took more of those careful steps, obviously trying to stay quiet, but then Grace gave him some cover with her voice.

"Cassie," Grace called out.

Dutton wouldn't be able to see Cassie from his position, but she might be able to hear Dutton. The woman obviously heard her because Cassie pivoted in Grace's direction. Hopefully, Dutton was staying down and out of sight just in case Cassie did have a gun or there were any of her henchmen around.

"You want your mother alive?" Cassie immediately responded. "Then, you and Dutton have to trade yourselves for her."

"So you can kill us," Grace concluded.

"You both deserve to die," Cassie shouted. "Dutton loved me until you ruined things by getting pregnant. I could have worked things out with him. He would have come back to me, but no. You had to have him, and you played dirty by using that kid to make sure he was done with me."

And there it was. The motive was all spelled out and wrapped in the rage he could hear in her voice.

Cassie seemed to have a battle with herself to regain her composure. "All I need is the two of you and a vehicle to get the hell out here, and Aileen will live."

Grace doubted that. If it came down to it, Cassie would probably prefer to murder them all.

"You killed innocent people to get back at us," Grace said.

No rage in her tone. It was disgust, and she hoped Cassie's confession wasn't putting Dutton through a nightmare of a guilt trip.

"Innocent," Cassie growled. "Andrea Selby was a dirty cop. She deserved to die."

"Dirty?" Grace asked.

"Yes," Cassie insisted. "When I was putting out feelers for someone to help me set up the fires and such, Andrea volunteered to help. Well, volunteered if I paid her a hundred thousand. If not, she was going to rat me out. So instead, I killed her. I stabbed her and then tied her to the fence post on Dutton's beloved ranch."

Grace silently cursed. Apparently, Cassie thought Andrea's criminal behavior should be punished with a death sentence. But it was entirely possible that Andrea had just been trying to set up a sting operation to stop a killer from getting started.

"And what about Elaine Sneed?" Grace pressed. "Bailey Hannon and Georgia Tate? You can't convince me they were dirty cops, too."

"They were necessary kills," Cassie answered. "Or rather attempted kills since Bailey survived. But Elaine had to die so I could set up Brian. I needed someone to take the blame for this when I went on with my life. Without someone being convicted, your deputies would have kept digging. Loyalty," she said, spitting out the word as if it was a profanity. "Georgia because she happened to see me when I snatched Elaine."

"You left her alive?" Grace shook her head in disbelief.

"No. I intended to dump her at your place, but she fought me and got away. If she hadn't died in the hospital, I would have had to take care of her."

That caused the bile to rise in Grace's throat. This woman had no empathy for an innocent woman.

"And as for Bailey, I wanted to fire up Wilson to go after you for not preventing his fiancée's death," Cassie added.

"So, Wilson and Brian aren't part of your revenge plan?" Grace asked.

Cassie laughed. "I wouldn't trust either of those idiots. And enough of this twenty questions. You're stalling. Get out here now, or your mother dies where she stands."

"You know if you kill Dutton and Grace, then I'll move in to kill you?" Rory called out.

"And me," Ellie echoed, followed by Bennie's confirmation to let Cassie know all the deputies were nearby. "We'll also take care of any thugs you've hired."

"The thug is dead," Cassie muttered. "Lunsford was trying to blackmail me so I put an end to him. Self-preservation," she added. "It doesn't matter now, but when you cops dig, you'll find payment to Lunsford that looks as if it came from Brian."

So that explained why the man was dead. Explained, too, how Cassie had planned to get away with murder, literally, while incriminating someone else. Brian wasn't a stellar guy, but he didn't deserve to be railroaded for murder. He would have just become another casualty in Cassie's vendetta.

"Cassie, this is over," Grace ordered. "Put down the knife."

Cassie gave a hollow laugh that seemed to turn into a sob. "I know it's over," she muttered. No rage this time. Worse. Resignation.

Grace had a bad feeling that Cassie was ready to die. And take them out with her.

"Dutton?" Cassie shouted. "What do you have to say about this? This mess that you started when you used me and discarded me for Grace."

It hadn't been that way, and Grace knew that Dutton wouldn't even attempt to reason with the woman. He would just keep moving until he caught sight of Cassie. Once Grace saw him in position, then she'd have to do more than just stall by talking to Cassie. She'd need to move closer, to make it seem as if she was surrendering.

The sound stopped her.

Not Dutton.

It was nowhere near where he was walking. This was to her right.

Grace shifted position, watching, holding her breath, and a moment later, Wilson stepped into view. Unlike Cassie, he was armed, and he had his gun gripped in his hand. And Grace took aim at him.

"Cassie!" Wilson roared at the top of his lungs.

Oh, mercy. That caused the woman to turn, and Cassie put Aileen in a choke hold with her left arm and kept the knife at her throat with her right.

"Move away from Aileen or I'll shoot you where you stand," Wilson snarled.

Wilson certainly sounded enraged and ready to kill. And probably not because of any devotion to his former boss, Aileen, but because Cassie had nearly killed Wilson's fiancée.

"Come closer, and I'll kill her," Cassie said, sounding very panicked now, and Grace knew time was running out. "Grace, get me that vehicle, and you and Dutton show yourselves now. Now," she repeated in a shout.

With Cassie's attention now on Wilson, Grace welcomed the fresh shot of adrenaline she got when she bolted toward the woman. But Dutton came out of the woods, sprinting toward Cassie. Cassie heard the movement and turned.

Not fast enough, though.

Cassie was still moving when Dutton reached out and caught hold of Cassie's right hand to get the knife away from Aileen's throat. Aileen helped with that. Even though she was tied up, she rammed her elbow into Cassie's gut and sent the woman staggering back.

Right into Dutton.

The body slam threw them off balance, and he and Cassie went crashing to the ground. Dutton kept a tight grip on her knife hand. And paid for it, since it gave Cassie the chance to punch and kick him. Howling like an animal, she sank her teeth into his arm.

Grace raced toward the fight even though she knew Dutton wouldn't want her anywhere near the knife. Dutton bashed Cassie's hand against the ground. Again and again. Until the knife finally went flying.

Losing her weapon seemed to break Cassie, and all the fight left her body. On a ragged sob, she went limp against him.

Dutton rolled Cassie off him, shoving her onto her stomach so she'd be easier to restrain. Then, he fired looks around, no doubt searching for Grace. She was there, alright, already in the clearing. So was Wilson. And the deputies were still a few yards away.

Wilson lifted his gun and took aim.

At Grace.

"Back off, Grace," Wilson snarled. "Cassie dies right now. I'm going to put a bullet right between her eyes."

Grace didn't feel much relief that she wasn't the man's target. That's because Wilson's eyes were wild, and he was clearly out of control. If Grace got in his way, he might shoot her.

"Don't do this, Wilson," Grace said. In contrast to Wilson's voice and expression, she was steady and calm.

"She has to pay. She nearly killed Bailey. And for what? Because she couldn't handle a breakup with the town's bad boy?"

"Dutton crushed me," Cassie yelled, clearly regaining some of her fight. "He treated me like dirt. He's a monster, and he has to pay." She began to kick and tried to wriggle out of Dutton's grip.

Grace hurried to them to assist. So did the deputies. Since Rory and Bennie stayed back with Wilson, Ellie was the one who charged forward with her handcuffs ready.

"Back away from her," Wilson yelled. "Let Cassie get up so I can kill her face-to-face. I'm going to make her pay for the hell she put Bailey through."

Cassie let out another howl of outrage, and when Ellie leaned down to cuff her, Cassie ripped the gun from the deputy's hand. She bolted to her feet, the gun firmly in her hand. Grace's heart went to her knees as Dutton automatically moved to put himself in front of her.

Just as the shot blasted through the air.

The moment seemed to freeze. One moment, when the hellish thoughts flew through Grace's head and nearly brought her to her knees.

Because during that moment, she heard the gasp of pain and shock. She heard the voice and believed it was Dutton. And in that moment, she knew she couldn't lose him. It wasn't solely because he was her baby's father.

It was because she was in love with Dutton.

And he couldn't die.

She looked at Dutton, at the shock on his face, and she frantically combed her gaze over him, looking for blood. But there wasn't any.

Not on Dutton, anyway.

The blood was on Cassie, spatters of it on her face, and despite the black clothes she was wearing, Grace saw the blood spreading across Cassie's chest.

The moment finally seemed to unfreeze, and there were

suddenly sounds, a lot of them. People running, Rory shouting, and Cassie dropping to the ground.

Wilson was still standing, still holding his gun that had delivered the fatal shot, and he didn't resist when Bennie ran to him and yanked the weapon from his hands. Wilson seemed to be in shock, too. He just stood there, not a drop of color in his face. But he wasn't remorseful, either.

"Call an ambulance," Grace shouted, and she lowered herself to the ground, ready to attempt to staunch the bleeding or do CPR.

But it wasn't necessary.

Cassie locked gazes with Dutton, and she seemed on the verge of spewing more venom. That didn't happen, though. The only sound that came from Cassie's mouth was a death rattle as she expelled a breath.

The last breath she'd ever take.

Chapter Eighteen

Dutton sank down onto the foot of the guest bed and felt the bone-deep exhaustion wash over him. Understandable, since he and Grace had been up all night, tying up some of the ends of the investigation, and it was now nearly nine in the morning.

And the tying up wasn't over.

Maybe never would be. Soon, Grace would need to go back into her office and deal with the aftermath. Deal with any trauma her deputies and mother might have experienced, too. Along with speaking to the ME, who now had Cassie's body, and interviewing Wilson.

Yeah, there was plenty to do.

First, though, he was hoping Grace could get some much-needed sleep once she'd finished her shower. Maybe a really long one, so the hot water could loosen what had to be tense muscles.

His muscles were certainly tense to the point of being painful. But there was relief, too, and he was certain once he could settle his thoughts, he would realize just how damn lucky they'd gotten. Cassie was dead, and that meant her killing spree had come to an end.

Later, he'd have to deal with the guilt that his breakup with the woman had spurred the string of deadly events. But

Dutton wasn't so drained that he couldn't see that he wasn't to blame for Cassie's extreme reaction.

He just wished he'd seen it coming.

Wished he'd been able to stop her before she'd gotten started.

So, yes, he'd feel guilt over that and how close Cassie had come to killing Grace, their baby and him. Heck, Aileen, Bailey and so many others as well. Thankfully, though, Aileen was safe in her own home. Bailey, too.

Wilson, not so much.

The man had been arrested, and depending on what the DA said, he was facing some serious charges. It was possible that with a good lawyer, Wilson could argue diminished capacity, and he might just get away with that. Still, Wilson had killed Cassie, and Dutton figured the man's life would never be the same because of it.

The bathroom door opened, and Grace came out, bringing the scent of his soap with her. She was wearing a bathrobe, one that his mom had given him for Christmas years ago, and it swallowed her. Maybe it would be comfortable enough for her just to fall into bed and sleep.

He stood, ready to relinquish the guest bed so she could dive right in, but he stopped when she lifted her phone. Hell. Dutton hoped something hadn't gone wrong.

"Just got a text from Livvy," she said. "Brian will be cleared of any charges related to the murders. I can't charge him with being a cheating, lying slime," she added and then shrugged. "We'll have to let karma deal with him."

True, and Dutton was betting Elaine's parents would be firing the man. That was a small victory at least.

Dutton went to her and brushed a kiss on her cheek. He avoided any of the small nicks and bruises from the airbags and purposely kept it chaste, since he didn't want anything interfering with her getting some rest.

"Go to bed," he insisted.

He moved away from her, ready to head to his own bedroom and attempt to do the same, but she caught his arm.

"Stay in here with me," she muttered.

Dutton felt some other emotions cut through the fatigue. One was hope. Another was lust. And dread, since he didn't want lust playing into this, not when Grace had to be exhausted.

"Stay with me," she repeated when she saw the hesitation in his eyes.

The hesitation would have stayed firmly in place had she not kissed him. Her lips didn't land on his cheek, but rather on his mouth. And there was nothing, absolutely nothing, chaste about it. It was filled with heat and oh, so much need. More than enough need and heat that something inside Dutton snapped.

His resolve vanished.

And he forgot all about such things as fatigue and sleep. He only remembered this. The kiss. Being with Grace.

The memories came. Of other times they'd been together like this. Except this time was different. They'd survived going through hell and back, and they were alive. So was their baby, and that had Dutton stopping and taking a step back.

"You're pregnant." He hadn't intended to make it sound like some startling revelation, but his mind was definitely questioning whether or not this was a good idea.

Grace smiled, a rarity with everything that had been going on, and she pulled him back to her. "Pregnant women have sex. We're having sex," she confirmed.

His pulse was already revving, but that amped it up even

more, and this time when her mouth came to his, he was the one who deepened the kiss. He hauled her into his arms, and let the heat and need take over.

The kiss was instantly hungry, jumping right out of foreplay and into something with an edge. An edge that was demanding the sex happen now. Dutton was all for that, but he wanted Grace to take the lead in case there were some restrictions.

However, if restrictions existed, Grace was showing no signs of it. Kissing him as if he was the cure for, well, everything, she backed him toward the bed, then lightly pushed him back onto the bed. She didn't break the kiss when she landed on top of him, all without breaking the kiss.

She didn't waste any time going after his belt, and with her clever hands, she got it undone, all the while touching him and firing up the heat even more. Dutton decided to do some firing up of his own, and he yanked open the bathrobe.

And found a naked woman.

Fully naked. And despite the fire urging him on, he took a moment just to savor the sight of her. Her breasts. Her belly. And her center, where she straddled him.

"Perfect," he muttered.

She made a yeah-right sound that he would have almost certainly disputed, but she kissed him again, lowered his zipper and slid her hand into his boxers. That gave him a jolt and he went rock-hard. Instantly ready, too, so he had to do more reining in just so he could stretch out the pleasure.

Dutton pulled her down to his side and immediately leaned in so he could kiss her breasts. Her stomach, too. And then he went lower, lower, lower, his mouth trailing over her skin until he reached the prize. She moaned, throwing her head back against the mattress and lifting her hips.

Yeah, this was stretching out the pleasure, alright.

And he would have no doubt continued to stretch it until she climaxed, but Grace made a sound of protest and moved away from him. Not far. Just so she could remove his shirt. Then, she tackled his jeans, boots and boxers. She didn't stop until she had him fully undressed.

Grace took a moment, too, her gaze combing over his naked body, and she must have liked what she saw because she smiled. Their gazes met. Held. And in that moment, so many things passed between them. Things he wanted said aloud, but that would have to wait until they sated this need that was clawing away at them.

She had a cure for the need. And it was a surefire one. Grace pushed him back on the bed and followed on top of him. With the eye contact still in place, she took him inside her.

The sensations were instant. Hot. And almost overwhelming.

She paused a moment, to let them both settle, to allow her body to adjust. And then she began to move. Slowly at first. So slowly. Stretching out the moments until all he could feel was wave after wave of pleasure.

Just when Dutton thought he could take no more, Grace gave him more. By moving faster, taking him deeper into her body. Revving up everything. The heat. The need. And their bodies' demand for release. He held on, waiting until he felt her climax. Until he felt her muscles squeeze against the full length of his erection. Then, he waited some more. Held out as long as he could.

Before Dutton let Grace finish him off.

GRACE WAS HAVING an amazing dream. One where she was having the best sex of her life with Dutton. Then again, *best* was the key word when it came to making love with Dutton.

That's why she was sliding into the dream, letting it play out while the heat consumed her.

But then, a sound woke her up.

Muttering a profanity under her breath, she slapped at the nightstand, the usual place for her phone. It was there, alright, but it wasn't her nightstand. That's when she remembered she was in the guest bed at Dutton's and that Dutton was still there.

Naked.

And she was snuggled in his arms.

No wonder she'd had the dream, and one look at his amazing face and body made her want to kiss him and go for another round of that great sex. But the phone didn't stop ringing, and it had woken him, too, so she reluctantly eased away from him and picked up her phone. Her heart got a jolt of a different kind when she saw her mother's name on the screen.

Since it hadn't been too long since Cassie had kidnapped Aileen and tried to kill them all, her mother could be dealing with the aftermath of that. Or maybe Cassie had had a henchman after all… Grace stopped with the worst-case possibilities and answered the call on speaker. Dutton would no doubt want to hear this conversation, since he could see her screen as well, and he was already sitting up. And judging from his expression, he was also bracing for the worst.

"What's wrong?" Grace immediately asked.

"I woke you," Aileen was equally quick to say. "I'm sorry. I probably should have let you sleep."

Grace checked the time and saw it was three in the afternoon. She'd been asleep for nearly five hours, and while her body felt as if it could use some more rest, that wasn't a high priority now. Her mother was.

"What's wrong?" Grace repeated, and she heard her mother gathering her breath.

"Nothing," Aileen insisted. "Are you with Dutton?"

Grace still wasn't convinced that nothing bad had happened, but her back went up a little at her mother's question. She hoped this wasn't about to turn into a lecture about her avoiding Dutton.

Because Grace wasn't going to do it.

No. No more avoidance. No more trying to convince herself she was better off without him. But that was something she'd deal with after she found out why her mother had called.

"Yes, I'm with Dutton," Grace said. "He's right here next to me and listening to this conversation." She left it at that, but her mother would know that meant she was in bed with Dutton, and since Aileen wasn't a fool, she'd know what had gone on.

"Good," Aileen replied, surprising Grace. "Because he'll want to hear this, too. The town council meeting just finished their vote about having a recall election."

Grace's chest went tight. She certainly hadn't forgotten about that, but she'd shoved it to the back of her mind. "And?" she pressed when her mother paused.

"And there'll be no recall vote. Grace, you got the endorsement of the entire town council. They think you're doing a solid job as sheriff."

That chest tightness vanished. "It probably helped that the killer is dead." And, yes, there was a tinge of sarcasm in her voice.

"It helped that members of the council realized they'd been letting a killer influence them about you. Added to that, the other person who spoke out against you, Wilson, is behind bars right now and will likely be charged with murder."

That helped with the remaining resentment that Grace felt over her badge being threatened. "Good," she muttered around the lump in her throat.

"I agree, and with Wilson and Cassie not spreading their hatred, I don't think any more questions will come up about you being at the reins," her mother concluded. "Oh, and I'm to tell you not to come into work tomorrow. That's from Rory. He's handling the postmortem on Cassie, and he and Livvy are doing the interview with Wilson."

Grace was mentally shaking her head. "I can't let them do that."

"Sure you can," her mother said. "Take tomorrow off. You've been doing nonstop duty to the badge. Now take a little time off for your baby. And for Dutton," she added. "Dutton, thank you."

"For what?" he asked.

"For keeping Grace and my grandbaby safe. I know that couldn't have been easy. It probably helps that you're in love with Grace. Yes, I can see that. I didn't want to see it for a long time, but I know you'll do what's right by both the baby and her."

With that, her mother abruptly ended the call, leaving Grace in shock. She figured Dutton was feeling the same, so she turned to him to give him an out. She would tell him her mother was wrong and that there was no need to do anything, no matter what her mother said.

She didn't get a chance to say any of that.

Because Dutton hauled her into his arms and kissed her. Really kissed her. It was long, deep and incredibly hot. The hotness went up a significant notch when he pressed his naked body against hers.

The remnants of the dream came rushing back. Remnants, too, of the scorching sex they'd had hours earlier. But Grace got a jolt of other memories, too. Of Dutton being there for some of the worst, and best, moments of her life.

"I'm in love with you," she blurted when they broke for air. "And I want you in my life."

He froze, and for one horrible moment, she thought she'd blown it, that she had ruined this moment. But then he smiled. It was that cocky grin that could be considered foreplay. It certainly gave her another dose of heat.

"I've waited a long time to hear you say that," he drawled. "Because, Sheriff Grace Granger, I'm in love with you, too, and I also want both you and our baby in my life…oh, let's aim for forever."

Forever suited her just fine.

He kissed her again. This one robbed her of all of the breath she'd just gathered. But Grace didn't mind one bit. Because in that moment, that wonderful scalding moment, she, too, realized she'd also been waiting a long time to hear and say those words.

I'm in love with you.

They were absolutely true words. Ones that she felt with her entire heart, and she knew from the way Dutton kissed her, that it was the same for him.

So Grace pulled him against her, kissing him, and taking everything Dutton, and only Dutton, could give her.

* * * * *

COMING SOON!

We really hope you enjoyed reading this book.
If you're looking for more romance
be sure to head to the shops when
new books are available on

Thursday 17th July

To see which titles are coming soon, please visit
millsandboon.co.uk/nextmonth

MILLS & BOON

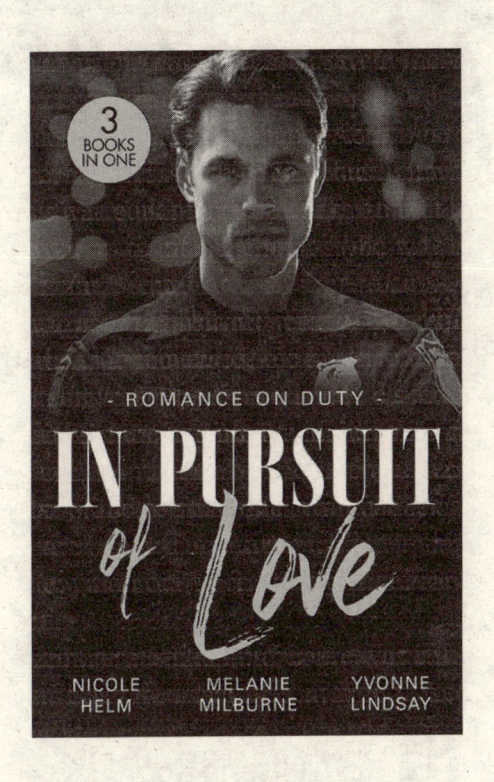

LET'S TALK
Romance

For exclusive extracts, competitions and special offers, find us online:

- **f** MillsandBoon
- **X** @MillsandBoon
- **◉** @MillsandBoonUK
- **♪** @MillsandBoonUK

Get in touch on 01413 063 232

For all the latest titles coming soon, visit
millsandboon.co.uk/nextmonth